"Where are the Romulans?" Riker asked.

The group was standing beneath a gigantic silver sculpture fashioned in the shape of a hawklike avian that loomed over the curved tiers of desks and chairs where the late Romulan Senate had done its deliberations for centuries. Surrounded by blue pillars and abstract, rust-colored wall hangings, the room's expansive stone floor was dominated by a circular mosaic of smooth marble, half blue and half green, and inlaid with lines and circlets of gold. A wavy ribbon of turquoise bisected the mosaic, at once separating and joining the two halves together. Golden icons faced one another across the length of the divide, arrayed like chess pieces.

On the green side, far off-center and larger than every other element on the mosaic, was the stylized image of a star and two nearby planets.

To Troi, the symbolism was both obvious and shocking . . . . and perhaps indicative of a disturbing cultural mindset. Here, at the very heart of their power, was the Romulan worldview: an image not of the empire entire, with Romulus at its center, but rather, a symbol of enmity, of its centuries-old antagonism with its old foe, the Federation.

And it dominated the very floor of the Senate Chamber.

Is this how they see themselves? Troi wondered. *Always on the verge of war with us? Or does the central placement of the Neutral Zone speak more to a feeling of confinement? A reminder of thwarted ambition? What does this say about a civilization, that it defines itself by its relationship to its longtime adversary?*

STAR TREK
TITAN™

TAKING WING
MICHAEL A. MARTIN
AND ANDY MANGELS

Based upon STAR TREK® and
STAR TREK: THE NEXT GENERATION®
created by Gene Roddenberry

POCKET BOOKS
New York London Toronto Sydney Ki Baratan

An *Original* Publication of POCKET BOOKS

POCKET BOOKS, a division of Simon & Schuster, Inc.
1230 Avenue of the Americas, New York, NY 10020

This book is a work of fiction. Names, characters, places and incidents are products of the authors' imaginations or are used fictitiously. Any resemblance to actual events or locales or persons, living or dead, is entirely coincidental.

ISBN-13: 978-0-7434-9627-8
ISBN-10:   0-7434-9627-2

First Pocket Books paperback edition April 2005

10 9 8 7 6

POCKET and colophon are registered trademarks of Simon & Schuster, Inc.

Cover art by Cliff Neilson
Cover design by John Vairo, Jr.

Manufactured in the United States of America

For information regarding special discounts for bulk purchases, please contact Simon & Schuster Special Sales at 1-800-456-6798 or businesss@simonandschuster.com.

Acknowledgments

The authors of this volume owe a debt of appreciation (or is that vengeance?) to several other *Star Trek* novelists: John Vornholt, Dayton Ward & Kevin Dilmore, Robert Greenberger, David Mack, and Keith R. A. DeCandido, the authors of the *A Time To* series of novels; Josepha Sherman & Susan Shwartz, the Romulan historians extraordinaire who named the Romulan capital; Judith and Garfield Reeves-Stevens, who *also* supplied a name for the Romulan capital; Michael Jan Friedman, who shepherded some of the characters who appear in (or are referenced in) this book through their very first post-*Nemesis* adventures; Dave Galanter, David Mack (again), and Josepha Sherman & Susan Shwartz (again), all of whom left some nifty little Easter eggs hidden for us in the *Tales of the Dominion War* anthology; and Diane Duane, who painted a great deal of the basic linguistic and cultural backdrop for the Romulan Star Empire.

Most of this story unfolds during the final days of the year 2379 (Old Calendar), shortly after the events of *Star Trek Nemesis* and the novel *Death in Winter.*

All violence, all that is dreary and repels, is not power, but the absence of power.

—RALPH WALDO EMERSON (1803–1882)

In politics, merit is rewarded by the possessor being raised, like a target, to a position to be fired at.

—CHRISTIAN NEVELL BOVEE (1820–1904)

We are going to have peace even if we have to fight for it.

—DWIGHT D. EISENHOWER (1890–1969)

CHAPTER ONE

"This must be your first visit to Ki Baratan," said the woman who stood behind the operative.

So much for hiding in plain sight, the operative thought, quietly abandoning his hope that she would pay him as little heed as had the throngs of civilians and military officers he'd already passed along the city's central *eyhon.* He turned and regarded her, averting his gaze momentarily from the graceful, blood-green dome of the Romulan Senate building. The ancient structure gleamed behind him in the morning sun, reflecting an aquamarine glint from the placid Apnex Sea that lay just beyond it.

"As a matter of fact, this *is* my first visit," the operative said. He smiled broadly, confident that the woman wouldn't sense how awkward this particular mannerism felt to him. "Before today, I had seen the greatness of Dartha only in my grandfather's holos."

As she studied him, he noted that she was old and gray. Her clothing was drab and shapeless, her lined countenance stern, evidently forged by upwards of two centuries of hard life circumstances. He watched impassively as she ran her narrowed, suspicious gaze over his somewhat threadbare traveling cassock.

"Dartha?" the woman said, still scrutinizing him. "Nobody has referred to the Empire's capital by *that* name since Neral came to power."

The operative silently cursed himself even as he concealed his frustration beneath a carefully cultivated mask of impassivity. Though his lapse was an understandable one—roughly akin, he thought, to confusing Earth's nineteenth-century Constantinople with twentieth-century Istanbul—he upbraided himself for it nonetheless.

"Forgive me, *'lai*," he said, using the traditional rustic form of address intended to show respect to an elder female. "I arrived just today, from Leinarrh. In the Rarathik District."

An indulgent, understanding smile tugged at her lips. "Just what I thought. I took you for a *hveinn* right away. A farmer who's never left the *waith* before."

The operative forced his own smile to broaden, reassured that she found his rural Rarathik dialect convincing. He maintained his caution, however; like him, this apparently harmless old woman might not be at all what she appeared to be. "At your service, *'lai*. You may call me Rukath."

She nodded significantly yet discreetly toward the dome—and the disruptor-carrying guards that walked among the green, ruatinite-inlaid minarets that surrounded it. "Then allow me to give you some friendly advice, Rukath of Leinarrh. Continue gawking so about the Hall of State, and I might have to call you 'dead.' Or perhaps worse."

The operative allowed his smile to collapse, which actually came as a relief. He feigned innocent fear, per his extensive intelligence and tactical training. "Do you really think those uhlans over there would actually *shoot* me? Just for *looking?*"

"Just pray that the cold fingers of Erebus find you too unimportant to snatch away into the underworld," she said with a pitying shake of the head. *"Daold klhu."*

Tourists, the operative silently translated the unfamiliar Romulan term as the old woman turned and walked away. "Jolan'tru, *'lai,"* he said to her retreating back.

He turned back toward the Senate Dome and watched as the guards made their rounds. He counted six at the moment, marching in pairs, their arrogant, disciplined gazes focused straight ahead. The old woman's warning notwithstanding, he might as well have been invisible to them.

But it's best not to become complacent, he thought, checking the chrono built into the disguised subspace pulse transmitter he wore on his wrist. Time was growing short. Since his surreptitious arrival on Romulus the previous day, he had taken in sights very few of his people had ever seen.

He'd just paid what might well turn out to be a once-in-a-lifetime visit to the Romulan capital of Ki Baratan. Now the time had come to venture beneath it.

The operative deliberately set aside unpleasant thoughts of the underworld of ancient Romulan mythology. Those old stories hadn't sufficiently described the noisome smells that were wafting up around him from the figurative—and literal—bowels of Ki Baratan. *Erebus, indeed.*

Guided through the stygian gloom by his wrist light, the operative was relieved to note that the venerable maze of *aekhhwi'rhoi*—the stone-lined sewer tunnels that ran below Ki Baratan—corresponded precisely to the maps the defector M'ret had provided to Starfleet Intelligence. Carefully stepping over and past countless scuttling, multilegged, sewer-dwelling *nhaidh,* he made his way to the appointed place. Once there, he pulled hard at a rust-covered, meter-wide wheel, laboriously opening up a narrow access hatchway that looked to be older than Surak and T'Karik combined. The corroded steel aperture groaned in protest, moving only fractionally as the muscles in his back strained. After perhaps a minute of hard coaxing, the wheel gave way and the hatch opened with a clang that reverberated loudly throughout the catacombs.

Releasing the wheel, he pulled a small disruptor pistol from beneath his cassock, then squeezed through the narrow opening without making any further pretense of stealth; by now whoever else might be down here, whether friend or foe, was surely aware of his presence.

He passed into the darkened chamber beyond the hatch, where air that reeked of stagnation, moldy old bones, and damp earth assailed his nostrils. Stepping forward, he heard a quiet yet stern male voice.

"Halt! Drop your weapon." Something cool and unyielding pressed forcefully into the small of his back.

The operative released his grip on the weapon, allowing it to clatter to the rough stone floor. A bright light suddenly shone before him, momentarily triggering his nictitating inner eyelids. He caught a glimpse of several humanoid silhouettes standing before him, several meters farther inside the cavern's depths.

"State your name," said the voice behind him. It sounded young, almost adolescent. *Or perhaps merely frightened?* "And state your business here."

The operative knew that this was the moment of truth,

and very possibly the last moment of his life. He faced that prospect with a Vulcan's ingrained equanimity.

"While on Romulus, I am known as Rukath."

"Of Leinarrh, in far-off Rarathik," someone else said, in a stern female voice. "By way of Starfleet Intelligence. Yes, we knew you were coming."

The operative nodded. "Then you already know my business here. I expected no less."

He felt the weapon at his back quiver slightly, and he calculated his odds of disarming the man behind him. They weren't at all good. Nevertheless, the time had come to end the standoff, regardless of the outcome.

"I also bring greetings from Federation starship *Alliance*. Captain Saavik sends her best regards to the movement. And to the ambassador, of course."

As the operative had hoped, the mention of the ambassador's wife prompted one of the silhouettes before him to detach itself from the others and step forward. The tall, lean form spoke in a graveled yet resonant voice that he recognized instantly, even though more than eight decades had passed since he had last heard it.

"Lower your weapon, D'Tan. Rukath is among friends."

"But how can we be certain this Rukath is a friend? If that's even his name."

The figure stepped forward another several paces, and waved an arm in what was obviously a prearranged signal. In response, the light levels diminished, allowing the operative to see the approaching man's face clearly, as well as the coterie of a half-dozen armed Romulan civilians, an even mix of men and women, who stood vigilantly all around him.

Ambassador Spock.

The tall, conspicuously unarmed figure came to a stop

only a meter away, his hands folded in front of his simple hooded pilgrim's robe as he studied the operative's face. The operative recalled his only previous meeting with the ambassador, whose saturnine visage was unmistakable despite the addition of a great many new lines and wrinkles. He wondered if Spock remembered him as well, after the passage of so many years. Perhaps the minor surgical alterations that had been wrought on his facial structure obscured his identity.

"Your vigilance is an asset to us, D'Tan," Spock said to the young man with the weapon. "But as Surak teaches us, there can be no progress without risk."

That evidently got through to the armed man, who withdrew his weapon and backed away. The operative spared a quick glance over his shoulder, nodding toward Spock's youthful bodyguard in a manner that he hoped would be taken as nonthreatening and reassuring. He noted the other man's response: a hard scowl and a still-unholstered disruptor.

The operative fixed his gaze once again upon Spock, a man who had achieved great notoriety back on Vulcan—as well as throughout the Federation and beyond—more than a century earlier. *How strange,* he thought, *that one who never even achieved* Kolinahr *now represents all of Vulcan here in this forbidding place—and attempts to bring such radical change to both Vulcan and Romulus.* He wondered if Spock would have taken on such a task had he attained the pinnacle of logic that the *Kolinahr* disciplines represented.

Would I have been so foolish to have followed him here had Kolinahr *not eluded me also?*

"Walk with me, please, Rukath," Spock said, then abruptly turned to stride more deeply into the rough-hewn cavern that stretched beyond the sewer hatch. The operative immediately fell into step beside the ambassador. He heard the crunch of gravel behind him, as Spock's followers tailed the pair at a respectful distance. *If I really were the Tal Shiar or military intelligence infiltrator these people fear that I am, this mission would surely be a suicide run.*

"You must forgive D'Tan," Spock said.

"There is nothing to forgive, Mr. Ambassador. His caution is understandable. The Tal Shiar's eyes and ears are everywhere."

"Indeed. And none of us have forgotten Senator Pardek's betrayal."

The operative thought he detected a touch of wistfulness in the ambassador's tone. Though it was a surprising departure from Vulcan stoicism, he could certainly understand it. Though he had studied Captain Jean-Luc Picard's reports about Romulus—one of which included Spock's own observation that reuniting the long-sundered Vulcan and Romulan peoples might take decades or even centuries to come to fruition—it was disappointing to think that Spock's efforts had yielded so little after eleven years of hard, often perilous work.

As though he had surmised the dark turn the operative's thoughts had taken, Spock came directly to the point: "Tell me, Rukath: Why have you come to Romulus?"

The operative was not surprised to learn that Starfleet Intelligence might not have briefed Spock thoroughly on his reason for visiting Romulus. Or perhaps Spock was testing him, despite his reassurances to D'Tan.

"I bear an offer from the Federation Council," the operative said.

Though the cavern's illumination remained dim, the operative could see Spock's right eyebrow rise. "And the nature of that offer?"

"The council has decided to give its official endorsement to your agenda of Vulcan-Romulan unification. But both the council and the new president will want you to return to Earth to make a formal report first."

Spock brought their walk to an abrupt halt. His dark eyes flashed with an almost fanatical intensity. The operative wondered what so many years living among Vulcan's hyperemotional cousins had done to the ambassador's emotional disciplines. Had he "gone native"?

"My work is here," Spock said.

The operative raised a hand in a placating gesture. "You would be returned here, Mr. Ambassador, to resume that work as quickly as possible. After you've addressed both the council and the president's office on your progress."

Spock turned his gaze downward and stared into the middle distance, a deliberative expression on his face. "I see," he said after a pause. "To avail myself of an Earth idiom, the council evidently wishes me to 'come in from the cold.' "

Thanks to nearly a century of at least intermittent association with humans, the operative was conversant with the idiom Spock had used. "Yes, Mr. Ambassador. And the council will almost certainly place Federation resources at your disposal, at least covertly."

Spock paused again before responding. "Indeed. That would be a significant change in Federation policy."

"We live in changing times, Mr. Ambassador."

"Unquestionably. President Zife's sudden resignation is but one sign." Spock clasped his hands before him, steepling his index fingers. "I cannot help but wonder whether the council's offer is related to Zife's abrupt departure."

The operative was impressed by Spock's knowledge of

the political landscape beyond the Romulan Neutral Zone, though he knew it shouldn't have surprised him; he reminded himself that the ambassador had made more than one brief return to Earth since beginning his work on Romulus.

"I'm afraid all I know about that is what's been on the newsnets," the operative said truthfully.

Spock nodded, his expression grave. The operative had no doubt that the ambassador was well acquainted with those same reports.

Sensing that the ambassador still required some additional persuasion, the operative said, "I will need to rendezvous with my transport this evening. If you will agree to accompany me, we can have you back in Federation space within days."

Something resembling a half-smile crossed Spock's face. "I trust, Rukath, that you aren't prepared to use force to return me to Earth."

The operative gestured toward D'Tan, whom he knew still stood—disruptor in hand—only a short distance behind him. "I am obviously in no position to force you to do anything, Mr. Ambassador. I had hoped you would agree to come to Earth voluntarily."

Spock very slowly shook his head. "I am pleased that the council has finally come to understand the necessity of the cause of reunification. But I cannot afford to abandon my work on Romulus, even temporarily. Especially now, while tensions between the Romulan Senate and one of the key Reman military factions continue to escalate."

The operative recalled yesterday's update about this very subject in his daily intelligence briefing. The mysterious Shinzon, the Reman faction's young leader, had led a number of successful military engagements against Dominion forces during the war. His sudden prominence in Romulan politics could cause unpredictable swings in the delicate balance of power within a senate now evenly divided on issues of war and peace.

"You wouldn't be away from Romulus for very long, sir," the operative said quietly.

"The local political landscape is far too volatile for me to leave now. In addition to the unpredictability of the Reman faction, there are rumors of unrest on Kevatras and other Romulan vassal worlds. I dare not leave Romulus now, even for a short time."

The operative decided that the time had come to risk goading the ambassador into cooperating. "Has your unification movement progressed so little over the past decade that you remain completely indispensable to it even now?"

But clearly Spock wasn't taking the bait. Sidestepping the question, he said, "I must also consider two other possibilities. One is that you actually *are* a Tal Shiar agent. The other is that the Federation Council's agenda is not truly as you have described it."

Despite this disappointing response, the operative still wasn't ready to accept failure. Taking a single step closer to Spock, he said, "Then I offer you access to my mind. I invite you to know what I know."

Spock's right eyebrow climbed skyward yet again. Then, after casting a reproving glance in D'Tan's general direction, the ambassador approached the operative. The operative closed his eyes, felt the steady, relentless pressure of the ambassador's fingers against his temples. Vibrant colors and orderly shapes began placing themselves in elegant arrangements across his mind's eye. It was a tantalizing glimpse into an extraordinarily powerful and well-organized mind.

And then it came: a *frisson* of recognition. *After all these years, he* does *remember me.*

"I believe you," Spock said, a moment after withdrawing his hand and breaking the mind-touch.

The operative's eyes opened, and he blinked away a momentary feeling of disorientation as the ambassador stepped away from him. "Then come with me back to the Federation."

Another shake of Spock's head. "I regret that I cannot."

"But you said you believed me."

"My faith in your sincerity is not the issue."

"Then what *is* the issue, other than Romulan politics?"

Spock's gaze narrowed as though he were beginning to lose patience with a willfully obtuse child. "*Federation* politics."

It was the operative's turn to raise an eyebrow in surprise. "I don't understand, Mr. Ambassador."

"The Federation president has just resigned. One of the two contenders to replace him can be charitably described as a political reactionary who wishes to adopt an aggressive posture toward former Dominion War allies. I find it difficult to believe that such a president would support the Unification movement on Romulus."

The operative needed no further explanation: Spock was clearly talking about Special Emissary Arafel Pagro of Ktar. And given candidate Pagro's already well-publicized anti-Klingon predilections, it was a safe assumption that he wouldn't support any peace initiatives on Romulus.

"The results of the special election are not yet completely tabulated," the operative said. "Governor Bacco of Cestus III may yet emerge as the winner."

Spock nodded. "In that event, I will consider returning

to Earth for a brief meeting with President Bacco and the council. Provided, of course, that Romulan-Reman affairs permit it."

At a wordless signal from the ambassador, D'Tan and the rest of Spock's retinue surrounded their leader. "Live long and prosper," Spock said, holding his right hand aloft in the traditional split-fingered Vulcan salute.

"Peace and long life," the operative replied, using his left hand to mirror Spock's ritual gesture.

Then the group spirited the ambassador away, vanishing with him around a darkened turning of the rough-hewn cavern walls.

The operative stood alone in the dim, rocky chamber, listening to the distant echoes of dripping water and his own frustrated sigh. Moving silently, he retraced his steps, recovered his disruptor from where D'Tan had forced him to discard it, and began his lonely ascent back to the cobbled streets of the *ira'sihaer*, Ki Baratan's ancient casbah.

He paused to take an afternoon meal in a shabby-looking inn built of gray-and-ocher bricks that appeared as old as time itself. Although his vegetarian order caused the servers to eye him with some suspicion, he was far too preoccupied with mentally preparing his official Starfleet Intelligence report to care.

Following the meal—Romulan cooks, the operative noted, did not seem to have the faintest notion of how to prepare vegetables—he booked himself into a private room on the inn's relatively secluded third floor. Once he'd settled in and run a tricorder scan for surveillance devices, he discreetly recorded his report, then used the transmitter mounted in his wrist chron to send it as an encrypted "burst" transmission that lasted only a minuscule fraction of a second. The chance that even the much-feared Tal Shiar would intercept it, much less decode it, were infinitesimally small.

Minutes later, he heard raised voices outside the window, at street level. For a moment he wondered if the Romulan authorities had indeed intercepted his transmission.

But one look out the concrete window casement told him that the people shouting on the streets weren't Tal Shiar, or even Romulan military personnel. A dozen people, all of them apparently civilians, were running from the direction of the Romulan Hall of State. He could hear little coherency in their cries, other than a few general references to death and murder.

Curious, he left his room and descended to the main lobby, and from there proceeded to the ancient cobbled street. Still more civilians were joining the steadily growing throng, adding to the noise, chaos, and general tumult. An increasing number of uniformed police and helmeted military uhlans began to appear among the frantic crowd as it surged down the street, away from the official state buildings. In the background of the low skyline of Ki Baratan's Government Quarter, the graceful dome of the Hall of State arced skyward, dominating the horizon like the perpetually sun-scorched face of Remus. A trio of fierce-looking *mogai* wheeled through the thermals high above the dome, making dirgelike shrieks as they circled on nearly motionless wings. The operative briefly wondered whether the carnivorous birds had sniffed out live prey or carrion.

A young woman ran along the sidewalk, nearly knocking him into an elderly man as she passed. Her jade-flushed face was contorted with panic and near hysteria. "They've murdered the Senate!" she cried, repeating the phrase incessantly.

The operative chased her for a few steps, grabbing her by the shoulders and turning her to face him. "Who? *Who* has murdered the Senate?" As he repeated her words, the notion of the entire Romulan Senate suddenly being struck down simultaneously sounded absurd to him.

The woman's only response was a terrified scream. At the same moment, something struck him from behind, hitting him hard enough to hurl him to the stone sidewalk. The impact drove all the breath from his lungs, and all feeling vanished from his left arm and both of his legs. Nevertheless, he managed to roll onto his back, hoping to face whatever had hit him.

A pair of uhlans in red-crested helmets and full armor raised their stun truncheons. The one closest to the hysterical woman silenced her scream with one savage blow. The other felled the old man whom the operative had nearly toppled by accident scant moments before.

"Leave them alone!" the operative shouted, though he could barely hear himself over the escalating melee. The uhlans moved toward him, their truncheons rising and falling like scythes harvesting ripe stalks of Rarathik-grown *kheh*. Countless other panicked civilians, ordinary folk who didn't even seem to know which way to run, were either scattered or felled by repeated blows from the weapons of a growing phalanx of police and military uhlans.

He fleetingly recalled what he'd read of the bloody riots that Archpriest N'Gathan's assassination of Shiarkiek, the Empire's aged monarch, had touched off more than five years ago. *Something really* has *happened in the Hall of State,* he thought. *Something* terrible. *Everyone here must think the same thing is about to happen to them as well.*

And judging from the behavior of the uhlans, they were every bit as panicked as the general populace.

Using his right arm, the operative laboriously pushed himself up into a sitting position, facing away from the two approaching uhlans. Pulling himself forward, he tried to navigate a sea of fleeing legs. Inadvertent blows landed by scores of running feet rained onto his ribs, chest, and belly.

Pulling his wrist chron to his lips, he shouted a pre-arranged command directly into the voice pickup, hoping that all the ambient noise wouldn't drown it out.

"Aehkhifv!" The Romulan word for "eradication."

He knew he was almost certain to be either captured or killed. If he was fortunate, his voice command had already set the purge program into motion, releasing a minute thermite charge intended to destroy every bit of Federation circuitry hidden within his wrist chrono.

Including the subspace burst transmitter that represented his best chance of getting off of Romulus alive.

Then came a bone-crunching impact against the back of his head. As he sprawled forward, tumbling over the edge of a darkened abyss, his last coherent thoughts were of the Romulan Erebus myths.

CHAPTER TWO

Among stars his kind had not yet traveled, Will Riker soared.

Scarcely feeling the observation platform of *Titan's* stellar cartography lab beneath his feet, Riker let go, surrendering to the illusion of gliding swiftly "upstream" along the galaxy's Orion Arm. Buoyed on the strains of Louis Armstrong's 1928 recording of "West End Blues," Riker seemed to move far faster than even his ship's great engines could propel him. The familiar stars of home had long since fallen away. What lay ahead and all around him was an unknown expanse whose mysteries he, his crew, and their young vessel were meant to discover.

So much to explore, he thought, at once humbled and exhilarated by the realization. *Who's out here? What will we find waiting for us? And what'll we learn along the way?* These were the same questions that had led him to join Starfleet years ago. Now, as then, he could think of only one certain way to unveil the answers.

Soon, he told himself. *Soon . . .*

"Will?"

Deanna. He was suddenly grounded again, the solidity of his starship sure and tangible once more, though the rushing star clusters and nebulae remained. Standing in the center of the spherical holotank, he'd been so immersed in the simulation that he hadn't noticed her entering the cartography lab.

"Computer, deactivate audio," Riker said, abruptly silencing the music of the immortal Satchmo.

Deanna came up alongside him, her eyes searching his as they met. "Are you all right?" she asked.

He nodded and wrapped an arm around her shoulders; she reciprocated, slipping one of her arms around his waist. "Just looking over the road ahead," he said quietly.

"And how does it look to you?"

The question took him off guard, forcing him to grope blindly for an answer. "Big," he said finally, unable to keep a slight laugh out of his voice.

"Then maybe you shouldn't take such a long view," she said lightly. "Just take it a step at a time."

Grinning, he asked, "Is that my counselor talking, or my wife?"

Deanna shrugged. "Does it matter? It's good advice either way."

His brow furrowed; he could read her emotions as clearly as she could anyone else's. "Is something wrong?"

She hesitated, then said, "I know what this assignment means to you, what you think it represents. I know you take it very seriously—"

"Well, shouldn't I take it seriously?" he asked, interrupting her, his words coming out more sharply than he had intended.

Deanna let it pass. "It shouldn't be a burden, Will. That's all I meant."

Riker sighed, leaning forward on the railing and looking down into the void, watching the stars as they continued to stream by below him. "I know. It's just hard not to think that there's a lot at stake. I look back on the last decade and I wonder how so much could have happened, how so much could have changed. Sometimes I felt like we were speeding through a dark tunnel, with no way to turn, and no idea what we'd hit next. The Borg, the Klingons, the Dominion . . . We spent most of those years preparing for the next fight, the next war." He didn't bother to mention this last difficult year aboard the *Enterprise;* he didn't need to. She knew as well as he what they had endured.

He turned to her again, saw that she was now watching him carefully. "Now we've come out the other side, and for the first time in nearly a decade, it feels like we have a chance to get back some of what we lost during those years. We can do the things we set out to do when we joined Starfleet in the first place—the things I grew up believing Starfleet was primarily about. The Federation's finally at the point of putting ten years of near-constant strife behind it. This mission, this ship, is my chance—*our* chance—to help. That burden is real, *Imzadi.* I'm not going to pretend it doesn't exist."

Deanna smiled gently at him, then reached up to touch the side of his face. "You shouldn't. But you can share it. That's why you have a wife, and a crew. So you don't have to shoulder it alone."

He took her hand, kissed the palm of it, and nodded. "You're right. And I won't. I promise."

"Bridge to Captain Riker."

Still holding his wife's hand, Riker tapped his combadge. "Go ahead, Mr. Jaza."

"Sir, the U.S.S. Seyetik *has docked at Utopia Station One. They report that Dr. Ree is preparing to beam over. We have transporter room four standing by."*

A small, puzzling smile tugged at the corner of Deanna's mouth. "Acknowledged," Riker said. "Tell the transporter room that Commander Troi and I are on our way. Riker out." Turning away from the railing, Riker reached out to the platform's interface console and deactivated the Orion Arm simulation.

He turned back toward her. "What's that smile for?"

"I'll tell you later," Deanna said, brushing the question aside.

Riker's eyes narrowed with good-natured suspicion, but he decided to let the matter drop. As the captain and counselor walked together toward the exit, the walls of the lab shifted, returning to their usual standby display of the visible universe surrounding *Titan*. Beyond the gridwork of the ship's drydock, the orange sunlit face of Mars dominated the space to starboard, the flat, smooth lowlands that were home to Utopia Planitia's ground installations obliquely visible to the extreme north; at *Titan*'s port side, the stations and maintenance scaffolds of Utopia's orbital complex stood out starkly against the yellow-white brilliance of Sol.

"Has the rest of the senior staff come aboard?" Riker asked Deanna as they exited the lab and strode into the corridor. He nodded at two of the ship's biologists as they passed, an Arkenite whose name he couldn't recall at the moment, followed by a lumbering Chelon of the palest green Riker had ever seen on a member of that species. The scientists nodded back.

"Almost," Deanna answered. "Dr. Ree is the last. Well, except for the first officer, of course. But assuming nothing goes wrong there, you'll be able to hold your staff meeting on schedule, and with everybody present."

Riker tried to keep his expression steady as they passed an exposed length of the corridor wall, where several techs from the Corps of Engineers were still working at replacing a faulty ODN relay in a replicator network that crossed half the corridor. The work looked considerably more complicated than it had half an hour ago, the last time Riker passed through this section.

"I'm less worried about having a quorum at the staff meeting than I am about launching on schedule."

"Don't be such a worrier, Will," Deanna said. "A few bumps along the way are natural. We still have two weeks. She'll be ready."

"Any new bumps I should know about?"

"Not really. Just the challenges you'd expect from trying to accommodate a crew this biologically diverse aboard a single starship. I was on deck seven while the construction team was putting the final section of Ensign Lavena's quarters into place. I must say it's a little unnerving to see a wall of Pacifican ocean water that extends from floor to ceiling. If we ever have a forcefield problem, her quarters will have to stay sealed, otherwise the rest of that deck will have a huge flood on its hands."

Riker smiled. *Titan*'s distinction as having the most varied multispecies crew in Starfleet history was one in which he took great pride. He was convinced it set the right tone, for the right mission, at just the right time in the Federation's history. Small wonder, then, that it was also an engineering and environmental nightmare. At least, until all the kinks were finally worked out.

"You're right," Riker said. "I'm not going to worry

about it. Besides, it wasn't all that long ago when we had to deal with ships that could have taken on a lot more water than that." *Our honeymoon on the Opal Sea,* he thought. *Quite an adventure* that *was.*

They reached a turbolift and stepped inside. "Transporter room four," Riker instructed it. The doors closed, and the lift started to move.

"There's something I do need to bring up," Deanna said. "It's Dr. Ra-Havreii."

"What about him?"

"He's asked to remain aboard *Titan* during its shakedown."

Riker frowned. "Did he say why?"

Deanna shook her head. "He wasn't specific, but I could tell he was troubled about something."

"A problem with the ship?"

"No, I asked him that immediately. He said he has no concerns about how *Titan* will perform, and his emotions bear that out. This is a personal request."

Riker nodded, considering the matter for a moment. "All right. Let him know he's welcome to remain aboard during the shakedown. No, wait, belay that. *I'll* tell him. A personal invitation from the captain is the least of the courtesies I can extend to *Titan*'s designer. And while he's with us, see if you can probe a bit deeper about his reasons for staying aboard—without offending him, of course. Maybe after Dr. Ree is settled."

"Understood," Deanna said, and there it was again—that small, restrained smile, the same one she had nearly released when Jaza had informed him of Ree's imminent arrival.

The lift halted, depositing them outside the transporter room. Riker stopped. "All right, Deanna, what is it?"

Her smile finally broke loose entirely, spreading across

her face until it became a grin. It was almost as though she was trying to keep herself from laughing. *Not a good sign.*

"You never read that file I left you on the Pahkwa-thanh, did you?" she said.

The Pahkwa-thanh, Riker thought. *Dr. Ree's species.* "I didn't see the hurry," he said aloud. "What's important to me about Dr. Ree are his talents and his record as a Starfleet physician, not where he comes from. I care about *who* he is, not *what* he is."

"But you've never met him," Deanna said, still smiling enigmatically. "Nor any other Pahkwa-thanh."

"Deanna," Riker said, then lowered his voice upon noticing a passing crewman. "If there's something about Ree I should know before I meet him, what is it?"

Deanna straightened his combadge as though preparing him for an admiral's inspection, her demeanor suddenly innocence itself. "As you said, it's probably not important. So let's just go meet him." Doing a quick about-face, Deanna marched into the transporter room before Riker could stop her. Now more than ever, he questioned the wisdom of captaining a ship whose crew included his wife as a senior officer and adviser. He knew he could trust whatever decisions Deanna might make on his behalf to be in the best interests of both himself and *Titan*'s crew. But he was also well aware that she wasn't above having a bit of fun at his expense in the process.

Riker sighed and followed her inside.

"Good evening, sir," said the young lieutenant who was standing behind the transporter console.

"Good evening, Lieutenant." Riker searched his mind, but still didn't remember the young man's name. "I'm sorry, but what was your name again?"

"Radowski. Lieutenant Bowan Radowski," the dark-complected technician said. "And no apology is necessary, sir. We all know who *we're* serving under, but I'm sure it's difficult learning so many new crew members' names."

Riker tried not to smile. He wasn't certain if the transporter chief belatedly realized that he had just insulted his captain's intelligence, but Riker knew no offense was meant. *Kind of reminds me of something I might have done in* my *younger days,* he thought.

A beep sounded from the console, and Radowski quickly ran his fingers over the controls. "Dr. Ree is standing by, ready to beam over."

"Energize, Mr. Radowski," Riker said.

On the transporter pad, the familiar luminal effect grew and coalesced into a solid being. As it materialized, Riker finally understood why Deanna had been so amused by his casual ignorance of Dr. Ree's species.

He had known from the head shot in Ree's personnel file that the doctor was quasireptilian. But he saw now that the little 2-D image, taken head-on, had been misleading. At his full height, Ree must have been over two meters tall, and was built like a running dinosaur. Ree's scaly, vivid yellow hide was accented by jagged stripes of black and red, and partially covered by an oddly configured Starfleet medical uniform designed to fit his unusual frame. A thick tail snaked behind two powerful legs, which had clearly evolved to chase down prey, and whose feet ended in talons and rear dewclaws. Ree's upper limbs more closely resembled humanoid arms, though it was hard to gauge their length because he kept them bent at the elbows, folding them close to his upper chest. His iguanalike head held a mouth full of sharp, finger-length teeth that glistened wetly.

Ree stepped off the transporter pad and approached Riker, staring at the captain with large, vertical-pupiled eyes that made him feel like a field mouse caught in the basilisk stare of a barn owl. "I am Dr. Shenti Yisec Eres Ree. Permission to come aboard?" the Pahkwa-thanh said. His diction was nearly flawless, though Riker saw that a forked tongue, as well as twin frontal pairs of upper and lower fangs—barely visible amid the rest of his formidable-looking dentition—were the likely source of the overly sibilant esses in his speech. Riker also noticed that the doctor was emitting a strange odor, something vaguely akin to burnt toast.

Not wanting to appear put off in the least by the doctor's appearance, Riker stepped forward and extended his right hand in greeting. "Permission granted. I'm Captain William T. Riker. Welcome aboard *Titan*, Doctor."

Ree extended one of his own hands and grasped Riker's with surprising gentleness. "A pleasure to meet you, Captain. I'm eager to get to know you better."

As Ree made contact, Riker almost flinched reflexively. Ree's manus was cold, with long, nimble digits that wrapped almost entirely around Riker's hand. The hard claws tipping the Pahkwa-thanh's fingers were, thankfully, filed down, but the overall experience of shaking Ree's hand raised the hair on the back of Riker's neck.

I'll get you for this, he projected toward Deanna, carefully schooling his features into poker-tournament mode and focusing his attention on *Titan*'s chief medical officer.

To his surprise, Deanna acknowledged having "heard" him. That seldom happened, except when they were in close proximity, or in times of exceptional emotional stress. The instinctive unease he had experienced at his first sight of Ree—perhaps an atavistic human fear-reaction—certainly qualified, Riker thought.

What's important is who *he is, not* what *he is,* Deanna quoted.

All right, lesson learned, he shot back. Clearly, despite his high-minded ideals and enlightened self-image, Riker could still be caught off guard by the unexpected, and by what he didn't yet understand. He realized now that Deanna had set him up in order to give him a wake-up call about the challenges that *Titan*'s crew—including her captain—would have to face in learning to live and work together. Riker resolved to read Deanna's files on the Pahkwa-thanh as soon as possible—as well as those of any other species represented among his crew about which he had a less than thorough familiarity.

Mastering his revulsion by sheer force of will, Riker withdrew his hand and gestured with it toward his wife. "This is *Titan*'s diplomatic officer and ship's counselor, Commander Deanna Troi."

Ree bowed slightly, though he did not offer his hand. "A pleasure." He looked at Deanna more directly. "I look forward to discussing empathic theory with you, Counselor. Some of us Pahkwa-thanh possess empathic sensitivities similar to those of Betazoids. While I have no measurable degree of this talent, I still like to think that it is my empathy that makes me such a good surgeon." He paused, then added, "It certainly isn't my humility." A dry laugh followed, sounding not unlike maracas being shaken.

Deanna beamed at him. "May I escort you to sickbay, Doctor?"

"That would be delightful," Ree said, somehow hissing and clicking simultaneously as he spoke. Riker thought of drawers full of steak knives when Ree's top and bottom teeth came into contact. "Since that is where I'll be spending half of each ship's day, I hope that I will bond with it immediately."

Deanna led the way out of the transporter room, with

Ree walking directly behind her, his head dipping to avoid hitting the doorframe, his claws clacking loudly across the deck as he moved. Out of Ree's line of sight, Riker started rubbing his right hand—which he imagined felt strangely clammy after Dr. Ree's handshake—when he "heard" Deanna in his thoughts again: *Just deal with it, Will.*

As he stepped into the corridor, a voice once again issued from his combadge. *"Bridge to Captain Riker."*

Watching Deanna and Ree disappear around a curve in the corridor, the captain tapped his combadge. "Go ahead."

"Sir, we've just been hailed by the runabout Irrawaddy, *on approach from Earth. She's requesting priority clearance to land in the main shuttlebay. Admirals Ross and Akaar are on board."*

"Thank you, Mr. Jaza. I'll be right there," Riker said as he headed for the turbolift, his poker face suddenly inadequate to the task of suppressing the frown that was creeping across his features.

A surprise visit from two of the most influential admirals in the fleet. This can't *be good news.*

CHAPTER THREE

U.S.S. TITAN

It had been four years since Lieutenant Melora Pazlar had left her brief assignment aboard the *U.S.S. Enterprise*-E and until two months ago she hadn't been back aboard a Federation starship. Her chief reason for staying so long in her native world's microgravity environment was personal. But now she realized that she'd had another legitimate rationale for having steered clear of Starfleet vessels for so long: physical discomfort. Even in the specially designed uniform she wore, adapting to the "normal" shipboard gravity could be a chore.

The uniform's exoframe servomotors let out a low, almost inaudible whine as Pazlar's willowy form progressed down the corridor. She moved forward deliberately, her garlanic wood walking stick assisting the exoframe's step-by-step redistribution of her weight. She saw a Vulcan and a Bolian approaching her, and politely nodded and smiled to them as they neared. She hoped she was concealing the constant pain and pressure *Titan*'s "standard" gravity settings caused her.

"Good afternoon, Lieutenant Pazlar," the young Bolian woman said as she came to a stop alongside her Vulcan companion. Her smile displayed a wide mouth full of bright teeth.

"Good afternoon, Ensign Waen," Pazlar said. Her mind raced, but she couldn't remember the name of the middle-aged Vulcan male, even though she had met him several days earlier. She noted that he seemed disinterested in her, so intent was he on the padd he carried. "I hope your day is going well," Pazlar said, at a loss to think of any other chitchat.

"Very well, thanks," Waen said. "We're on our way to the arboretum to see how Savalek's new *Kylo* orchid is faring." She gestured toward the Vulcan as she spoke the name, then back down in the direction from which they had just come. "I suppose you're off to see what they've done to your quarters?"

Pazlar nodded. "I have to confess I'm a bit anxious about that."

Waen leaned in closer, bringing her hand up to her mouth in a conspiratorial gesture. Pazlar doubted that she needed to bother whispering, since Savalek seemed absolutely absorbed by whatever was on his padd. "I heard some fairly loud swearing coming from the open doorway as we passed. I think it was that Ferengi geologist."

The Ferengi? *What is she talking about? Why would— what's her name, anyway?—why would Bralik be in my quarters?* Pazlar shifted her cumbersome weight, wincing slightly as her body settled into a new position. "Well, I'd best get down to see what all the swearing is about."

"We'll see you soon," Waen said, her tone jolly.

"Good grace," Pazlar said, remembering the Bolian term for a friendly farewell. As she made her way down the corridor, she heard Waen whispering to the Vulcan behind her. She turned her head slightly, and caught Savalek staring back at her with a strange look on his face. The Bolian woman, caught whispering, waved to Pazlar with slender blue fingers.

What were they whispering about? And what was that look in Savalek's eyes? Melora was used to such whispers; as the first Elaysian to join Starfleet, she had initially been confined to a gravity-negating mobile chair, and had later worn an exoframe even more cumbersome than the current model. Early in her career, she had often felt—fairly or unfairly—as though "high-g species" regarded her as a cripple. Despite the subtly contoured brow ridges that marked her as a member of a nonhuman species, it had always seemed that many of her fellow Starfleet Academy cadets had had a difficult time fathoming the essentially gravity-free environment from which she had come. Granted, the existence of a place such as Gemworld— whose null-gravity humanoid habitat had been maintained since antiquity by automated machinery—seemed at first glance to defy every known law of planetary science. Still, Pazlar was always frustrated when others apparently failed to understand that she was no more out of place in one g than, say, an oxygen-breathing Terran would be in Pacifica's undersea city of hi'Leyi'a.

Early on during her time among humans, all the whispers and "special" treatment had made her extremely defensive. By the time she had been assigned briefly to head stellar cartography aboard space station Deep Space 9 some nine years ago, she had developed a decidedly antagonistic attitude. The station's doctor, Julian Bashir, had offered her a neuromuscular adaptation therapy which could have acclimated her motor cortex to standard gravity—permanently. But she had decided against the therapy, having learned by the end of her short stint on DS9 that her attitude, not her physiology, had needed adjustment.

She had spent the next several years honing her skills, acquiring new ones, and then being tested on numerous short-term "specialty" assignments, ranging from stultifyingly mundane mapmaking junkets to some truly harrowing missions in which she had piloted shuttles. During the Dominion War, she had helped save 192 of her shipmates, and had been decorated for valor afterward. Immediately following the war, she had accepted an assignment aboard the *Enterprise* to conduct a low-gravity science study on Primus IV.

But fate had made other plans for Pazlar. After she had been contacted by the Lipul, one of her homeworld's six sentient races, she convinced Captain Jean-Luc Picard to divert the *Enterprise* to the artificial planet known as Gemworld. Although Pazlar and the starship's crew had succeeded in preventing Gemworld's destruction, she had been forced to take the life of another Elaysian during the mission. In the aftermath, Picard had granted her extended leave from Starfleet to face her homeworld's Exalted Ones, and to atone for her crime. She had spent a seeming eternity drifting in cloistered meditation, fasting and contemplating her deeds on that mission—actions that weighed heavily upon her even now, and probably always would.

Although even the Exalted Ones had finally declared the death of the renegade engineer Tangre Bertoran justifiable and unavoidable, Pazlar had continued her atonement rituals for many months—intervals known as "shadow marks" among the Elaysians, whose world lacked a natural satellite from which to construct a lunar calendar—before making her decision to reconnect with Starfleet. She had been on assignment with the science vessel *Aegrippos* when Captain Riker had invited her to join the crew of *Titan.*

Pazlar thought her initial meeting with Riker last week had gone quite well. He was fresh from what had apparently been an unusual honeymoon on Pelagia, and had seemed eager to accede to Pazlar's requests.

"If I take this job, the stellar cartography lab *is* going to be micro-g most of the time," she had said firmly. "Not to put too fine a point on it, sir, but I've adapted to everyone else's need for gravity for a long time now. I think it's time that my colleagues began to adapt to some of my more . . . free-floating needs."

"Agreed," Riker had said, smiling. "There's something else, Lieutenant."

"Sir?"

"We've got a pretty radical structural idea for your quarters," he had said with another disarming grin. "I've had the engineering teams working on cabin retrofits for several members of the crew who have special environmental requirements. I think you'll like what they've come up with for you."

Now, a week later, Pazlar neared the alcove that led to the door to her quarters. Or, more specifically, one of the doors. As the Bolian had said—*why am I so bad with names?*—the entryway stood open, and several blue-banded engineering hover platforms were visible just inside the alcove.

As Pazlar stepped into the alcove, a growing feeling of comfort washed over her. Using the wall keypad, she manually closed the outer door behind her, to avoid causing discomfort to anyone who might be inclined to pop across the entryway's threshold to say hello. Next she made sure that the hover platforms were locked into place against the wall, and that no loose tools were lying atop them, since the slightest bump could send them flying after she lowered the artificial gravity. "Computer," she said, "drop gravity in alcove to one-sixty-fourth g."

Immediately, the pain and fatigue in her joints dissipated. Pazlar pushed off against the deck beneath her feet and rose into the air. Dodging the hover platforms, she glided effortlessly over to the inner door on the ceiling, arrested her motion there, and touched the palm pad set into the bulkhead beside it. The door slid open, and Melora entered her quarters.

The lights were bright inside. Coming to a halt against the curvature of the far wall, she looked straight upward to the next level, where her bathroom facilities were located. She saw Chief Bralik, the noncom Ferengi geologist, exiting the room with surprising grace, considering the room's low-g environment.

"Whew!" Bralik said, a sour look on her face. Then again, maybe that was an entirely normal expression for a Ferengi.

"Doctor Bralik," Pazlar said. "May I ask what you're doing in my quarters?"

Bralik pivoted to look down at Pazlar, her eyes wide and her sharp, uneven teeth bared. "Oh. Sorry. Chief Engineer Ledrah invited me to tag along."

Pazlar grabbed a handhold and pushed herself smoothly upward, trying to keep the look of puzzlement off of her face. "Why exactly did Ledrah invite a geologist to inspect the retrofit of my quarters?"

Scratching one of her ears—Pazlar wasn't certain, but it seemed to her that male Ferengi had far larger ears than did the females—Bralik seemed nonplussed by the question. "Probably because I used to work at the micro-g Karcinko mining facility back in the Ferengi Alliance. I got used to these kinds of long, vertical spaces there. Most of the ones down the mines had a lot more *grak* floating about, though."

"You were a miner there?" Grasping another handhold, Pazlar oriented herself alongside Bralik. The diminutive Ferengi woman did indeed seem to handle herself very well in low g, a knack that even some seasoned Starfleet veterans never acquired. "Please don't take this the wrong way, but I'd always thought that those sorts of jobs were off-limits for Ferengi women."

Bralik snorted. "A lot has changed during the last few years, thanks to Zek and Rom. On the other hand, some people are still stuck in the past. Take the mining trade, for instance. Once I helped the senior engineer work out the flaws in his construction plans for the Karcinko facility, he dumped me for a more bountifully figured *chava*. My reputation was already ruined, so I decided to stay on at the facility rather than slink back home."

"So you went there as a mining engineer?"

Bralik chortled again. "No. I went there as the senior engineer's property. Wasn't even allowed to wear clothes. But I picked up my interest in geology there, and started studying it on the sly." She paused for a breath. "I'm older than I look, you know."

"I'm not sure I follow," Pazlar said, confused.

"I mean, I'm not some genius child prodigy geologist. I've paid my dues. After that horrible accidental cave-in that killed the senior engineer and his *chava*, I went to other mining facilities to study, and eventually went out-system. This is all before all of Zek's reforms, you understand. Ferengi females almost *never* went off on their own back then."

"Ah," Pazlar said, nodding. *Why is she telling me all this?* She pointed up to the third level of her narrow, silo-shaped quarters. "Is Nidani up there?"

"Yeah," Bralik said, pushing herself upward. "Come on. I think she's up there patching up a Jefferies tube that runs behind the bulkhead right past your sleepsack."

Pazlar glided up after her. She wasn't surprised there was still work to be done. Her living space was, as far as she knew, the only vertically oriented crew quarters ever built into a Federation starship. She supposed that "built" was probably the wrong term; Ledrah and her staff had actually retrofitted a narrow space spanning three decks in order to fashion living quarters suitable for an Elaysian.

"Hey, Ledrah!" Bralik bleated loudly, her voice echoing up and down the shaft. Pazlar made a mental note to apply some sound-dampening fabric or foam to the walls.

A familiar face emerged from an open access hatch. Ledrah looked harried, gripping a tool of some sort between her teeth. Her shock of bluish hair was matted with sweat; it would have been free-floating except that the Tiburon had it clipped to one of her large, seashell ears.

Ledrah mumbled something, releasing the tool from her mouth as she did so. It drifted forward and down in a lazy ellipse, but before the clearly micro-g-unaccustomed engineer could snatch it, Pazlar had already done so.

"Thanks," Ledrah said. "Sorry it's still such a mess in here. I'd hoped we'd be farther along on the reconstruction by now." She lowered her voice slightly, gesturing with one hand up to the fourth—and highest—level. "I'm starting to think having Paolo and Koasa on the job might be more trouble than it's worth. If I'm not having to redo something they've done wrong, they're arguing about which way to do it right the first time."

"But they're handsome," Pazlar said, smiling. "And they're twins."

Ledrah carefully extricated herself from the Jefferies tube hatch, laughing. "You're right. And they aren't any-where as bad as I make them out to be." She cautiously kept one hand on the rail, to steady herself in the micro-g environment.

"My understanding among your type is that hostility often masks attraction," Bralik said, her toothy smile showing. "Better be careful. They're junior officers."

With a mock scowl, Ledrah waggled a mottled, salmon-colored finger at the Ferengi. "You just watch yourself there. I know some of your secrets, too!"

As Bralik put her hands up, as if to protest her inno-cence, Melora spoke up. "I really appreciate all the work you're putting into the place, Commander."

"Well, it is a challenge, but it's about time we tried something new," Ledrah said. She looked around guiltily and dropped her voice. "Not that there's anything *wrong* with Ra-Havreii's basic design, mind you. It's just nice to see a few of my own ideas integrated into this ship, too."

"I've never met a chief engineer yet who didn't want to make the ship she's serving on her own," Pazlar said.

Engineers. She thought for a moment of Reginald Barclay, the shy man with whom she had shared a brief romance while serving aboard the *Enterprise.* She under-stood that in the time since then, he had been an active part of Project Pathfinder, which was instrumental in bringing the lost starship *U.S.S. Voyager* back to Earth. She hadn't spoken to Reg in years, and wasn't certain even now whether she was avoiding him, or vice versa. Or if their protracted mutual silence was mere happenstance.

Perhaps once she was fully settled aboard *Titan,* with a

mission or two under her belt, she would make the time to contact him.

"Hellooooo," a pair of heavily accented voices called from above them, in unison. Ensigns Paolo and Koasa Rossini came swimming down toward them, pulling along a cart of tools between them.

"Ooooh, your favorite junior officers are here," Bralik said, not quite quietly enough.

Ledrah flushed a bright pink, particularly along the vertical ridge of tiny horns that bisected her forehead, then lobbed the small instrument in her hand straight at Bralik.

Pazlar stifled a laugh as the object bonked the Ferengi woman directly between the twin lobes of her cranium, then ricocheted off into the room's lower levels.

I think I'm going to like this crew, she thought. *For once, I'm not the only outsider who has to adapt. We're all going to have to adapt to each other.*

Nurse Alyssa Ogawa watched the rhythmic, repetitive motions of Xin Ra-Havreii's long, wispy white mustachios. She found the effect almost hypnotic.

He's trembling, she realized with no small amount of surprise. *Why is he so nervous?*

"How long did you say this had been bothering you, Commander?" Ogawa asked.

Idly playing with the pips on the collar of his standard Starfleet duty uniform, Dr. Ra-Havreii swayed unsteadily toward one of the biobeds and reclined heavily on it. He assayed a laugh, but its apparent breeziness was belied by a subtle deepening of his slightly rusty complexion. "It comes and goes. I can usually cope with it, but it's flared up since I came aboard. One of my stomachs seems to have remained behind at the Utopia ground station."

Ogawa reflected on how ironic it was that a designer of starships had such wobbly space legs.

Offering him what she hoped was a reassuring smile, she said, "Then let's see what we can do about that. Short of sending a search party down to look for that missing stomach, that is."

He returned a pale reflection of Ogawa's smile as she walked to an interface console, where she checked the pharmacological database for broad-spectrum antinausea agents that were compatible with Efrosian physiology. Selecting one, she retrieved the proper vial and a hypospray from one of sickbay's equipment shelves and returned to her patient.

She touched it to the commander's neck and released the drug into his system.

"Feeling better?" she asked after a moment.

He nodded tentatively, his long, shimmering white hair undulating with the motion like some undersea reef-creature as he sat up slowly on the biobed. "Thank you, Lieutenant. I'm most grateful."

"Happy to help. You still need to see one of the doctors, though," she cautioned. "I recommend doing it as soon as possible."

Ra-Havreii nodded again, hand to abdomen as he breathed.

"I take it you don't make it out of the lab very often," Ogawa said.

Ra-Havreii seemed to hesitate before answering. "Not for several years. Nearly four decades of theoretical engineering for the Skunkworks seldom required that I leave Mars."

"The Skunkworks?" Ogawa said, unable to keep the laugh out of her voice as she repeated the odd word.

"A nickname among us engineers for Utopia Planitia.

Apparently it's an homage to an organization with a similar function from Earth's history." Ra-Havreii's elaborate eyebrows drew together. "I'm surprised you're unfamiliar with the term."

Ogawa smiled and shrugged. "I don't think there's any Terran who knows every obscure detail of our history. Surely not every Efrosian knows his own that well."

That seemed to take the commander aback. "Forgive me, Lieutenant. I'm afraid I have a bad habit of imposing my own cultural norms on my associates. I meant no offense."

"None taken," Ogawa assured him. "But does that mean Efrosians generally do having a working knowledge of those kinds of details?"

"It's culturally mandated," Ra-Havreii revealed. "You may be aware that my world is in the final stages of a prolonged ice age. My people evolved in the forests of the temperate band straddling Efros Delta's equator. Because of the difficult conditions there, our road to technological advancement was longer than it was for many other humanoid civilizations. As a result, we developed a highly structured and fiercely observed oral tradition to pass information from one generation to the next. Such practices are still observed, even though there is no longer a practical need for it."

Ogawa was intrigued. "If you don't mind my saying so, Doctor, it sounds like a very problematic and imprecise way to convey and preserve information."

"You'd be surprised," Ra-Havreii said with a soft laugh. "Abstract knowledge, after all, may be stored and communicated in any number of ways. *Meaning* is a different matter altogether. Our oral tradition has allowed us to preserve not only very ancient knowledge, but, where relevant, its emotional context. We've found that to be a powerful advantage when it comes to learning and, more importantly, to understanding.

"You must understand also that the idea of a written language had not yet occurred to my kind when all this was taking hold. Our oral tradition evolved out of necessity, not by choice. To this day, our method of data storage is aural, not optical. Our libraries have more in common with symphonic archives than they do with, say, this ship's databases. Rather than utilizing visual symbolism, we've created tonal vocabularies for history, science, philosophy, even mathematics. Similarly, our spoken language includes a range of vocalizations, imperceptible to most other species, that may contain many layers of subtext."

"Music," Ogawa realized. "Your entire culture is music-based. I've heard of such things, but the species that evolve along those lines are always aquatic. Never those that evolve on land. That's fascinating."

Ra-Havreii seemed delighted by her amazement. "We've come to understand that we're unusual in this regard," he admitted, "but it has served my kind well."

Ogawa wanted to ask more—she craved to, in fact—but at that moment the main sickbay door hissed open, drawing her attention toward the sound. She smiled as Commander Troi entered.

Then Ogawa's eyes widened as she focused on the large, sharp-toothed reptiloid who accompanied *Titan*'s diplomatic officer.

She quickly recovered herself. "Dr. Ree, I presume?" Ogawa said, smiling broadly.

Ree righted his head, blinked his opaque inner set of eyelids, then the transparent outer ones. His wide mouth pulled back in an approximation of either a grin, or a look of predatory hunger. "Unless you have another Pahkwa-thahn on your medical staff, that must be me." His clawed feet barely clicked against the floor as he stepped forward and extended one arm toward Ogawa. "You must be my indispensable chief nurse, Lieutenant Ogawa."

She grasped his hand and shook it, struck at once by the smoothness of his scaly skin and the gentleness of his touch. "At your service, Doctor. A pleasure to meet you. I look forward to our working together."

"As do I, Nurse." Ree's head suddenly swerved to face Ra-Havreii, who flinched slightly at the motion. "And who have we here?"

"Doctor Shenti Yisec Eres Ree," Troi said, "may I present Doctor Xin Ra-Havreii of Utopia Planitia."

"Ah, one of Starfleet's shipwrights," Ree said, then peered at Ra-Havreii more closely. "You seem a bit waxen for one of your species, Commander. What seems to be the matter?"

"Nothing serious," Ra-Havreii said. "Just an upset stomach."

"Chronic?"

The engineer looked surprised. "As a matter of fact, yes."

"Let me guess: replicated *levithi* nuts."

Ra-Havreii shrugged, embarrassed. "I've been waiting on a shipment of the real thing from Efros, but I don't expect it to arrive before *Titan* leaves the Sol System."

"You'll be with us awhile, then?"

Ra-Havreii glanced briefly at Troi, who nodded ever so slightly. "That was my intention, at least until *Titan* stops over at Starbase 185."

"A ten-day voyage, assuming there are no complications, not to commence for another two weeks," Ree said. "That's an unacceptable amount of time to go without health-sustaining nutrients that are obtainable only from foodstuffs native to your homeworld, Commander."

"I've managed through similar periods in the past," Ra-Havreii said. "The most difficult part is the nausea, but Nurse Ogawa has been very helpful in that regard."

Ogawa took that as her cue to tell Ree, "I've administered two cc's of peratheline, Doctor."

"An efficacious choice," Ree said. "But while peratheline will alleviate the symptoms, it will not address the underlying problem." Ree picked up a nearby padd and deftly tapped it with the tips of his blunted claws.

"I appreciate your concern, Doctor, but really, I can tough it out," Ra-Havreii said. "Besides, the replicated nuts—"

"Are unfit for Efrosian consumption," Ree finished. "Not that the dieticians who program Starfleet replicators don't try hard, but there are certain complex organic molecules the technology still has trouble with, the unique essential oils in *levithi* nuts being a prime example." Ree finished tapping the padd and handed the device to Ra-Havreii. "This should take care of the problem."

The commander looked at the padd. "I don't understand. Who is Chief Moreno?"

"One of the engineers aboard the *Seyetik*. We got to know each other quite well during the voyage from Deep Space 7. Quite an amiable fellow, and if I may say, an absolute fiend for Efrosian *levithi* nuts. He boasted having four containers in one of the ship's cargo bays. Since the *Seyetik* has put in to Utopia for upgrades that should extend well beyond *Titan*'s departure, I expect Chief Moreno may be amenable to cutting a deal whereby he takes possession of your expected shipment in exchange for a good portion of his present supply."

Impressed, Ogawa exchanged a look with Troi, who winked at her. Ra-Havreii seemed speechless. "Doctor Ree . . . I don't know what to say. Thank you."

"You're quite welcome, Commander. Now, off you go."

Ra-Havreii thanked Ogawa one more time, then left sickbay with Troi to pursue whatever was next on each of their no doubt busy itineraries, leaving the main sickbay area empty except for Ogawa and her newly arrived superior officer.

"Now then, Nurse, do you happen to know whether my medical supplies have been brought aboard?" Ree asked in his raspy, sibilant voice.

Ogawa nodded. "The quartermaster received your materials late yesterday. I've already arranged to have most of them transferred to sickbay, and they should be here by day's end. As you requested, a portion of the arboretum has been set aside for your pharmacological plants, but I strongly recommend you supervise any retrofitting yourself."

"You anticipate problems?"

Ogawa hesitated. "I took the liberty of reviewing the list of plants and the environmental modifications you specified," she admitted, "and let's just say I suspect the complexity of your proposed greenhouse and the precision with which it'll need to be balanced will present the engineers with a few new and potentially unwelcome challenges."

Ree's laugh sounded like an overturned rain stick. "Nurse Ogawa, that has to be the most gently worded critique of my complete unreasonableness that I've ever heard. I rather think I'm going to like it here."

Ogawa beamed. "Please, Doctor, call me Alyssa."

"Very well, Alyssa," he said, pronouncing the name with a lengthy hiss. "And you may call me Ree. Now, while I await the arrival of my personal effects, I should like to begin scheduling the crew physicals to ensure that the reports will be complete and filed before we launch.

I understand we have eighteen civilians on board, is that correct?"

"Soon to be nineteen," Ogawa said, thinking of Ensign Bolaji, a shuttle pilot now in the middle of her second trimester of pregnancy. "But yes, that's correct."

"Then I would like to begin with the civilians. Get a taste of them, as it were."

Ogawa laughed aloud at Ree's joke. She was beginning to find his enthusiasm infectious. Nodding, she said, "I have just the person in mind to be your first patient, Doctor."

Ogawa walked across the sickbay toward her office. The door slid obediently open, revealing two figures seated behind the desk. Her young son Noah was staring down at a padd, his brow crumpled in concentration. Hunched over it with him, his Trill spots only just visible on his thickly bearded face, was Ranul Keru.

"You can do it, all you have to do is think it through," Ranul said in an encouraging tone. "Just remember to cancel out the terms on both sides of the equation."

"But it doesn't make sense," Noah complained.

"It only seems that way. Take your time."

Ogawa paused in the doorway for a moment to watch them work. She felt a surge of gratitude for Ranul's continued presence in Noah's life. Like Ranul, Ogawa and her son had suffered a terrible loss while serving aboard the *Enterprise;* over the past two years, that shared grief had drawn the three of them together, almost as a de facto family. Ranul had lost Sean Hawk to the Borg more than six years ago; two years later, Ogawa had lost Andrew Powell, Noah's father, during the Dominion War at the Battle of Rigel. Sometimes she likened the three of them to ionized atoms brought together out of a desperate need to share their few remaining electrons.

Though Andrew had been dead for nearly five years, Ogawa saw her late husband's kind, strong face every time she looked at Noah. The child was both a comfort to her and a painful reminder of her loss, though thankfully much more the former than the latter.

"Sorry to interrupt the math lesson," she said.

Ranul grinned at her. "That's all right. I think we both needed a break."

Ogawa stepped into the office. "Good. Because there's somebody here I want you to meet." She swept her arm toward the open doorway behind her, where *Titan*'s new chief medical officer crouched so as not to bump his scaly head as he entered. "Lieutenant Commander Keru, Noah Powell, say hello to Doctor Ree."

Ranul looked startled for a split second. Then he smiled an easy smile, and introduced himself as he leaned forward across the desk to offer his hand in greeting. The doctor briefly took the hand in his gentle, hyperarticulated grasp. Then the reptiloid surgeon disengaged from the handshake and fixed his serpentine gaze on her son.

She squinted and held her breath for a moment, hoping that Dr. Ree's decidedly alien appearance wouldn't startle her son into saying something embarrassing. Noah was, after all, only eight years old.

Noah rose, goggle-eyed and silent as he stared at Ree. A long beat passed. "Wow," he said at length, drawing out the word and brushing a shock of jet-black hair out of his eyes. His voice was breathless, but without a trace of fear. "A Pahkwa-thanh. Cool!"

"So, you *still* don't have your exec, then?" Admiral William Ross asked, a concerned look on his face as he snatched the steaming cup of *raktajino* from the replicator.

Riker maintained a neutral expression, though he inwardly counted to ten before answering. If he didn't know better, he'd swear that Ross and Akaar were second-guessing him. *Maybe they're just testing me for prelaunch jitters. Better not disappoint them.*

"No, sir. But I can't afford to rush a decision as important as this one," Riker said evenly, seated behind his heavy Elaminite desk. "My XO needs to be someone that I know I can trust implicitly before we even clear the moorings."

Seated in one of the chairs in front of Riker's desk, Admiral Akaar uncrossed and recrossed his long legs, almost grazing the side of the desk as he did so. Though the towering Capellan seemed less tightly wound than Ross, Riker still couldn't shake an uneasy feeling that whatever news they were bringing him could not be good.

"And none of your *Enterprise* confederates fit the bill?" Akaar asked.

"Yes, and no, sir. I had three candidates from the *Enterprise*. All of them turned me down." He had more or less expected Geordi and Worf not to take the position, though either man would have excelled in it. But he was still stunned that Christine Vale had turned him down not once, but *twice*.

Of course, I turned down three captaincies before I finally saw the light, he thought. If he could finally change his mind, then why couldn't she?

Akaar and Ross exchanged a glance, then looked back at Riker, neither saying anything. Ross blew on his *raktajino* and sipped cautiously.

"There were exigent circumstances behind their decisions," Riker said, feeling defensive in the silence. "In fact, I'm going to pay a visit to one of them shortly. This time I feel certain that the candidate in question will accept my offer." *Please, Christine, take the job!* Riker thought to himself.

Akaar's mahogany-brown eyes focused on Riker like a pair of mining lasers. "May we assume, Captain, that the unnamed person who eventually becomes this ship's executive officer will not be another member of your immediate family?"

He's trying to bait me, Riker thought, though he wasn't about to allow either admiral to provoke him into losing his cool. "I assume, Admiral, that you're referring to the presence of my wife on my senior staff."

"I am, Captain," Akaar said. "I have seen other command officers make similar personnel decisions, often to their great regret. They frequently have great difficulty maintaining their objectivity."

Riker wondered if Akaar was referring to Lieutenant Nella Daren, who had served as the *Enterprise*-D's head stellar cartographer about a decade ago. Daren's brief romance with Jean-Luc Picard had resulted in both her and the captain going their separate ways over the very issue Akaar was raising now. *But my relationship with Deanna is different,* Riker told himself. *We didn't just meet and start a relationship from scratch. We've known each other for twenty years. And we're* married *now.*

Families serving together on starships was nothing new to Starfleet, but seldom the captain's family, and Riker knew that was Akaar's point.

"I am well aware of the pitfalls, Admiral," Riker said evenly. "Nevertheless, I'm completely satisfied that Commander Troi is my best possible choice for the dual role of diplomatic officer and senior counselor. Her record speaks for itself. As does mine, I think."

Riker had been shifting his gaze from one admiral to the other as he spoke. He made certain his next utterance was directed squarely at Akaar. "The fact that Commander Troi and I are married will have absolutely *no* bearing on any decision I might make."

Both admirals sat impassively, concealing their reactions with the skill of master poker players. A moment of silence passed, and Riker decided to take the bull by the horns. "Please forgive my bluntness, but I find it hard to believe that the purpose of your surprise visit was to quiz me about my senior-officer roster."

Akaar leaned forward, uncrossing his legs again and resting his large hands on his knees. "No, it is not, Captain. The reason we came was to discuss your first assignment."

Riker's brow furrowed. "It was my understanding," he began, "that I would be receiving specific orders about our mission from Admiral de la Fuego, once we arrived at Starbase 185."

"No," Ross said tersely, interrupting—and making Riker's heart sink precipitously. "There's going to be a delay, Captain. Admiral de la Fuego has already been advised that you won't be reporting to Starbase 185 on schedule. You have a new mission." He set his mug down on the desktop and leaned in slightly, drawing closer to Riker. "Understand that for now, most of the information about this mission is being distributed on a purely need-to-know basis, and all you need to know at this moment are the basics. You may inform members of your senior staff and your crew what we're about to tell you. However, many of the details are quite sensitive, based on intelligence that's currently in flux, and therefore may not be made completely available to you or your crew until this ship is ready to sail."

Riker leaned back in his chair, pulling away from Ross in the process. "I take it that despite this ship's stated purpose, the mission we're about to undertake will be neither exploratory nor scientific?"

"You are to proceed to the Romulan Neutral Zone, Captain," Akaar said emphatically, pointedly not responding to Riker's obvious but not-yet-stated concerns. "In response to Praetor Tal'Aura's request for a Federation-Romulan dialogue, the Federation Council and Starfleet Command have placed *Titan* at the head of a small multilateral diplomatic and humanitarian convoy. I do not need to tell you how dangerous it would be if the Romulan Empire were to dissolve. The resulting political upheavals could spread large amounts of unaccounted-for weaponry across the quadrant. But this is a very real possibility. Your mission, in part, is to alleviate the social and political chaos that now threatens to sweep Romulus, Remus, and the rest of the Empire because of Shinzon's assassination of the Romulan Senate, and the power vacuum left in the wake of his own subsequent demise."

Riker was already regrettably all too well aware of Shinzon's crimes; the crew of the *Enterprise*-E had been directly involved in stopping the mad, self-anointed praetor's murderous bid for galactic power.

"We expect that the task force will be greeted by a contingent of Romulan ships in the Neutral Zone," Akaar said. "And we anticipate that they will then conduct *Titan* and her convoy to Romulus itself, where you will conduct the diplomatic phase of your mission."

"I'm curious as to why we're sending relief ships," Riker said, already beginning to get over his initial surprise at this sudden change to his mission. "I wasn't aware that things had gotten so desperate on the other side of the Neutral Zone." If they had, he reasoned, then it was doubtful that the crew would have the luxury of spending the next two weeks completing *Titan*'s launch preparations.

"Romulus has not descended into complete chaos— *yet*," Akaar said. "But the supply chains within empires are notoriously vulnerable to political instabilities. Should the regime on Romulus topple altogether, the aid supplies carried by your task force may well become essential, at least in the short term. We anticipate, in that event, that whichever Romulan and Reman leaders emerge from the subsequent power struggles will respond to our goodwill with the appropriate gratitude."

Running one hand through his brown-and-gray hair, Ross continued after Akaar paused. "The Romulan Star Empire, or what's presently left of it, now stands vulnerable not only to outside attack, but also teeters at the edge of a potentially apocalyptic civil war as various Romulan and Reman political factions squabble over the reins of power. At the request of Praetor Tal'Aura, you will mediate power-sharing talks between the various opposing sides. Though the Romulans have been committed Federation adversaries for the last two centuries, the Federation Council and Starfleet Command are both greatly concerned about the ramifications of political chaos in the Romulan Empire."

Chaos. Riker found his own mind verging on it at this moment. The *Enterprise*'s last mission to Romulan space had been traumatic enough for that ship and her crew, bringing about the deaths of Lieutenant Commander Data and scores of others. Not to mention the psychic rape that Shinzon himself had inflicted on Deanna. Though Riker had no doubt that his wife and diplomatic officer would do her duty without hesitation, he could also guess how hard it would be for her to return so soon to the very place where Shinzon had violated her.

He was about to be sent into one of the most politically volatile places in the galaxy, with an untried new ship and an untested crew—nearly all of them dedicated explorers who had prepared for, and expected to undertake, a mission of an entirely different order.

CHAPTER FOUR

U.S.S. TITAN, STARDATE 56941.9

"I officially pronounce her fit and ready to fly, sir," Lieutenant Commander Nidani Ledrah said as she replaced the access panel to the *Armstrong*'s port engine nacelle. She rose from a crouch and strode alongside the spotless new type-11 shuttlecraft, and beamed with professional pride.

Riker returned Ledrah's smile, delighted by her enthusiasm.

"I'm curious about something, Captain," Ledrah said, her voice echoing across the high, vaulted spaces of *Titan*'s primary hangar deck. Nearby was parked the runabout *Irrawaddy,* which had brought Admirals Ross and Akaar aboard. Shuttlecrafts *Ellington, Gillespie, Holiday, Handy, Beiderbecke, Marsalis,* and *Mance* were all arrayed neatly beyond, positioned farther away than both the *Armstrong* and the *Irrawaddy* from the forcefield barrier that prevented *Titan*'s atmosphere from rushing out into the airless void. Beyond the hangar's yawning aperture, Mars presented its ancient, sanguine, crater-pocked face.

"Ask away, Commander," Riker said, slowly walking around the sleek auxiliary craft, admiring its simple, tapered lines. Of the eight shuttlecraft aboard *Titan,* the *Armstrong* had already become his hands-down favorite.

"I heard you're taking her to Earth, sir."

"You heard correctly, Commander. Why? Are you that eager to have her back?"

"No, sir, not at all," Ledrah said, sounding almost flustered.

Riker raised a hand reassuringly. "Don't worry, Nidani. I promise not to scratch her up."

"No, sir, that isn't what I meant at *all.* I was just wondering if you were coming back with a new exec."

Riker nodded, understanding. "As opposed to offering the job to somebody who's already aboard."

"Not that I was planning on spreading it around, sir." Ledrah had grown beet-red. She clearly wished she'd approached this conversation with half as much care as she'd just taken getting through the *Armstrong*'s preflight checklist.

"Of course not, Nidani," Riker deadpanned. "I like to think of *Titan* as a 350-person village. So you can imagine how shocked I'd be if any gossip started making the rounds."

Ledrah looked embarrassed. Changing the subject, Riker returned his attention to the *Armstrong*'s white hull metal, which was utterly smooth and unblemished.

"She's a real beauty, isn't she?"

Ledrah seemed relieved at the shift in conversational trajectory. "She certainly is, sir. Cruising speed of warp nine, warp nine-point-four max. She can even manage warp nine-point-eight for up to thirty-six hours in an emergency. Though I wouldn't recommend it if you don't absolutely have to."

"Good to know. But with any luck I won't have any need to reach near-transwarp speeds between here and Earth orbit."

Ledrah now looked abashed by her brief technological rhapsody, though Riker assumed such things to be an occupational hazard to chief engineers everywhere. "Right, sir. Of course. I was, ah, just trying to say she's definitely worthy of her name."

Guessing what was coming next, Riker suppressed a mischievous smile. "Her name?"

Ledrah returned the smile with an enthusiastic grin of her own. "Yes, sir. Armstrong. The first human to leave his bootprints on Luna. Makes sense, since *Titan* is a *Luna*-class vessel, after all." She was clearly proud of her knowledge of Earth's aerospace pioneers.

Riker manually entered his access code into the keypad located on the forward starboard hatch, which obediently hissed open. "I'm afraid that's not who she's actually named after, Nidani."

"She's not named after Neil Armstrong, sir?" Ledrah's grin suddenly dimmed by several hundred gigawatts.

"Nope. Neil was already spoken for when Starfleet issued us our shuttlecraft. There's already a *Challenger*-class starship named after *that* particular Armstrong." Riker entered the cockpit and took a seat behind the spotless black flight controls. He looked through the open hatchway and relished the engineer's escalating confusion.

"So . . . which Armstrong *is* she named for, sir?"

Riker quickly tapped a series of commands into the flight console. "Louis," he said a moment before the hatch hissed shut, mercifully cutting off whatever response Ledrah might have made. He wondered briefly whether she recognized the reference, or if she would immediately run to a computer terminal to look it up.

Shortly thereafter the great Satchmo's namesake glided with a momentary flash through the atmosphere-retention forcefield of the hangar deck, cleared *Titan*'s drydock, accelerated, and took wing across the ruddy face of Mars, quickly leaving her mothership and Utopia Planitia behind. Then Riker guided the craft along a graceful, gentle arc down the Solar gravity well toward Earth.

Earth grew quickly from a pale dot to a small blue disk to a great azure orb. Descending to an altitude of about three hundred kilometers over the eastern coastline of Africa, Riker matched the shuttlecraft *Armstrong*'s velocity with that of the orbiting McKinley Station. As the open spacedock facility drew steadily nearer, Riker began to make out fine details on the hull of the great *Sovereign*-class starship inside. The majestic leviathan was suspended, gently cradled between the drydock's duranium struts and girders.

He had a visceral sensation of having come home, if only for one last visit. *But the* Enterprise *isn't my home anymore,* he thought with a wistfulness that surprised him.

At least a dozen environmental-suited repair techs could be seen working at various points on the dorsal area of the starship's saucer section, while nimble one- and two-person work bees methodically transported personnel and components to and fro. Though the exterior repairs and inspections were clearly continuing, there remained almost no trace of the hideous damage inflicted on the *Enterprise* during her head-on collision with Shinzon's flagship, the *Scimitar.* Angling the *Armstrong* beneath the starship's ventral surface, Riker noted that the captain's yacht, the *Calypso II*, was back in its customary place, integrated seamlessly into the saucer. The auxiliary vessel, the replacement for a predecessor that had been destroyed during the previous year's disastrous Rashanar mission, displayed not so much as a scratch.

It's good to see that the repairs to the captain's yacht went so well. Riker smiled, thinking back to the honeymoon he and Deanna had begun on Pelagia less than a month ago. As a wedding gift, Captain Picard had lent them the *Calypso II* for that excursion, a voyage that had subjected the craft to more than a few bumps and bruises. Though Picard hadn't made any mention of the damage afterward, Riker would have been able to sense the captain's displeasure even without the help of Deanna's Betazoid empathy.

A message from the saucer's aft hangar deck interrupted his reverie, and he swiftly acknowledged and brought the *Armstrong* into line for final approach and landing. Less than three minutes later, after setting the shuttlecraft down and securing it within the familiar cavernous hangar, Riker strode across the busy deck toward the inner pressure doors, noting the presence of perhaps a dozen engineers who were going about various shuttlecraft-maintenance–related tasks. Each of them paused and adopted attentive postures as he passed, and he told them all to remain at ease. Though almost all of them looked quite young, they struck him as an efficient, disciplined group of officers. But that wasn't the first thing he noticed about them.

I've never met a single one of them before, he thought, pausing near the hangar's inner doors. Certainly, the calamitous events on Dokaalan, Delta Sigma IV, and Tezwa had claimed the lives of large numbers of *Enterprise* security personnel; but a large proportion of engineers, medics, and others had died during those harrowing missions as well, and the presence of so many new faces here served as a stark reminder of that painful fact. It also brought to mind the more recent battle against mad Shinzon, whose failed attempt to annihilate Earth with a forbidden thalaron weapon had claimed the lives of dozens more of Riker's former shipmates.

Including Data, Riker thought.

"May I help you, Captain?" said a familiar voice behind him.

Riker turned and saw the grinning visage of Geordi La Forge. Behind him stood Lieutenant Commander Worf, a sly half smile slightly contorting his characteristic dour expression as he towered over the *Enterprise*'s chief engineer.

Riker returned the grin and grasped Geordi's extended hand. The handshake immediately became an unabashedly sentimental bear hug. Releasing La Forge, Riker took a half step backward and regarded them both.

"Did I look lost?" Riker said in answer to Geordi's question as he released the engineer.

"Not lost, sir," Worf said. "But you do appear . . . nostalgic." The Klingon officer relaxed his posture, apparently satisfied that Riker wasn't going to try to hug him as well.

Riker beamed at Worf. "Commander, one of my final acts as this ship's executive officer was to recommend you as Counselor Troi's replacement. Your sensitivity shows me that my judgment was sound." He considered commenting on the stray cat hairs he saw clinging to Worf's metallic baldric, but held his tongue; he knew that Data's cat Spot was now sharing Worf's quarters, an arrangement that was surely a significant imposition on the loyal yet solitary Klingon.

Worf's passing look of confusion gave way almost immediately to one of comprehension. Riker recalled that when he had first come aboard the *Enterprise*-D fifteen years ago, human jokes had left Worf utterly at sea. Though he would never be the life of the party, the utterly humorless warrior Worf had been in those days was no more.

"I regret that circumstances have forced me to settle for other duties instead, Captain," Worf said dryly.

"There are always other jobs in the fleet if this one doesn't work out, Worf," La Forge deadpanned to Worf. "I know that *Titan* already has a pretty darned good head counselor. But from what I hear, the exec position there is still open. Maybe there's still time to change your mind." He turned his blue-white optical implants back on Riker with an insouciant wink.

Riker allowed his smile to fall ever so slightly. *Geordi would know if Christine had changed her mind about not taking the job. If I can't persuade her this time, I'm just going to have to move on. Go through the candidate list again, and then settle for someone else.*

He hated to settle. And he'd already been thwarted on this particular quest too many times.

"Actually my ongoing executive-officer audition is one of the reasons I'm here," Riker said aloud. *"Titan* won't ship out for almost two whole weeks, so I have that long to finish filling out my roster. But don't worry. I'm not going to try to steal either of you again."

La Forge chuckled at that, no doubt recalling that he had been Riker's first choice for the exec job. Geordi had opted instead to remain aboard the *Enterprise* as chief engineer, a job to which he felt better suited. Worf, who had been prematurely invited to take *Titan*'s exec job by Admiral Ross, had looked forward to serving under Riker's command . . . until Picard, following Data's death, had sought Worf's permanent assignment to the *Enterprise*. The change in circumstances had led Riker to make his second overture to Vale, which she proceeded to turn down *again*.

La Forge's tone grew suddenly serious. "Do you think she'll say 'yes' this time, Commander?"

Riker shrugged. "I'll let you know. But if later you see me scowling in a dark corner of the crew lounge, order me another drink, stat."

And with that, he stepped through the inner hangar doors and into the corridor that led to the rest of deck six. A few moments later he entered a turbolift, which he momentarily placed on pause.

"Computer, locate Lieutenant Commander Christine Vale."

The door chime sounded, startling her.

Seated cross-legged on the low sofa in her quarters, Christine Vale set the replicated hard-copy book she had been reading down on her lap. The volume, a biography of Thelian, the Federation's president during the time of Cardassian First Contact, wasn't succeeding in holding her interest. At last count, she'd read the same paragraph five times.

Is it already time?

"Come," she said to the closed door. Already aware of her visitor's identity, she moved the book onto the coffee table and rose from the sofa, only belatedly becoming aware that her boots lay in a heap beside her bed. Though her uniform was otherwise virtually inspection-ready, her feet were bare.

The tall form of William Riker stepped confidently into the room. "Hello, Christine."

"Hello, Captain," she said, trying not to let her lack of footwear make her feel awkward, even though she was entitled to be comfortable in her own quarters. She reminded herself that he had once seen her lying on a South Pacific beach wearing nothing but a skimpy swimsuit. *But today we had a meeting scheduled, and I lost track of time. Not a very auspicious start for a prospective first officer.*

Finger-combing her short, sandy-hued hair, Vale gestured to a nearby chair. "Would you like anything to drink, Captain?"

"No, thank you," he said, taking the offered seat. "And you can call me Will. Why don't you have a seat yourself?"

Nodding, Vale resumed her place on the sofa and tried very hard not to fidget. Silence stretched between them.

"So," Riker said finally.

"So."

Throats cleared. More silence followed. Once again, Riker was the one to break it. *"Titan* won't head out for another thirteen days, Christine. I'd still like to have you aboard as my exec."

She inhaled, then released her breath in a long, nearly inaudible sigh. "The last time you asked me to my face, I gave you a 'no.' "

"But when I called you again a little later, you revised it to an 'I need to think about it some more.' Unfortunately, I really can't wait any longer. So have you given my offer any more thought?"

She nodded. If she were to be completely candid, she would have to admit that she had found it difficult lately to think about much of anything else.

"Rimward through the Orion Arm, beyond where anyone's been before," she said before another conversational lacuna could develop. "The idea certainly sounds . . . exciting." She knew she was keeping her reaction under restraint, hiding her cards, as it were. The job sounded even better than exciting—it sounded *perfect*. Pure exploration was the dream of virtually every officer in Starfleet, at least at some point in their careers. *Even for someone who never really wanted to be anything other than a cop.*

And another ship, a vessel with a wholly new mission, might allow her to put some distance between herself and the ghosts of Tezwa.

She watched as he shook his head gently, his expression taking on a somewhat wistful cast. "I'm afraid I've been forced to set aside the Orion Arm mission, at least temporarily. Instead, our maiden voyage will take us to the Romulan Neutral Zone, and probably to Romulus itself. We'll be heading up a special task force. Extending an olive branch while helping the Romulans maintain order until they can get their government back up and running."

Despite Riker's evident disappointment over the delay in exploring the Orion Arm, Vale found her interest even more piqued than it had been before. That surprised her, since she had lost so many of her people trying to keep the people of Tezwa from plunging into the abyss of societal collapse and civil war. She knew that keeping the peace on post-Shinzon Romulus would be vital to the Federation's security—and that it could end up making the Tezwa mission look easy. *I guess I'll always be more peace officer than explorer.*

"Is your answer still at least a 'maybe'?" Riker said,

breaking into her reverie. He was leaning forward, his eyebrows raised in expectation, though the rest of his features remained poker-game neutral.

She rose. In spite of herself, she began to pace, her hands clasped behind her back, her bare toes flexing and grabbing at the carpet, a nervous habit she'd acquired as a little girl growing up on Izar, waiting for her mother to return home from night patrols. After another protracted silence, she stopped herself and faced Riker.

"I've told Captain Picard about your offer," she said. She knew she was only stalling, and she hated herself for it.

Riker nodded, his hands pressed against his knees. "I know. I've already discussed this with him. I didn't want him to be blindsided, or feel that I'm poaching. But what you still haven't told either of us yet is whether or not you really *want* to take the job. So are you interested?"

She knew the time had come at last to display all her cards, face up. "I *am* interested . . ." She trailed off.

"Ah, I hear a 'but' coming."

She favored him with a wan smile. "But I can't. I'm sorry, Will. I'm afraid I have to turn it down."

Riker seemed to deflate, at least a little. Vale knew he wanted very badly to add her to his senior staff. And she was flattered by his persistence. But why couldn't he see what a terrible idea it was?

"Do you mind telling me why?" he said finally.

She sighed again, then plopped herself back down on the couch so she could look at him at eye level. Noticing that she had been playing idly with the newly awarded hollow third pip on her collar, she forced her hands down into her lap.

"Permission to speak freely, Captain?"

"Always. And it's Will."

"Will, you're not going to like what I have to say."

His lips turned upward in a wry smile. "I guessed that. I already don't like the 'no' part."

"I think you'll like the rest even less. But I suppose I wouldn't be a worthwhile first-officer candidate if I were ever to be anything less than perfectly honest with you."

"That's why I need you on my bridge, Christine," he said. "What's on your mind?"

"Commander Troi."

He blinked several times, his forehead corrugating slightly in puzzlement. "Deanna has been hoping for weeks now that you'd change your mind and join us. She never mentioned any problems between the two of you."

"Please don't misunderstand me," Vale said, holding up a hand. "I don't have any problem at all with Counselor Troi. My problem is with your relationship with her."

"You mean the fact that she and I are a married couple? I'm afraid the time to object to that was just before that first wedding ceremony back in Alaska. We're well past the 'forever hold your peace' period."

Ack! she thought. *Not what I meant!*

She moved her right hand in a quick wiping gesture, as though erasing an old-style blackboard in front of her, and did her best not to grimace. After pausing for a moment to compose herself, she said, "Deanna is more than simply *Titan's* senior counselor. According to the tentative crew roster you sent me, she's also the ship's diplomatic officer. That's an extremely important post aboard a ship whose main purpose is exploration, don't you think?"

His puzzled frown appeared to be heading rapidly toward scowl territory. "And I can't think of anyone better suited for it."

"Me neither. Trust me, Captain—Will—I'm not second-guessing your judgment in assigning her that job."

Now it was Riker's turn to stand. Towering over her, he

was beginning to look truly irritated. "It seems to me that's *exactly* what you're doing."

Nettled, Vale decided to stop trying to sugar-coat what *really* needed to be said here. She rose as she spoke, never breaking eye contact with him. He still towered over her, but she didn't so much as flinch.

"No, sir. I simply don't feel comfortable serving under a captain who has made his own wife such a critical part of his senior staff. If you'll forgive me for saying so, I don't think it's a wise arrangement for you to have made."

Riker's brow slackened as he lapsed into a thoughtful silence, evidently mulling over her words with great care. At length, he said, "You know, you're right. I can't escape the reality that a captain employing his wife as a senior adviser defies most conventional command wisdom. As a matter of fact, Admiral Akaar just spoke to me about it."

Her eyes widened at the mention of Akaar's name. The regal Capellan numbered among the highest ranking admirals in Starfleet, and was also one of the oldest.

"And what did you say to him?" she said.

Riker's benign smile returned. "The same thing I'm about to tell you. That it's all about discipline and faith. It's about my ability to keep my family life separate from my professional career. It's about my having the discipline to make tough decisions without allowing family considerations to cloud my judgment. And it's about the faith of the people around me that I won't waver in maintaining that self-imposed discipline. I'm confident I can supply the discipline. Hell, I wouldn't have had much of a career in Starfleet without that.

"But I need *you* to supply a lot of the faith. As well as the courage to be completely honest with me whenever you're having doubts. Just like you're doing right now."

Vale let his words hang in the air, and found herself

marveling at his easy gift for oratory. Had he always had that ability? She'd never noticed it before. She wondered how it was that the addition of that fourth pip always seemed to enable a command officer to deliver such stirring speeches.

"Did you really say all that to Akaar?" she said once she had collected her thoughts.

He chuckled. "Of course not. I wish I had. So I rehearsed that little speech all the way from Mars to here. Not that I really expected it to convince you."

"What *did* you expect?"

"That I'd at least reassure you that I've already made an effort to understand your misgivings. And that I sincerely believe this will be a nonproblem. The fact that Commander Troi and I are married will not affect my command judgment. Especially if you're sitting at my right on *Titan*'s bridge, keeping me honest."

She nodded mutely, impressed by his sincerity and his utter openness. His awareness of his own fallibility, balanced by a steely determination not to allow himself to fail. And his very real need for her own perfect candor, which was perhaps the best quality she could offer him.

What more could she ask of a CO?

"Besides," Riker added, "do you really think *Titan*'s head counselor would have let me get away with ignoring an issue like this?"

Vale found herself chuckling, suddenly far more at ease about the prospect of venturing into the strange, unknown world called "the command track."

"All right. I think you've just sold me. *Mostly.*"

"Mostly?"

"There's still another problem. And I'm afraid it's also Commander Troi–related." Before he could respond, she pressed on: "If I'm going to be your exec, that means that

Commander Troi is going to have to report to me, just like the rest of the crew."

"That's right," he said, his mien serious.

Vale's left hand went back to her collar, and her finger once again traced the outlines of the two and one-half pips that identified her rank as that of lieutenant commander. "But Deanna's a full commander. She outranks me."

An almost impish grin suddenly crossed his face. "I've already come up with a solution to that problem. Report to *Titan,* and you'll have that third pip—Commander. But you'd better hurry. Offer's good for a limited time only."

Vale took a step backward, momentarily stunned. She couldn't have been more surprised if he had just sprouted wings.

"But I only got promoted to lieutenant commander a few weeks ago," she said after the seeming eternity it took for her voice to return.

"So?"

"But you can't just . . . *promote* me again."

His grin broadened.

"Can you?" she added.

"Never tell the captain what he can and can't do," he said. "Didn't we just establish, yet again, that I'm infallible?"

Laughing, she extended her right hand. He took it in a firm grip. "Looks like I'd better inform Captain Picard that he's going to need to find a new chief of security," Riker said.

"If you don't mind, sir," Vale said, disengaging from the handclasp, "I really ought to be the one to do it."

He nodded. "I'll leave you to it, then."

"Will you be heading back to Utopia Planitia now, Captain?"

"Not right away." He turned and moved toward the

door, which hissed open for him. "There are a few . . . farewells I want to make first."

She nodded, surmising that he would want to see Geordi and Worf again before departing. And sometime before his return to *Titan* he would need to have some time alone with Captain Picard.

Thoughts of the *Enterprise*'s rock-steady captain, who was even now breaking in an almost entirely new crew, precipitated a renewed surge of guilt over her decision to leave. *Get a grip on yourself, Christine. Didn't the captain say he'd support whatever decision you made?*

Riker paused in the doorway. "Oh, and Christine?"

"Sir?"

For the first time, he made a show of looking directly at her bare feet. "When you report to *Titan,* don't forget to bring your boots."

CHAPTER FIVE

"Look out!" yelled astrobiologist Kenneth Norellis as the tool kit slipped from his grasp. Reacting instinctively, he grabbed vainly for the falling implements—and simultaneously lost his grip on the ladder. The artificial gravity took him, and he plunged nearly two meters straight down through the vertical shaft of the Jefferies tube.

He landed in a heap at the bottom, a moment after his tool kit sprayed its cargo of spanners and stem bolts in every direction. The impact forced a surprised yelp out of him, in addition to abruptly pushing most of the air from his lungs.

"You okay?" said Melora Pazlar, poking her head into the Jefferies tube's shaft from a horizontal access tunnel.

"Dammit!" Norellis said, massaging his right knee, through which pain was now flaring with near-nova intensity. "I can't believe I just did that," he hissed through clenched teeth. *And for what? A diagnostic analysis of a tertiary backup holographic imaging relay. I might be walking wounded, but it's pretty damned certain nobody's gonna pin a medal on me for* this *particular injury-in-the-line-of-duty.*

"You mean you can't believe you took a fall just now?" she said. Norellis was certain that the willowy Pazlar had never made a graceless move in her life—her cane and gravity-compensating exoframe notwithstanding. He saw in her barely suppressed smile that she was politely refraining from reminding him about the other tumbles and minor accidents he had suffered in his rush to make *Titan* ready to study the cosmos by her scheduled departure date. *As though this couldn't have happened to* anyone, he thought, his rising indignation almost—but not quite—distracting him from the lancing pain in his right knee.

"Good thing I happened to be nearby," she said after he followed her out into the corridor, she walking with a smooth economy of motion, he advancing in a tentative, painful crawl. "Need any help, Kent?"

He winced, praying silently that he wasn't badly hurt. "I think I'm okay. Just need. A minute. To catch my breath. And gather up my tools."

She nodded, standing beside where he half sat and half lay on the deck. The delicate Elaysian planted her cane firmly with one hand and extended the other down toward him. "Let's see if you can stand first."

He took her hand, using it to steady himself as he slowly rose, while Pazlar's exoframe whined with the effort of keeping them both steady. As soon as he reached his feet, his already-throbbing right knee felt as though it had just entered *Titan*'s matter-antimatter annihilation chamber.

He settled back onto the deck plating with a sharp cry and a resounding thump.

"Let me help you get to sickbay, Kent," Pazlar said. "You need to have Dr. Ree look you over."

"No!" he said, somehow finding enough wind to shout before he even realized what he was doing.

"I think you may have sprained more than your pride, this time, Ensign," said another voice, deep and rich and resonant.

Norellis turned in the direction of the voice and met the concerned gaze of Lieutenant Commander Ranul Keru, the tall, burly unjoined male Trill who served as *Titan's* tactical officer and chief of security.

Crap, Norellis thought. *Why does he have to see me like this? The universe must really hate me today.*

"I'm fine, Commander, really," he said aloud, struggling up into a crouch that made a Cardassian interrogation chamber seem like mercy itself. "No need to bother Dr. Ree. Really. I mean, he's a very busy man—er, dinosaur."

"Ree isn't a dinosaur," Keru said. "He only looks like one."

"Ah, so *that's* what this is about," Pazlar said, a look of understanding crossing her fair features. "I have to confess, even I find Dr. Ree a little scary-looking. But he's extraordinarily gentle. I even heard Nurse Ogawa telling Olivia Bolaji that Ree is a world-class obstetrician."

The astrobiologist smiled lamely, hugging the bulkhead as his breathing normalized and he continued trying to straighten his knees. "That's a lucky thing for Olivia. And if I ever get pregnant while I'm serving on *Titan*, I promise that Dr. Ree will be the second one to know."

His flexing knee reached a critical angle, and the pain once again dumped him deckward. Keru's thick forearm caught him before he completed his latest pratfall.

Pazlar favored Norellis with a sympathetic gaze. "Take some friendly advice from an expert, Kent. Next time you have to crawl around at the top of a Jefferies tube, disable the artificial gravity in there."

He nodded. "Great idea." *Fat lot of good that does me now.*

"Come on, Ensign," Keru said in mock-stern tones. "To sickbay with you."

"You might outrank me, Commander, but I'm not sure you can make me go to sickbay." But he knew he was losing the argument. Keru and Pazlar had already flanked him and were supporting him, effectively frogmarching him down the corridor toward a turbolift.

"Consider it an order if you like," Keru said, smiling, "or think of it as a strong suggestion from someone who never goes anywhere without a sidearm."

What remained of Norellis's spirits fell at least as quickly as his tool kit had. *Great. Now Keru thinks I'm a coward. And probably a xenophobe, too.*

As the doors of Dr. Ree's sickbay drew near, Pazlar whispered in his ear. "Don't worry, Kent. Dr. Ree hasn't eaten any member of this crew."

Not yet, Norellis thought as he passed through the gates of Hell, and abandoned all hope.

But once inside sickbay, he was heartened by the sight of a kindly, familiar face. Instead of a savage lizard-man, he saw Nurse Ogawa turn toward him. Except for her young son, Noah, the head nurse was the only other person in the sickbay reception area.

"Please tell me Dr. Ree is out," Norellis whispered, his jaw drawn tight from the agony in his knee as Keru and Pazlar helped him sit on the edge of a nearby biobed. "Maybe one of the other doc—"

"As a matter of fact, Dr. Ree *is* out at the moment," Ogawa said, cutting him off. "He's trying to boost morale by making a few 'house calls' among the crew."

Norellis sighed in relief at her confirmation of Ree's absence, then winced again as jagged lightning bolts of pain shot through his right knee.

Then he noticed Ogawa watching him in silence, her expression baleful. She brandished a medical tricorder as though it were a hand phaser. "Would anyone mind if I have a word with Mr. Norellis? *Alone?*" As Keru and Pazlar beat a tactful retreat, the nurse placed a gently restraining hand on little Noah's shoulder. "Not you, Noah. I want you to hear this, too."

Oh, crap, Norellis thought again, wishing he could run after his two shipmates. *I've really stepped into it this time.*

"Tell me, Kent, what do you know about Dr. Ree?" Ogawa said as she ran a quick scan of his injured knee. "How much can you tell my son about him?"

"Not a lot," he confessed.

She exchanged the tricorder for a hypospray, and injected him on the side of his knee. The pain immediately abated, and he flexed the joint cautiously. Still no pain. He heaved an appreciative sigh. Then he noticed Noah regarding him with his dark, curious, almond eyes.

Acknowledging Norellis's grateful smile with a small smile of her own, she continued: "So you aren't aware of all the new surgical techniques Starfleet has acquired thanks to the Pahkwa-thanh in general, and to Dr. Shenti Yisec Eres Ree in particular."

"Um, no."

"Or the dozens of papers he's had published in Federation medical journals."

He knew his face was heating up, warming and tinting

itself to the precise color of shame. "Ah. Not, er, not as such. No."

"So all you *do* know about him amounts to the fact that he belongs to a species that superficially resembles an extinct Earth reptile."

Norellis nodded. "A very scary, carnivorous Earth reptile. Yes." He remembered meeting Ree the night before in the arboretum; the doctor's long, crazily articulated fingers alone had made Norellis want to jump out of his skin. This morning Norellis had watched in mortified fascination as the doctor took a meal in the main mess hall. He wondered when the dripping red contents of Ree's plate would stop haunting him—

"Are you even *listening* to me, Kent?"

He shook off his unpleasant memories, wondering just how much of Ogawa's dressing-down he had missed. "You're right. I suppose I haven't been exactly fair to Ree. I took the same Academy diversity training you did."

"That's exactly what I was trying to remind you about."

He nodded. "I guess I'm just not used to being part of such an obvious minority. Being a human on a ship with a crew as varied as this one, I mean." It suddenly occurred to him that he himself had been a minority of quite another sort for as long as he could remember—a fact that had never bothered him, nor anyone else in his life.

To Norellis's intense relief, Ogawa broke off her attack and answered his frank admission with a smile. She began waving a deep-tissue regenerator over his injured knee. "I'm glad we're seeing eye to eye then."

Though he returned the smile, he thought, *But I can't promise you I won't flinch if Ree tries to touch me.*

That notion made him feel rather disappointed with himself. He remembered his Starfleet Academy diversity training, of course, and recalled how very seriously he had taken it at the time; he'd just never expected to have to put it to so much practical use so very often. Between his anxieties about *Titan*'s CMO and a score of other nonhumanoid crew members aboard, not to mention the cultural differences among the rest, Norellis was beginning to think diversity was easier in theory than practice.

"Is this what you mean by 'conflict resolution,' Mom?" Noah asked, brushing his dark bangs from his bright, coal-colored eyes.

Ogawa beamed at her son. "Yup. And it's the best kind."

"Huh. I wonder if it'll be this easy with the Romulans."

Norellis saw that her smile faltered then, though not completely. "We can only hope, kiddo," Ogawa said as she tousled the child's hair, then told him he was free to go now if he wanted. Noah wasted no time taking his mother up on the offer, leaving sickbay at a brisk trot.

Now alone with a woman whom he knew he'd just given good reason to chew him out, Norellis was more desperate than ever to change the subject. "So will I ever play soccer again?" he said, pointing to his knee.

Ogawa had already turned back toward the biobed and was putting her instruments away. "Stay off it as much as you can for the rest of the day. And try not to fall down any more Jefferies tubes the next time you're on duty."

Rising cautiously to his feet, Norellis wondered how she knew exactly how he'd injured his knee. Had Keru or Pazlar called ahead while he'd been distracted by his blinding pain? Or had Ogawa just made a lucky guess? In the short time he'd known her since he had left Starfleet Academy for *Titan*, she had always struck him as an extremely intuitive person.

"Alyssa, what do you know about Ranul Keru?" He was glad now that she'd insisted ever since joining *Titan*'s crew that everyone stay on a first-name basis with her.

"Anything in particular you're looking to find out, Kent?"

Norellis cleared his throat, silently cursing himself for his nervousness. "Is . . . Is he single?" He felt his cheeks beginning to flush again.

Casting a glance over her shoulder as if to make certain they really were alone, Ogawa pulled up a chair. The junior engineer resumed his perch on the edge of the biobed.

"I don't want to get a reputation as being *Titan*'s resident *yenta*," she said. "So you haven't heard anything from me. Got it?"

He nodded, silently making a lock-and-key gesture across his lips.

"He's single. But he's also kind of a loner."

"Are you saying I shouldn't, you know, pursue him?" Norellis wanted to know, feeling some genuine confusion.

"No. I'm just saying you need to proceed with caution. He lost a lifemate during a Borg attack on the *Enterprise* six years ago. And he's been carrying around a lot of grief ever since then. So my advice is to proceed with caution. Go slow, Kent."

Thanking her, he moved toward the door. He wondered if he was about to exchange the pain in his knee for pain of a wholly different sort.

"It's nice of you to make a house call like this, Doc," Olivia Bolaji said, resting on the sofa in the center of the quarters she shared with her husband, Axel Bolaji. "I know how busy you are."

"I am never too busy to check up on *Titan*'s very first hatchling-to-be," Ree said, his voice a leathery rasp. "So, how is the unborn youngling today?" Ree placed one of his nimble, superarticulated hands gently on her abdomen.

Olivia fought to keep from flinching away from his touch. Shamed by this, she hoped he hadn't noticed.

"Our newcomer has been kicking a lot lately," Axel said, a proud parental smile spreading across his deep brown Australian aborigine features. "It's hard to believe the due date is only fifteen weeks away now."

That seems like an eternity, Olivia thought as she looked down at her inexorably expanding belly. Her only regret about their decision to have a child was the time it would force her to spend away from her job. Olivia loved her work, and she knew she was going to have to begin curtailing it sometime in the next couple of months, if not sooner.

"You can level with me, Doc," she said. "Are you sidelining me?"

Ree blinked several times—the outer, rough-textured eyelids closed and opened first, followed in alternation by a moist white inner membrane—as he appeared to digest the unfamiliar human sports idiom. Then he displayed several rows of serrated, daggerlike teeth in what had to be the Pahkwa-thanh equivalent of a benevolent smile. "Not yet, Olivia. I will maintain your flight and duty certifications for at least the next month. Let's schedule another examination for thirty standard days from now. I will reevaluate your duty status then."

Ree bid the couple farewell and exited into the corridor, carefully but quickly negotiating the narrow doorway, his broad tail tucked up tightly behind him.

Olivia breathed an involuntary sigh of relief after he had gone.

She glanced down once again at her distended abdomen, then smiled at Axel, gratified that *Titan* had turned out to be so family-friendly, at least so far. Being a much smaller vessel than the *Venture*—the *Galaxy*-class star-

ship on which she and Axel had most recently served—
Titan had nowhere near as many married couples and
children living aboard her. But Olivia felt that their bur-
geoning family was more than welcome here nevertheless.

But maybe it's not so welcoming to Ree, she thought,
her thoughts abruptly darkening. Why hadn't Ree asked
her to report to sickbay for today's prenatal examination?
Could it be that other members of the crew were flinching
in his presence, just as she had? Was Ree picking up on
those feelings of alienation, and therefore making an extra
effort to reach out to the crew?

She contemplated the child that was steadily growing
within her. *Let's hope you and Noah Powell will get these
things right more often than the rest of us do.*

"Okay," Vale said as the azure limb of the Earth dropped
away from the *Armstrong*'s forward windows, "how about
this one: 'We hold it in our power to begin the world
anew.' "

Riker nodded solemnly. Though he'd served with Vale
aboard the *Enterprise* for the past four years, he had never
realized just how well read she was. "Where did that one
come from? Ben Franklin?"

"Thomas Paine." She appeared pleased to have
stumped him.

"I like it," he said. When he saw her triumphant grin, he
amended his statement with, "So I'll put it on the short list
with the other contenders."

"Can you recommend a *better* one?" she asked, ap-
pending a "sir" a beat later as an obvious afterthought. She
was clearly taking this business very seriously.

After pausing to enter a minor course correction into

the flight control console, Riker decided he had no choice other than to take up the gauntlet she had thrown down.

"All right: 'Among the map makers of each generation are the risk takers, those who see the opportunity, seize the moment and expand man's vision of the future.' "

"Emerson," she said with unflappable confidence. "Not bad. I think you ought to short-list that one, too. How about this one: 'My guide and I came on that hidden road to make our way back into the bright world and with no care for any rest, we climbed—he first, I following—until I saw, through a round opening, some of those things of beauty Heaven bears. It was from there that we emerged, to see—once more—the stars.' "

Riker was so impressed with that one that he actually let out a long whistle. "Beautiful, though I think it's a little long. Milton?"

"Dante."

He made a face. "Let's pass on that one. Maybe we ought to go heavier on brevity and lighter on metaphysics: 'O Stars and Dreams and Gentle Night; O Night and Stars return!' "

Once again absently tracing a finger across the three solid pips on her collar, Vale silently focused her gaze on some undefined portion of the shuttlecraft's ceiling.

Ha! he thought. *Got you. You can't get 'em all right.*

"I didn't figure you for a fan of Emily Brontë, Captain."

He slumped in defeat. "Well, much as I like Cab Calloway's song lyrics, I couldn't find any I thought would pass muster with Starfleet Command. So I went back to the classics."

"I'm not criticizing, sir. The Brontë is a good choice. Maybe as good as the Magee: 'And, while with silent, lifting mind I've trod the high untrespassed sanctity of space, put out my hand, and touched the face of God.' "

They lapsed into contemplative, companionable silence for several minutes. Mars hove into view, growing rapidly from a ruddy marble to a broad, rust-colored disk.

"Deanna can help sort this out," Riker said. "After all, we don't have to come up with *Titan*'s dedication plaque epigram today. We still have almost two weeks of final preparations to make before we launch."

Mars grew huge, and Utopia Planitia's orbiting starship assembly facilities swung across the terminator into the planet's sunward, daylit side. Floating in orbital freefall along the open spacedock facility that surrounded it was the graceful, twin-nacelled shape of the *U.S.S. Titan*.

Though she was of an entirely new design, one of the very first of her type to be built, *Titan* was by no means the most impressive ship in the fleet. A *Luna*-class long-range exploration vessel, *Titan* massed somewhere between the *Intrepid*-class vessels introduced nearly a decade earlier and the old *Ambassador*-class. And she was fast, well-staffed, and could more than hold her own in a fight, if need be. But mostly she seemed eager to glimpse what was out there.

And she's my *ship,* he thought, his chest swelling with pride. *My first real command.*

As Vale deftly piloted the *Armstrong* toward *Titan*'s main hangar deck, Riker noted with some relief that something had changed there. He tapped a command into the panel before him, opening up a voice channel.

"Riker to bridge."

"Bridge here, Captain," said Jaza. *"Welcome back, sir."*

"Thanks, Mr. Jaza. When did the *Irrawaddy* depart?"

"Admiral Ross took the runabout back to Earth several hours ago, sir."

Riker was pleased to hear that the admirals' visit was over. Though he didn't exactly hold a grudge against

Ross—he regarded him as an accomplished, competent officer who certainly deserved every laurel he'd earned during the dark days of the Dominion War—Riker nevertheless wasn't anxious to spend a lot of time in the man's presence. He hadn't forgotten that William Ross had very nearly filled *Titan*'s first-officer position without consulting him first. Not that Ross's choice of Riker's own longtime friend and shipmate Lieutenant Commander Worf was by any means a bad decision; it simply had not been *his* decision.

"Thank you, Mr. Jaza. And please advise Commander Troi that our crew is now complete," Riker said as Vale began securing the craft.

"I'm happy to hear that, Captain," came the musical voice of Deanna Troi, which immediately brought a small smile to Riker's face. *"Welcome aboard, Christine."*

"Thank you, Commander," Vale said, sounding somewhat uncomfortable with Deanna's familiar tone. *Maybe she's still got some misgivings about my command structure,* Riker thought. Still, he felt confident that his diplomatic officer and his new exec would end up working well together, despite the concerns that both Vale and Admiral Akaar had raised earlier.

Deanna must have been thinking along similar lines. *"I think Admiral Akaar will also be delighted to hear that you've decided to join* Titan*'s crew."*

Riker's smile collapsed like the core of a neutron star as the *Armstrong*'s hatch hissed open. "The admiral's still aboard?"

"He's coming along with us on the Romulan assignment," Deanna said, using her most carefully neutral "poker night" tones. *"In the meantime, he'll be staying aboard* Titan*."*

Riker's eyebrows rose in a manner that would have

spoiled his luckiest poker night. "Commander, has the admiral been made aware that the 'meantime' prior to *Titan*'s departure will last nearly two weeks?"

"Yes, sir. He says he's looking forward to spending that time here, so I've assigned him VIP quarters for the duration."

"That's . . . wonderful. See you on the bridge. Riker out." He and Vale rose and exited the shuttlecraft.

At least it doesn't sound as though he's going to try to rush our departure date, he thought with no small measure of relief as he mentally scrolled through a nearly endless list of essential yet still only partially completed prelaunch tasks.

But as he walked alongside Vale toward the nearest turbolift, he began wondering if he was about to discover what a thirteen-day inspection tour felt like.

CHAPTER SIX

After the first week passed, Troi noticed that she was feeling increasingly restive, so much so that she booked a couple of sessions with Counselor Huilan, one of her two subordinates in *Titan*'s Mental Health Services department. She was glad for the presence of the hardworking male S'ti'ach. The nearly meter-high sentient, who resembled a fat, blue-furred, bipedal bear with extra arms and dorsal spines, smiled with his saberlike white incisors bared as he regarded her with his huge, fathomless black eyes, all the while patiently listening to her problems and offering occasional encouragements. Despite his small size, Huilan easily did the work of any two humanoid counselors, which was a real asset on a ship whose widely varied crew carried so much potential for interpersonal friction. After Starfleet had halved Troi's original request for a four-person counseling staff—Starfleet Command, in its infinite wisdom, had decided that a total of three counselors, including Troi, ought to be more than adequate to handle any 350-person crew, regardless of its composition—she was doubly grateful for the little S'ti'ach's tireless efforts on behalf of *Titan*'s morale.

Nevertheless, Troi was feeling uneasy by day thirteen of Admiral Akaar's stay aboard *Titan*. It wasn't that Akaar was particularly overbearing, or even overtly impolite. But the tall, imposing Capellan was omnipresent, and his constant watchful propinquity had proved palpably unnerving to more than half the crew as they struggled to finish making the ship ready for its altered mission—a new agenda that was, all by itself, creating a great deal of anxiety in a ship's complement selected more for its scientific credentials than for its diplomatic expertise. Lieutenant Pazlar had told Troi of her frustration with the admiral, who had essentially turned the stellar cartography lab into his personal command post during much of each day's alpha watch. Because of its variable-gravity capabilities, the delicate Elaysian had come to regard the lab, with its unique, low-g window on the universe, almost as her own private domain. Troi knew how much Pazlar valued the few places aboard *Titan* besides her own quarters where she could comfortably dispense with her ever-present exoframe. Akaar was literally weighing the lieutenant down, even as he more metaphorically burdened the rest of the crew.

Troi also couldn't help but notice the admiral's fascination with *Titan*'s crew composition, particularly the ship's unusually large proportion of nonhumanoid species. Personnel such as Orilly Malar of Irriol, a double rarity in that she was both nonhumanoid and an expert in exobiology, and the partially cybernetic Choblik engineering trainee Torvig Bu-Kar-Nguv, seemed particularly fascinating to Akaar. The admiral would no doubt have also spent more time closely observing the Pak'shree computer specialist K'chak'!'op—whom virtually everyone on *Titan* simply called "Chaka" as a compromise between the arachnoid's complex mouthparts and the limitations of the speech apparatus of most humanoids—had the large sentient arthropod not exhibited a tendency to retreat for protracted periods into her quarters. Ensconced behind the earthen and organic-silk walls of her shipboard living space, Chaka could do her work as easily as she could anywhere else on the ship. Troi made a mental note to visit her soon and make a real effort to draw her out of her exoskeletal shell, as it were.

Is Akaar trying to prove that we can't make such a diverse crew work? she wondered, as she discreetly watched the iron-haired fleet admiral in one of the ship's common eating areas, where he was taking a meal on dishes that looked absurdly small before such a large man. The Capellan's face gave nothing away, though, and he was nearly as opaque to her empathic talents as a Ferengi.

At least he doesn't insist on making all the mission specialists posted upstairs hop up and shout "admiral on the bridge" whenever he appears, she thought. There was always something to be thankful for, however small.

As the day and hour of *Titan*'s departure from Mars orbit came and passed, she was grateful that the admiral's staff, comprised of several extremely dour Vulcans, hadn't even come aboard until scant hours before the ship's launch, which occurred on time and without any significant glitches. Despite an understandable apprehension over what lay ahead for *Titan* and her crew, Will's sense of relief as Ensign Lavena finally put the ship on a heading for the Romulan Neutral Zone had enfolded Troi like a warm down comforter. As she accompanied him afterward into the forward observation lounge for Akaar's official Romulan mission briefing, Troi breathed silent thanks to the founders of the Fifth House for these small mercies.

Titan's senior staff quietly took their seats before a backdrop of star-strewn blackness. Troi noted with some satisfaction the calm attention and curious anticipation they were all radiating, sentiments that almost entirely drowned out a small but unmistakable undercurrent of apprehension coming from most everyone present, at least to some degree.

"Thank you, Captain Riker, for the cooperation that you and your crew have given me and my staff," Akaar said, his voice a low rumble. The admiral sat ramrod straight at the opposite end of the table from Riker, and Troi watched with interest as the two leaders' eyes met. They were clearly evaluating each other.

"Not at all, Admiral," Will said. "I'm sure I speak for everyone here when I say we're eager to get our new mission under way." *Even if the nature of that mission has changed completely since I accepted this command,* Will's cerulean eyes seemed to add wordlessly.

Troi sat at Will's immediate left. Seated counterclockwise around the table starting from the captain's right were First Officer Vale, Security/Tactical Officer Keru, Senior Science Officer Jaza, and Dr. Ree, who occupied a specially customized seat designed to accommodate both his unusual height and his thick, muscular tail. Turning her gaze clockwise from her left, Troi glanced at Chief Engineer Ledrah, whose wrinkled Tiburonian ears spread nearly as wide as poinciana blossoms. Beside Ledrah, and at Akaar's immediate right, sat Dr. Ra-Havreii, attending the briefing at his own request.

Behind Akaar stood three stone-faced Vulcans, two of

them women. Though Troi found their ages difficult to determine, she judged from their bearing and salt-and-pepper hair that the youngest of the trio was well over a century old.

"Some of you are doubtless wondering why I have elected to come along on this mission," Akaar said, addressing the room. "I have come less in a military capacity than in what Starfleet Command and the Federation Council would no doubt describe as 'humanitarian.' " His brief pause made the irony of his last word conspicuous; everyone present was well aware that humans comprised a distinct minority aboard *Titan*. "Since the fall of its Senate, there has been a great deal of political chaos in the Romulan Empire, and this has grown more acute in the past several days. The Romulans need outside help, and—more importantly—they are finally willing to admit it.

"Among my staff are several experts in Romulan sociology, politics, and culture." Akaar continued before briskly introducing T'Sevek and T'Rel, the two Vulcan women, and Sorok, the lone Vulcan male. Each was dignified, almost regal in bearing, though their earth-tone civilian suits were elegant in their unadorned simplicity. "T'Rel?"

Nodding her curt, decidedly Vulcan acknowledgments to both the admiral and the captain, T'Rel took a single step toward the conference table before speaking. "Thank you, Admiral. Captain. Members of *Titan*'s crew. I trust you have all read the background documents we transmitted to you last week." She acknowledged the round of nods that answered her with a peremptory nod of her own. "Very good. Among the strongest of the numerous Romulan factions to emerge from the post-Senate Romulan geopolitical landscape is—"

"Excuse me." Nearly everyone in the room seemed surprised at the almost brusque interruption. Except, Troi noted, for the man to whom the voice belonged: Will Riker.

Based more on her private conversations with Will than her Betazoid talents, she knew exactly what was coming.

T'Sevek replied in an almost chiding tone. "Captain, we would prefer that your questions be held until *after* our briefing presentation."

"That's a fine idea, ma'am. However, there's one question I really need to get out of the way *first*. And that's because nobody has answered it to my satisfaction yet, even though I've already asked it more than a few times over the past two weeks."

Clearly becoming irritated, all three Vulcans turned as one toward Admiral Akaar, who sighed as he spread his hands in capitulation. "All right, Captain Riker. Which question are you speaking about?"

"The most fundamental one, Admiral. Why is *Titan* being sent on this mission rather than the *Enterprise?* I don't mean any disrespect, sir. But *Titan* has been a ship of exploration from drawing board to final crew roster. It seems to me the Federation's flagship would be far better suited to this mission—as would its commander, who is a much more accomplished diplomat than I am."

Troi suppressed a smile. *My, but you* are *still eager to get out to the far reaches of the Orion Arm, aren't you, Will?*

But she also knew very well that far more was at play behind Will's wrinkled brow than simple frustration over *Titan's* recent change of orders and mission. He was clearly suspicious that the loss of personal prestige his former captain had suffered following last year's Rashanar catastrophe had had something to do with Picard's being passed over for this historic diplomatic assignment—a job that Will clearly believed that Picard should have drawn.

Troi was forced to ask herself if Akaar might not be holding Rashanar against Picard, despite his subsequent multiple vindications at Dokaalan, Delta Sigma IV, and Tezwa, not to mention Picard's aiding Klingon Chancellor Martok in recovering the clone of Emperor Kahless after he had mysteriously gone missing several weeks ago.

Frowning, Akaar nodded and regarded Will in silence for a protracted moment. Still unable to read the guarded Capellan very deeply, Troi began to wonder if Will had finally pushed him too far.

Then the admiral spoke with surprising mildness, in tones tinged with regret. "That is a fair question, Captain. But it is one that your former commanding officer has already answered, during his recent mission into Romulan space."

Will scowled. "I'm afraid I don't understand, sir."

"Let us simply say that Captain Picard's . . . uncanny resemblance to the late Praetor Shinzon did not go unnoticed on Kevatras," Sorok said, stepping forward. "Word of the unfortunate relationship between Picard and Shinzon has already spread far and wide throughout the Romulan Star Empire."

Troi suddenly understood, even as she noted the look of comprehension that was spreading across Will's face.

"You think Captain Picard's presence would destabilize the Romulan Empire even further," the captain said.

Sorok nodded solemnly, one eyebrow slightly raised. "Of course, Captain. As the man who assassinated the Romulan Senate, Shinzon is widely viewed as the author of virtually every difficulty the Empire currently faces. The fact that he was a clone of Jean-Luc Picard is just as widely known throughout the Romulan sphere of influence."

"Our primary mission is to assist the Romulans in the

creation of a sustainable political power-sharing agreement," T'Sevek added, speaking in professorial tones. "Picard's presence would be antithetical to this goal."

"Is that *really* our primary goal?" Troi was startled to note that she herself had been the one to voice this question. Every head in the room had turned in Troi's direction; her crewmates' emotions ran the gamut from surprise to expectation, while the Vulcans, eager to get on with their briefing presentation, only seemed quietly annoyed.

"What do you mean, Commander?" Akaar said. Though he remained difficult to get a precise empathic "read" on, Troi perceived little other than patient curiosity coming from the large man.

Still, she decided it was best to proceed with utmost caution. "Just," Troi began slowly, "that the political chaos in the Romulan Empire presents the Federation with a unique opportunity."

"Ah," Akaar said with a knowing nod. "You are speaking of the opportunity to neutralize the Romulan Empire's potential as a threat to us by splitting it up. The same opportunity that some say we failed to exploit with the Klingons nearly a century ago, after the Praxis explosion threatened Qo'noS itself with destruction."

Troi shook her head, intensely uncomfortable with being compared to the flinty-eyed cold warriors of a thankfully bygone era. "Not precisely, sir. But surely some of the Empire's former subject worlds—Nemor, for example, or perhaps Miridian—might be amenable to voluntarily entering the Federation sphere of influence now that Romulus can no longer effectively rule them."

"True enough," said Akaar. "And had Arafel Pagro prevailed in the recent presidential election, our current mission might well have been to secure exactly that result.

But President Bacco has chosen instead to build trust with the Romulan Empire by assisting it in its efforts to remain essentially intact, in no small part to maintain the Federation's security along the Neutral Zone."

"Meaning we're just going to prop up Praetor Tal'Aura's regime?" said Vale, clearly unhappy with that prospect and apparently addressing the entire room.

T'Sevek shook her graying head. "That is a gross oversimplification of our mission, Commander. The goal of our task force is to assist the new praetor in reaching an accord with several rival factions that have emerged to fill the dangerous power vacuum created by the sudden absence of the Romulan Senate."

T'Sevek's fleeting mention of the task force reminded Troi that Akaar still had yet to fill anyone in on precisely which other starships had been assigned to accompany *Titan* into the Romulan Neutral Zone, aside from the trio of aging *Miranda*-class supply vessels that had escorted her all the way from Utopia Planitia Station. It seemed rather late in the game for this particular detail still to be unannounced. Was it possible that Starfleet Command actually expected *Titan* to prevent the dissolution of the Romulan Empire essentially on her own?

"I was under the impression, Admiral," Dr. Ree said, interrupting Troi's reverie with his oddly sibilant almost-purr, "that Romulan praetors never share power willingly."

"You are correct, Doctor," Akaar said. "But Praetor Tal'Aura is nothing if not a pragmatist. Both she and the newly appointed Proconsul Tomalak are creatures of necessity, well aware that today's oppressed dissidents can be tomorrow's desperate assassins—like Shinzon. Along with a few key survivors among the behind-the-scenes backers of the now-defunct Senate, they understand that it is better to strike deals with their political opponents sooner, rather than risk sharing the Senate's fate later."

T'Rel shot an expectant look in the direction of Akaar, whose silent nod invited her to resume the prepared briefing. "Over the past two weeks, a number of rival political factions have gained prominence on Romulus."

Two weeks, Troi thought, coming to a sudden realization about Akaar's presence aboard the ship. *No wonder the admiral has spent so much time alone in the stellar cartography lab since he came aboard.* She reasoned that he must have been using it as a "war room" for modeling the volatile Romulan geopolitical situation—and that Akaar's strangely unhurried attitude toward *Titan*'s departure date had a purpose behind it as well. *Maybe he didn't* want *to get us under way too quickly. Perhaps he preferred to allow Tal'Aura's opponents some additional time to gather their strength—or wanted Tal'Aura herself to simplify the game by taking a few of her rivals out of the picture.*

"These rival factions," continued T'Rel, "had heretofore lived in fear of both the Romulan Senate and the late Praetor Hiren. Despite Tal'Aura's emergence as the first praetor of the post-Shinzon era—she may have actually aided Shinzon in assassinating her Senate colleagues— these factions now seek to pick up the Empire's pieces and seize the reins of power themselves."

Sorok spoke next, as though the Vulcans had decided in advance to take turns during the presentation. "The most powerful of these factions is a breakaway party of former Senatorial backers. This group previously supported a 'war hawk' minority camp within the Senate, which endorsed preemptive attacks against both Vulcan and Earth. In the past, the Senate's moderate majority kept them in check. I trust I needn't explain how dangerous it would be to Federation security should this group gain any significant influence over the Romulan military. Pardek, a former Romulan senator, has emerged as the most visible advocate for these political hard-liners."

"Pardek?" Will said, frowning. "I remember Captain Picard having some dealings with him. Pardek never struck me as a hawk, or as aggressive toward the Federation. I thought he was a peace activist, and a populist."

"That may have been true at one time," Sorok said with apparently strained patience. "Though he was always a loyal subject of the Romulan Star Empire, his participation in the Khitomer conferences of 2293 was instrumental in the creation of the initial peace accords between the Federation and the Klingon Empire. However, his attempt eleven years ago to disrupt the Vulcan Reunification movement on Romulus made plain that Pardek was far from incorruptible. And Starfleet Intelligence believes that he blames his daughter's murder more than five years ago on alleged Federation–Tal Shiar intrigues. As a result, Pardek has become a staunch enemy both of the Federation *and* of his own Empire's intelligence service."

Stepping into Sorok's brief pause, T'Sevek spoke next, apparently trying to keep the briefing moving along. "The Romulan military comprises the next faction. Intelligence reports that Commander Donatra and Commander Suran, both former followers of Shinzon, have emerged in co-leadership roles since the recent death of Admiral Braeg."

Will allowed himself a grim smile. "Donatra. I'm glad there's going to be at least one friendly face among the rival faction leaders."

Troi recalled that Donatra had risked her own life—as well as the lives of her subordinates aboard the warbird *Valdore*—to help the crew of the *Enterprise* defeat Shinzon.

"Do not count on Commander Donatra's easy cooperation, Captain," T'Rel said with a deep scowl. "She appears to have had a . . . domestic relationship with Braeg. Since Romulans are notably vindictive people—blood feuds are quite common among them—Donatra may therefore continue the late admiral's bitter opposition to Tal'Aura's praetorship."

One of T'Sevek's silvered eyebrows shot skyward at this. "Or she may not. All we know for certain about the military faction represented by Donatra and Suran is that it has yet to throw its support behind either Tal'Aura's praetorship or the so-called 'war hawk' contingent."

"The military faction may merely be waiting for its own chance to seize power," T'Rel said.

T'Sevek shook her head. "I believe we should regard the fact that Donatra turned against Shinzon in order to assist the *Enterprise* as a hopeful sign, an indication that the Romulan Empire—specifically its military—is capable of changing for the better."

Obviously trying to dampen the rekindling of an old argument between his two colleagues, Sorok seized the conversation, speaking loudly. "The *fourth* most significant faction is also the least visible one: the Tal Shiar, the Romulan Star Empire's elite intelligence bureau. For many years this covert, semi-independent organization has been the most feared bureau in the Romulan government. The Tal Shiar seems to have been thrown briefly into disarray by the fall of the Senate. A man named Rehaek has figured prominently in recent Starfleet Intelligence reports on Tal Shiar leadership. As Tal Shiar director Koval's successor-by-assassination, Rehaek's importance in whatever power-sharing arrangement eventually emerges on Romulus cannot be overstated."

Troi could not help but agree. Ten years earlier, Romulan dissidents had forced her to impersonate a Tal Shiar officer. Though a Romulan commander named Toreth had ultimately seen through her disguise and exposed her imposture, Troi had tasted in others the hot fear that a Tal Shiar operative could generate, even among hard-bitten Romulan military veterans.

"Two other important factions remain to be discussed," T'Rel said. "The first of these has benefited hugely from the power vacuum created by the sudden removal of the Senate, as well as from the deaths of Praetors Hiren and Shinzon. I speak of the newly emancipated Remans. Formerly exploited by the Romulans as slave laborers in the dilithium mines of their all-but-uninhabitable homeworld of Remus, the Remans have used the current political turmoil to add to the pool of ships and weaponry they apparently began assembling quietly during the manifold distractions of the Dominion War. The Remans are quite angry, and their leader—one Colonel Xiomek, a decorated Dominion War veteran who fought for the Alliance alongside Shinzon—expects to accomplish a great deal of very rapid social change on his people's behalf."

Akaar spoke at this point, apparently surprising T'Rel and the other two Vulcans. "The final group has also taken advantage of the recent social upheavals in order to obtain political prominence." The admiral fixed his gaze squarely upon Will. "I believe both you and your former captain are well acquainted with its leader."

Will answered with a sober nod—and a single syllable.

"Spock."

After Akaar signaled with a hand gesture that he was finished for the moment, T'Rel resumed the briefing. "This group, which was founded some thirty-five years ago and has since come to be known as the Unification movement, has been an underground, countercultural force until recently. Federation ambassador Spock assumed its mantle of leadership more than eleven years ago, and since that time the movement has come to venerate Vulcan logic above the traditional martial values of Romulus."

Sorok chose that moment to make it clear that he did not share T'Rel's apparent approval of the Unificationists. "Ambassador Spock's faction claims to seek the cultural, political, and philosophical reunion of the sundered worlds of Vulcan and Romulus. It is Spock's stated belief that this development represents the *only* viable path toward a permanent peace between the Romulan Star Empire and the Federation."

"I take it you don't exactly agree with Spock's appraisal of Romulan-Vulcan relations, Sorok," said Commander Ra-Havreii, a wry smile crossing the Efrosian's usually melancholy countenance.

After exchanging cryptic yet clearly significant looks with both T'Sevek and T'Rel, Sorok turned to face the starship designer. "Proponents of Ambassador Spock's Unificationist viewpoint see remolding Romulus in Vulcan's image as necessary and desirable—"

"As well as inevitable," T'Sevek said, interrupting.

Troi noted that Sorok's composure remained unassailable—but only on the outside. "That inevitability is open to debate, T'Sevek. In truth, any effort at reuniting Vulcan and Romulus may just as 'inevitably' lead to Vulcan's transformation into a second Romulus. In fact, a poll taken only days ago reveals that a majority of Vulcans stands with me on this issue. That is to say, most Vulcans believe that Spock's endeavors on Romulus are far too risky."

"A political majority can be transitory," T'Sevek said coolly. "Particularly such a narrow one."

T'Rel remained silent, though the cold glare she was casting at Sorok betrayed a deep belief in Vulcan logic—a belief that wouldn't yield to Sorok's obvious apprehensions about Romulan conquest, however well justified they might be.

Vulcan must be split right down the middle on this, Troi thought. And she wondered, not for the first time, why her first official mission as *Titan*'s diplomatic officer had to be such a damned tough one.

"The debate regarding Vulcan-Romulan unification is not confined to Vulcan," Akaar said, reasserting control over the proceedings. "Since the fall of the Romulan Senate, even the Federation Council has begun considering the issue very seriously. In the wake of the political instability within the Empire, some on the Security Council have even suggested withdrawing the official assistance the Federation recently offered to the Unificationists. That, in my view, would be an *enormous* mistake, since the Unification movement may well prove to be the only Federation-friendly political bloc able to wield power of any consequence—assuming we are there to assist them when they need us."

"For what it's worth, Admiral," Will said, "I agree with you completely. We have to help the Unification movement gain enough political traction to become a major player in whatever power-sharing arrangements emerge on Romulus."

"I hate to be the one to bring this up, Admiral," said Science Officer Jaza, a Bajoran, "but we technically haven't even been *invited* to Romulus yet. As far as I can tell from the background briefing material, the new praetor has agreed only to have her representatives meet us and the other ships in our task force at specific coordinates inside the Neutral Zone."

Once again, Troi was tempted to ask Akaar whether any more ships were coming to join them, but she held her tongue as Jaza held his ground against Akaar's stony stare.

"Fortunately, Commander," the admiral said in measured tones, "I have access to somewhat more up-to-the-minute information than you do about the Romulan praetor and her willingness to do business with us—as well as the temperament of the other faction leaders. With the assistance of members of the Federation Council, I have already set up an introductory meeting on Romulus between Captain Riker, Praetor Tal'Aura's faction, and the senior Reman leadership."

Speaking directly to Will, Akaar added, "Your first task, Captain, will be to run that initial meeting and see to it that everyone is still willing to negotiate and compromise at the end of it. You will carry the negotiations forward from there, with the full support of me and my staff."

And make sure the Romulans and Remans don't immediately start killing each other, Troi thought, swallowing hard.

"I'm looking forward to it, sir," Will said without hesitation. Then he turned slightly to his left and cast an almost pleading glance directly at Troi, who could feel apprehension radiating from him in waves. She had to admit that she was producing a goodly quantity of that same emotion herself. *I'm going to need you like I've never needed you before,* Imzadi, he seemed to be saying, though he hadn't spoken aloud.

"I'm curious, Admiral," said Vale. "Why isn't Ambassador Spock's group being represented at this 'pre-meeting'?"

Troi immediately felt herself responding to a surge of renewed hope coming from Will. Surely the former Federation ambassador's vast experience would be an asset at any Romulan power-sharing meeting, however preliminary it might be.

But Will's newfound sense of optimism began receding like the tide as Akaar sadly shook his head. "Ambassador Spock's communications with the Federation have been sporadic at best since his most recent sojourn across the Neutral Zone more than two standard years ago. And we appear to have lost contact with him altogether some six weeks ago. He failed to show up for a scheduled meeting with President Bacco, but sent no messages to explain his absence."

"Do you think he's dead?" Will asked.

"Just prior to the slaying of the Senate, one of our on-site operatives confirmed that Ambassador Spock was alive and still in charge of the Unification movement. After President Bacco was sworn in, Spock once again contacted the Federation to schedule meetings with the president and the security council. But he never attended those meetings, and never contacted anyone to explain why.

"What has become of him during the intervening seven weeks, we simply do not know. Every subsequent attempt to contact the ambassador, or to ascertain his condition, has met with failure. Even the operative who made the most recent face-to-face contact with him—a meeting confirmed by Spock himself shortly before his own disappearance—has vanished."

"If I may, Admiral," said Sorok, who patiently waited for Akaar's nod before continuing. "Even if Ambassador Spock were a confirmed participant in the upcoming diplomatic meetings with the Romulans, I believe it would be a mistake to place too much reliance on his political influence."

Troi couldn't resist following up on this. "Why?"

"Because Ambassador Spock was merely a figurehead for a charismatic movement. Such causes tend to lose momentum in the absence of the strong influence of their founder-leaders."

Do you mean charismatic, flash-in-the-pan "founder-leaders" like Surak? Troi wondered wryly. She was tempted to ask the question aloud, but saw no reason to go out of her way to bait Sorok or the other Vulcans. They seemed peevish enough without being needled deliberately. Though Vulcans generally worked hard to present a phlegmatic aspect to outsiders, Troi ranked them among the most emotional species she had ever encountered.

"Even if he still lives," the male Vulcan continued, "Spock cannot lead the Unificationists forever. He will inevitably succumb to old age, or the frequently lethal intrigues of Romulan politics."

Troi picked up an immediate and strong undercurrent of sadness coming from Akaar in response to Sorok's words. That didn't surprise her in the least; from what she'd read of his service record, the Capellan admiral had always maintained close ties not only to the Vulcan ambassador, but also to many of Spock's closest friends and colleagues. It was a relationship that went all the way back to Akaar's birth 112 years ago.

"Spock is not yet ancient enough for natural death to draw near to him, Mr. Sorok," Akaar said. "And I sincerely hope that he has yet to fall prey to the other dangers you describe."

"As do I, Admiral," the Vulcan replied, his voice appropriately quiet and grave. "As do I."

Troi's attention was suddenly drawn back in Will's direction. His emotional "color" strongly resembled the hope and optimism she had read in him moments earlier. But another, even stronger sentiment burned brightly beneath it all, and she felt heartened when her mind touched it.

It was determination.

"Until I am presented with proof to the contrary, Admiral," Will said, "I'm going to consider the ambassador alive and well. I find it difficult to believe that a man of Spock's accomplishments would allow his enemies to sneak up on him. Especially when he's in the company of people as courageous as the Romulan dissidents who risked everything to follow him over the past eleven years."

But Sorok was evidently not ready to relinquish his pessimism entirely. "As I tried to make clear, Captain Riker, it would be foolish in the extreme to count on help from Ambassador Spock."

Will smiled broadly at the Vulcan, and Troi noted it was the same smile he reserved for newbies on poker night. "Mr. Sorok, with six rival political factions mixed up in this, it would be foolish to count on *anything.*"

Now Troi could sense the caution and trepidation that quietly roiled just beneath the surface of Will's emotions. But these feelings were securely chained down by his resolve to come to terms with all the complexities of the Romulan political landscape, with or without the help of Spock or his followers.

He'll figure it all out on the fly, just like always, Troi thought as she traded glances with both Will and Christine, and then met the expectant, hopeful gazes of each of the other members of *Titan's* senior staff. *We all will.*

"Now, if there are no further questions . . ." Akaar said,

trailing off to signal an end to the briefing as he rose to his full, two-meter-plus height.

Will rose from his chair as well. "Actually, Admiral, there's still a bit of unfinished business. I need to know—"

His combadge cut his query short. *"Bridge to Captain Riker,"* said an urgent yet tightly controlled female voice.

"Go ahead, Lieutenant Rager," Will said after tapping his badge.

"Sir, three Vor'cha-*class Klingon attack cruisers have just decloaked within fifty kilometers of us. They appear to be loaded for bear. And they're closing."*

"Yellow alert, Lieutenant, until we know what they're doing here. I'm on my way up." Will moved briskly toward the door without waiting to be dismissed. Troi was already up and following him, as were Vale, Jaza, Keru, and Ledrah.

"Yellow alert, Captain?" Akaar said as he followed Will out into the corridor, ducking slightly to avoid brushing his broad head across the top of the doorway. "Is that any way to greet the rest of our humanitarian task force?"

Troi now realized that Akaar had just supplied the answer to Will's interrupted final question. Incredulous at the answer, she could scarcely keep from tripping over her own feet as she raced her husband and Christine Vale to the turbolift.

CHAPTER SEVEN

U.S.S. TITAN

The sides of the cramped turbolift seemed to close in on the group as the doors whisked closed and the lift raced toward the bridge. Vale suppressed a slight wave of claustrophobia. She was the shortest one on the lift, between Troi and Commander Jaza, with Captain Riker, Commander Keru, and especially Admiral Akaar towering above all of them. Of the others from the briefing not on the lift, Ledrah and Ra-Havreii were on their way to engineering, Dr. Ree was heading to sickbay, and Vale didn't know, or particularly care, where the trio of Vulcan aides had gone.

"Care to explain how the Klingons are a 'humanitarian task force,' Admiral?" Riker asked, his eyes steely as he looked across to Akaar. He didn't need to point out that there was no love lost between Qo'noS and Romulus, wartime alliances notwithstanding.

"We have recently been advised that the Remans have requested assistance from the Klingon Empire," Akaar said evenly. "These three ships are therefore to be part of the relief convoy that will be traveling with you to the Romulan Neutral Zone."

And when were you planning on telling us this? Vale wanted to ask, remembering that just minutes ago, Akaar had attempted to close the meeting without disclosing the information about the Klingons. She left her thoughts unvoiced, though she was wondering exactly what game Akaar was playing with Riker. *If he's testing the captain somehow, this hardly seems like the right time or place.* On the other hand, in her newly promoted position, she wasn't about to openly challenge the behavior of one of Starfleet's most prominent admirals. *At least, not yet.*

"Are there any *other* convoy ships coming that we should know about?" Riker asked, sounding nettled.

The turbolift stopped, and the doors opened onto the bridge as Akaar said, "None of which I am aware, Captain. Truthfully, I did not expect the Klingons to arrive quite so early, nor that they would be brandishing their weapons openly on a diplomatic mission such as this."

Diplomacy, Vale thought, *isn't exactly the Klingons' strong suit.*

Riker acknowledged Akaar's statement with a brief glance, then strode onto the bridge. Per his standing orders, there were no announcements of "captain on the bridge" from the crew, though Vale saw several of them stiffen their posture a bit at their stations. Vale smiled as she saw this; Starfleet Academy grads, even the science specialists, were creatures of habit.

"Report, Lieutenant," Riker said crisply as he settled into his slightly raised command chair. The configuration of the bridge was not unlike that of the *Enterprise*-E, though it was smaller, and the deck sloped between its upper and lower levels. The chairs for the captain, the XO, and the diplomatic officer were all equipped with retractable armrest consoles. The new seats also employed emergency harnesses, in case of a collision or some unexpected failure of the inertial-damping system. Vale knew that Riker wasn't wild about the restraints, but had been gratified when the captain had acceded to their potential necessity should a battle situation arise.

Seated next to flight controller Chief Axel Bolaji, Lieutenant Sariel Rager didn't turn from her ops station as she ran her brown fingers quickly over several controls. On the large central viewscreen, a trio of predatory-looking *Vor'cha*-class cruisers hovered in formation. "The Klingons have disengaged their weaponry and are standing down," she said. On the screen, a graphic overlay of a red circle glowed brightly around one of the ships for a moment, corresponding to commands Vale saw Rager giving to her ops panel. "This is the *I.K.S. Quv,*" she said, then the second ship lit, and she added, "and the *I.K.S. Dugh.*" The central ship was highlighted now. "The lead ship is the *I.K.S. Vaj.* Her commander has already hailed us and asks that you return the honor, Captain."

As Vale took her seat on Riker's right, her mind raced to retrieve the Klingon she had studied at Starfleet Academy. She pointed to each of the ships in turn, and said, "I believe that *'Dugh'* means 'to be vigilant,' *'Quv'* means 'honor,' and the lead ship, *'Vaj,'* is 'warrior.' "

"That's got to be the seventeenth ship named *'Vaj'* that I've heard of," Riker said, half smirking. He turned his head slightly, speaking over his shoulder to address Keru, who was stationed behind him on the upper level. "Stand down yellow alert."

"Yes, sir," Keru said, tapping the tactical panel in front of him.

"Hail the lead ship," Riker said, leaning forward.

The image of the ships shrank to occupy a small portion of the upper viewscreen as the main view switched to show the bridge of the Klingon vessel. Seated at its center was a corpulent, uniformed Klingon, eating messily from what appeared to be some kind of gourd.

"This is Captain William Riker of the *U.S.S. Titan.* With whom do I have the honor of speaking?"

The Klingon handed his gourd to a smaller Klingon nearby, wiped his sleeve across his mouth, belched loudly, and stood. *"I am Khegh, son of Taahp, commander of the* I.K.S. Vaj *and her escort vessels. I emerged the victor in thirty-seven engagements during the war against the honorless* Qatlh *of the Dominion."* Then, as if to underscore his point, he belched heartily yet again.

Riker nodded slightly, standing as well, mirroring Khegh. "Then you are a great warrior indeed, General."

Vale squinted, and noticed the Klingon's rank insignia, barely visible underneath a pile of spilled gourd glop. *Good eye,* she thought, looking back toward Riker.

"Wars do not make one great," Khegh said. "Victory *makes one great!"* He grinned, his crooked teeth looking as though they hadn't been cleaned in weeks.

"I appreciate your standing down your weapons after you decloaked," Riker said evenly. "I'm certain you only had them charged in the event we encountered some unforeseen danger."

Vale sneaked a quick glance at Troi, and imagined the counselor was thinking the same thing she was. *Smooth.*

"Either that, or we just wanted to give you a good scare," said Khegh, punctuating his utterance with a phlegmy belly laugh.

"We would like to extend an invitation to you, and the captains of the other two vessels, to join us for dinner," Riker said with an ingratiating smile. "We can discuss the coming mission, and how best to serve the cause of the Remans *and* the Romulans, as well as our respective governments."

Khegh squinted. *"We'll consider it and get back to you."* The screen went dark, and the corner image of the trio of Klingon ships immediately enlarged to fill it.

Riker turned, his smile quickly fading. "Well, *he* was certainly a charming customer."

Troi put her palm up to her chin, brushing a finger over her lips. "There's more to him than he's showing, Captain. I suspect that his uncouth mannerisms were a ruse calculated to make him easy for us to underestimate."

"Could you sense any hidden agendas regarding the Romulans?" Riker asked.

"Not yet," Troi answered. "Perhaps something will reveal itself if we can have some closer contact with him."

"Of course, he'll already know you're half Betazoid, so he'll be on watch for you 'reading' him," Vale said.

Akaar moved down the sloping ramp toward Riker. "What do you hope to accomplish by sharing a meal with the Klingons, Captain?"

Riker raised an eyebrow and smirked slightly. "Beyond having an exhilaratingly disgusting dining experience?" A more serious expression replaced the flippant one. "Truthfully, I'm concerned that the presence of Klingon warships alongside us might make the Romulan military nervous, especially if the Klingons are known to be siding with the Remans. It seems very much as if it will be poking unnecessarily at an open wound."

"True," Akaar said, nodding. "Except that you are discounting the importance of having better-armed Klingon vessels riding shotgun alongside *Titan* and her convoy. You do have a fair offensive capability, but *Titan* is certainly no warship. You and the less-well-armed aid ships might be more vulnerable without Khegh's presence if rogue elements of the Romulan fleet decide to mount a sneak attack."

"It's also likely," Troi said, "that the presence of the Klingons as allies of the downtrodden Remans will pressure the competing Romulan factions into agreeing to treat them fairly in whatever power-sharing arrangement ultimately emerges from the talks."

Akaar stepped in closer, lowering his voice. "Regardless, Captain, if any conflagration begins out here, it is better that it be initiated by the Romulans or the Klingons than by a Federation vessel."

Riker gazed up intently into the eyes of the Capellan. "If I have anything to say about it, Admiral, neither my ship nor the Klingons' will be engaged in *any* battle. As Khegh just said, 'Wars do not make one great.' And as the product of a warrior society yourself, I'm sure you must feel the same way, sir."

Akaar looked impressed. "Let us hope you are correct, Captain," he said, then exited the bridge, perhaps to confer with his staff.

Vale settled back into her chair, at the immediate right of the center seat. She still wasn't sure what to make of the hostility Riker seemed to harbor toward the admiral, but she felt a surge of new confidence in her CO after witnessing how firmly yet discreetly he had stood up to his superior officer. *I've made the right decision,* she thought. Titan *truly is my home now.*

It had taken another day and a half for the Klingons to make their decision about supping with the *Titan* crew, and a good half hour to decide on an appropriate menu. Then, ten minutes before the appointed dinner time, Khegh had hailed the Starfleet vessel and requested that the venue be changed to his own flagship.

Seated behind the Elaminite-wood desk in his ready room, Riker was a bit taken aback by the request. "May I ask why, General?"

"The captain of the Dugh *does not wish to eat replicated Klingon food,"* Khegh said glibly. *"It upsets his digestion and makes him gassy, if the truth be told."*

"Ah, quite understandable, then," Riker said, nodding. He was certain that there had to be other reasons, but wasn't sure it would be worth trying to ferret them out now. "I accept your offer, General. I will prepare my officers to beam over to your ship."

"Wait!" Khegh said, his voice emphatic. *"I understand that one of your officers is a Betazoid?"*

"My diplomatic officer is half Betazoid, yes," Riker said. "She is among my most valued—"

"Leave her on your ship," Khegh said, interrupting. *"I do not trust Betazoids, or Vulcans, or any of the other thought readers."*

Mental alarms went off inside Riker's head. *What is he trying to hide?* But there was nothing to be gained by pushing the point. "Agreed," he said, nodding. "I will bring along only my executive officer and my security chief. A human and a Trill."

"Acceptable, Captain. I hope the three of you have the stomach for gagh *and bloodwine in copious quantities,"* Khegh said with a leering smile, after which the tabletop screen went dark.

Riker looked up at Deanna, Keru, Vale, and Akaar, all of whom were waiting there in the ready room, having heard the entire conversation.

"I don't like this, sir," Vale said.

"Nor do I," Keru said, nodding. "We could be walking into a trap."

"I don't think they have any cause to trap us," Riker said, standing. As far as anyone knew, the Klingons had never learned of the Khitomer Accord violations former Federation President Min Zife had secretly committed on the planet Tezwa; therefore, no Klingon general in good standing had any reason to break the Klingon-Federation alliance that had served both peoples so well before, during, and after the Dominion War.

Riker looked at his wife. "Did you get any better 'read' off Khegh this time?"

"Nothing that suggests danger," Deanna said. "But I still feel fairly certain he's hiding something—something I'm intuiting may have nothing whatsoever to do with *us*. Either he's being secretive out of deference to the prejudices of his convoy captains, or else he's doing it out of sheer enjoyment of being manipulative."

"Manipulative? Imagine that." Riker looked directly toward Akaar. "Admiral, is there anything else you may have . . . omitted from the mission briefing that might have some bearing on this?" He knew that he was skirting the edge of insubordination, but the Capellan officer had been getting on his nerves increasingly the longer this mission went on. If he had fully informed Riker of all the particulars before they had gotten under way, preparations for the mission would have gone so much more smoothly.

Akaar treated him to a stern gaze that acknowledged the insubordination, but then answered him without any rebuke. "Nothing that comes immediately to mind, Captain."

Riker clapped his hands together. "It's settled, then. The only thing we know we have to fear is their cooking."

" 'Cuisine' might be a better choice of words," said Deanna. "Don't count on a lot of it being cooked."

"That scares me more than any phaser fight," Vale said, blanching visibly.

Vale felt her stomach roiling as a boisterous male Klingon set a second mug of warm *raskur* down in front of her. Following the truly unappetizing dinner of live and wriggling *gagh*—she was grateful that Riker had warned her to avoid acquiring a persistent intestinal parasite by chewing the nasty things to death before allowing them to wriggle down her esophagus—overcooked roasted *targ,* and a salad that seemed to undulate under its own power, it was all she could do to keep from heaving the meal back up, blasting their warrior hosts right across their ridged foreheads with gut-churning peristalsis.

Keru seemed far less affected. Although he wasn't a joined Trill, she imagined that any species physiologically capable of allowing a symbiotic life-form to join with them via a belly pouch probably could ingest just about anything. Amazingly, with three tankards downed, he still seemed as sober as a Federation magistrate, even as the Klingons around him got progressively sloppier and drunker.

Captain Riker was seated at the head of the table, to General Khegh's immediate left. The task force had entered the Neutral Zone a mere ten minutes ago, and as a strategy session, the meal seemed less than successful. Every time Riker tried to steer the discussion to the arena of the brewing Romulan-Reman conflict, Khegh just as quickly diverted it with boasts, blusters, and heavily embroidered tales of past battles. The Klingon wanted to discuss anything, it seemed, but their coming mission to Romulus. He seemed especially interested in hearing stories about Lieutenant Commander Worf, whom he claimed to have known during his pre-Starfleet days in Minsk, unlikely though that might be.

Sitting between the boisterous male Klingon commander, Tchev, and a female Klingon named Dekri, who looked as if she were about to spill right out of her bustier-like top, Vale felt a rough hand pressing on the small of her back.

"So, what do you consider to be your greatest triumph in battle?" Tchev asked, turning toward her with a snaggletoothed leer.

Vale's mind raced. Over the last year alone, she had spearheaded the *Enterprise*'s rescue operations on Dokaal, led efforts to calm the social chaos on Delta Sigma IV, and had coordinated several ground assaults during the guerrilla war on Tezwa. She wondered if any of those incidents might strike this Klingon as worthy of song or story.

"While I think I respect honor in combat and life as much as any Klingon," she said, "I'm not certain that—" She stopped as she felt the hand on her back slip lower, onto her rear.

She looked first at Tchev, then at Dekri, both of whom were smiling and listening intently—or at least as intently as they could, given how drunk they clearly were.

"If whoever has his hand on my ass doesn't remove it immediately, *he* will become my greatest triumph in battle," Vale hissed, low enough that only her immediate companions were likely to have heard.

As Tchev looked at Vale blankly, Dekri moved away, bringing her arm back to the table to grasp her mug. Vale shot her a withering glance, then said, "As I was saying—"

The chirping of a combadge interrupted her. She saw

Riker hold up his hand apologetically toward Khegh before tapping the gleaming metal device on the front of his tunic.

"Riker here."

"Captain, several Romulan ships are decloaking only a few klicks from the convoy." Vale recognized the voice as that of Chief Axel Bolaji, the gamma-shift flight controller. The Klingons went silent, rising to their feet in reaction to Bolaji's warning.

"Understood," Riker said as the Klingon ship commanders and junior officers exited the mess hall, apparently shaking off the effects of their gluttony. He stood and addressed Khegh, who seemed somewhat slower on the draw than some of his officers. "Thank you for your hospitality, General. But I think we both need to return to our respective bridges now."

Khegh got unsteadily to his feet and raised a dirty flagon that might have contained *warnog* in Riker's direction. *"Qapla',* Captain!"

Vale and Keru took up positions beside Riker as he spoke again into his combadge. "Riker to *Titan.* Three to beam directly to the bridge."

Another male Klingon junior officer suddenly burst into the room, shouting something in rapid-fire Klingon just as Vale felt the familiar shimmering tug of the transporter beam. As the dingy room faded from view, she saw Khegh react angrily, and imagined that he wasn't happy that the *Titan* crew had been more alert to the approach of the Romulan ships than had his own warriors.

Maybe he ought to cut back on the shipboard partying, she thought.

A moment passed, and the three of them were materializing on *Titan's* bridge, in an alcove near the door that led to the head. Vale immediately wished she could excuse herself to divest her stomach of its objectionable contents, but duty was duty.

"Yellow alert. Ready shields, but keep them down for now," Riker said urgently, intent on the viewscreen. It displayed a quintet of the sleek new *Mogai*-class Romulan warbirds—to Vale's eye they looked like a cross between the huge, biframed *D'deridex*-class warships and the Klingons' *Vor'cha* attack cruisers—arrayed in an attack pattern. Any one of them must have dwarfed *Titan* by at least a factor of four, and their weaponry had to be at least as potent.

Riker immediately pointed to a particular warbird that he evidently recognized. "That's the *Valdore*. Her hull's still damaged from the pounding Shinzon gave her weeks ago."

"Let's hope she and her friends haven't changed their praetor's plan to roll out the welcome mat for us," Vale said.

"They're hailing us, Captain," Keru said, not turning his head from the tactical console in front of him.

Riker looked quickly over to Vale. "Did I splatter any Klingon food on my shirt?" he asked with a wry grin. After Vale shook her head, he turned back to the screen, tugging his uniform jacket downward and puffing his chest up. Vale quietly hoped she wouldn't discover that she'd accidentally let a live *gagh* worm wriggle into her sleeve.

"On screen," Riker said.

The face that appeared on the viewer was one that Vale recognized from the images from the after-action report Riker had filed immediately after the Shinzon affair. To her everlasting regret, she had been taking shore leave on Earth at the time the *Enterprise* and her crew had been forced headlong into those events.

"Commander Donatra," Riker said, favoring the stern yet attractive young Romulan woman on the viewer with a reserved smile. "You look well."

Donatra offered a wan smile in return. *"If that is so, then I am fortunate indeed. Congratulations on your new command, Captain Riker. And welcome to the Neutral Zone."*

A place where nobody is supposed to be, Vale thought, feeling her heart thump heavily in her chest. *Including the Klingons.* She hoped that nobody on any of Khegh's or Donatra's vessels was spoiling for a fight.

"Thank you, Commander," Riker said simply. "We have come on a mission of aid. I'm sure you have been informed that our presence has been requested by both the Romulan and the Reman peoples."

"I have, Captain," Donatra said, raising an elegantly arched eyebrow. *"Do you recall what I told your former captain when last we saw each other?"*

He nodded. "You said that he had made the first of what you hoped would be many friends in the Romulan Empire."

Donatra smiled with what Vale took to be genuine warmth, an intuition confirmed by Troi's smile. *"Very good, Captain. And despite the fact that Picard is not here, I extend that friendship to you and your crew. There are more than a few ... rogue elements in the Empire who might wish to interfere with your mission here. Therefore, I shall assign three vessels from my squadron to escort you and your entourage directly to Romulus."*

"Rogue elements." That's the exact term that Akaar used earlier, Vale thought with a start. *Is that just a coincidence, or is it something more?*

Riker bowed his head slightly toward the screen. "For that, you have our gratitude." Vale knew that Riker must also be considering the briefing that Akaar and his three Vulcan aides had conducted the previous afternoon. T'Sevek had warned them that Donatra was in league with Commander Suran in the leadership hierarchy of a powerful independent military faction. T'Rel, in particular, had seemed to distrust Donatra's motivations quite a bit.

"Your people, as well as your Klingon escorts"—a subtle, momentary sneer seemed to creep into Donatra's voice at this point—*"may feel the need to be . . . cautious while we escort you. Feel free to raise your shields or adopt whatever mode of readiness you deem appropriate. I certainly can understand the sense of unease that all of you must be experiencing."*

She paused for a moment, then added adamantly, *"But do* please *inform the Klingons that appropriate readiness does* not *include fully charging their weapons."*

Riker nodded again, his face as impassive as Akaar's. "I appreciate your candor, your discretion, and your assistance, Commander."

"Then we shall speak again soon, on Romulus," Donatra said. A moment later, the screen image changed back to that of the various ships—Romulan, Klingon, and Federation—that were arrayed around *Titan* as she proceeded inexorably toward Romulan space. And plunged headlong toward whatever fate awaited her there.

Riker turned to Vale.

"Rogue elements," he said. "Curiouser and curiouser."

CHAPTER EIGHT

U.S.S. TITAN

"We're being hailed again, Captain," said Cadet Zurin Dakal, who was currently backing Keru at tactical by manning communications.

It had been less than twenty minutes since Commander Donatra and her squadron had appeared to escort the convoy toward Romulus—and since then Donatra's warbird had reactivated its cloak, vanishing from sight, though perhaps not from the general vicinity of the convoy.

Riker turned his chair in the direction of the youthful Cardassian trainee. "Who's calling us this time, Cadet?"

"Romulus sir." Dakal glanced down at his readouts, and the young Cardassian's eyes suddenly became enormous. "The signal is coming directly from the Romulan Hall of State. It's Praetor Tal'Aura."

Riker felt his own eyes widen involuntarily as well. Then he noticed that both Deanna and Vale, seated in the chairs that flanked his own, had turned their expectant gazes upon him.

"Should I call Admiral Akaar back to the bridge?" Vale asked.

Riker shook his head, though he wouldn't have been surprised if Akaar were discreetly monitoring the incoming message from stellar cartography. "He did say this was *my* mission."

Vale nodded in agreement, then pivoted her chair in Dakal's direction. "Are the Klingons able to pick up this transmission?"

"Almost certainly, sir," Dakal said.

Riker chuckled. "That's fine. There's no point in antagonizing our Klingon escorts by hiding things from them. I'm sure being this far inside Romulan space is making them twitchy enough." Turning back toward the viewscreen that almost entirely covered the forward segment of the circular bridge, Riker said, "Put the praetor on the screen, Cadet."

A moment later, the image of a regal, stern-faced Romulan woman of early middle age appeared in the center of the screen. Her slim figure was perched on an ornate chair that was the approximate color of Romulan blood. A wall made of ancient-looking green stone was visible several meters behind her.

But Riker's eyes were drawn more urgently to the steel-eyed Romulan male who stood attentively beside the praetor.

Tomalak. Riker tensed as he recognized the other man. He silently noted Tomalak's aristocratic civilian suit, cut to accentuate the broadness of his shoulders, and the senatorial sigils that were attached to his dark tunic. Tomalak had always been trouble when he'd served as a commander, and more recently as an admiral, in the Romulan military. Riker felt certain that Tomalak's presence here and now alongside his beleaguered empire's praetor couldn't bode well for the coming power-sharing talks.

"Praetor Tal'Aura," Riker said, rising and making a respectful half-bow. "We are honored."

"Welcome to the Romulan Star Empire, Captain Riker," the praetor said. *"Allow me to introduce Proconsul Tomalak, my trusted right hand."*

His eyes bright but cold, Tomalak smiled, a gesture that Riker found anything but reassuring. He hadn't forgotten any of his previous encounters with Tomalak. Thirteen years ago, the Romulan officer had engaged in some rather brazen espionage on the remote Federation planet Galorndon Core. Then, only a few weeks later, the commander had used faked intelligence to convince a Romulan defector, Admiral Alidar Jarok, that a Romulan sneak attack on the Federation was imminent. Jarok, who had wanted only to preserve the lives of innocents on both sides—as well as his Empire's honor—had taken his own life after learning of Tomalak's cynical manipulations. Riker wasn't sure he could ever find it in himself to forgive Tomalak for that. And he was absolutely certain he couldn't trust him.

"The proconsul and I have met before, Praetor," Riker said without elaboration.

"Indeed," Tal'Aura said, leaning forward, her expression hard but earnest. *"Let us hope that this familiarity will make our preliminary meeting go more smoothly."*

Not very damned likely, Riker thought, though he kept his expression carefully neutral.

He glanced down at Ensign Lavena's flight-control displays before returning his gaze to the main viewer. "Our convoy is only about sixteen hours away from Romulus at our present speed, Praetor. Once we arrive, will the

Reman leaders require our assistance in getting to the first meeting?"

Tal'Aura blinked several times before replying, as though confused. *"Captain, perhaps we do not yet completely understand each other. Before we involve the Reman leadership in any power-sharing talks, I wish you to mediate a . . . prefatory conference between us and the other Romulan efvir-efveh who now contend for influence within the Empire."*

"Efvir-efveh," Riker repeated soundlessly, taking only half a beat to recognize the Romulan term that translated, at least approximately, to "power groups" or "factions."

Tal'Aura continued: *"Any Reman presence at our first meeting would make this necessary preliminary meeting far more . . . tense than it needs to be. I'm sure you can understand that."*

Riker nodded slowly. *Certainly. You don't want to have to worry about your former slaves quietly drawing their knives under the negotiating table. Especially when you and the rest of the former slaveholders are still busy trying to outmaneuver each other.*

Still, he had to admit that the praetor did have a legitimate point. The Reman faction's absence from the first session might arguably ease some of the intra-Romulan tensions, though actually holding a meeting without the Remans posed some very real problems.

As would flatly refusing to go along with the praetor's plan. *A rock and a hard place,* he thought grimly.

Riker slowly paced toward the starboard side of the bridge as he addressed both Tal'Aura and Tomalak. "Can I assume that you'll take every precaution to keep this . . . preliminary meeting *entirely* secret? If the Remans were to find out about it—"

"The Remans will learn only what we wish them to

learn," said Tomalak, interrupting in unctuous tones. "*Their demands will be considered in due course, to be sure. At the start of the general negotiations between* all *the competing* efvir-efveh."

As his motions carried him back toward the center of the bridge, Riker noticed that both Deanna and Vale were still looking up at him. But now they were regarding him with unconcealed trepidation. Both were clearly asking him, without words, whether he understood the implications of what he was about to do.

He knew there was another important consideration as well: If the Klingons were indeed listening in, then they, too, already knew of the Romulans' intention to exclude the Remans from the first meeting. The Klingons had come at the request of the Remans; might they not be inclined to spill Tal'Aura's secret immediately?

But wouldn't Tal'Aura and Tomalak have anticipated that, too? he thought. *They must be gambling that the Klingons don't want a Romulan-Reman war any more than they do.*

Riker met the praetor's hard gaze without wavering. "Who else is going to attend this . . . preliminary meeting?"

"*The proconsul and I will receive Commanders Donatra and Suran, the most prominent leaders of our military. And Senator Pardek.*"

"*Receive*" them, Riker thought, silently weighing the significance of this verb. *Because she can't just command them to attend. It must be killing Tal'Aura to have to appear so weak in front of old adversaries.*

But he also knew that Romulans were nothing if not pragmatic. And a Romulan praetor who did not face reality forthrightly surely could not hang onto her power and position for very long.

"Pardek, for one, will be most disappointed if we cannot arrange the initial meeting we are proposing," Tomalak said.

Pardek, Riker thought. *He would probably be attacking the Federation right now if he had access to enough personnel and firepower.* He was glad that Commander Donatra would also be present; if she were still as honorable as she had proved herself to be during the battle against Shinzon, then she would certainly do everything possible to prevent Pardek from waging war against anyone.

Riker knew that he had a decision to make, and that it had to be done quickly. He spared a quick glance at Deanna, whose dark, fathomless eyes offered no hint of a solution. Vale, still seated at his other side, was completely poker-faced. Nor was there time to adjourn to confer about what was to be done—not without risking giving insult to the praetor.

Am I about to grant de facto *Federation recognition to a single Romulan faction?* Riker thought, carefully keeping his rising anxiety from reaching his face. However legitimate Tal'Aura's claim to power might be, there would be hell to pay with the other factions were they to perceive that the Federation was in any way predisposed in Tal'Aura's favor. The Federation had to be perceived by all sides as an "honest broker," or else the entire mission was doomed to failure.

Hell, he thought. *Sometimes playing fair means asking annoying questions.* Aloud, he said, "I can certainly understand why you might want to start the talks without having the Remans in the room. But I wonder why you're also excluding some of the other important Romulan constituencies."

Tal'Aura studied him quietly for an elastic moment before replying. *"If you're concerned about snubbing the Tal Shiar, Captain, you probably needn't worry."*

"With respect, Praetor, the Tal Shiar always seem to learn things that would be better kept quiet. I believe it would be a serious mistake to count them out. I very much doubt that the Empire's current ... difficulties have slowed them down much."

"You are probably correct, Captain," Tal'Aura said.

Riker couldn't restrain himself from frowning slightly. "Praetor Tal'Aura, you seem to be saying that you don't expect our secret meeting to stay that way. Doesn't that concern you?"

Tal'Aura chuckled, then settled back in her chair. *"Not terribly, no. If there's one thing the Tal Shiar excels at, it is the ancient art of keeping secrets. Provided, of course, that they are secrets the Tal Shiar wants kept. But I sense that the Romulan Star Empire's much-feared shadow army isn't really what concerns you, Captain."*

Riker nodded. Deciding that a little flattery couldn't hurt, he said, "You are very perceptive, Praetor."

She didn't seem overly impressed. *"Then please speak plainly, Captain."*

"Very well. Nearly three years ago, Ambassador Spock's Unification movement—and the many Romulan citizens who have quietly supported it over the years—received the approval of one of your predecessors. Why weren't any Unificationists invited to this initial meeting?"

Tal'Aura inclined her head toward Tomalak, who stepped forward. *"Captain Riker, much has changed during the past three years, as I'm sure you're aware. Praetor Neral was replaced by Praetor Hiren fairly quickly. And I can't overemphasize the damage the subsequent ... praetorship of Shinzon has wrought."* Tomalak's expression looked especially sour as he fairly spat Shinzon's name. *"In light of the current troubles within our borders, our new praetor has wisely assigned a much lower priority to Romulan-Vulcan relations."*

"I see," Riker said. He had to admit to himself, however grudgingly, that Tomalak's rationale actually made a great deal of sense under the present circumstances.

"I hope we have answered your questions satisfactorily, Captain," Tal'Aura said in a clipped tone that brooked no further delay. *"Now will you agree to mediate the initial meeting, as we have described it?"*

Riker felt as though his boots were poised at the crumbling verge of a bottomless abyss. And he knew that the time had come for him to take a deadly, yet necessary, step over the edge. He briefly thought of his late father, who'd been killed during the recent civil unrest on Delta Sigma IV. Though Kyle Riker had possessed more than a few less-than-admirable traits, indecision wasn't among them.

Squaring his shoulders, Captain William Thomas Riker made up his mind.

"All right, Praetor Tal'Aura. Proconsul Tomalak. My senior staff and I will agree to conduct the prefatory meeting as you suggest—without the Remans and the Unificationists."

"Excellent, Captain," said Tal'Aura, dipping her head slightly. Something approximating a smile pulled at the sides of her narrow, patrician face.

"With *one* small proviso," Riker continued, raising a hand.

She lifted an eyebrow in an almost Vulcan manner. *"Say on, Captain. What is your proviso?"*

"That the Federation's participation in this early meeting is not to be taken as an official endorsement of any of the leaders present," Riker said coolly. "Including you, Praetor Tal'Aura."

Tal'Aura bristled visibly at this, but remained silent. After a lengthy pause, she said, *"Very well. My staff will contact you again in sixteen of your hours.* Jolan'tru, *Captain Riker."*

"Jolan'tru, Praetor," Riker echoed, though the praetor's image had already vanished, to be replaced immediately by the infinite depths of star-bejeweled space.

"Well, we already knew the praetor wasn't likely to agree to share power quickly or easily," Vale said, rising from her seat.

Deanna nodded. "Taking that into account, I think that went fairly well. We'll soon be dealing with three of the most powerful factions in the Romulan government. You went a long way toward ensuring that our first full Romulan-Reman meeting goes smoothly, Captain."

"As long as we can keep this first meeting off the Reman newsnets," Vale said.

"Of course," Deanna said. "But at least Tal'Aura is cooperating with us. That's a very positive sign."

"She needs us," Riker said.

Deanna nodded. "No question. She must have serious doubts that she can successfully handle all the chaos that could come her way from breakaway subject worlds, or from hostiles beyond the Empire's borders, without our help."

Vale favored Deanna with a smile, obviously agreeing with her analysis. "Did your Betazoid empathy tell you that?"

"There's a whole lot of interstellar space between Tal'Aura and my Betazoid empathy," Deanna reminded her, looking amused. "My diplomatic instincts will have to do until we get just a tiny bit closer to Romulus."

Riker returned to his seat in silence, disconcerted by what felt like his complete inability to predict the outcome of the mission he faced. Accustomed to far more straightforward tactical situations, he felt decidedly uncomfortable being saddled with such a handicap.

Such is diplomacy, he thought, simultaneously gratified and regretful that his Starfleet career hadn't been more preoccupied with that particular discipline. He could only hope that he hadn't just helped create yet another dangerous power clique by inexpertly meddling in the chaos Shinzon had left in his murderous wake.

"We're being hailed *again,* sir," Dakal reported, sounding surprised.

Riker sighed. "Who is it this time?"

"It's General Khegh. He's coming through on a secure channel."

Suppressing an even bigger sigh, Riker said, "Put him on the screen, Cadet."

General Khegh's visage greeted him a fraction of a second later. The Klingon flag officer grinned, again showing off his impressive array of jagged, discolored teeth. Unsurprisingly, his skin was still florid from excessive drink.

"Romulans will be Romulans, won't they, eh, Captain?"

Riker nodded. "After we shake their hands, we'll be sure to count our fingers."

Khegh reacted with another belching belly-laugh. *"And we shall—how do you humans say it?—we shall watch your backs, Captain."*

"Thank you, General." Riker found Khegh's drunken martial conviviality anything but reassuring.

"And you needn't worry about our alerting the Remans to Tal'Aura's machinations to exclude them from your first

meeting. We will keep your confidence, so long as Tal'Aura agrees to receive the Reman leaders in subsequent talks."

"You are a wise leader, General." *He's a lot smarter than he looks,* Riker thought. *Of course, he'd almost have to be.*

"But make no mistake, Captain," Khegh said, his lips suddenly curling into a snarl. *"We will not passively endure further Romulan treachery. If those pointy-eared* petaQ *attempt to waylay our convoy with their cloaked vessels, we will swiftly make all nine of their Hells very crowded places indeed."*

Lovely, Riker thought, wondering if it wasn't likelier that the general would hit *Titan,* or perhaps one of the other ships in the convoy, were he actually forced to open fire. "Thank you, General. We appreciate your vigilance."

"wa' Dol nIvDaq matay'DI' maQap, 'Aj," Vale said to the Klingon, whose hawklike eyes widened in surprise. Riker found it hard to tell if he was pleased or offended.

After a pause, Khegh shouted, *"Qapla'!"* before vanishing from the screen.

Though Riker had picked a word or two out of Vale's stream of rapid-fire Klingon, his own command of the language wasn't quite up to parsing the idiom she had just used. Curious, he turned to face his exec. "Exactly what did you say to him, Commander?"

" 'We succeed together in a greater whole.' It's an old Klingon aphorism that seemed appropriate to the situation."

"I had no idea you were so fluent in Klingon," Riker said, impressed.

"I'm not. I nicked it from a phrase book I memorized during my Academy days for an extra-credit assignment. *Affirmations* by General BoQtar."

Riker chuckled. "Sounds like a pretty quick read."

"Judging from Khegh's ever-so-slightly chastened emotional reaction," Deanna said, "it served as a polite reminder that we need him to restrain himself. Or 'keep his powder dry,' as they used to say in Earth's Wild West."

In spite of his own dark thoughts, Riker found himself chuckling again. "Nice shooting, pardner," he said to Vale. Anticipating a difficult series of negotiations between several exceedingly contentious and cantankerous parties, he felt a surge of gratitude at having two senior officers with such finely honed diplomatic instincts.

"We are now leaving the Neutral Zone, Captain," Axel Bolaji reported from behind the conn. "Entering the periphery of Romulan space."

Riker stared straight ahead into a firmament ruled by the dangerously splintered Romulans. Despite his confidence in both Deanna and Christine, he found himself wishing that Ambassador Spock could also be at his side when all the shouting finally began down on Romulus.

Chapter Nine

VIKR'L PRISON, KI BARATAN, ROMULUS

Throughout the past week, Tuvok had been completely unable to focus his attention, as his fever rose ever higher. As closely as he could tell, he had been imprisoned for fifty days, though in the dark, windowless dampness, it was difficult to reckon time accurately. He couldn't even keep track of the cycles by counting mealtimes, since food arrived irregularly, with entire days sometimes elapsing between meals.

But neither the interrogators, the guards, nor the other prisoners had found out that he was *not* Rukath, the lowly farmer from Leinarrh, in the Rarathik District. The minor surgical alterations he had undergone before making landfall on Romulus had held up. Only the most detailed scan, to which he had apparently not yet been subjected, could have revealed that he was actually Vulcan rather than Romulan.

Between his Starfleet intelligence training, his Vulcan disciplines, and the tricks he had learned while on deep cover assignment with the Maquis, Tuvok was confident in his ability to maintain his assumed identity under repeated questioning and even torture. But fatigue, and perhaps even a recrudescence of the early-stage Tuvan syndrome he thought he'd beaten two years earlier, had taken their toll; he had made several mistakes about Romulan geography and history during his more recent interrogations, evidently arousing enough suspicion among the prison authorities to motivate them to keep him in custody, placing him in solitary confinement in a cold, dismal space all but indistinguishable from a stone casket. Languishing in the darkness, he cursed his faltering memory. He still didn't know if the guards really thought he was a spy, or if they were merely having fun torturing a simple-minded *hveinn* who had wandered too far from his crops.

Today—*What day is it?* he wondered yet again—despair was creeping in at the edges of his consciousness, and no amount of meditation seemed to help, even when he could muster sufficient concentration to attempt to enter a state of *aelaehih'bili're,* or mind-peace. With his wrist chrono destroyed, Starfleet had no sure way to locate him, and rescue seemed unlikely anyway, given that so much time had passed already since his capture. He thought repeatedly of his wife, his grown children, his grandchildren, but even picturing their faces was already growing difficult.

Defying all logic, he found he was actually beginning to look forward to brief glimpses of, or contacts with, his jailers, no matter how badly they mistreated him. Save for the screams and moans he heard coming from other stone cells in the catacomblike underground prison complex, his captors were now the only intelligent beings with whom he could interact.

Since the initial wildfire-like rise of his fever several days ago, he had begun to lose control of both body and mind. When he wasn't shivering, he was laughing or crying, the normally suppressed emotions ripping at his being far more than had the physical discomfort of imprisonment. Mostly, he tried to sleep, escaping into a black pool of oblivion. Dreams came to him rarely, and he found their absence a great comfort. When they did come, they were vivid, disturbing, and illogical.

A dark, beetlelike insect scuttled across the moist stone-and-brick floor toward his foot, then up into the rags that shrouded his legs. He watched and waited, his need and desperation overcoming decades of studied discipline. As it came within striking distance, his hands thrust out like *le-matya* pouncing on a desert *ferravat*. His shackles clinked as he grabbed the beetle. He felt it attempt to gore his flesh between the pincerlike horns on its head, but he squeezed it until its carapace split. The insect died instantly.

In the dim light, he checked the belly of the beetle, but did not see the distinctive markings of the female. He had started to eat one of them weeks ago, and learned that the females carried a deadly poison in their belly sacs. Twisting this beetle's head by the horns, he decapitated it, then tossed the head aside. He took a bite of the crunchy body, which immediately suffused his taste buds with a dry, acrid tang. He closed his eyes as he slowly chewed another bite, and felt darkness and despair wash over him again.

"Get that creature out of your mouth," his mother, T'Meni, *said sharply, glaring down at him.*

He looked down at his hands, and saw his stubby fingers clutching a half-eaten geshu *bug. "Why? Wari was eating it first."*

She bent over and slapped the insect from his hands, into the desert sand. "Wari is a sehlat. You are a Vulcan boy. Vulcan boys do not eat insects."

"That isn't logical, Mother," he said. "We feed Wari food that we no longer want. If he can eat what we do, why can't we eat what he does?"

"Vulcan boys do not eat insects," she said firmly, then turned to walk away.

Tuvok looked over at the half-eaten bug. It began to squirm, and turned what was left of its head toward him.

"Romulan boys eat insects," it said, its voice thin and reedy. "Are you a Romulan?"

"No," Tuvok said, his voice suddenly deepening into that of an adult. He stood and backed away from the writhing insect, then turned. Standing before him was Captain Spock, who was flanked by Captain James Kirk and Captain Hikaru Sulu.

"I'm not certain I understand your objection, Ensign," Spock said to him. "We are discussing an alliance between the Federation and the Klingon Empire, not a unification between Romulans and Vulcans."

Tuvok shook his head, trying to clear his thoughts. "The Klingon ideal is conquest and expansion," he finally said, slowly and deliberately. "This worldview is antithetical to the very foundations of the Federation. Klingon culture is based on violence and brutality; Klingons exist to conquer, destroy, and subsume."

"Quite a firecracker on your crew, Hikaru," Kirk said with a smile, gesturing toward Tuvok, but looking at Sulu.

"They want nothing more than to destroy the very fabric of our ideals," Tuvok said, continuing, though his thoughts seemed jumbled. "They want to blend their chaotic emotional society into ours, and you're being *duped into helping them, Captain Spock. Pardek is using you.*"

"*Who is Pardek? Are you feeling all right, Ensign?*" Sulu asked. A mug of hot tea was in his hand and he threw it at Tuvok.

Instinctively, Tuvok put up his hands to protect his face. The tea splattered against them and clattered to the floor in front of him, suddenly transformed into a pile of randomly scattered t'an rods.

"*Clearly, you aren't quite into this game of kal'toh,*" a familiar voice said, and Tuvok looked through his splayed fingers. There, in Tuvok's wrecked quarters aboard the U.S.S. Voyager, squatted Lon Suder, the starship's psychosis-addled Betazoid crew member. Suder reached down with bloody hands to grab some of the t'an rods. "*What are you afraid of, Tuvok? That your mind will collapse before your society does?*"

"*I can control my mind,*" Tuvok said, backing away. "*I have trained to achieve Kolinahr.*" He stepped back through the door outside his quarters, and stumbled into the searing desert of Vulcan's Forge, pitiless Nevasa baking him from almost directly overhead.

"*But you never finished your training,*" intoned the Vulcan master who now stood before him. The robed adept then turned his back on Tuvok, who began to follow. Sand swirled around him, propelled by a swift, insistent wind.

"*I can complete my training,*" Tuvok cried out. He saw his wife, T'Pel, and his children and grandchildren. Other masters were escorting them away from him.

T'Pel turned and called to him. "*You left your Kolinahr training incomplete. You left your family incomplete. And you do not support the progress of our people.*"

He saw that the masters were leading his family toward

a phalanx of Romulan warbirds that had settled in the desert, looking as though they had always been there.

He felt a hand on his shoulder, and turned to see Admiral Kathryn Janeway. She smiled at him sweetly. "Even if you didn't complete your training, I thought you had learned your lesson, Tuvok."

"Which lesson?" he asked her. His head felt as if it were splitting open, and sweat ran down his face.

"You engineered the melding of the Maquis with the Starfleet crew aboard *Voyager*," Janeway said. "Despite all logic, despite the conflicts between two groups that had every reason never to work together, you managed to bring them into accord. Just like Ambassador Spock is doing on Romulus."

Tuvok wiped the sweat away with the tattered sleeve of a robe he hadn't recalled ever having worn before. "I no longer oppose Spock's Unification movement," he said. "That is why I volunteered for the mission to Romulus." Now, he knew where the robe had come from.

"You *don't* oppose Unification?" Janeway asked, looking peevish. "Then why aren't you helping Spock *now*?"

Tuvok was about to answer, when he felt his stomach buckle with immense pain. He cried out and fell, sprawling onto a hard surface. Janeway was gone. The blowing sand was gone. Only the random pattern of rough-hewn stones and bricks of his cell floor remained.

The last thing he saw before his eyes closed was the severed head of a beetle as it was crushed under the toe of a heavy boot. Then hot darkness came, mercifully enfolding him.

Mekrikuk heard the guards before they even entered the hallway. He knew that many of his Reman brethren had allowed imprisonment and deprivation to dull their senses, but he had worked hard to keep his sharp and honed. He was thankful for the prison's lack of light. Remans, after all, were creatures of the darkness.

Exercising at Vikr'l Prison wasn't an easy option. The prisoners were kept underfed and overaggravated, and any Reman who showed open contempt for the Romulan jailers was taken away and never heard from again. Rumors were that troublemakers were processed into food after their executions, effectively getting rid of any evidence of wrongdoing on the part of the guards while demeaning the captive Remans even further by forcing them into cannibalism. Mekrikuk chose not to eat on the days after someone had been taken away, no matter how tempting he found the intense food-smells.

Mekrikuk was used to hardship. His earliest memories were of being beaten in the dilithium mines, when he was barely four years old. Several of his siblings had died in the mines, either from exhaustion or disease, although Bekrinok had been killed for daring to stand up to a Romulan taskmaster who was sexually assaulting his teenage mate.

Of the rest of his family, Mekrikuk was the only one to have survived the Dominion War. Like many Remans, he had served as cannon fodder, but somehow, he had survived and emerged victorious in engagement after engagement. Mekrikuk had even saved the life of Delnek, the favored son and aide-de-camp of Senator Varyet.

That act had secured Mekrikuk a favored place in the senator's household. Varyet was a progressive politician who championed the rights of downtrodden provincial races; Mekrikuk was technically a slave in her household, but had been given unprecedented freedom, as long as he remembered "his place" while in public.

Not long ago that freedom had been cut short. A human named Shinzon, allied with the Remans, had assassinated the Romulan Senate, including both Varyet and Delnek. In the days that followed, the military forces rounded up every Reman they could find in and around Ki Baratan, as well as more than a few Romulan civilians, for "questioning."

Given his closeness to such a well-known political figure, Mekrikuk had received greater scrutiny than most. He had survived brutal torture, but told his interrogators nothing of value, largely because he didn't *know* anything of value, other than the location of some of the late senator's hidden valuables. By the time they were done with him, he would have sacrificed anything—or anyone—to get them to stop, or put him out of his agony.

Finished with him after only a few days, the military dumped him in Vikr'l, where he appeared to have been forgotten. He often wondered why they hadn't killed him, and sometimes wished he had the courage to end his own life. But he had learned many things in the prison, not the least of which was the burning desire to pull his life back from the brink yet again, as he had done so many times before during so many harrowing battles against the Jem'Hadar.

Reman legend was replete with tales of Tenakruvek, a great warrior who had returned from the brink of death five times, only to grow stronger each time. He eventually ascended to the Reman afterlife, to become a part of the pantheon worshipped by those few Remans who still prayed to the harsh deities responsible for placing them on their barren world of ever-day and ever-night.

Although he knew that many would see it as blasphemous, Mekrikuk now sometimes fancied himself a modern successor to Tenakruvek. After all, he had survived the mines, the war against the Dominion, and now torture and imprisonment. "Only two more deaths left," he often said to himself whenever he felt his spirits sinking too far.

Whether because of his large size or his heavily scarred body, the others in the cellmaze mostly left Mekrikuk alone. Some newcomers had offered themselves to him in exchange for protection; twice he had taken the offer, less from any carnal desire than because it was an expected trade, merely the way of the world. The two under his protection hadn't been abused by any other inmates, and they worked to keep themselves as fit as Mekrikuk did. They also kept their ears open for interesting news or opportunities.

Especially opportunities to escape.

They were away now, as the guards brought another new prisoner down the hall, using their dazzling handtorches to light their way and blind any Remans who got too close. Many of the others pressed forward to the bars of their cells, but the smarter ones stayed back. The chance to see the newcomer would come soon enough, and those nearest the bars were often sprayed with caustic *xecin* in addition to having their light-sensitive eyes dazzled by the handtorches; Mekrikuk found it odd, but he knew that some of them had actually come to enjoy the burning and stinging sensation of the *xecin*, if not the blinding lights.

As expected, the guards ordered everyone back from the bars, then sprayed the chemical at any who were slow to comply. They dumped a slight, rag-clad body in the center of the cell block, then turned to leave. After the outer cell-block doors had clanged shut behind the retreating guards, the individual cell doors opened automatically, allowing the other prisoners to inspect the new arrival.

Mekrikuk looked over at the body as the others began to move in closer. He saw immediately that this was not another Reman. It was a dark-skinned Romulan. Despite the kindness Varyet and Delnek had shown him, the sight of the bedraggled Romulan stirred something very close to hatred within Mekrikuk, as he was sure it did with all the other Remans in the cell block.

He remembered gentle Varyet, and felt shame.

What has this man done to deserve this? Mekrikuk reached out with his mind, concentrating hard to read the man. His telepathic talents were limited, but he knew that the mind of a sickly or infirm person was often easier to "touch" than that of someone in full health.

Moving into the Romulan's mind, he saw a Romulan woman and a family arrayed around her, but they were trapped behind a smoky wall. On the wall was a swooping symbol that Mekrikuk recognized as that of the Federation's Starfleet Command.

Startlement. *These aren't Romulans. They're* Vulcans.

He saw a dark-skinned Vulcan man sitting on the floor, his legs crossed, his crisp black-and-gray uniform clean and pressed. A small construct of sticks sat in front of him, intricate and fragile.

Mekrikuk looked at the pastel-hued walls that surrounded the dreamscape Vulcan, and saw images there of starships, of a group of officers in red tunics, another ragtag group of men and women led by a man whose face was tattooed, and a third group, dressed in uniforms identical to the one worn by the Vulcan who was seated on the floor.

The Vulcan looked up at him, and held up one of the sticks he had stacked before him. *"You* can help me complete my mission," he said.

"Your mission is to complete this device?" Mekrikuk asked.

"No," the man said simply. "My mission is to help those who wish to reconnect the Romulan Empire with its progenitors. It is not unlike the construction of the *kal-toh."*

Suddenly, the walls seemed to come alive, the images and people displayed there disappearing. Mekrikuk saw that the walls were now covered with beetles, their chitinous mandibles and carapaces beating in an insistent rhythm. As the carpet of insects moved inexorably toward the Vulcan, he looked at Mekrikuk and said, "To help me would be logical, Tenakruvek."

Mekrikuk shook himself out of his telepathic trance, the insect-covered walls dissolving into the harsher reality of the cellmaze. He saw the crowd leaning in toward the new Romulan, grasping and pulling, stealing from and bruising the unconscious man further. He was sure to be dead within moments.

"H'ta fvau, riud ihir taortuu u' irrhae alhu kuhaos'-ellaer tivh temarr!" Mekrikuk's voice thundered through the cellspace, and his outburst had the desired effect. The prisoners, having just been duly warned that the next person to touch the new prisoner would be eaten for dinner that night, backed away, some fearfully, some sullenly, some respectfully.

Mekrikuk approached and knelt beside the far-too-warm man who lay on the stone before him. He turned the man's bruised, battered head and felt his weak, thready pulse. Even though the man looked like a Romulan, he could see that this was the very same Vulcan he had seen in his mind-link.

The man whom he knew was not named Rukath, but *Tuvok*.

"I will help you," Mekrikuk said, hoping that Varyet was watching him from the Halls of Erebus.

CHAPTER TEN

"This isn't exactly what I signed up for," Kent Norellis said, watching the streams of green bubbles that rose like inverted meteor showers inside his glass.

Cadet Zurin Dakal looked up from his tray of sushi—an obsession he had acquired during his freshman year at Starfleet Academy—and was relieved to see that Norellis, seated at right angles to Dakal on the left, had apparently addressed the comment to no one at the table in particular. Dakal had feared that he personally would be expected to respond to the ensign's newest complaint, and that was one challenge he was not yet ready to undertake.

All things considered, Dakal knew he should have felt honored to be here. Not only did he have the distinction of being the first Cardassian in Starfleet, not only was his Academy class the first to begin in the aftermath of the Dominion War, not only was he one of only four fourth-year Starfleet cadets privileged to fulfill his required field studies on a new starship at the start of its mission, but now he also seemed to have been unofficially adopted by what was quickly emerging as a tightly-knit and bewilderingly eclectic group of science officers and noncommissioned specialists.

But while he had accepted the group's invitation to join them for dinner at the Blue Table—the crew's nickname for the informal weekly gathering of members from the science department in the mess hall, a custom which had started a month prior, after the first of them had come aboard at Utopia—he felt guarded and wary among aliens his kind had so recently conspired to dominate. Dakal was far more comfortable sitting quietly and observing the group dynamics among the gathered scientists than he was participating in their discussions. It was only prudent, he believed, to approach this new experience as he had every other since leaving Lejonis—with caution.

"Kent, what are you going on about?" asked Lieutenant Pazlar, who was seated opposite Norellis, on Dakal's right. A Martian aquifer fizz—naturally carbonated water drawn directly from the subsurface permafrost outside Utopia Planitia—and a Tarkovian broadleaf salad sat on the table before her.

"Romulus," Norellis said. "It's just not the kind of mission I expected this ship to go on, much less on its maiden voyage. And it certainly isn't what I had in mind when I chose my scientific specialties at the Academy."

Next to Norellis, Lieutenant Eviku, one of the ship's xenobiologists, turned his hairless, swept-back head toward him. "Not this again," the Arkenite said. "I thought we agreed you wouldn't use these dinners as a venue for your complaints?" Eviku's domed forehead dipped toward Norellis with a slight air of menace.

Norellis held up his hands. "Hey, I'm not complaining. I'm just feeling a little . . . impatient, is all. After all the

emphasis the captain put into outfitting and crewing this
ship for exploration, sending us to Romulus feels, I dunno,
like a slap in the face. It's like we're all on hold until this
political nonsense is over."

"For what it's worth, Kent, I don't completely disagree," Pazlar said. "Don't get me wrong. Since I joined
Starfleet, I've had to deal on the fly with everything from a
major war to a full-blown, planetary-scale disaster. So I'll
cope with whatever weirdness *Titan*'s missions throw at
us with only minimal griping. All the same, I'd rather be
charting unexplored solar systems and new stellar phenomena than settling power-sharing treaties."

"*I second that,*" Dr. Cethente said, situated next to
Pazlar. Cethente's simulated voice, translated from the
bioelectric impulses that constituted its normal mode of
communication, emerged from the combadge belted
around the center of its unusual body with an undertone of
wind chimes.

The only nonhumanoid scientist present at the Blue
Table, astrophysicist Se'al Cethente Qas was also the one
that Dakal found the most disquieting—though not for the
reasons some of the crew seemed to be reacting to Dr. Ree
or the other nonhumanoids aboard *Titan,* none of whom
bothered Dakal at all. What troubled him was the fact that
Dr. Cethente looked suspiciously like a lamp that had once
belonged to Dakal's paternal grandmother back on Prime.
Cethente was a Syrath, whose exoskeletal body had the
same fluted quality that was prevalent in Cardassian design. The astrophysicist was shaped, in fact, a great deal
like a three-dimensional sculpture of the symbol of the
Union: a high dome on top, tapering downward almost
to a point before bottoming out in a diamond formation
that Dakal knew was the Syrath secondary sense cluster.
Like the primary cluster that was the dome, the diamond

was dotted with bioluminescent bulges, glowing with the telltale green light of its senses at work, soaking up information about its environment omnidirectionally. Four slender, intricately jointed arachnid legs extended in four directions from the body's narrowest point, giving Cethente a solid footing on the deck, while an equal number of tentacles emerged at need from equidistant apertures just under the dome.

In repose, and with its tentacles retracted, Cethente seemed quite the inanimate object. But to Dakal, the doctor looked so much like the lamp in his grandmother's dwelling—and which had so consistently unnerved him as a child—that after first being introduced to it, Dakal briefly suspected the Federation of having sent a Syrath operative to spy on his grandmother.

Norellis took a sip of his bubbly drink—some form of synthale, Dakal suspected—and turned to the Bajoran who sat quietly at the head of the table, directly opposite Dakal. "You've been conspicuously silent on this subject, Commander."

Without looking up from his salad, Jaza smiled and said, "I'm still collecting data."

"Surely you have some opinion," the ensign said.

Unhurriedly, Jaza set down his fork, took a sip from his glass of water, and looked thoughtfully at Norellis. "Someone once observed that 'Worlds turn by politics as surely as they do by gravity.' "

Dakal's chopsticks, holding a *maki* roll of dark red Ahi, stopped halfway to his mouth. He could feel his neck ridges flushing. The Bajoran wasn't looking at him, but Dakal refused to believe his choice of words had been accidental.

Norellis's brow furrowed as he tried to place the quote. "Who said that?"

Jaza had already recovered his fork and returned his attention to his salad. "Cadet?"

Suddenly all eyes were on Dakal. He swallowed hard, unsure how to proceed, and angry that Jaza had put him on the spot in this manner. Finally, he admitted, "It was written by Iloja of Prim, a Cardassian poet, over two hundred years ago."

The revelation seemed neither to impress nor to incense anyone at the table. *So far, so good.*

"So what does it mean?" Pazlar asked Jaza. But when it became clear that the lieutenant commander would not be diverted from his salad again, the group's attention refocused on Dakal.

"Ah," he began. "Well, Iloja believed that the evolution of the sentient mind was merely a way for the universe to know itself, and that therefore no understanding of the universe can be complete without understanding sentient behavior."

Norellis snorted. "That's not science, it's philosophy."

Dakal was ready to launch into an elaboration of his point, but hesitated. His eyes darted briefly at Jaza, hoping for a clue as to what the senior officer expected of him. But the commander gave no sign that he was even listening.

And yet it would be a mistake to think that he is not. I'm being tested. Very well, then. I'll rise to this challenge as I have every other.

"Iloja is best remembered as a serialist poet, but before his exile he was an eminent astronomer and natural philosopher," Dakal explained. "As such, he understood that one's vantage point affects one's understanding of the observable universe. A different point of view may lead to a different understanding—or a deeper one, when taken in conjunction with one's original observations."

"Where does the quote about politics and gravity come in?" Norellis asked.

"In understanding first that Iloja was speaking as a Cardassian expatriate, having come from a world where politics was as fundamental a force as any found in nature. And second, in considering the possibility that his observation may not have been exclusive to his particular circumstances, but might have been applicable universally."

"I'm not sure I see what any of this has to do with *Titan* going to Romulus when we should be exploring."

"But we *are* exploring," Dakal said.

Norellis just stared at him blankly.

"Look at it another way," the cadet continued. "Your fields of expertise are astrobiology, the comparative study of life and its origins everywhere in the universe, and gaia-planetology, the study of planetary biospheres and ecosystems. Correct?"

Norellis smiled patiently. "A little oversimplified, Cadet, but I'm willing to accept those definitions for the purpose of our discussion."

"Thank you," Dakal said. "Can we also agree that the study of biospheres relates specifically to what may be described as the living zones within or surrounding a planet?"

"I suppose that's close enough. So?"

"So isn't the realm of politics merely another zone that has evolved to enclose a living world?" Dakal asked. "A 'politicosphere,' if you will. And *Titan* is about to begin the process of exploring that zone. And perhaps even experimenting on it."

"Oh, I like this kid, Najem," Pazlar said to Jaza, a smile spreading across her face as she turned back to Dakal. "I think Iloja wasn't the only natural philosopher to come out of Cardassia. Tell me again, Cadet, why you're training to be an operations specialist?"

Dakal shrugged his wide shoulders. "It seems to be where my strengths are, Lieutenant."

"Then think again," Eviku said. "Stick around long enough, Cadet, and we'll make a scientist of you yet."

Dakal smiled. "I'll accept that as a compliment, sir. I do have a great respect for science, and I admire the enthusiasm of its practitioners. I've just never had much patience for the fine details."

Norellis rolled his eyes. "Which is why you're a far better candidate than I am to push buttons up on the bridge."

Nodding, Dakal said, "With respect, sir, I *prefer* that you science specialists leave the driving to others."

"Really," Pazlar said dryly, at which point Dakal realized his misstep: In addition to her credentials in stellar cartography, the Elaysian was also one of *Titan*'s better shuttle pilots.

"Only so you specialists can concentrate on the *really* hard work," Dakal added quickly.

"Excellent save, Cadet," Dr. Cethente said. *"You ought to make admiral in no time."*

"If Bralik were here, I'm sure she'd have a few choice thoughts on the subject," Eviku said.

Pazlar chuckled appreciatively. "Bralik seems to have choice thoughts on *every* subject."

"Where *is* Doctor Bralik?" Dakal asked as he finished the last of his sushi. "I had thought she would be joining us."

Kent nodded past Dakal. "A few tables behind you, slumming with the yellowshirts."

"I heard that!" came the sound of Bralik's voice from across the mess hall, which prompted laughter from around the Blue Table. *Ah, of course: Ferengi ears,* Dakal noted. *I must remember that.*

"I have to admit," Pazlar said after the laughter had subsided, "I never would have thought of politics as a field of scientific inquiry. I never thought much about it before."

"Then it should be ripe for exploration," Cethente chimed, unexpectedly taking up Dakal's argument. The Syrath was not eating—at least, not in any obvious way; Dakal suddenly realized he hadn't the faintest idea how Cethente took its nourishment.

"As interesting as all this is," Norellis said, "I'm still skeptical that what we're doing on Romulus can have any relevance to our mission into the frontier, assuming we ever get there."

"Everything is connected, Kent," Jaza said, speaking up again at last. "Even when you think it isn't. Sometimes it's obvious, sometimes it's subtle, and sometimes it's paradoxical. It may take generations to see those connections, and longer still to understand them. Or those things may simply come all at once in a flash of insight. You just never know. So don't make the mistake of pursuing knowledge arrogantly. Keep an open mind."

"Always good advice, Commander," Norellis said with a nod, and drained his glass. Then he added with a grin, "But I'll still take a subspace singularity over a Romulan political confab any day of the week." He excused himself from the group, moving to join the table where Bralik was dining with Chief Engineer Ledrah and several members of the security department. Shortly thereafter, Pazlar, Eviku, and Cethente said their goodnights and left the Blue Table as well, leaving only Dakal and Jaza. Dakal decided this was the ideal opportunity to confront his superior head-on about his reference to Iloja.

"Did I pass your test, Commander?"

Finishing the last of his water, Jaza's brow furrowed. "My test, Cadet?"

"You wished to see how I would handle a discussion of my culture, did you not?"

"No, I did not," Jaza said mildly.

Dakal frowned. "Then why—?" Dakal stopped, realizing his emotions were taking hold. "Permission to speak freely, sir?"

Jaza leaned forward and, resting his elbows on the dining table, steepled his fingers before him. "Permission granted."

"If you were not testing me, then why did you single me out as a Cardassian during dinner?"

"I didn't, Cadet," Jaza said calmly. "You've singled yourself out by constantly being on your guard against any sign of interest in you as a representative of your species. You deliberately avoid the subject, I believe, because despite Starfleet's acceptance of you, you keep expecting the other shoe to drop."

Dakal was familiar with the human expression; he'd heard it at the Academy. "Respectfully, sir, you should have discussed the matter with me privately rather than ambush me as you did."

Jaza smiled. "The point was to have you deal with it publicly, Cadet." The Bajoran gestured expansively at the rest of the mess hall. "Look around you, Dakal. Do you really think the people who choose this life are inclined to judge you based on your species? They're more interested in *you* than in your accidental relationship to a longtime foe of the Federation. And as you saw during the meal, we're certainly capable of separating whatever lingering ill feelings we may have about the Cardassian Union from our interest in Cardassian culture, or in one Zurin Dakal.

"But I think you know that, or you'd never have enrolled in Starfleet Academy in the first place. Am I wrong?"

Dakal considered Jaza's words, reflecting on the long road he had traveled from the refugee camps on the neutral planet Lejonis, the world to which he, together with his parents and siblings, as well as scores of other families, had fled after they had been perilously smuggled off Cardassia Prime five years prior, during the height of the Dominion occupation there. Raised in a culture that revered duty to the state above all other virtues, even familial devotion, leaving Cardassia behind at such a difficult time, culminating in the carnage that had marked the war's costly end, had felt conflictingly like both treason and patriotism to the refugees on Lejonis. Treason because they had, in a very real sense, turned their backs on their homeworld during her darkest hour; patriotism because the planet of their birth had been distorted by corrupt opportunists and alien invaders almost beyond recognition. But dissidents and conscientious objectors had never fared well on Prime, even in the best of times, so the refugees on Lejonis had resolved to be patient, to preserve and stay true to the values and ideals that had first made Cardassia strong, in the hope that, one day, they would make her strong again.

Cardassia's billion dead at the war's end had shaken that hope among the refugees, but hadn't extinguished it. Most of the families soon returned home to help restore their fallen civilization any way they could. But a small number—young Zurin Dakal among them—had reasoned that there was much good that could come from showing the rest of the galaxy a Cardassian face different from the one that had brought so much pain to the Alpha Quadrant. Those individuals—mostly academicians and artisans of one sort or another—had resettled on worlds throughout the Federation, teaching at universities, joining organizations devoted to the arts, or helping with the postwar rebuilding efforts. Dakal alone had elected to join Starfleet, though he had hoped others of his kind would eventually follow. In all but name those self-exiled Cardassians were Prime's cultural ambassadors, hoping in some small way to begin healing a rift that they believed had grown too wide and too deep for far too long.

Perhaps Jaza is right, Dakal thought, *and these last four years as a solitary Cardassian among all these aliens have made me forget the reasons I chose Starfleet. Perhaps I should not be reluctant to share my heritage with my shipmates, or to celebrate it. How better to prove my fears false? Or to confront any fears I may encounter?*

"No, Commander, you aren't wrong," Dakal said. "In fact, you've helped me to remember a few things I should not have forgotten. Thank you, not just for your interest, but for inviting me to this evening's Blue Table."

Jaza smiled again. "It's an open invitation, Cadet. Join us any time."

"Thank you, sir," said Dakal, suddenly experiencing a sense of home for the first time since separating from his family. *Perhaps trust can turn worlds as well.*

As he entered deck seven's multipurpose mess hall–cum–recreation center, Ranul Keru tried to tamp down his mounting worries. For reasons he had yet to identify, recurring feelings of self-doubt had plagued him during his past few duty shifts. He wondered repeatedly if he was really capable of serving effectively as both chief of security and tactical officer.

Of course he still believed, at least intellectually, that he was the right person for this dual job. Though he had served in the far less action-intensive role of stellar cartographer during his first tour of duty aboard the *Enterprise,* he had also been trained in multiple techniques of unarmed defense, had achieved some of the highest marksmanship scores of his Academy class, and had already proven himself during real-world tactical crises on Trill, Tezwa, and Pelagia.

When he had returned to the *Enterprise* two years ago following an extended personal leave on Trill, he had transferred to security, joining the department that was then headed by Christine Vale. Had Lieutenant Commander Worf still been in charge of ship's security then, Keru knew he couldn't have worked under him; the Klingon officer was the one who had, albeit out of necessity, shot Keru's lifemate, Lieutenant Sean Hawk, and then let his corpse drift off into trackless space.

No, it was the Borg *who killed him,* he repeated to himself for perhaps the billionth time. *Worf was only doing his job, protecting the ship. Sean was infected with nanoprobes, and would have used them to assimilate the rest of us.*

And yet, every time he made that argument to himself, he saw the face of Captain Jean-Luc Picard, who had also once been assimilated by the Borg, only to be rescued later and cured of his nanoprobe infection. More recently, the long-lost *U.S.S. Voyager* had returned to Earth, bringing along a human woman who had also been successfully deassimilated from the Borg collective. Both Picard and the woman *Voyager*'s crew had repatriated had been nanoprobe-infected for far longer than Sean had been.

He could have been saved, too. Worf was too quick to sacrifice a fellow crew member, battle conditions or not.

It was an ugly doubt to be carrying around, but he had been unable to put it to rest for more than half a decade now. There had to have been another way. Sean Hawk would still be alive today if Worf had simply put forth a better effort to find it.

He knew that this nagging bitterness, this shard of blame that remained lodged in his soul like old shrapnel, was one of the underlying reasons that Keru had accepted the role of security chief aboard *Titan* when Captain Riker had extended the invitation. He had not said it aloud, but inside, he'd fairly screamed it: *I won't sacrifice anyone on my team. No one is expendable.*

During the past few weeks, he had worked his security crew hard, probably harder than they'd ever been worked at the Academy. On the physical side, he had them running simulations in the holodeck, training in multiple exotic forms of hand-to-hand combat, including Vulcan V'Shan, Terran Tai Chi, and Klingon *Mok'bara,* while practicing with a medley of weapons that ranged from standard phasers to Klingon *bat'leth*s to Capellan *kligat*s to Ferengi energy whips. On the academic front, he had them immersed in language studies to free them from total dependency on the universal translator, and introduced meditation techniques from several different cultures in order to bring their minds and bodies into closer alignment.

He knew that some of them resented the extensive training, no doubt feeling they had already "made their bones" serving in their previous postings. He had even heard a few whispered comments about his own previous "cushy" job as a stellar cartographer. So he worked himself hard, right alongside his crew, doing everything they did, as long as his other duties didn't call him away. Lately, even with the Romulan talks looming, he hadn't had a lot to do other than continue drilling.

Now, even though he was off duty, he had decided to

wear his uniform into the mess hall. Relaxed dress code or no, he felt he ought to at least set an example. Besides, he hadn't really wanted to take the time to change clothes after the beta shift crew had assumed their stations on the bridge.

As he headed toward the mess hall's food-service area, he surveyed the entire room quickly. The dining area had attracted a few small clusters of people, three to four per table. At one table, he saw flight controller Axel Bolaji and his very pregnant wife, Olivia, seated with two of his security guards, Rriarr and Hutchinson. He smiled and nodded, and Axel Bolaji smiled back. Keru noted that Rriarr and Hutchinson looked decidedly unhappy.

They must be self-conscious about my seeing them out of uniform, he thought, noting their civvies, which were perfectly acceptable in the mess. *Guess I've given them good reason to see me as a hard-ass.*

He neared the buffet area, and smiled as the various smells wafted toward him. Ebriscentil, *Titan*'s civilian Ktarian cook, had prepared another fabulous repast, as he had been doing since the ship launched. Keru was glad that Riker had requested a combined galley, bar, and recreational area aboard *Titan;* not only did it give the crew more encouragement to socialize, but it also allowed them a respite from replicated foods. Riker had apparently learned the value of such a venue in the *Enterprise*'s crew lounge.

Keru served himself some Kaferian apple-glazed Maporian rib-eye, a salad of Denuvian sprigs, and a breadlike Bolian pastry that came with a spicy dipping sauce. Hefting his tray, he remembered to snatch a handful of extra napkins; while eating, he always had a napkin handy to keep his bushy mustache clean.

Before looking for a seat, he sidled up to the bar.

The bartender, a Mars-born human named Scot Bishop-Walker, was his favorite of those aboard who dispensed drinks. Not only was he one of the few humans who was almost as tall as he was, but he was easy on the eyes as well, with high cheekbones and a dark, neatly trimmed goatee.

"Ranul! What can I get you?" Bishop-Walker asked, a bright smile on his face.

"I'm feeling a little adventurous tonight," Keru said, smiling back. "Give me a tankard of that dark Orion beer."

The bartender raised an eyebrow. "One tankard coming up. But you'd better handle it with care."

Keru laughed. "You ought to know by now how tough it is to get me drunk."

"Someday I'm sure one of my concoctions will defeat that stout Trill constitution," Bishop-Walker said, sliding a large, foamy drinking vessel across the counter toward Keru. "Enjoy. You can work it off with me on the velocity court tomorrow."

"Thanks," Keru said. "You still owe me a rematch." The bartender had trounced him at velocity three days earlier.

"Some people can never get enough punishment," Bishop-Walker said over his shoulder as he moved to help another crew member farther down the bar.

Keru turned away with his tray of food and drink, scanning the crowd for an appropriate place to sit. He saw Ensign Norellis beckoning to him from a table next to one of the large observation windows. As he neared the table, he saw that Ledrah and Bralik were seated with him.

"Hi, Commander," Norellis said, moving up and gesturing toward the sleekly curved window. "Why don't you sit on the inside? The view there is lots better."

Odd offer, but nice, Keru thought. He took a seat beside

the bulkhead, lifting his tray over Norellis's food. "Thank you, Ensign."

"Please, call me Kent," Norellis said, perhaps a bit too eagerly.

"Oh, yes, *please* call him Kent," Bralik said. She chortled until a look of pain abruptly crossed her face. "Ow! Watch those boots, kid!"

Keru realized that Norellis had indeed kicked Bralik under the table, but couldn't imagine why. Ledrah was pointedly looking out at the stars, apparently trying to stifle a grin.

"Am I missing something here?" Keru asked.

"No," Norellis said quickly. "It's Bralik that's missing her manners."

"Manners are just another form of societal domination intended to crush all individuality," Bralik declared.

Ledrah made a mock-shocked face. "Is that a new Rule of Acquisition?"

"Just a cutting social observation," Bralik said. "Listen, and grow wise."

"Oh, come on, Bralik," Ledrah said, idly fingering one of her outsize wrinkled ears. "Just because you've spent your whole life rebelling against Ferengi society doesn't mean you have to rebel against everybody else's."

"Why not? We live in a galaxy that supports thousands of sentient species. Here aboard the *U.S.S. Melting Pot,* we've built a sort of cultural atom-smasher—a laboratory designed to create clashes of customs and manners, if you really think about it."

Keru found himself troubled and intrigued at the same time. Bralik may have been loud and coarse, but he had to concede that she had a point. *There's no shortage of opportunities for conflict with a crew this diverse.* But he still tended to think of *Titan*'s diversity as a strength rather than a weakness.

"So, what are you saying, then?" Norellis asked.

Bralik set down her drink and said, "If we're supposed to be out here looking for new life and new civilizations, then what are we learning if we don't take parts of their customs away with us? Isn't the best aspect of exploring the chance to take away the knowledge that things can not only be different, but also that those differences can be celebrated?"

Everyone at the table sat quietly for a moment. Keru realized he had forgotten to chew his last bite of salad, and resumed. Ledrah finally looked his way, then gestured toward Bralik. "Before you ask, yes, she *is* always like this."

Norellis scooted out of his seat. "I'm off for another round. Would you like another drink, Commander?"

Keru smiled, gesturing toward his still mostly full tankard. "Not just yet, thanks."

"Get me a Core Breach," Ledrah said.

As Norellis wandered toward the bar, Keru looked back at Bralik. "That's a very progressive way of thinking for a Feren—"

"He likes you," Bralik said, interrupting. "He's too shy to say it himself, so I figure I'd better tell you before he gets back to the table."

"Excuse me?" Keru asked, confused.

Bralik tilted her head to one side. "For someone who came out of stellar cartography, you're surprisingly inept at connecting the dots, Ranul," she said, speaking slowly as though addressing a willfully obtuse child. "He wants to court you."

"*Court* me?"

Ledrah put her hand over Bralik's mouth, stifling what-ever her next comment was. "Bralik shouldn't have said anything, Commander. Just forget it."

Keru's mind whirled. The last thing he expected during dinner was to be told that a junior officer wanted to "court" him. Much less one in whom he had zero romantic interest.

"Okay," he sighed. "Let me just say that I appreciate your efforts at matchmaking, however unorthodox they might be. But Ensign Norellis and I are not, and *will* not, be involved in anything other than a professional relation-ship." He stared intently at Bralik. "And if you're his friends, you'll find a way to tell him that, without being so unmannerly as to hurt his feelings."

Bralik's eyes locked with Keru's, then moved over to Ledrah. The engineer finally removed her hand from Bralik's mouth—whereupon the Ferengi woman began speaking immediately. "Sorry if we misjudged your pref-erences, Commander. Nidani is single, too, if she's more to your liking. She also—"

Ledrah clapped her hand back over Bralik's mouth, a look of murder flashing in her eyes.

Norellis reappeared, holding a tray with drinks for him-self and Ledrah, as well as a second hefty tankard that ap-peared to be intended for Keru.

"Hey. What did I miss?"

"You are rarely exasperating, Will Riker, but when you are, you are in a *very* big way."

Troi plopped down on the settee in a huff.

"What?" Will asked, throwing his hands in the air. "I'm just not sure it's such a good idea."

Troi was glad that they were meeting in the senior

counselor's office rather than in their quarters. At least here, where her spirits were buoyed by the room's soothing light-blue color scheme, an aquarium stocked with freshwater fish from a dozen worlds, and shelves crowded with hardcopy books and Betazoid art objects, she felt far more comfortable adopting a professional tone with her husband. She took a deep, cleansing breath through her nose, then exhaled through her mouth before continuing.

"Look, Will, you were the one who pushed for the inclusion of the mess hall, and you did so for all the right reasons. Chief among those reasons was that it would provide a social atmosphere on a ship that had not been designed with social interaction as one of its top priorities. But how can you expect the crew to develop an appropriate relationship with their captain if you won't even eat with them?"

"I'm just concerned about it looking wrong," Riker said, sitting down next to Troi. "I don't want Akaar, or anyone else, to accuse me of being too familiar with my staff."

Troi's eyes widened as she released another puff of air. "I promise not to ask you to sleep with any crew members other than me, Captain."

"Very funny. You know perfectly well what I mean about propriety. Besides, I thought we were talking about socializing in the mess hall."

Troi softened her tone. "Maybe we are, maybe we aren't. What's this really about, Will? Akaar? You can't allow his presence to undermine your command. He is on this ship for one mission, and one mission alone."

"Sure," Will said, his expression sour. "It just happens to be my very *first* mission."

"True. But once it's over, he'll be gone and you'll have to live and work with everyone else on board for all the other missions that will follow. By then you and the crew need to have done some . . . bonding."

"Bonding."

She hated to compare captains, but felt he still needed some convincing. "Remember how your life was on the *Enterprise?* On *two Enterprises?* You played poker. You drank in Ten-Forward. You played in your jazz ensemble, with subordinates. You were a friend to the entire crew— or at least friendly to all of them. Captain Picard was almost *never* that way."

He smiled at that. "No. But he mellowed over time."

"But only up to a point. His command style was always very cool and reserved. Nobody on board doubted his leadership, his competence, and his genuine concern for every member of the crew. But only those of us who were closest to him saw him as a friend. To everyone else, he was only their captain, however exceptional. And *his* style can't be *your* style."

"But I was a first officer then, Deanna. Not a captain. I may have to put a bit more distance between myself and the crew than I'm used to."

She took his hands in hers, and looked into his eyes. "Do you, *Imzadi?* Are you prepared to sacrifice the unique command style you've spent your entire career cultivating? I don't think so. If you were, you wouldn't have left so many of your fingerprints all over this ship already."

He frowned. "Fingerprints?"

"Oh, please. A shuttlecraft named after Louis Armstrong?"

The frown melted, and flowed into an appreciative smile. His emotions felt like a rainstorm receding before a rising sun.

"Be their friend *and* their captain," she continued. "Give them a chance to be loyal, and give yourself a chance to earn their loyalty. And their friendship. Not just their respect." She smiled back at him, then said, "Don't wait seven years to join the poker game, Will."

He suddenly leaned in and kissed her, then pulled her into a close embrace. *Thank you*, he thought, and she heard it in her mind, and felt his love fueling the senti-ment.

After several minutes, they disentangled themselves. He smiled. "Let's head for the mess. Deal the cards, and see what happens."

They stood and walked toward her office door. He stopped and caressed her hair. Earlier today, she had gotten the ship's stylist to braid her luxuriant, reddish-brown mane into a dozen or so rows, twisting it into a single mass at the back. She felt that this style—which she had worn briefly during her recent honeymoon with Will on Pelagia's Opal Sea—gave her a sleek look, while still allowing her to maintain a wholly professional demeanor.

"We would have had to go anyhow," he said. "If for no other reason than to show off your quite alluring new hair-style."

Troi chuckled, then pushed her husband closer to the door. "Flatterer," she said.

Entering the corridor, they walked the twenty paces or so that separated Troi's office from the mess hall. Before they could step inside, the doors slid open, and two engi-neers quickly exited and made their way quickly to the turbolift. Neither had acknowledged the captain's pres-ence, and both had looked nauseated.

"Wonder what's wrong," he said.

"Perhaps they ate something that didn't agree with them," Troi said, keenly aware that something had truly bothered the engineers. She gestured toward the buffet. "It certainly all looks good."

As they made their way over to the buffet, Troi saw that Will was making eye contact with everyone he could. Since this was his first meal there in two weeks, it made sense that most of the people present were surprised to see him. She was happy to note that several crew members were already feeling increased respect for their captain because of his appearance here.

After serving themselves—she taking an Andorian tuber root salad with Betazoid oskoid fronds, he assembling something he described as an improvised Lycosan Reuben sandwich—they began looking about the room for seating. They saw several empty tables in one corner, although Akaar's trio of Vulcan advisers was seated nearby. At another table only a little farther off, Dr. Ree squatted, his long, thick tail partially coiled beneath him, his chair pushed to the side to accommodate his long frame. His back was turned to everyone in the room.

"Let's sit with Dr. Ree," Will said.

Troi smiled, feeling a surge of triumph. Will had really warmed up to his CMO—as had many aboard *Titan*—though there were still some among the crew who remained almost viscerally troubled by his fearsome look.

As they neared the table, Ree looked up at them, his nested double eyelids blinking in alternation, first vertically, then horizontally.

"Mind if we join you, Doctor?" Will asked.

"If you can stand the gruesome sight," Ree said. As Will and Troi sat down, he added, "I seem to have scared a few of the more sensitive diners away."

"Nonsense," Troi said, then cast her gaze onto the meal Ree was eating.

On a large platter was a bloody pile of raw meat, still attached to a long, curved bone. Mottled, bile-colored gobbets of fat and gristle festooned the edges of his plate.

"What is that you're eating?" Will asked. Troi sensed no serious discomfort coming from Will; as a survivor of many a Klingon meal, very few things could turn his stomach.

Ree gestured at his repast with a single long, sharp foreclaw. "Freshly-killed *targ*. The Klingons have been most hospitable in sharing their comestibles. I had to convince our chef that he should *not* cook it before serving it to me."

After lustily tearing off, chewing, and swallowing another large bite, Ree cocked his head to one side, then swiveled it to take in all the other faces in the mess hall. Troi did likewise.

Though the people in the room were the products of perhaps a score of distinct worlds and cultures, they had achieved an unprecedented degree of emotional unanimity. Troi also noticed that most of them were looking in Ree's direction.

They were staring. Some were plainly horrified. But most were making a heroic effort not to let their revulsion show. *Good. We're making some real progress here.*

Ree looked back at Riker and Troi. "I believe that I shall finish this in my quarters later," Ree said, standing. "Thank you for sitting with me."

Turning, Ree carried the platter of meat with him as he crossed the room and exited into the corridor. The room was utterly silent until the doors hissed closed behind him.

Ree's sadness hung in the room like a cloud of smoke. Clearly, he was becoming sensitive to those who had not succeeded in hiding their distaste.

Maybe that constituted some sort of progress as well. Bridges, after all, had to be built on both sides of any biological or cultural divide.

"Damn," Will muttered.

"What's wrong?" Troi wanted to know.

"Looks like we picked this table for nothing," he said, simultaneously radiating disappointment and mischief.

"It's all right, Will," she said very quietly. "Integrating this crew is going to take work."

"No, that's not what I mean at all."

She frowned, not at all sure where he was going. "Then what *do* you mean?"

"Khegh didn't serve *targ tartare* during the meal on his flagship. I was hoping Ree was going to leave a joint or two for me."

Chapter Eleven

The Hall of State, Ki Baratan, Romulus

The massive ruatinite-inlaid doors swung quickly inward, as though propelled by some implacable, irresistible force. The great doors crashed jarringly against the polished volcanic stone walls, casting a harsh echo throughout the praetor's audience chamber.

You will learn respect one day, Rehaek, Praetor Tal'Aura thought as two black-clad figures entered the wide doorway and resolutely approached her, their *hnoiyika*-leather boots clacking loudly on the gleaming black floor.

Tomalak moved forward from Tal'Aura's side to intercept the two interlopers.

"Jolan'tru, Director Rehaek," the proconsul said in even tones. "I do wish you had called ahead. We would have prepared some appropriate . . . hospitality for you."

Rehaek came to a stop less than a single *dhat'drih* from Tomalak, and perhaps only four times that distance from the praetor's chair. The man who had entered beside

Rehaek stopped obediently alongside his master, glowering at Tomalak with undisguised contempt. Rehaek's vulpine features, however, bore an almost neutral expression that would not have looked out of place on a Vulcan.

Until he favored both Tomalak and Tal'Aura with a singularly lubricious smile.

Then the man who stood beside Rehaek spoke for his master, as though Rehaek himself did not wish to sully himself by directly addressing those he regarded as his inferiors. "Unnecessary, Proconsul," said Torath, Rehaek's adjutant, his hard gaze focused squarely upon Tomalak. "We did not wish to take up much of the praetor's valuable time."

Tal'Aura had always particularly detested Torath, perhaps even more than she disliked and distrusted Rehaek himself. The proconsul's obviously laborious effort at restraint made it apparent that Tomalak shared the praetor's antipathy. Oddly, Tomalak and Torath looked enough alike to be first cousins, or perhaps even half siblings. Both were tall, pale, and broad in the shoulders, with thick black hair cut in a severe fashion that emphasized both men's prominent brow ridges. Tal'Aura knew that they were of an age as well, each man rapidly nearing the midpoint of his second century. Perhaps their mutual enmity had arisen organically, cultivated by both of them over the last several decades. Or maybe it had materialized abruptly, the way Torath's master had so suddenly appeared within—and had almost as quickly conquered— much of the Romulan Empire's military intelligence apparatus.

Of course, Tal'Aura thought with no small amount of bitterness, *the destruction and disorder loosed by Shinzon no doubt helped you seize control of the Tal Shiar itself.*

She hated the fact that Shinzon's unprecedented disruption of the Romulan political system had elevated someone as unworthy as Rehaek to such power and prominence. She hated that nearly as much as she loathed facing the unpleasant reality that her own claim to the praetorship had arisen from those selfsame catastrophic circumstances.

As usual, thoughts of Shinzon threatened to send her into a tailspin of regret. Four years earlier when she'd served in the Senate, she had tried to have the surface of Goloroth laid waste before Shinzon and his savage Remans could escape into space with an all but omnipotent thalaron weapon in their possession. She had failed, and that failure had forced her into an unholy alliance with Shinzon during his recent brief tenure in the praetorship. While that alliance had allowed her to avoid being turned to thalaron ash along with the rest of the Senate, it had caused the weight of a crumbling Empire to settle squarely on her shoulders.

If only those shapeless hhwai'il *in the Gamma Quadrant had crushed the Tal Shiar a bit more thoroughly during that ill-conceived joint venture with the Obsidian Order eight years ago. Had that occurred, there might never have been a thalaron weapon for Shinzon and his barbarian hordes to steal.*

"Praetor?" Torath said sharply, shattering Tal'Aura's almost penitent reverie.

Not deigning to rise from her chair, Tal'Aura ignored Torath, instead locking her gaze with that of Rehaek. "Since you are so concerned with my schedule, Director Rehaek, allow me to help you expedite your business here. After all, I know well how very valuable *your* time is."

Rehaek made a perfunctory bow to Tal'Aura, coming

perilously close to mocking the rituals and protocols that had surrounded the praetorship for centuries. Those rituals and protocols had, sadly, fallen increasingly into disuse during the five years that had passed since the craven assassination of Emperor Shiarkiek.

"Then I shall be brief, my Praetor," Rehaek said. "I have come because I know you are about to conduct a . . . private preliminary meeting with Starfleet personnel, Romulan military leaders, and former Senator Pardek."

Tal'Aura was not the least bit surprised by the extent of the young Tal Shiar director's knowledge of her plans. Indeed, she would have been nonplussed had he failed to catch wind of it. "I suppose it won't be such a private gathering after all, then."

His smile broadened, though his eyes retained the patient intensity of a mountain *sseikea* that had scented its prey and hungrily awaited an opportunity to strike. It was no wonder he'd succeeded in outmaneuvering and disposing of Koval, his ailing predecessor.

"That is entirely up to you, my Praetor," Rehaek said. "I merely wish to assist all parties concerned in achieving a mutually acceptable . . . political understanding. One that we can all build upon for the future—and that will ensure that the Empire will even *have* a future."

Tal'Aura nodded. From the moment he had entered the chamber, she'd expected something like this. "That is a generous offer indeed, Director. But I presume that it does not come without a steep price."

"Your many decades on the Senate Intelligence Committee were well spent, my Praetor. However, my price is hardly what I would call 'steep.' "

She was beginning to grow weary of Rehaek's circumlocutions. "Speak plainly. What exactly is it you want?"

She saw that her blunt tone had garnered a glare from the insufferable Torath. She ignored it, and continued to focus her concentration on the Tal Shiar leader's sharp gaze.

"I wish only to forge a mutually cooperative relationship with you, my Praetor, and your regime. Openly, and in public. I am certain I can help you moderate the aggressive predilections of Pardek's faction, as well as those of the unruly elements within the military. You know that Pardek would attack Earth and the Federation, had he the opportunity. Commander Suran might even be inclined to provide him with the military support he requires."

Pardek, Tal'Aura thought ruefully. *Such a sad, bitter man.* She had always believed that the machinations of Koval, Rehaek's immediate predecessor as Tal Shiar director, deserved the blame for Pardek's rage at least as much as did the Federation's spies.

Tal'Aura nodded in bleak acknowledgment of Rehaek's assessment. She considered what a disaster another rogue Romulan attack against Earth would be, so soon after Shinzon had tried to destroy that planet. Such a thing could well seal the doom of an Empire that was already well on its way to tearing itself asunder.

Aloud, she said, "But why would you support my praetorship in such an overt manner? After all, you have never been . . . appropriately deferential to the office of the praetor."

"I have always had only the highest esteem for the *office,* my Praetor."

Tomalak reacted to that insult by taking a single angry step toward Rehaek. Tal'Aura instantly halted the proconsul with a sharp command and a frosty glare. There was nothing to be gained by allowing the current face of Tal Shiar treachery and terror to goad her. Despite the throne she now occupied and the resources she now controlled, she knew that her position was far too tenuous to risk tempting the fates. Besides, she wasn't at all certain that Tomalak would survive an encounter with Torath. Tomalak was too valuable to her praetorship to place him at risk. At least for now.

Despite the still-incensed proximity of Tomalak, Rehaek didn't flinch. Nor did he need to use more than a glance to restrain Torath's evident desire to take some aggressive action of his own against the proconsul.

Rehaek looked to Tal'Aura, as though the other two men no longer even existed. "Surely, my Praetor, you can appreciate the grave danger that Pardek's faction poses to the Empire."

After a pause she smiled, having come to a realization. "Yes. And I don't imagine a hard-liner war against the Federation would be good for you, either, Director." *There is such a thing as too much chaos. Even for one who often depends upon it to keep his adversaries confused in order to maintain his own power and position.*

The spymaster nodded. "Then we understand each other well, my Praetor."

"I understand that you need me, Director Rehaek. Perhaps more than I need you." Triumph surged within her breast, as it rarely ever did in the presence of senior Tal Shiar officials. *He feels the need to flex his muscle visibly, right in front of the leaders of the other factions. Perhaps he thinks they are losing their ingrained fear of the Tal Shiar. He needs to demonstrate the length of his reach. And that the Tal Shiar still wields power to be reckoned with, Koval or no Koval.*

"I wish to help you contain the threat that Pardek represents, my Praetor," Rehaek said, not rising to her jab. "And I think you'll agree that the intelligence support I can provide will be invaluable to you in maintaining your . . . authority."

You mean such intelligence as you deign to share with your esteemed praetor, she thought.

"And I think you'll also agree, my Praetor," Rehaek continued, "that what you will require most immediately from me is my silence. You may, in fact, find that indispensable—if you are to maintain whatever hold on Imperial authority you now possess."

"Your silence?" Tal'Aura sensed that Rehaek was about to pounce like a rain-jungle *zdonek*.

"Come now, my Praetor. The Remans are unaware of the early power-sharing conference you are about to host. The one that excludes them. Imagine how much more vulnerable your position would become were they to learn of this. The Remans would believe you are trying to deceive them. And deceit motivates Remans to break things. Sometimes even things that have yet to be built, such as political alliances.

"Commit to an alliance with the Tal Shiar, my Praetor, and I will see to it that the Remans learn nothing untoward before the first full power-sharing conference."

Tal'Aura felt her earlier sense of triumph evaporating. Her throat felt drier than the sunward side of Remus.

"I prefer that my friends and adversaries alike state their threats in plain language, Director Rehaek."

He nodded, an ironic smile tugging at his lips. "Very well, my Praetor. In the absence of a formal understanding between us, I can state with almost perfect certainty that the Remans *will* discover your upcoming secret meeting—and in plenty of time to wreak havoc across both of the Two Worlds, and perhaps far beyond. Such an outcome would be most . . . distracting to your praetorship, to say the least."

She slumped back in her chair, feeling defeated.

"Do not listen to him, Praetor," Tomalak said. *"Let* him stir up the Remans. That might force the hands of Donatra and Suran. A new Reman uprising could reveal the actual extent of Donatra and Suran's control over the Empire's military forces. It might drive a wedge between the two commanders. It could even send a large proportion of their men and matériel over to *our* side."

Tal'Aura shook her head and spoke in tones scarcely above a whisper. "But at what cost?"

Tomalak began an angry rejoinder, but she silenced the proconsul with a peremptory wave of her hand. His silence encouraged her; she knew he would not have relented so easily had he not known that she was right.

Rehaek held the advantage, at least for the moment.

"Very well," Tal'Aura said, addressing the spymaster and his far-too-pleased-looking lackey.

But the unending struggle between the praetorship and the Tal Shiar is by no means resolved, she thought. *It is merely postponed until more convenient circumstances arise.*

Glancing down at the palm of his pudgy right hand, Pardek saw the time displayed on his chrono-ring, and noted that the meeting would not begin for nearly four full *veraku.* He loitered in the Hall of State's vast library, alone except for a half-dozen extremely vigilant armed uhlans and a handful of nervous-looking scholars who were clearly trying to look completely intent upon their various academic research projects. The sun streamed in through windows high in the domed roof, casting long shadows across the towering ancient bookshelves and the low-slung modern computer terminals in the otherwise unlit chamber. Everything looked peaceful enough, though Pardek could hear the emergency vehicles, their echoing klaxons reminding him of the cries of distant seabirds. A slight ozone tang hung in the air, evidence of the fires that had raged for weeks across much of Ki Baratan's South Quarter, and which still smoldered in the nearby ancient district known as the *ira'sihaer.*

During his first term in the Senate more than a century earlier, Pardek had developed the habit of arriving early for critical meetings such as the one scheduled for today, the better to size up his adversaries from some unobtrusive nearby waiting area before following them into the meeting chamber proper. He rose from the chair where he had sat beside one of the computer screens and deactivated his link to the newsnets. There was still ample time for another stroll around the spacious courtyard that surrounded the Hall of State. Within a few minutes, he had circled the courtyard and stepped into one of the secluded alcoves that led back inside the great domed building that held the praetor's audience chamber.

"Senator," a sharp voice intoned from a short distance ahead of him.

Pardek saw two men in civilian clothes approaching him from the direction of Tal'Aura's audience chamber. He recognized the shorter of the pair immediately as Rehaek, the current leader of the Tal Shiar. This was the man who had killed the hated Koval, the Federation-tainted criminal who had slain Tai'lun and Talkath, Pardek's wife and only daughter. As such, Rehaek could almost be considered an ally. Almost.

"*Jolan'tru,* Director Rehaek. I wasn't aware you were to be present at the coming meeting." Pardek was confident that Rehaek knew of the meeting, and that he was therefore revealing nothing that the clever young Tal Shiar chief hadn't already discovered for himself.

After nodding to his impassive companion, Rehaek turned his gaze back upon Pardek. He smiled with surprising mildness. "I won't be present . . . at least, not directly."

Ah, Pardek thought. *The Tal Shiar need not send a representative. They have eyes and ears everywhere, not all of them living ones.* He shuddered involuntarily, recalling how casually Koval had thwarted his security system more than six years earlier, invading his home and threatening the life of his only child in an effort to intimidate him.

Pardek reminded himself not to allow the satisfaction he had taken in Koval's recent death to lull him into lowering his guard. The Tal Shiar was still the Tal Shiar. And he had no assurance that Rehaek's Tal Shiar was any less likely to get into bed with the Federation, or perhaps even other far more dangerous foes of the Empire.

"It appears you have the praetor's ear, Director Rehaek," the former senator said, choosing his words cautiously.

"All loyal Romulans should rally around our new praetor, particularly when the Empire is in jeopardy. Should we not?"

Pardek sniffed, allowing the other men a glimpse of the political outrage he usually kept tightly wrapped, except perhaps in Tal'Aura's presence. "The legitimacy of Tal'Aura's praetorship is still open to debate, Director. In fact, I find her automatic inclusion in today's Federation-mediated talks to be highly questionable. Prior to the assassinations of Praetor Hiren and the Senate, Tal'Aura was merely yet another senator. Her claim to the praetorship is therefore no better than that of any *other* senator."

"Except that she *is* alive, whereas almost all of those other senators are not, including the entire Continuing Committee. That fact alone gives Tal'Aura a decided advantage over her erstwhile peers, I should think."

Pardek tried to ignore Rehaek's smirk. "Regardless, I am surprised to see that you've embraced Tal'Aura's claim to the praetorship—especially before the debate over its very legitimacy has even truly begun."

"I see," Rehaek said, a look of inexplicable sadness crossing his sharp features. "But one of the essential functions of the Tal Shiar is to prevent such debates from becoming dangerous distractions from our Empire's larger objectives. Therefore such debates must sometimes be settled preemptively."

Pardek noticed only then that no uhlans were visible from the alcove in which he and the two spies stood. That was strange indeed; ever since Shinzon's attack on the Senate, it had seemed that not a single square *dhat'drih* of downtown Ki Baratan was left unguarded by the praetor's uhlans.

A violent shiver slowly climbed the rungs of Pardek's spine. The former senator took an instinctive step backward.

"Do it now, Torath," the spymaster said quietly, sounding weary and far older than his years.

Pardek turned, tried to run, but the man called Torath was faster, stronger, and perhaps an entire century younger. A slightly curved length of gleaming metal appeared in the younger man's hand as though conjured by a sorcerer out of Romulan myth. Before Pardek could raise his arms to defend himself, Torath had inscribed a deep horizontal furrow across the older man's throat.

His legs suddenly too weak to support his weight, Pardek tumbled to his knees, then sprawled onto his side on the alcove's gleaming floor.

His vision quickly turning green-tinged and hazy, Pardek watched with a peculiar sense of detachment as Rehaek approached, then crouched beside him. "The humans your faction plots against would describe you as a 'hawk,' Senator. Rather like the late, unlamented Shinzon. But the time for reflexive aggression has passed. It represents an unacceptable variable. That makes the future impermissibly chaotic, and thus far more difficult to predict than it needs to be."

You don't care about the future, Pardek thought. *You only care about power. Just like Koval.* He tried to speak the words aloud, but succeeded only in making moist gurgling noises.

Rehaek adopted a curiously beneficent-looking smile. "Therefore I need to send the other members of your faction a very clear and unambiguous message. *You* will be that message, Senator."

Pardek knew with utter certainty that he was mortally wounded. He felt his blood flowing in a hot, emerald torrent from the gash across his neck, rapidly cooling as it pooled on the floor all around him. He looked directly up at his killers through rheumy, dimming eyes.

"That was untidy, Torath, but necessary," he heard Rehaek say to his associate. "Have the senator's body transported back to his own office. His like-minded associates are sure to find it quickly there."

"Immediately, sir," said Torath, who then spoke a few

terse commands into the communications device that was evidently hidden in his lapel.

Darkness enfolded Pardek at the same time the transporter beam came. Though he knew it wasn't a rescue, he still rejoiced at its cold embrace.

For he would soon walk the Halls of Erebus, where his wife and daughter were surely awaiting his arrival.

CHAPTER TWELVE

U.S.S. TITAN

Christine Vale arrived on the bridge for her shift early, as was her habit. The extra time gave her a chance to be fully briefed by the gamma shift bridge commander, who, in this case, was Lieutenant Commander Fo Hachesa, a Kobliad with an infectiously pleasant personality—as well as a sometimes offputting propensity either to drop suffixes from gerunds and adverbs, or to add superfluous ones.

"Not much to report, Commander," Hachesa said. "Perhaps their heavy drink has render them unable to bother us."

Vale gave him a slight smile, remembering the meal aboard the *Vaj*. She saw some of the other bridge crew members grinning at his statement as well, indicating that scuttlebutt about Khegh and his crew must already have traveled far and wide throughout the ship.

"We have also receiving a request from Commander Donatra that the captain contacting her at 0900," Hachesa said. "It wasn't appearing urgent, merely a query into the details of our delivering of aid supplies. But you know how hard it is to judging these shifty Romulans."

That's two racist slurs he's made in one minute, Vale thought. While she hated to call such an otherwise competent and eager young officer on the carpet, she couldn't allow such behavior to continue. She debated whether to speak to him about it now versus waiting until after she'd consulted either Captain Riker or Commander Troi about the problem.

"Other than that, Lieutenant Rager said she needed to visiting sickbay, so I've asked Chief Bolaji to take over ops until she returning to duty." Hachesa handed her a padd. "That's all, Commander. Have an enjoy shift."

Vale made a quick decision. "Hold on just a moment, Fo. May I see you in the ready room, please?"

He looked puzzled. "Certain."

They stepped into the captain's empty ready room, the doors sliding closed behind them. Despite the fact that she was specifically authorized to use the room when she had control of the bridge, this was the first time she had been in the room without Riker. She immediately felt uncomfortable. But rather than appear indecisive—*and I do have the right to be in here,* she reminded herself—she decided to just sit on the edge of the desk instead of in the large chair behind it.

She looked Hachesa squarely in the eyes. "Commander, I noticed that you made two references that were denigrating to other species just now. First the Klingons, then the Romulans."

He looked wounded. "I didn't meaning anything negative by it, sir. I was just try to be humorous."

"I realize that," Vale said, "but that doesn't make it any more acceptable. When you are in command of the bridge, *especially* in the absence of any immediate provocation, species-related slurs set a bad example for the crew. It would be one thing if a drunken Klingon had just hailed us, but to cast all Klingons as drunkards undermines the trust this crew needs to have in them during this mission. The same with the Romulans. We're in their space, and Donatra represents one of our few allies here. We need to be supportive of her."

"I understanding, Commander," Hachesa said, though his eyes narrowed a bit, giving him a defiant, sullen aspect.

Vale wasn't certain that he *did* understand, but pressing the point further seemed futile. If interspecies amity was indeed a big part of *Titan's* ongoing mission, she knew she had to lead by example. With a tolerant smile, she said, "Good. I don't expect it will be an issue any longer, then. Thank you, Commander."

"Am I dismiss?"

"Yes. Go get some sack time or some grub."

"Yes, sir." Hachesa spun on his heels and stepped toward the door.

Vale watched him leave. *He needs to learn to handle criticism a bit better, too,* she thought. *Otherwise he's not going to do well on the command track, no matter how many other crew members actually seem to enjoy his kidding around.* Again she considered making Troi aware of the situation.

Stepping through the ready room doorway and back onto the bridge, Vale saw that the gamma-to-alpha shift change was under way, though there were still several minutes left until the gamma shift officially ended.

She approached Science Officer Jaza, who was working at his station on the bridge's starboard side.

"How goes the deployment of the new sensor nets,

Mister Jaza?" she asked. Although *Titan*'s current mission was one of interstellar diplomacy, there was no reason the science staff had to sit on its hands. Romulan space was filled with objects and phenomena about which Starfleet wanted to gather information.

"Most of the work was done by Ensign Ichi on the gamma shift," he said, "though it appears that K'chak'!'op was an invaluable aid as well." Jaza pronounced the name crisply as "Chaka."

"K'chak'!'op was *on* the bridge?" Vale asked in wonder. The Pak'shree computer specialist so rarely left her quarters.

"No," Jaza said with a smile. "She worked from her den, as usual. I truly think she feels a lot less clumsy there, without us bipedal humanoid types around to distract her."

"So, what do the new sensors tell us?"

On Riker's orders, Vale had tasked the crew with deploying a series of wide-band, high-resolution sensor nets, specially calibrated to detect cloaked Romulan ships as well as other dangers. While these instruments couldn't locate or track such ships directly, they could, at least in theory, detect anomalies such as the moving "blank spaces" created by their warp fields, or the telltale gravitons that leaked from even the most heavily shielded cloaking systems.

Unfortunately, the energy required to sustain such a heightened state of sensor acuity placed significant demands on *Titan*'s power output, effectively compromising her shields and weaponry. *Another reason to be thankful for Klingon escorts,* Vale thought. Though the idea of lowering *Titan*'s defenses while moving ever deeper into Romulan space didn't sit well with her, she had to agree that the security trade-off Captain Riker had made was a wise one, under the circumstances; *Titan* would spot any approaching dangers, advise the Klingons, and then let them do what they did best, should the need arise.

Vale knew that Dr. Ra-Havreii, *Titan*'s designer, was even now working with Lieutenant Commander Ledrah and several members of her crack engineering staff on reducing the sensor net's energy cost, though they had failed to tumble onto any significant breakthroughs since *Titan* had left Utopia Planitia. Still, as far as she knew, *Titan* was the only Starfleet vessel currently using this experimental technology.

Jaza interrupted her thoughts, pointing out several multicolored graphics that were scrolling by on the wall-mounted monitor screen. "So far, we haven't detected any ships other than those of our convoy. We're mostly encountering dust, rock, and ice particles, ranging from microscopic to about the size of your head. Nothing much different than the flotsam that appears in the Denorios Belt whenever the Celestial Temple burps."

Jaza's casual reference to the home of his people's alleged gods reminded Vale momentarily that he was one of the Bajoran faithful. Not that it wasn't obvious—he did wear the traditional Bajoran earring on his right ear—but she wasn't particularly religious herself, so she tended not to dwell on such things.

"Only this flotsam is a little less, um, sacred," Vale teased.

Jaza shrugged. "Flotsam is flotsam. It's no different when the Prophets sweep it out of the Temple than it is when it's carried off of an asteroid by the stellar winds. Are the contents of the trash cans in human churches, mosques, or temples touched by some Terran or Izarian deity?"

"I've never had much time for gods or goddesses myself," Vale said. She wasn't certain why she was admitting this right on the bridge. But Jaza's serene presence made her feel utterly at ease.

"Understandable," he said, nodding. "Many who work in the sciences feel similarly." He placed his hands upon his heart. "I try instead to integrate my faith in science with my faith in the Prophets. Truth is truth, whether spiritual or scientific. As long as I seek truth in either sphere, I will continue to grow and evolve, as does the universe itself."

Vale smiled, touched by his sincerity. *How very Zen he is,* she thought. *Not to mention attractive and single.* Perhaps when they weren't preoccupied with an urgent mission she could arrange to spend some time with him. She couldn't remember the last time she'd gone on a date.

She forced the thought aside. Jaza wasn't just a colleague—he was a subordinate. Dating him would therefore be absolutely inappropriate.

As inappropriate as marrying him? asked a peevish voice in the back of her head—the same voice that had raised her initial objections to Captain Riker's decision to make his wife a member of his senior staff.

She noticed then that Jaza was staring at her curiously. Had he been having any of the same thoughts?

Before the awkwardly silent moment could stretch further, the computer let out a staccato series of beeps. New blocks of text and graphics began scrolling in columns onto Jaza's monitor.

"Hmm, this is odd," he said, frowning as he studied the emerging data. "Our long-range scans are picking up some kind of spatial anomaly. It appears to be located inside Romulan space only a few hours away from Romulus itself at high warp."

"What kind of spatial anomaly?" Vale asked, resisting

the urge to immediately tap the combadge on her chest and call the captain to the bridge. It was the kind of move she would have made without hesitation while serving as security chief aboard the *Enterprise*. But she was in command in Riker's absence, and he was probably on his way up to check in with the newly arrived alpha shift anyhow.

"Readings are all over the place right now," Jaza said. "I'm picking up spatial and gravimetric distortions. Also intermittent signatures of duranium, tritanium, and polyduranium."

Vale tensed. "Hull metals. Ship debris?"

"Possibly." Jaza shrugged. "There's too much spatial distortion right now for me to say for certain. I'll try to boost the sensor net's resolution further, but I'm not sure how much more I'll be able to squeeze out of it. It's too bad the anomaly doesn't lie directly along our present heading." He resumed working over his console, intent on his stream of scrolling data. On Jaza's monitor, a false-color image of the anomaly began to take shape between the columns of numbers. It was an irregularly shaped green-and-orange cloud that reminded her of an angry lobster.

"Keep me apprised," Vale said. Something about the anomaly's appearance nudged at the back of her mind, giving her a vague feeling of unease.

Spatial anomalies and starships never seem to be a good mix, she thought, considering the hull metals Jaza had detected. She found she was unable to think of any pleasant, happy ways they might have gotten there.

Leaving Jaza to his work, Vale stepped down from the science station and took a seat in the command chair. Her eyes trained on the wide forward viewscreen, she studied the void that lay between *Titan* and Romulus, grateful for the sight of its countless—and mercifully non-anomalous—stars.

"I'm certain he didn't mean anything by it, Will," Troi said in a hushed tone. She was nearly overwhelmed by his intense feelings of frustration.

"I wish I could believe that, Deanna," Will said just as quietly, his brows rising like thunderheads as he walked alongside her down the corridor. "But he's been critiquing my command style since the moment he came aboard."

Troi put her hand up to his arm, stopping him. "No, Will," she said once she was satisfied that they were alone in the curved passage. "I'm *certain* he didn't mean anything by it. You have to grant that I can read into these things a bit more reliably than you can."

She could hardly wait for this element of their first mission to be over with. This morning, uninvited, Admiral Akaar—all spit-and-polish, as usual—had joined them for breakfast in the mess hall. His unsolicited criticism of *Titan's* off-duty casual clothing policy had rankled Will, leading to their hasty departure after the meal.

Troi lowered her voice. "Look, Will, I'm not wild about his presence here either, and neither is Christine. And I know how he feels about your placing me in your command crew. But until the conclusion of this mission—*your* mission—you need to ignore his slights and to focus. It's not worth the frustration to dwell on this."

Will let out a long breath through his nose, his puffed-up chest and shoulders deflating a bit. His expression softened as well, and he appeared to be about to say something when an odd gurgling noise came from the doorway just ahead of them down the corridor.

The door slid open, and the gurgle became louder as Ensign Aili Lavena stepped out, drops of water from her boots spattering the carpet in the corridor. She was attired in her modified uniform, which included the hooded hydration suit that kept her skin from drying out in *Titan*'s standard M-class environment areas. The door to her quarters closed behind her, once again muffling the aqueous background noises coming from within.

Lavena looked down the corridor and saw Will and Troi standing there. "Good morning, Captain. Counselor." Her voice sounded slightly muted behind the transparent rebreather mask that loosely covered her face. A small cloud of vapor rose around its edges as she spoke. "I hope the waterlock system didn't startle you. Some of the landlubbers seem to find it a little disturbing."

Troi recalled having seen the engineers making the retrofits that had enabled the Selkie conn officer to enter and exit her nonstandard-environment quarters. But neither she nor Will had actually heard Lavena's customized ingress/egress system in operation before. It certainly stood to reason that the tons of Pacifican seawater the system had to restrain wouldn't be completely unobtrusive. It sounded disconcertingly like the flushing of a humanoid commode.

"Not at all," the captain said. "We were just having . . ." He paused momentarily, and Troi noticed a peculiar if fleeting emotional undercurrent that almost broke the surface before vanishing utterly.

"We were just having a conversation," he said, his composure once again rock solid.

"Very good, sir," Lavena said, her head cocked to one side. "I'll see you both on the bridge." As the ensign turned and walked away, Troi glimpsed a transitory emotional highlight coming from her as well.

Though short-lived, it was not unlike the one Will had just quashed.

Will began walking forward again, but Troi placed a hand on his arm, holding him in place. Once Lavena had rounded a bend in the corridor, she turned him toward her.

"What was *that* about?" she said, keeping her voice low even though no one else was within earshot.

He surprised her by actually blushing slightly. "Leave it alone, Deanna. It's nothing."

She smiled, her eyes narrowing involuntarily. "It's *not* nothing. I felt something coming from both of you." The sentiment she had barely glimpsed in them both was finally beginning to make sense to her. "It was almost . . . *carnal,* for lack of a better word."

"Deanna," Will said, his voice deepening, imploring. He was clearly becoming intensely uncomfortable.

No wonder Pacifica was always such a popular shore-leave destination for dashing, unattached young Starfleet officers, she thought. Grinning, she slugged her husband playfully on the shoulder. "You *dog!* You and Lavena on Pacifica?"

Will resumed moving forward down the corridor, his blush intensifying and spreading to his ears. "It was a long time ago, Deanna," he said in a near-whisper. "Just once, and right out of the Academy. And I only just *now* recognized her."

She hurried to catch up with him, savoring the all-too-rare discomfiture her otherwise easygoing husband was displaying. "Ah, so now there are *two* people in your bridge crew you've been intimate with. I wonder what the admiral would think about that?"

Will shot her a withering glance, but said nothing else aloud. *I'm embarrassed enough about this,* Imzadi, she felt him say through the empathic bond they shared. *Leave it alone, Deanna. Please.* His chagrin burned in her mind as brightly as a sodium flare.

Arriving with him at the turbolift, Troi struggled to stifle the fit of giggles that had arrived unbidden. They stepped aboard, and as the doors closed, the empathic bond they shared delivered her an actual concrete image; it was a crystal-clear shard of memory.

It surprised her, but somehow failed to shock her. After all, she knew he'd occasionally been something of a "wolf" very early in his Starfleet career. But because their level of mutual trust and sharing had been so deep and intimate for so long, she simply couldn't justify holding a more than twenty-year-old incident against him.

It happened before we even knew each other, she thought. *And he must not have given Lavena a second thought after he and I met during his assignment to Betazed.*

But that didn't mean she found his charming emotional roil any less enjoyable.

Riker hoped that his flushed face wouldn't be noticeable as the turbolift doors opened and he stepped onto the bridge. Despite his request, he knew Deanna wouldn't let his decades-old liaison with Lavena stay buried completely. Her job revolved around talking, and she would certainly want to talk with him further about this. On top of that, she seemed to love to tease him, and often wouldn't let go of embarrassing facts for years, if ever. At least he could count on her professionalism and public discretion as his diplomatic officer and chief counselor, not to mention as his spouse.

Fortunately, he already knew from experience that she wasn't unduly bothered by his bygone romantic entanglements. One couldn't easily keep such old episodes hidden from her Betazoid empathy anyway, and he was grateful that she had the good sense not to be scandalized by them. She had, after all, been raised by the unabashedly free-spirited Lwaxana Troi; Deanna therefore demonstrated very few sexual inhibitions.

At least that had been so until recently, he reflected glumly. Ever since the psychic assault that Shinzon, through his viceroy, had committed against Deanna while she and Riker had been making love nearly two months ago, she had become far more sensitive and introspective than usual in the bedroom. Even their honeymoon had been haunted by the specter of Shinzon's violation, and Riker sensed that she still had some healing left to do even now.

As Vale stepped toward him and handed him a padd, Riker re-focused his thoughts on the business of running *Titan*. Taking his place in the command chair, he scanned the reports on the padd and listened as his exec told him about Donatra's cargo information request and a number of other matters that would demand his attention during his final duty shift prior to *Titan*'s arrival at Romulus.

"Captain, Commander, I have some additional readings from the anomaly we've been observing," Jaza said, calling over to Riker and Vale from the main science station.

"Put it on the screen, please, Lieutenant," Riker said.

The forward viewscreen's default image of warp field–distorted stars was replaced by a long-range view of another, more static, starfield. The image was of lower-than-usual resolution, but glowing, crackling, gracefully tapered and braided ribbons of energy were clearly visible despite the somewhat grainy quality of the picture. Text and numbers scrolled at the bottom of the screen, fed directly to the viewer from the Bajoran science officer's console.

"It's producing some truly powerful spatial and subspatial distortions, as well as a great deal of gravimetric shear at its event horizon, Captain," Jaza said.

"Does it pose any danger to the convoy?" Riker asked, though he knew Vale would have advised him were there any real cause for concern.

"Negative, sir. Our current heading won't take us close enough to it to cause us any problems. But thanks to some pretty exotic chemistry in the debris cloud surrounding the anomaly, it'll probably give us some fairly spectacular fireworks displays."

Riker nodded. The shifting bands of colors and lightning-like discharges reminded him of the thunderstorms and auroral displays he used to see in the skies over Valdez, Alaska, during his childhood.

"What sort of 'exotic chemistry' have you found, Mr. Jaza?" Riker asked.

"Heavy transuranic elements and alloys that probably couldn't have occurred here naturally. Duranium, polyferranide, polyduranium."

"Materials used in building starship hulls and engine components," Vale said.

"Exactly," said Jaza. "And I've also detected traces of cobalt, molybdenum, tripolymers, highly ionized cortenide, and something that strongly resembles polyalloy."

Riker recognized several of the chemical compounds Jaza had listed. And he knew of only one source from which they all might have come. Something very cold slowly ascended his vertebrae.

"It's amazing," Jaza continued. "I only wish I had a chance to take our new sensor nets a lot closer to this thing."

"Maybe you will, Jaza," Vale said, "on the way back to Federation space."

On the way back to Federation space, Riker thought. *Of course.*

"I certainly hope so, Commander," Jaza said to Vale. "This thing's almost as mysterious as the Celestial Temple. I haven't been able to find any previous record of this specific anomaly anywhere. Even Lieutenant Pazlar's stellar cartog section is stumped. It's apparently a spatial rift of some sort. And it has a background thalaron radiation signature that's unlike anything I've ever seen before."

Thalaron, he thought, closing his eyes momentarily as he considered how close Earth had come to being flensed of all life by this lethal form of radiation, which had been harnessed by the mad usurper Shinzon.

Opening his eyes again, Riker slowly swiveled in his chair and took a long, slow look around his bridge. He saw looks of sad recognition on Deanna's face, as well as on those of Ranul Keru and Christine Vale. Although Vale had not been aboard the *Enterprise* during the battle against Shinzon, Riker knew that she had made herself almost obsessively familiar with everything that had occurred on that fateful day. Only Lieutenants Jaza and Rager seemed oblivious to the subdued feelings of everyone else.

Of course. Neither of them were part of the crew of the Enterprise *that day.*

"The reason this anomaly hasn't been charted yet, Mr. Jaza, is because it wasn't even here until a few weeks ago. You're looking at the remnants of the late Praetor Shinzon's illegal thalaron weapon."

And the echoes of the explosion that took Data from us forever.

Jaza bowed his head momentarily in apparent prayer. Riker thought the Bajoran must have just realized that he had been observing a graveyard. He wondered which losses of his own Jaza was now contemplating.

Riker resumed studying the phenomenon on the screen. His eyes moist, he bade his dear, dead friend Data a silent farewell. Though his longtime shipmate had been vaporized rather than buried, he now had a permanent monument of sorts.

Deanna, her eyes also bright with unshed tears, silently reached out and squeezed Riker's hand.

He hoped that neither *Titan* nor her escort convoy would suffer any similar losses before this mission was finished.

Chapter Thirteen

Somewhere Deep in Romulan Space

Space itself twisted into gigantic shimmering whorls and glowing iridescent loops before Commander Donatra's fascinated eyes. What she saw was a thing of both beauty and power. A monument to the heroism of many.

And to the overweening ambition of one.

The Great Bloom. Here is where the thalaron explosion finally rid us of Shinzon, she thought, *along with his plans to spread still more death and destruction across the galaxy.*

Surveying the bridge of the warbird *Valdore,* she watched her crew as they busied themselves scanning and monitoring the phenomenon displayed on the viewer. Turning back toward the Great Bloom's spectacular image, she reflected that this region of space had nearly become a cemetery for her own ship and crew, as well as for Shinzon. How many noble Romulan soldiers, as well as subordinates of Captain Picard, had died in the battle to stop the upstart praetor's dishonorable rampage?

Now, many weeks after a truly dreadful weapon had been turned back upon its wielder, the site of Shinzon's denouement still blazed furiously. Commander Suran had recently confided to her that he regarded the Great Bloom as a cosmic warning about the deadly consequences of wielding power unwisely—and of choosing allies poorly. It was obvious now to Donatra that she and Suran had chosen poorly indeed when they'd made their initial alliance with Shinzon and his Reman faction.

Just as Tal'Aura chose poorly, she thought, *when she threw in with Shinzon.* She remained convinced that Tal'Aura could never have assumed the praetorship without first conspiring to enable Shinzon to eliminate Praetor Hiren and every important member of the Romulan Senate save herself.

Donatra continued staring into the ever-shifting recesses of the great tear in the spatial fabric known as the Great Bloom. She couldn't bring herself to disagree with Suran's assessment of the thing's significance. But she preferred to see another dimension to it as well: it was also a testament to the sacrifices that both Romulan and Federation nationals even now stood ready to make for the ever-elusive cause of peace.

Perhaps it is also a monument to redemption. Donatra wondered if she would ever expiate the guilt she still felt for having once supported the man who had slain every member of the Romulan Senate except for the one who now called herself the Empire's praetor.

It is indeed a hopeful sign that we have found a constructive use for this remnant of Shinzon's folly, Donatra thought, watching in silence as orderly patterns of dots carefully arranged themselves at strategic positions between the glowing loops of thalaron-tortured space-time. She sincerely hoped that taking advantage of the phenomenon's newfound utility would give additional meaning to the lives of all the soldiers and senators whom Shinzon's horrible weapon had slain.

Each of the more than two dozen tiny shapes on the viewer's tactical display represented a *D'deridex*-class or *Mogai*-class warbird, every one of them equipped with armaments, shields, and engines comparable to those of their flagship, the battle-scarred *Valdore*. Those potent armaments included not only scores of disruptor banks and hundreds of photon torpedoes, but also large complements of small but lethal attack fliers.

Every one of these vessels had already been officially written off as seized or destroyed during the brief Reman uprisings that had flared up immediately after Shinzon's assassination of the Senate. If the commanders and crews of these vessels took care to maintain their distance from the spatially-riven event horizon that lay close to the center of the Great Bloom's expanse, those ships would find a safe and discreet port here, remaining undetectable from any appreciable distance. The space-time distortions caused by the Great Bloom's intense gravitational lensing effects would see to that. *Now our "ghost fleet" but awaits either my or Suran's command to pounce upon whoever prevails in the struggle for civilian power, be it Tal'Aura, Pardek, political moderates, or even those vile, cave-dwelling* uaefv'digae *from Remus.*

The aft turbolift door hissed open. Out of the corner of her eye, Donatra saw Commander Suran enter at a breathless near-run. "We need to speak, Commander. Privately."

Donatra suppressed a harried sigh. She wondered how many more times she would have to soothe Suran's misgivings about hiding so many ships within the Bloom's energetic shadow. He had objected from the beginning that the Bloom, as good a hiding place as it was, lay too far away from Romulus to allow for a sufficiently fast deployment should the need to do so arise unexpectedly. But he had never presented a better alternative. Although Suran was ostensibly on her side in the Empire's ongoing power struggles, there were times when she wished she could simply pull rank on him rather than having to explain and persuade. *But even if I could just order him about, what assurance do I have that he would do as I command?*

Then she saw the look of real concern in his eyes, which blazed with a sincerity she hadn't seen since Tal'Aura had engineered Admiral Braeg's death. Though she respected Suran's tactical prowess, she didn't credit him with enough artifice to counterfeit such passion. Whatever was on Suran's mind now, it was clearly nothing trivial.

"Of course," Donatra said, keeping her voice even as she gestured toward the bridge's starboard side.

"It's about former Senator Pardek," Suran said as soon as the plain gray duranium door had slid shut behind them, ensuring their privacy. "He's just been found dead."

She dropped heavily into the chair behind her desk, and gestured toward the empty seat in front of it. "I assume he didn't die peacefully in his sleep."

"Not unless he enjoyed taking his rest with something very sharp on his pillow," Suran said as he took the offered seat. "His own people found him in his office with his throat slashed. My sources indicate that the deed was apparently done within the last half *verak* or so."

The news of Pardek's murder brought Donatra up short, though it didn't truly surprise her. Deaths by misadventure hadn't exactly been uncommon in and around the Empire's centers of power, even before Shinzon's elimination of the Senate. Discreet assassinations of political adversaries had become almost routine under Praetor Dralath many years earlier. She had read accounts of Dralath himself slashing the throat of a dissenting senator—a murder committed in the Council Chamber, right before the startled eyes of the victim's legislative colleagues.

But a slashed throat hardly seems like Tal'Aura's style, she thought. And Romulan praetors, aside from the bloodthirsty Dralath, usually demurred from such naked violence. They tended to favor instead convenient happenstances such as hovercar crashes, sudden acute "illnesses," and other similarly improbable—though plausibly deniable—mishaps.

Still, she knew that Tal'Aura's culpability in Braeg's death was undeniable. The late admiral had not only been Donatra's beloved, he had also been Tal'Aura's chief rival for the praetorship of the Romulan Empire. Thoughts of Tal'Aura's foul act of treachery revived the dull pain that had never entirely departed from her right leg and the entire right side of her torso. Though the superficial plasma burns she had suffered on the day of Braeg's death were within Dr. Venora's capacity to heal completely, Donatra had decided to leave the scars intact; they remained as tangible reminders both of her enduring love for Braeg and of her abiding hatred for Tal'Aura.

Donatra hoped that the nagging aches of her wounds would ensure that she never again risked showing her back to the Empire's newest self-appointed praetor. Her side tingled uncomfortably as she wondered if Tal'Aura had seen Pardek as yet another dangerous rival for power. Like Braeg, who might well have ascended to the praetorship himself but for Tal'Aura's perfidy.

"Do you see the praetor's hand in Pardek's murder, Suran?" Donatra asked.

"It is certainly possible. Tal'Aura may see genuine danger behind the rhetoric of Pardek's faction. His confederates Durjik and Tebok have made no secret of their desire to make war on the Federation."

A desire that you, my ally of convenience, once shared not only with Pardek, but also with Shinzon. Did Suran now truly see his erstwhile association with Shinzon as a blunder, as she did? Not for the first time, Donatra wondered whether Suran's current alliance with her was motivated by his decades of loyalty to the slain Admiral Braeg—and therefore at least partly from their shared hatred of Tal'Aura, Braeg's killer—or if it was merely a marriage of expediency. Could she really afford to trust Suran any more than she could Tal'Aura?

But can I really afford not to?

"Pardek's group has been rattling its tarnished Honor Blades for another war against the Federation for some time now," Suran continued. "I'm sure that even Tal'Aura would agree that the Empire can ill afford such a conflict, especially now. But I seriously doubt that even she would have resorted to such a crude means of assassination."

"It cannot be the Remans," Donatra said, stroking her chin. "Their involvement would imply knowledge of the impending power-sharing meeting—the one from which we all agreed to exclude them. Were they aware of the initial secret conference, they surely would have made a great deal more trouble than slaying a single retired Romulan senator."

"Thank Erebus for small mercies." He sighed, obviously resigned to the identity of the only other likely culprit. "The Tal Shiar, then."

Donatra nodded. "I suspect the bureau's young new director might be arrogant enough not to care overmuch about subtlety. He probably even saw to it personally that you became aware of the murder as quickly as you did."

Suran nodded. "If that's so, then Rehaek would appear

to be a rank amateur. Under his leadership, the Tal Shiar may give us significantly less trouble than it did under Koval."

Or Rehaek may merely be maneuvering us into under-estimating him. "Perhaps. But the main question now is, will the other members of Pardek's faction overreact to the former senator's murder?"

"There is little they can do to advance their plans. Not without the support of the military." With a predatory smile Donatra rarely saw outside of all-out combat situations, Suran added, "Fortunately, we have a good deal to say about that, thanks to our hidden fleet."

"He who rules the military rules the Empire," she thought, silently quoting Amarcan's *Axioms,* a text she had all but memorized during her Imperial War College studies.

Answering Suran's battlefield grin with one of her own, she said, "I take it you no longer question the wisdom of using the Great Bloom to conceal the bulk of our forces."

His head dipped in an abbreviated parody of a courtly bow. "I withdraw most of my earlier objections. Though we still may need to move the fleet quickly, I will concede that the necessity of keeping our strength secret has grown ever more urgent. I only wish we could afford to position our fleet closer to Romulus. We may have to mobilize it very soon, and I remain certain we will receive very little prior warning when that occurs."

She considered trying to reassure Suran yet again that their "ghost fleet" could indeed be deployed in time to do whatever might be required of it, and that Romulus itself wasn't completely undefended, even without the extra forces. Instead, she merely regarded him in silence. Though she felt relieved that they finally seemed to be in fairly close accord—a rare thing, despite their mutual loyalty to the late Braeg, and their shared hatred of the pretender Tal'Aura—Donatra also found herself wishing she could derive more satisfaction from it. *Perhaps,* she thought, *that requires more trust than either of us is capable of giving.*

Centurion Liravek's voice suddenly issued from the comm terminal on Donatra's desk. *"Bridge to Commander Donatra."*

Donatra touched a control on her comm panel. "Go ahead, Centurion."

"You instructed me to alert you shortly before the time of our scheduled departure for Romulus," the centurion said, his manner crisp and professional. *"If we go to maximum warp during the next five* siure, *we will just arrive at Ki Baratan by the designated time."*

"Very good, Centurion. Leave the fleet here, in concealment. But take the *Valdore* to Romulus now. Best speed."

"At once, Commander."

Donatra rose from her chair, signaling that it was time to get back to work. Suran did likewise.

"Don't worry, Suran. The *Valdore*—and the entire fleet—stands ready to take back the Romulan Empire. Together they will restore all the honor that Shinzon and Tal'Aura have squandered."

Suran approached the door, which obligingly hissed open. "Provided the Senate factions, Tal'Aura, and the ravening hordes of Remus do not tear the Empire to pieces in the meantime—thus rendering all honor irrelevant."

With that, he departed from the ready room. The door closed again, leaving her alone with apprehensions that were growing increasingly difficult to tame.

Though the Remans remained relatively calm for the

moment, an all-out clash between them and what remained of the Romulan Empire's traditional power structure might well prove inevitable. Perhaps the die had already been cast by the dead hand of Shinzon. And could she truly rely on her recently acquired Federation allies not to take advantage of the coming chaos? Surely the Klingons, wartime alliance or no, would move to seize the Empire's resource-rich border worlds should Romulus descend into civil war.

Whatever comes, we must be ready. Or the Empire will surely be lost.

Another of Amarcan's *Axioms* sprang from her memory then, providing at least some small measure of comfort: *"Fear only fear."*

CHAPTER FOURTEEN

U.S.S. TITAN

"Thank you, Commander Ledrah."

"All part of the service, Captain," said the chief engineer, her voice filtered through the combadge. *"But be careful, sir. This admiral is a sneaky bastard, if you don't mind my saying so."*

"I don't mind a bit, Nidani. But you're lucky he hasn't got here yet. Now, try to stay out of trouble, all right?"

"Always, sir. Ledrah out."

The ready room fell silent. Riker stared out the observation window at the distant stars. But he felt none of the joy and exhilaration he had experienced barely two weeks ago when he had immersed himself in the holographic projections of the stellar cartography lab. Instead of reveling in the unrestrained freedom of deep space, its dark beauty illuminated by countless distant fires, he found himself searching for naked-eye stellar distortions.

It was a poor trade-off.

His sharp gaze sought out disturbances that were as

likely to be the products of drifting debris as cloaked vessels. As he watched, one of the trio of *Miranda*-class Starfleet aid ships, *Der Sonnenaufgang,* moved gracefully past the outer port-side edge of *Titan*'s hull, headed toward the brilliant azure limb of Romulus, about which the convoy had entered orbit less than thirty minutes previously. According to Vale, the other two vessels, the *Phoebus* and the *T'rin'saz,* were already well into the process of beaming down food, medical supplies, and heavy-duty industrial replicator equipment, along with a cadre of Starfleet medical, engineering, and security personnel to render aid and oversee distribution of the convoy's provisions to Romulan civilians dispossessed by the recent social unrest. *Der Sonnenaufgang* was concentrating on using her cargo transporters to send particularly heavy matériel, such as construction equipment, down to the planet's surface.

Despite apprehensions to the contrary from their respective crews, the Federation-Klingon convoy had crossed Romulan space completely unmolested. Even so, there were a large number of small Romulan cruisers and scout ships in the immediate vicinity of Romulus and its four moons, though not nearly as many warbirds as Riker would have expected. Either the Romulans were playing host to their visitors with utmost sincerity, or they were keeping the bulk of their fleet carefully concealed, at least for the moment. He wondered idly if they were lying in the weeds, watching and waiting for the right moment to pounce either on *Titan,* General Khegh's vessels, or the Starfleet aid ships.

But that possibility seemed far-fetched given the reception the aid convoy had received so far—and what Romulus stood to lose if the Romulan military were to attack, considering the obvious evidence of the unreliability of the Empire's internal lines of supply. *Senator Pardek and his followers may want to move against the Federation,* he thought, *but Praetor Tal'Aura seems to be keeping things calm, no matter how unstable her power base might be.*

The door chimed, and Riker turned from the window. "Come," he answered.

Stooping his head slightly, Admiral Akaar stepped through the doorway and into the ready room. Like Riker, he had not yet changed into his dress whites; the secret meeting with the Romulan leaders was still nearly two hours away.

"You asked to see me, Captain?" Akaar said, straightening to his imposing full height once he was inside the ready room.

Riker felt himself tense up, and hoped it didn't show outwardly. He gestured toward one of the chairs. "Yes, thank you, Admiral." He sat down behind his desk, and leaned forward as the large Capellan wedged his wide frame into the chair.

Riker paused to take a deep breath, preparing to launch into the speech he had been practicing over and over in his mind; he had debated for hours whether it would accomplish the goal he intended, or if it would instead cost him the admiral's respect.

"Admiral, normally I wouldn't speak quite so frankly to someone who outranks me, but this is my ship, my command, and my ready room," he said finally. "Even though it's lousy poker strategy, I've decided not to wait until the end of the game to put all my cards on the table."

Akaar betrayed not the slightest hint of emotion as he stared impassively back at Riker. "Your point, Captain?"

"My point is this: since you first came aboard *Titan,* you have been openly critical of my command style and command decisions," Riker said, holding the admiral's intense, dark-eyed gaze. "You have also, in my considered opinion, been less than forthcoming with information vital to the success of this mission and crucial to the safety of my crew. These actions jeopardize my staff's confidence in me, and, quite frankly, in *you.* If we are to succeed here, I need you to be honest and forthright about *all* of the intelligence you have regarding the Romulan political situation. I ask only that you confide in me and let *me* decide what facts need to be distributed to the crew and when."

Seeing that Akaar was making no move to reply, Riker took another deep breath. *In for a slip, in for a brick.* "Admiral, I turned down three commands before accepting this one. I have been a decorated Starfleet officer for better than twenty years now. I know that hardly compares to the eighty-some years you've served, but it's not inconsequential. And neither is the fact that Starfleet continued to offer me command positions until I finally accepted. Whatever doubts you may have about my authority or my methods, you should take them up with *me* instead of my staff."

Riker settled back into his chair, and looked across the uncluttered desktop at Akaar. The older man's expression remained inscrutable, and the quiet seconds that followed seemed to drag into minutes. *Have I gone too far?* Riker wondered. *Was that a spectacular case of career suicide?*

Finally, Akaar leaned forward. "Thank you for bringing this to my attention, Captain. I shall try to be more circumspect in acknowledging your authority in the future." His lips formed a grim smile. "When *Titan* left Utopia Planitia, I was still receiving many conflicting intelligence reports regarding the Romulans. I made the decision then, rightly or wrongly, to keep intelligence matters purely on a need-to-know basis. I was not trying to keep either you or your staff out of the loop. Rather, I was attempting to determine precisely what you needed to know and when. Trust me when I say that you would likely have been infinitely *more* frustrated had you been forced to sit in on many of the interminably long conferences I held with Sorok, T'Sevek, and T'Rel." He rubbed a knuckle across one of his thick gray eyebrows, as though wearied by the memories.

"I see, Admiral," Riker said, nodding. Still not content to let go of his anger entirely, he continued in a low, almost perilous tone. "Commander Ledrah has just informed me that Dr. Ra-Havreii has installed an illegal cloaking device aboard one of *Titan*'s shuttlecraft. I assume this was done on your order."

Akaar seemed to take Riker's charge completely in stride. "It was."

Riker felt his face redden, suddenly awash in memories of similar treaty violations that he had been a party to more than two decades ago under Captain Erik Pressman. "And exactly when did you intend to bring me into *that* particular loop, Admiral?"

To his credit, Akaar didn't appear flustered in the least. "Whatever you may believe about me, Captain, I did intend to inform you about the cloaking device as soon as it became necessary."

"That's very reassuring, sir. It's good for a captain to know when he's been made responsible for breaking one of the Federation's oldest treaties with the Romulan Empire."

Akaar's tone grew more than a little sarcastic. "The Romulan Empire itself is in flux, as you have no doubt noticed, Captain. As are the treaties it has made with the Federation."

In other words, we're stronger than they are now, Riker

thought bitterly. *So if we decide to tear up those treaties, the Romulans had damned well better take it and like it.*

Aloud, he said only, "Why?"

The admiral's steel-gray eyebrows seemed to thicken like rising storm fronts. "Patience, Captain. I would prefer to clear up a more general matter first."

Though he was no less frustrated now than moments ago, Riker knew there was nothing to be gained by pressing the issue. The admiral was clearly saying that he would explain whatever he decided to explain when he felt damned good and ready to do so, and not a moment sooner.

"All right, Admiral."

"It may surprise you to learn that I believe that your perception of me may be as much right as it is wrong," Akaar said. "I am an old man, and I have served under many starship captains, and with many crews. Therefore when I enter any new command situation, or interact with a new commander, I suppose I do tend to subject him or her to considerable scrutiny. I can certainly understand how that scrutiny, combined with your own understandable apprehensions about facing your first command assignment—especially on *this* particular mission—could stir up feelings such as those you have expressed."

Akaar shifted back in his chair, and suddenly looked even taller. "But I must tell you, Captain, that I find your command style to be wise, decisive, and intuitive. You have also made great strides with your crew. Usually it takes several missions for a crew to fully bond with its CO, but I already sense that your staff has developed a strong loyalty toward you . . . and I am not merely speaking of your fellow *Enterprise* alumni, or your wife."

Despite his righteous anger over the cloaking device,

Riker could feel the stress begin to pour out of his body like steam escaping from a volcanic fissure. He had expected Akaar to bellow angrily and pull rank on him, or perhaps even to threaten to strip him of his command for having taken such an insubordinate tone with him.

Instead, the Capellan seemed cordial and almost apologetic, even allowing Riker a glimpse of something akin to gentle humor. Riker felt that he was receiving something extraordinarily rare. With an almost stunning shock of recognition, he realized what that something was. *It's almost like getting praise from Dad.*

Forcing his thoughts back to the present, Riker said, "Maybe I *have* allowed my perceptions of you to be colored by my own . . . apprehensions. And by the sensitive nature of this mission."

Akaar extended a large hand. "I hope we have arrived at a mutual understanding, then. You should be satisfied that I am not a deskbound paper-pusher sent here for the express purpose of 'busting your chops.' And I will conclude, unless you give me reason later to further revise my opinion, that you are no neophyte in need of supervision. Now shall we move forward, Captain?"

Riker took Akaar's hand and shook it firmly. "Agreed, Admiral."

Akaar nodded his head curtly, his earlier grim smile now returned. "Before we break out into a Risan peace song, let me ask: Have you had any luck finding Vulcan life signs on Romulus?"

Riker withdrew his hand and frowned. "No, I'm sorry, sir. Not yet, at any rate. Scanning the Romulan homeworld for Vulcan life signs makes the naked-eye search for a needle in a haystack look pretty easy by comparison."

"The biosigns we seek are more than likely in, under, or near Ki Baratan."

"Ki Baratan and the surrounding area have come up dry so far," Riker said, nodding. "I've had Commander Jaza and several of Commander Ledrah's techs working on refining the resolution of the new sensor nets. But the central problem remains: distinguishing two Vulcan biosigns from those of several billion Romulans."

Akaar's brow furrowed, and he stared past Riker at the distant glowing limb of Romulus that was visible through the observation window to the left of the desk. "Your search may be complicated by the fact that one of those two Vulcans has been microsurgically modified to pass as a Romulan."

"Your missing agent?" Riker asked. He remembered that Akaar had mentioned a missing intelligence operative during the first mission briefing, but the admiral hadn't elaborated when he had later ordered the search for Vulcan life signs.

Akaar nodded, then looked Riker directly in the eyes. "Captain, it is very important to me that we find that agent, whatever fate may have befallen him. I must confess that I have a personal stake in the return of both Ambassador Spock and our operative."

Akaar's haunted expression explained why the admiral was willing to play so fast and loose with treaty law. *He's planning to run a surreptitious rescue raid down on Romulus,* Riker thought, *just in case we fail to arrange a quiet, unobtrusive rescue via transporter.*

"Who is the agent you sent to track down Ambassador Spock?" Riker asked, already beginning to bristle again at the admiral's apparently ingrained reticence about sharing information.

"The agent is Commander Tuvok," said Akaar.

Riker's eyebrows furrowed. "The name sounds familiar . . ."

"Tuvok is a career tactical specialist and intelligence operative, as well as having served aboard the *U.S.S. Voyager* during that vessel's unplanned detour to the Delta Quadrant. Most recently, he was an instructor at Starfleet Academy. Admiral Janeway of Starfleet Command and Admiral Batanides of Starfleet Intelligence agreed with my assessment that he was the officer best qualified to infiltrate Romulus and make contact with Ambassador Spock for the purpose of persuading him to leave Romulus for a conference with the president and the Federation Council. So Tuvok was tapped for the job a few months ago."

Once again, Akaar looked past Riker at the observation window and the planet that lay beyond it. "I first served with Tuvok long ago, back when we were both much, much younger. We were both assigned to *Excelsior* for a time, under Captain Hikaru Sulu." A wry smile slowly spread across his lips. "I think you would have liked Captain Sulu. He, too, tended to favor unconventional command methodologies. And he probably would have reacted as you did when faced with a secretive, overbearing admiral. Hikaru was brought up on insubordination charges more than once, but he always managed to beat them somehow. Results count for more than protocol, after all."

"So you and Tuvok are friends," Riker said.

"We were friends, once," Akaar said quietly. "But we had a . . . disagreement many years ago. We have said scarcely a word to each other over the past three decades."

Riker didn't need Deanna with him to conclude that Akaar was rehashing old regrets. The admiral's need to search for Vulcan life signs was not purely professional, but also deeply personal. Riker was already aware that Spock had known the admiral since the day of his birth;

the rightful hereditary leader of Capella had been named "Leonard James Akaar," after two of Spock's closest friends, the chief medical officer and captain, respectively, of the old *Constitution*-class *U.S.S. Enterprise*. And now that he was aware that the missing Tuvok also had a personal connection to the admiral, Riker empathized. Not only had he recently lost one of his closest friends, Data—right here in Romulan space—but Riker also had to acknowledge, if only to himself, that his own father's recent violent death remained a painful, unhealed wound.

"Whatever we do, we must make contact with Ambassador Spock," Akaar said. "He may provide indispensable assistance in stabilizing the political situation on Romulus—Sorok's low opinion of the Unificationist movement notwithstanding."

"I agree," Riker said, his voice strong and steady. Still, he wondered what else about this mission Akaar might still be holding back from him. Not twenty minutes earlier, Deanna had reiterated yet again her opinion that the admiral was being less than forthright concerning Spock. "We'll find them, sir."

But even as Riker made this assurance, a chill of dread entered his mind.

How do I know we'll find them? They may both already be dead.

And he was sure he saw the same misgivings reflected in Akaar's dark, downcast eyes.

Chapter Fifteen

The Hall of State, Ki Baratan, Romulus

Deanna Troi kept her eyes open as the familiar sparkling blaze of light intensified and engulfed her, before rapidly dimming to twilight levels. The eager Lieutenant Radowski and the worry-radiating Commander Vale, along with the rest of *Titan*'s compact transporter room four, were abruptly replaced by the cavernous, vaulted spaces of the Romulan Hall of State. Radial, crescent-shaped windows set high into the domed ceiling admitted the waning sunlight into the otherwise unlit room, obscuring the chamber's periphery with curved, inky shadows.

Hello, again, Troi thought, forcing down a shudder of foreboding as she looked around the spacious room. Thanks to her still-green memories of Shinzon—and his viceroy Vkruk—she couldn't help but feel foreboding in this place that Shinzon had so recently occupied.

Yet no matter how uncomfortable this chamber made her feel, she knew this was no time to allow herself to become distracted.

She noticed then that both Will and Admiral Akaar were watching her, their emotional auras blazing brightly with concern for her even though their faces remained impassive. The only other member of the four-person away team who *wasn't* studying her was Security Chief Keru, who had eyes only for the large empty chamber in which they had materialized. Though Keru hadn't produced a weapon—Will and the admiral had agreed that it wouldn't be wise to do anything to make the Romulans any more nervous than they already were—he was clearly ready for anything.

She could see that he had good reason. The dark wood and stone walls, though resplendent with ornate red tapestries and elegant green statues of predatory birds set into high sconces, cast shadows that could have hidden a dozen snipers.

Will stepped to Troi's side, straightening his white dress-uniform jacket as he moved. "Are you all right?" he asked quietly.

"Don't worry about me," she said, a bit more tartly than she had intended. She was sensing a great deal of apprehension and confusion coming from beyond the room from just about every direction, almost like a pall of smoke rising above a fire. She found the emotions difficult to sort out, and had to focus her attention very tightly to prevent them from getting in the way of the business at hand. The confused intensity that she sensed reminded her that the city of Ki Baratan had been experiencing social upheavals of various kinds ever since Shinzon had killed the Senate.

"Where are the Romulans?" Will asked, looking around the empty room.

As if cued by the captain's words, a quartet of hard-faced, uniformed uhlans appeared, each soldier entering the chamber from a different cardinal direction. The disruptor pistols in their hands told everyone that they didn't share Keru's reticence about openly brandishing weaponry.

"You will accompany us directly to the Senate Chamber," said one of the uhlans before turning on his heel and leading the way into and through a branching corridor.

Moments later, the group was standing beneath a gigantic silver sculpture fashioned in the shape of a hawk-like avian that loomed over the curved tiers of desks and chairs where the late Romulan Senate had done its deliberations for centuries. Surrounded by blue pillars and abstract, rust-colored wall hangings, the room's expansive stone floor was dominated by a circular mosaic of smooth marble, half blue and half green, and inlaid with lines and circlets of gold. A wavy ribbon of turquoise bisected the mosaic, at once separating and joining the two halves together. Golden icons faced one another across the length of the divide, arrayed like chess pieces.

On the green side, far off-center and larger than every other element on the mosaic, was the stylized image of a star and two nearby planets.

To Troi, the symbolism was both obvious and shocking . . . and perhaps indicative of a disturbing cultural mindset. Here, at the very heart of their power, was the Romulan worldview: an image not of the Empire entire, with Romulus at its center, but rather, a symbol of enmity, of its centuries-old antagonism with its old foe, the Federation.

And it dominated the very floor of the Senate Chamber.

Is this how they see themselves? Troi wondered. *Always on the verge of war with us? Or does the central placement of the Neutral Zone speak more to a feeling of confinement? A reminder of thwarted ambition? What*

does this say about a civilization, that it defines itself by its
relationship to its longtime adversary?

Troi looked up from the star map, forcing herself once
again to focus on the immediate—and on the two high-
ranking Romulans who now strode to the room's center,
stopping at the precise spot from which Romulan senators
had delivered their orations for more than two centuries.
She noted that the dull gray floor was spotless, showing no
evidence of the potent thalaron radiation that she knew
Shinzon had used to obliterate all life within this august
chamber.

"Welcome to Ki Baratan," said Praetor Tal'Aura with a
beneficent smile that incompletely concealed a world-
weary mixture of ambition and caution. Her dark gray rai-
ment was simple and unprepossessing, not unlike that of a
junior member of the Senate. "I thank you all for coming."

Troi returned the smile as best she could, managing to
do so only by sheer force of will. *And thank you so much
for the enthusiastic welcoming committee.*

"We're happy to assist you in any way we can, Madam
Praetor," Will said, sounding utterly self-assured as he
introduced the away team, beginning with the admiral
and ending with Keru. The captain's carefully managed
feelings of apprehension spiked momentarily when he
exchanged bows with Proconsul Tomalak, the tall, wide-
shouldered man who stood at the praetor's side.

"You have already gone a long way toward demonstrat-
ing the truth of your words, Captain," Tal'Aura said. "The
medical supplies and industrial replicators your convoy
ships have delivered will relieve untold suffering among
my people. I thank you on behalf of the entire Romulan
Star Empire."

Though the praetor's outward expression had not
changed, Troi noticed an emotional turbulence roiling be-

neath her words. *It is costing this woman a great deal to be forced to accept our help,* she thought. *And she knows as well as we do that she can't really do or say anything "on behalf of the entire Romulan Star Empire." At least not unless and until things get a lot better for ordinary Romulans, and soon.*

A door on the east side of the room slowly opened, interrupting Troi's reverie. She watched as three other Romulan civilians and a pair of high-ranking military officers entered the room, accompanied by yet another small contingent of armed, stern-visaged uhlans. Troi noticed immediately that former Senator Pardek was not among this group, and she exchanged a silent yet significant glance with Will, who had clearly made the same observation.

"Allow me to introduce the other participants in this conference," Tomalak said, gesturing toward the newly arrived Romulans, all of whom were already taking seats around what was clearly a newly installed conference table set a few meters back from the circular room's center.

As Tomalak completed the introductions, Troi quietly surveyed the other negotiating parties, "reading" their emotional states even as she studied their uniformly guarded facial expressions. She and Will were already acquainted with the tall, dark-haired female military officer, Commander Donatra.

When Donatra's warbird had vanished from the *Titan* convoy's Romulan escort squadron, Troi couldn't help but wonder what the commander had been up to. Had she kept the warbird *Valdore* cloaked nearby, to keep watch over the convoy? Or had she left the area on some urgent errand? Because Jaza's new sensor net had failed to detect the slightest trace of Donatra's cloaked vessel, Troi had made the latter assumption, as had Will. Though she still sensed, unsurprisingly enough, that the commander was hiding something significant, Troi hoped that Donatra could be counted on as an ally, someone who would help keep this meeting from becoming overly contentious.

At Donatra's side sat Commander Suran, an older man whose hair was the color of duranium deck plating. Both he and Donatra wore medal-bedecked dress uniforms that included medium-length ceremonial swords that Troi immediately recognized as Honor Blades; though both Suran and Donatra displayed some degree of apprehension at being in the presence of both the praetor and a contingent of former adversaries from the Federation, they bore themselves with a quiet pride and dignity that matched their exterior martial decorations quite well.

But Donatra's every glance at Tal'Aura was freighted with a hatred so pure and terrible that Troi experienced it almost as physical pain. Troi could sense that Suran harbored a strong antipathy toward the new praetor as well.

The third member of the newly arrived party took up a position on the other side of the wide sherawood table. And though soft-spoken, the man whom Tomalak had introduced as a former senator named Durjik radiated anger the way a fast-spinning neutron star gave off X-rays.

"So," Durjik said without waiting for Tal'Aura's formal leave to begin speaking. He paused to stare appraisingly around the table at each member of *Titan*'s away team, who had taken their seats moments after the Romulans had. Then he allowed his contemptuous gaze to settle on Akaar. "We meet the enemy face to face at last."

Will spared a quick glance at Troi. She nodded almost imperceptibly, thereby telling him that Durjik wasn't speaking hyperbolically; as a member of Pardek's "attack-the-Federation-preemptively" faction, he seemed utterly sincere in his fear and hatred of the Federation.

And why isn't Pardek himself here?

Her attention suddenly drawn to the smoldering anger whose fires Akaar was keeping prudently banked, Troi began watching the admiral closely.

"When I look at you, Senator," Akaar said slowly and deliberately, "I do not see an enemy."

"Then you are a liar or a fool, human. Which is it?" Deanna felt haughtiness, with a sprinkling of surprise.

The admiral allowed a small smile to emerge. "I am no more human than you are."

"Immaterial. Whatever your species, you are of the Federation. One of its many mongrel races, no doubt." Durjik pointed aggressively toward the admiral's dress-white tunic and the two small rows of decorations that crossed its front. "You wear the Federation's uniform, and those bangles tell me that you will do anything to defend it. Just as *I* would do anything to preserve the Romulan Star Empire."

Including going to war against the Federation for no reason, even if that means there'll be no Empire left to preserve afterward. The former senator's increasingly palpable anger was beginning to make her head throb. And yet she felt a pang of sympathy for him as she studied his craggy, careworn face. Had he, like Pardek, developed his penchant for belligerence only recently, because of some grievous personal loss? It struck her then that counseling and diplomacy might be two sides of the same coin.

Will leaned forward, asserting a degree of quiet control over the meeting that Troi found soothing. "In fact, the admiral's homeworld is not yet a member of the Federation," he said. "But I think we all agree with you in one very important respect, Senator. There is very little that Admiral Akaar, or any of us, wouldn't do to defend and preserve the Federation. We'll even risk coming open-handed before people who hate us—if that's what it takes to build a peace that both our civilizations can live with."

Troi noticed immediately that the net level of tension in the room was noticeably decreasing, at least among Donatra, Suran, and Tal'Aura, as well as among the Star-fleet contingent.

Durjik's outrage, however, now blazed even more brightly than it had before. *Something besides our presence here is bothering him,* Troi thought.

"If I may, Senator," Troi said, tamping down her own rising apprehension. "Wasn't Pardek supposed to represent your faction at this meeting?"

Durjik fixed her with a glare as sharp as Donatra's Honor Blade. She "felt" his answer before he spoke it aloud, and it confirmed her growing suspicion.

"Surely you must know already, Commander Troi. Your people are on the short list of suspects, after all."

Troi felt Durjik's hostility intensifying even more. Though Keru sat still and quiet, he was throwing off waves of caution and vigilance. Donatra's emotional temperature was rising as well, while Suran seemed as intent on studying Donatra as he was on Durjik's accusations. Though outwardly impassive, Akaar fumed quietly inside. And Tal'Aura and Tomalak, whose temperaments Troi thought were probably more alike than either would like to admit, both seemed alternatively appalled and amused by Durjik's bitterness.

"I'm afraid I don't understand," Will said.

"Ah. Of course. The inevitable wide-eyed protestations of innocence. You would claim to be unaware that I discovered Pardek's murdered corpse not four *veraku* ago."

Will nodded, keeping the shock he felt from reaching his face. Mostly. "I claim exactly that," he said. "Because it's true."

Troi wondered why Durjik was so certain the away team should know of Pardek's death.

"With respect, Praetor," Keru said in a low but confident voice, "I wish we had been advised of Pardek's murder prior to our arrival. Security is my responsibility, and the timing of Pardek's death implies that none of the rest of us is safe until his murder is solved."

"We can discuss that later, Commander," Will said to Keru, who immediately fell silent.

Troi knew that Keru was rightly making this meeting's security his highest priority. But she also knew that the Romulans, being driven in large part by pride, were famously loath to make themselves appear vulnerable before the Federation, about whose presence even the most liberal of Romulans harbored ambiguous feelings. She understood that for the Romulans to reveal Pardek's assassination immediately prior to the start of negotiations as delicate as these would not only wound their pride, but would also aggravate their already heightened sense of vulnerability. This potential loss of face was more than any Romulan could bear—especially after their new, self-installed praetor had already accepted several tons of humanitarian aid supplies from the *Titan* convoy.

"Only a fool would expect security here, where Shinzon slew the entire Senate," Durjik said to Keru before turning his glare back upon Will. "And I would be equally foolish to expect you to provide it, Captain Riker. After all, you would no doubt say or do anything to suppress Pardek's political viewpoint." Durjik punctuated his words by jabbing an accusatory finger at *Titan*'s captain from across the expansive table.

Remaining admirably calm, Will said, "Suppress? No. But I had hoped to *convince* him that there's no longer any need for hostilities between our Federation and your Empire. Just as I hope to convince *you* that we can establish peace."

Durjik snorted dismissively. He leaned forward across the sherawood table, his beefy forearms supporting his considerable weight. "My congratulations, then, Captain. Whatever your other shortcomings might be, you have certainly succeeded in pacifying Pardek."

"*Ahlh* droppings, Senator," Donatra said to Durjik. "*Titan* was several light-*veraku* away from Romulus when Pardek was killed."

"As were we," Suran added, gesturing toward Donatra.

Suran's comment piqued Troi's curiosity. Where had the *Valdore* been at the time of Pardek's murder? The *Titan* convoy could move only as fast as its slowest ship; unlikely as it was, the *Valdore* might have made a high-speed diversion to Romulus while cloaked, its absence from the convoy undetected.

True, you helped the Enterprise *crew bring down Shinzon,* Troi thought as she studied Donatra and considered her cautious, guarded emotional aura. *But can we really trust you?*

"If so, that would seem to leave our esteemed praetor as our prime suspect, would it not?" Durjik said.

Both Donatra and Suran immediately seemed to warm to the notion of Tal'Aura-as-murderer. Tomalak was just as quickly on his feet, a short curved sword appearing in his hand as if conjured by magic. Troi was suddenly at the center of an emotional whirlwind. Somehow, Will remained cool, though he was as taut as a coiled spring. Akaar held himself back, but only barely. Keru seemed about to throw himself between the two angry Romulans.

Damn! Everything was about to come apart, right before her eyes. Her first outing as *Titan*'s diplomatic officer seemed unavoidably headed toward outright violence.

"Kroiha!" Tal'Aura shouted in Romulan, filling the room with her voice without so much as rising from her chair. *"Tharon!"*

Tomalak froze, as he had been commanded. "Forgive me, my Praetor." Sheathing his sword, he returned to his seat, though with evident reluctance. And he continued to glare at the former senator, never letting his hand venture far from his blade.

"My apologies," Durjik said, bowing his head slightly. Troi sensed not a shred of sincerity behind his words, and she seriously doubted he was fooling anyone else either.

Will broke the ensuing silence, clearly eager to get the meeting back on track. "Does anyone here seriously believe that anybody present at this meeting was involved with Pardek's death?"

"We shall see," Durjik said, scowling at Donatra and Suran.

"I suspect what we'll see," Troi said, "is that Pardek probably ran afoul of one of the factions not represented here today."

Tal'Aura chuckled humorlessly. "As brutal as Pardek's murder was, it was far too subtle an act to have been carried out by the Remans."

"I'm not talking about the Remans. I'm referring to the Tal Shiar."

Troi immediately sensed an almost reflexive wave of apprehension radiating from the praetor's hindbrain. That was understandable, given the fear that the Romulan Star Empire's semi-independent military intelligence bureau had so carefully cultivated for so many years. But something else lurked beneath Tal'Aura's apprehension as well, a secret she was holding more closely than one of Christine Vale's poker hands.

The praetor was hiding something critical. And it was related to the Tal Shiar.

Tomalak spoke up, his tone and manner insincerely patronizing. "And what special expertise might you possess regarding the Tal Shiar, Commander Troi?"

Should I come right out and tell him? Troi thought. Focusing her gaze for a moment onto the chamber's high ceiling, she decided on forthrightness. "I used to *be* in the Tal Shiar."

All the Romulans in the room seemed greatly amused by this. *Good. At least they're less likely to kill one another now that they've shared a joke at the expense of an old adversary.*

She saw then that Will was flashing a warning glare in her direction. "Commander."

"Forgive me, Captain," she said in her most professional tone. She was determined to continue. "Let me be more precise. Ten years ago, I posed as a Tal Shiar agent in order to help a high-ranking Romulan senator defect to the Federation."

The captain's eyes looked like dinner plates, and she met his incredulous stare with a warning glare of her own. *I know what I'm doing here, Will. If these people don't start focusing their hostility onto targets other than each other, this entire mission is doomed before it even starts.*

Troi looked at Donatra, who was regarding her with hard, appraising eyes. Though her countenance concealed it well, she was clearly revising her opinion of the Starfleet contingent. Troi sensed that her frank admission of espionage—performed during an entirely different astropolitical era—was beginning to generate some real respect from Donatra.

"Vice-Proconsul M'ret," Suran said to Troi. In sharp contrast to Donatra, his voice and manner were frosted with anger and contempt. "M'ret the traitor. You were one of those who helped him betray the Empire's security."

Because of Suran's intense negativity, Troi found she had to work harder than she'd expected to keep her own rising pique from coloring her reply. "During the decade since his defection, M'ret has helped prevent a tremendous amount of bloodshed between your people and ours. If the talks we are beginning now succeed in making further progress toward peace—if they build upon M'ret's work—then your histories may make a far kinder appraisal of him someday."

"The sun will grow dark and cool long before that day arrives," Suran said, as stonily as any Vulcan. "M'ret is a traitor, now and forever."

Durjik guffawed almost explosively. "Such steadfastness is ironic indeed, coming from you, Suran—a man who once believed, as Pardek did, that the best way to secure peace with the Federation is to conquer it while it sleeps."

Troi wondered if Suran was going to reply to Durjik with cold steel, as Tomalak had nearly done moments earlier. Then she felt Donatra's patience shatter like a dam blown apart by the inexorable pressure of some great sea.

"*Akhh!* Durjik, you act as though you have never erred, learned from the error, and then changed your ways!"

Durjik responded without so much as a pause for breath, exhibiting debating skills he had no doubt honed over countless years of service in the Senate. "Like Suran, error is evidently the major focus of *your* expertise, Commander Donatra. You and Suran both sided with Shinzon, whose plans of conquest came to naught."

"As did our noble praetor," Donatra said coldly, turning her angry gaze on Tal'Aura.

The praetor bristled, but remained silent, as did the increasingly angry Tomalak.

"You have argued Commander Donatra's point well, Durjik," Suran said evenly, though his outrage was limned in Troi's empathy as brightly as a disruptor bank being fired. "You and Pardek weren't always bent on preemptive war. Time and circumstance have changed you both greatly. Why, Pardek even once supported that ridiculous Vulcan Unification movement, until Neral drove it back into the hole from which it crawled."

"Whatever errors you may impute to our praetor, Commander Donatra, you will note that she still lives, Shinzon notwithstanding," Tomalak growled. Turning to Durjik, he added, "Unlike your beloved Pardek, whose own errors have made him *kllhe* fodder at long last, and deservedly so."

Durjik rose, throwing his chair backward. Tomalak mirrored Durjik's sudden movement, despite another sharp protestation from Tal'Aura. Supercritical tempers detonated. Steel blades flashed. Troi had missed the precise instant when the two antagonists had lost control, so overloaded had her empathy become by their relentless emotional "heat." Will, Akaar, and Keru were already rising in an effort to intercede, but it was clear that none of them could act in time to prevent a second act of murder.

Time stretched. Drawing on her decade-old experience living among Romulans *as* a Romulan—as well as on the past several weeks, during which she'd acted as the primary social lubricant among *Titan*'s highly varied crew—she quickly grasped the last diplomatic arrow in her quiver.

Troi shouted with a vehemence and volume that would have impressed even her mother. "The Remans will tear the flesh from your bones!"

Tomalak and Durjik hesitated, then slowly lowered their blades. As one, they both turned to face Troi. She noticed then that every eye in the chamber was upon her. *I'd better keep this going, now that I finally have their attention.*

"The Remans won't care about your political differences!" she said, maintaining a commanding tone that she somehow kept just a few decibels short of shrillness. "They won't care about who served Shinzon and who opposed him! They won't care about your internal grudges and petty feuds! All they will care about is what you represent to them: oppression! You show them this kind of weakness and disunity, and they will scoop out your brains and eat them! If you expect to make long-term peace with them instead of more war, then you'd better start setting aside your differences. Now. Sit. Down."

Her words hung in the air. The room was quiet, though Troi's empathic senses were numbed beneath a deluge of conflicting reactions.

"Please," Will said gently, breaking the silence. He gestured toward the empty chairs that lay upended and scattered on the floor. Despite the empathic "noise" that still crowded the room, Troi found his sense of relief unmistakable. She noticed then that something else lay beneath that emotion as well.

Admiration. He was greatly impressed with her performance. She had to force herself not to smile, though she felt both relief and cool satisfaction.

Tal'Aura had remained seated. Her face impassive despite her distraught emotional state, she chose that moment to rise and address the room. "We shall adjourn for now."

The praetor turned to face Troi. "You have pointed out some of our most critical weaknesses, Commander Troi, and for that I thank you. Those weaknesses will be addressed prior to the first full conference among all the factions." Next, she faced Tomalak. "Come, Proconsul. You and I have much to discuss." It was obvious to Troi that their discussion was likely to be quite loud and one-sided; Tal'Aura no doubt took a dim view of mortal combat in the Hall of State, and demanded better self-control from her subordinates.

After Tal'Aura and the chastened yet still-angry Tomalak exited the chamber, Durjik, Donatra, and Suran did likewise, escorted to separate exits by the small group of armed uhlans who had been discreetly guarding the room's perimeter during the meeting.

Now the away team stood alone in the Senate Chamber, at least for the moment.

"Well," Will said, heaving a sigh of relief. "I suppose that could have gone a lot worse."

"Your diplomacy was inspired," Akaar said to Troi, a small appreciative smile crossing his normally dour features. She could tell that he, too, was sincerely impressed. "If more than a little dangerous."

"Betazoid empathy can help a negotiator avoid pushing too hard," she said. *Sometimes, anyway.* Empathy or no, she still felt as though she'd just made a successful bluff while holding only threes and deuces, beating the odds because of blind chance as much as skill. "Maybe it was just a lucky gamble."

"I'm not sure what you did was a gamble at all," Keru said. "It's almost as though you switched your empathic abilities into 'offensive' mode."

She frowned slightly. "I'm not sure what you mean."

"I mean," Will said, grinning, "that you were giving off what a jazz musician would call a very strong 'vibe.' "

"It's not something I like to do very often," she said quietly. She recalled the extremely unpleasant ordeal that she had shared with her mother five years earlier. They had been part of a large group of Betazoid telepaths that had used a highly dangerous invasive empathy technique against the Dominion forces that had invaded and occupied Betazed. Use of the technique had ultimately freed Betazed, at the cost of too many Betazoid lives. She shuddered at the memory.

"Perhaps," the admiral said, "you should speak to the Lesser Teers of Capella's Ten Tribes after this mission concludes. You might speed my homeworld's admission to the Federation by a generation or more."

Troi noticed then that Keru had taken his tricorder out and was once again slowly scanning the room, obviously taking advantage of the peculiar absence of armed guards. After turning once in a full circle, he scowled and breathed an inaudible curse.

"Find anything?" Will wanted to know.

The big Trill nodded. "Something very interesting, Captain. Evidently one of the excluded power factions *did* find a way to attend this meeting after all."

"Meaning?"

"Meaning this place is crawling with tiny listening devices. Literally. I want to scan everybody closely before we beam back aboard *Titan*."

Will gave Keru a crisp nod. "Do it." Keru immediately got busy, beginning with Troi.

A moment later the security chief reached between the braided rows of her hair and grasped something there. He took a step back and revealed that he was holding something tiny between his thumb and forefinger. "Could you hold this thing so I can scan it?" he asked her. She nodded, and he dropped it into her open hands.

She found she had to grab the pinhead-size, hard-shelled object quickly between her own thumb and fore-finger. The thing was made of metal, and its dozen or so legs were trying frantically to carry it away, no doubt back to its secretive masters. She handed the squirming "bug" to Will and silently mouthed the words "Tal Shiar." Then she shuddered, unnerved by this new violation of her person. *Their eyes and ears really* are *everywhere.*

A few minutes later, after some careful scanning and grooming, the away team materialized back in *Titan*'s transporter room four, where the group underwent a second series of scans, which turned up negative.

"Interesting that we were left unguarded just long enough to find and disable those Tal Shiar 'bugs,' " Will said after they had all been certified "bug-free."

"Did Tal'Aura know they were there?" Keru wondered aloud as he tucked his tricorder away. He placed it beside the shielded sample vial in which he had stored the captured listening device in the hope that *Titan*'s science and engineering staff could use it to develop enhanced tactical countermeasures.

"Perhaps this little discovery makes the Tal Shiar a likelier culprit in Pardek's murder than Tal'Aura or Tomalak," Will said.

Troi nodded in agreement. "Or Donatra."

"I certainly hope so," Will said.

The group left the transporter room and entered the adjoining corridor, whereupon Akaar and Keru went one way—presumably intent on getting the captured Tal Shiar bug to Jaza and Ledrah—while Troi followed Will the other way into a turbolift she knew would take them straight to the bridge. Despite the reassuring arm he placed around her shoulders after the doors closed and the lift began to move, a wave of sadness swept over her. "Vibe" or no "vibe," building trust among such hardened, suspicious, and cynical people as these Romulan leaders could very well prove to be the single biggest challenge of her Starfleet career.

She prayed silently that it was a challenge she could meet.

Chapter Sixteen

"Mnean partrai hra' yy'a hwi hvei h'rau na gaehl!"

Mekrikuk's deep voice echoed down the corridor. Generally, the Romulan *klhus* ignored the yelling and screaming from the Remans, but when someone yelled that there was another dead body back in the cells—as Mekrikuk had just done—they paid slightly more attention. Whether the corpses ended up in the food or in a mass grave somewhere outside the prison was a matter of constant debate. Mekrikuk had always suspected that the Romulan corpses were treated with slightly more dignity than the Reman dead were afforded, and he hoped this would be the case now.

The Romulan known by others as Rukath, but to Mekrikuk and his protected ones as Tuvok, lay motionless on the ground. Tesruk and Kachrek were guarding his body to prevent any postmortem molestation by the other prisoners, but Mekrikuk knew that it was not his protected ones that really kept the others at bay. His own menacing presence accomplished that.

By the seventh time that Mekrikuk thundered the notice to the guards, he finally heard movement coming from the far end of the dimly illuminated cell block. It wasn't so much the sound of the guards that had alerted everyone to their arrival; none of the Reman prisoners in his tier needed their extra-sensitive hearing to divine the guards' presence, since the cacophonous noise from the prisoners in the first tiers nearest the entrance had effectively alerted everyone in Vikr'l Prison.

Moments later, the handtorches of the approaching guards blinded those foolish enough not to avert their eyes.

"Ihnna uaenn na itaeru!" the lead guard roared, but the crowd had barely begun complying by moving backward when the quartet of guards flanking him let loose with sprays of *xecin.* Those caught in the vapors immediately began gasping for air, retching and convulsing. The faster-moving prisoners had already fled deeper into the relative safety of the cellmaze.

Two of the guards came into the cell cautiously, while a pair of their fellows watched their backs, plasma rifles at the ready. The guard closest to Rukath/Tuvok kicked him in the ribs, causing his lifeless body to roll partially to one side. The other sprayed *xecin* full-force directly into Rukath/Tuvok's face. Seeing that it had no effect on the body, the two men grabbed the corpse's ankles and began pulling it from the cell.

"Farewell, and good fortune on the Other Side," Mekrikuk said, loud enough for the guards to hear. One of them immediately trained his rifle and handtorch on Mekrikuk. Kachrek stepped into the path of the rifle, but the guard didn't fire.

The heavy doors clanged shut, and the guards moved away in a group, pulling Rukath/Tuvok by his ankles toward the cell block's outer doors.

Mekrikuk took a deep breath and began to prepare himself. Though his psionic abilities had always been fairly limited, he pushed out with them aggressively, reaching toward the one particular mind that offered any prospect of freedom and salvation.

The gray stillness was infinite. It held neither memories nor ghosts from his former life. Though Tuvok was aware that his body was being kicked, the sensation didn't register as pain so much as a lighter shade of gray.

He had not gone so deeply into a healing trance in more than half a century. To any who might examine him, he was functionally lifeless. Only a deep-tissue tricorder scan would reveal the persistent vestiges of life within him, a state not very far removed from suspended animation. He was well aware that such a low level of metabolic activity couldn't be maintained for long; were his heart rate to decline any further, or the balance of gases in his bloodstream to alter in the slightest, his mimicry of death would become far more perfect than he had intended.

Tuvok found the trance more difficult to maintain than usual for several reasons. Although the Reman Mekrikuk had helped to restore him somewhat from his earlier malnourished condition—thus aiding him in regaining a degree of control over his mental disciplines—Tuvok knew that his current condition was far from ideal. More important, those in a healing trance often found it difficult to return to full consciousness unaided.

For this reason, Tuvok had worked with Mekrikuk on a specialized form of hypnotic command, to be delivered telepathically. The Reman's esper abilities were untrained and limited, but Tuvok had mind-melded with Mekrikuk—a terrible mutual lowering of personal barriers, but a deed thought necessary by both men under the current dire circumstances—and had given the Reman clear, unambiguous instructions.

Time passed, all but unreckonable in the gray infinite, before Tuvok saw the silent flash of color that represented Mekrikuk's mental burst, far away, coruscating and crackling as it moved inexorably toward him. Eventually, with an almost agonizing slowness, it engulfed Tuvok, and he saw in it the path that would lead his mind toward a fully conscious state. Tuvok wondered idly whether the characters in the ancient stories of *fal-tor-pan*—the re-fusion of a Vulcan's immortal *katra* with its still-living body—had experienced something similar. Though Ambassador Spock was rumored to have undergone just such a re-fusion once, Tuvok had never quite been able to bring himself to believe it.

As he gradually drifted back to himself, Tuvok began to regain some rudimentary awareness of his physical body. He realized with some discomfort that he was being dragged by his feet, the rough-hewn stone floor tearing away at his bloodied back through the rags that draped his emaciated body. He felt a burning sensation in his nostrils, mouth, and eyes, and realized that his captors had sprayed him with something caustic, probably to make certain that he truly was as dead as he appeared. He was careful not to react to the smell or the pain, keeping his breaths shallow, willing his countenance to remain just as lifeless as it had looked while he had been in the healing trance.

"*Dii Pangaere tohr ve reh nubereae,*" he heard one Romulan guard say to another, and he felt a twinge of pride that he had outlasted their expectations.

His captors suddenly stopped dragging him, and Tuvok heard one of them bark a sharp command. *"Aihr Arrain Vextan. Abrai na iaaeru!"*

As if the grinding mechanical sounds of the prison doors weren't clue enough that they had reached the outer gates, Tuvok felt the floor vibrating beneath him as the great metal barriers rolled open. Seconds later, he was dragged into the area beyond the doors, where the floor was smoother, and the air cooler and less fetid. Though his eyes remained closed, he could sense a considerable increase in the ambient illumination.

After the guards had dragged him another twenty paces or so, Tuvok felt them let go of his body, which he allowed to collapse limply. One of his handlers kicked him in the ribs, rolling him none too gently onto his side. Focusing past the pain, Tuvok cautiously opened his right eye, the one nearest the smooth white floor, and saw the booted feet of four uniformed prison guards. From this and the position of the voices he heard before him and behind him, he quickly concluded that a total of five other people were in the room with him; one of them was located behind him, out of his line of sight.

He waited patiently, still as a corpse as the guards laughed and bragged about their casual, habitual abuses of the Reman prisoners, and speculated about the indignities the dead Romulan farmer must have suffered while incarcerated with them. One of them wondered aloud about exactly how the farmer had died, and another said that he would run a quick scan to find out.

Knowing his interval of "laying low" had just about reached its end, Tuvok gathered his energies and focused his mind as clearly as he possibly could. A moment after the guard rolled his body over yet again, flopping him onto his back, Tuvok opened his eyes. Out of necessity, the pacifism of Surak gave way to the ancient survival instinct, decades of special tactical training, and no small amount of rage at his captors.

Before the guard could react, Tuvok jammed his right palm sharply upward and into the man's chest. The Romulan was dead before he could utter a sound, his eyes bulging in mute surprise.

Tuvok heard the others react with shock and horror, but he was already moving, his attention tightly focused on his grim task. He instantly took in the room around him, seeing three men grouped to one side, and another behind him, as he had surmised moments ago. He flung the sharpened rock that he had been clutching in his "dead" left hand at the sole guard behind him, aiming it for his forehead.

One of the trio brought his rifle to bear, but Tuvok had already moved, scissoring his legs out and connecting with the knees of two of the guards. They both screamed and fell backward onto the equipment and computer banks that lined the nearby wall.

The guard with the weapon fired once, and the disruptor blast flashed by harmlessly over Tuvok's right shoulder. The Vulcan rolled and brought himself upright as the other man fired his rifle again. Gambling that the armed guard wouldn't expect him to approach, Tuvok launched forward with a savagely purposeful *ke-tar-yatar* maneuver, crushing the man's windpipe with a kick to the throat.

Tuvok turned his attention back to the other two guards, both of whom were attempting to reach their rifles and sidearms, despite their fractured knees. He reached the nearer of the two first, put both his hands on the guard's neck, and executed him swiftly by means of a *tal-*

shaya, then used the man's corpse as a shield while the other guard fired at him.

Grabbing the weapon-holding hand of the guard he had just killed, Tuvok pushed the man's dead fingers, firing a triple burst at his attacker. Two of the shots connected, throwing the guard backward and leaving a smoking hole in his tunic.

His senses keen, Tuvok surveyed the situation. In the last eleven seconds, he had dispatched four of the guards present, while the one he had struck with the rock lay convulsing in a corner, a thick black bruise spreading across his forehead and green blood running freely into his eyes. He was still alive, but posed no threat. The discipline of Surak began to reassert itself, accompanied by an almost overpowering wave of self-disgust. He brutally pushed the latter aside; there would be time for self-recrimination later, assuming he somehow managed to reach safety.

Appraising the computer terminals against the wall, Tuvok realized that he was in a control chamber that ran the prison cell block's systems. Large wall-mounted monitors displayed infrared images of the prison's mazelike passageways, perhaps the very ones through which he had just been dragged.

Though he hadn't yet heard an alarm, he knew he couldn't afford to take the time to figure out the layout of the prison, and probably lacked the time even to map out his most efficient escape route. The guards' disruptor rifle blasts had undoubtedly been detected by other Romulan troops, so it was likely that he had only minutes of freedom left, if that. But he knew of someone who almost certainly *did* know the best way out, though accessing that information would be almost as dangerous as facing the rest of the prison's armed personnel.

Tuvok approached the bleeding guard and pulled his crumpled form into a sitting position. The man's dark eyes were open but unfocused, and his body still twitched. He was dying, but not yet dead. At least not completely. Tuvok forced aside another wave of self-loathing as he contemplated what he was about to do. *What I have to do.*

Placing his left index finger beside the dying man's nose, his thumb under his chin, and splaying his other fingers against his bloodied cheek, Tuvok stared deeply into his erstwhile captor's rapidly glazing eyes.

My mind to your mind, he thought, placing every iota of his will into the mind-meld. If he could extract the information he needed before the final dissolution of the guard's mind, then everyone confined in this horrific labyrinth might stand a fighting chance of escaping.

Mekrikuk felt the gentle touch of Tuvok's mind before he even heard the Vulcan's thoughts. The brief contact allowed him time to warn Tesruk and Kachrek and several other Reman prisoners—though they were not exactly friends, Mekrikuk regarded them almost as equals—of what was about to transpire.

Then the cell doors opened, and Mekrikuk knew that the Trayatik dice had finally been cast.

At first, no one seemed to react. But within seconds, the Reman prisoners began a mad en masse rush to the corridors. Finding themselves suddenly outside the cellmaze doors for the first time since their arrival at Vikr'l, many of the Remans pushed forward toward the prison's outer perimeter, which some of them had not even seen in years. Some stayed behind, scrapping and brawling with prisoners from other tiers, their anger over real or perceived slights now exploding with furious intensity.

Mekrikuk and a handful of Reman prisoners from his immediate circle of intimates stayed back in the cell, biding their time as the noise of the rapidly escalating riot grew almost deafening. The shouts and screams reached an earsplitting volume as the doors to the chambers beyond their tier also opened. Approaching the duranium bars, Mekrikuk squinted, watching as hordes of Remans surged forward into the well-lit areas that lay beyond the outer doors.

He grinned in satisfaction, imagining that this scene was being repeated in every confinement wing in Vikr'l Prison, thanks to the machinations of Tuvok. Until the Vulcan's newly scrambled security codes could be deciphered, this entire maximum security facility had been effectively turned into an open courtyard. Mekrikuk had no pity for the guards he was certain were now attempting to flee the prison as the angry masses surged toward them, their minds brimming over with thoughts of revenge.

And of freedom, which was Mekrikuk's foremost desire. Assuming he survived the events of this day, there would be time and opportunity later to exact vengeance against his captors. For now, he knew he would have his hands full just keeping himself alive and in one piece.

Mekrikuk noted that the outer corridors were mostly empty now that the rioting crowd had moved toward the prison's periphery. *The storm is always calmest in its center,* Mekrikuk thought, echoing the sentiment that Tuvok had instilled in him during their brief psionic contact. All that remained in the cell block's deeper recesses were the broken bodies of the dead and those too badly injured to take advantage of the opportunity to escape.

"Denae!" Mekrikuk said, and his small retinue of Reman compatriots followed him cautiously out into the corridor. The rough stone floor was slick with emerald blood as they exited the cellmaze.

"Bont na batlem saith," he commanded, and the group moved among the wounded. As he had instructed, they quickly and cleanly killed any who would otherwise have died a lingering, agonizing death from their injuries. Mekrikuk had learned to practice this judicious compassion during the Dominion War, on Goloroth and other battlefields. He knew well that wars were anything but noble enterprises, and that their corpse-strewn killing fields were among the least glorious places to die. Having looked into perhaps hundreds of haunted, pain-racked eyes, he understood the grateful release of those whose journeys to the next world he had mercifully expedited.

His grim task complete, Mekrikuk led the group down the corridor. They blinked and squinted as they entered the more brightly-illuminated rooms and corridors that lay beyond. *"Keisa,"* Mekrikuk said, instructing his people to enter the small chamber on the right.

They entered, and Mekrikuk saw five Romulan guards lying dead on the floor. They were the same guards who had taken Tuvok away. He saw that they had been savaged after death by the prisoners who had moved through this room. Stupidly, the rioters had also smashed most of the monitors and computer equipment in the room before they had moved on.

"Tuvok?" he called out. There was no sign of the Vulcan, but his mind told him that his ally was somewhere in the room.

He heard a sound above and behind his group. He

whirled to look, as did the others, each of whom possessed hearing no less acute than Mekrikuk's.

Mekrikuk looked upward. From behind the dark latticework of pipes that ran across the ceiling, Tuvok emerged. The rags he wore were encrusted with dirt and blood. He held several disruptor rifles, tied together with a length of cord.

Tuvok jumped down, his legs coiling beneath him as he landed, like those of a particularly agile *arark*.

"You are unharmed?" Mekrikuk asked.

"Essentially," the Vulcan said. "I have not been injured beyond repair. Thank you." He turned to face the others and began distributing the captured Romulan energy weapons, handing one to Mekrikuk and another to Tesruk.

Despite Tuvok's assurances, the Vulcan's dark, sunken eyes were twin pools of pain. Mekrikuk supposed he was unaccustomed to such violence as he had seen today.

"The Romulans will already have locked down Vikr'l's outer perimeter," Tuvok continued, speaking in the Romulan common tongue. "We will have to overcome that problem once we reach it. There are other entrances and exits, if we can find them. But our way will be blocked there as well, by other prisoners, by guards, and by whatever security measures they will soon take to quell this riot. It's likely that they will take lethal measures, and perhaps even try to eliminate the entire population of the prison. We will have to make our escape before that happens."

"Voi mnaeri mnean ihra corr Rihanha?" asked Fapruk, a portly older Reman male. Mekrikuk had always regarded Fapruk's so-called revolutionary crimes—the nominal reason for his incarceration at Vikr'l—as the consequence of spontaneous vandalism rather than the result of any coherent plan.

"We should trust him, Fapruk, because he got us this far," Mekrikuk answered. "And because I said so," he added in a more menacing tone.

His expression determined, Tuvok motioned toward a side doorway.

"Let's get out of here."

Chapter Seventeen

U.S.S. TITAN

"Captain, I believe I've isolated Commander Tuvok's life signs."

Riker turned his chair, feeling hope surge within him. "Good work, Mr. Jaza. Put what you've got up on the screen, please."

The image on the bridge's central viewscreen shifted. It had been displaying Romulus in the center, along with images of the Federation relief ships and their Klingon escorts; the scene now displayed a map overlay of the planet, which swiftly zoomed in on a sparsely populated area just outside the capital city of Romulus. As the image zoomed in further, Riker saw a large circular facility in an aerial view, and recognized it as a highly secured, bunkerlike facility.

"Tuvok appears to be inside Vikr'l Prison, which is located within one of the outlying districts of Ki Baratan," Jaza said. "The readings are pretty thready, though. I'm picking up indications of kelbonite and fistrium inside the prison walls. Not a lot, but enough to cause some interference with our scans, even with the new high-res sensor nets. We might have better luck if we could get our sensors closer to the prison."

"Seems like quite a stroke of luck that you happened to find him," Vale said as she rose from her chair and approached Jaza's science station.

"He may have been located in a deeper section of the prison before now," the Bajoran said, frowning as his fingers moved deftly across the console in front of him. "If he's just been moved toward the perimeter, that might explain why the scanners couldn't find him until now."

"Can we get a transporter lock on him?" Riker asked.

Ranul Keru spoke up from the tactical station, aft of the captain's chair. "I'm afraid not, sir. The prison appears to be equipped with wide-dispersal transporter scramblers. All we'd get back would be a pile of protoplasmic sludge."

Riker studied the image on the viewscreen, his eyes narrowing. *If I send a rescue team down there, I put the Romulan-Reman power-sharing negotiations in jeopardy. I'd risk giving Durjik and his followers a* real *reason to reject the Federation.* And it didn't help matters that the prison was so close to the capital city of the Romulan Star Empire.

"Sir, I'm also detecting what appear to be weapons discharges within the prison perimeter," Keru said. "The Romulan and Reman life signs we're reading are all moving around quite a bit."

"A prison riot?" Vale said, looking up from the data she was reading at Jaza's station.

Which means this may be our only opportunity to get Tuvok out of there alive, Riker thought. As wary as he was, he knew he couldn't afford to delay taking action any longer.

"Commander Vale, Commander Keru, assemble an extraction team," Riker said, an edge in his voice. "I want your *best* people on this. Go in, get Tuvok out, and *don't* get caught. I do *not* want anyone to know that Starfleet was ever there. Use the *Handy*. She's already been outfitted for this sort of thing."

Vale's eyes widened, but she nodded crisply. "Yes, sir." A moment later she and Keru were sprinting to the turbolift. Keru was already calling into his combadge for his security team.

Riker felt a twinge of regret; had this been the *Enterprise, he* would have been the one leading this rescue mission. But now, he had larger responsibilities. Despite his half-joking promise to Captain Picard that he intended to ignore the advice of his new first officer, he understood the wisdom of keeping a ship's captain on the bridge.

"Mr. Jaza, patch everything over to my ready room, and then take the bridge," Riker said, rising from his chair. "Inform Dr. Ree that we may have injured coming within the hour. Lieutenant Rager, I want you to monitor the Romulan communications channels. Find out everything you can about this riot, and get the information directly to the away team, encrypted and scrambled."

Riker moved toward his ready room, tapping his combadge as he walked. "Admiral Akaar, Commander Troi, to my ready room, please."

Dusk was deepening into night over the Romulan capital city. The shuttlecraft *Handy* dipped through the low-rolling clouds toward Vikr'l Prison. The sleek type-11 craft was the only one of the ship's complement of eight that Admiral Akaar had authorized—illegally—to be equipped with a cloaking device.

Vale and Keru both agreed with the unorthodox decision, especially given the potentially volatile nature of their interaction with the Romulans. Vale thought it made little sense that both the Romulans and the Klingons were permitted cloaking technology, while the Starfleet convoy was hampered by decades-old agreements with a Romulan government that no longer even existed.

Vale looked around the shuttle at the assault team that Keru had assembled. It included the Caitian lieutenant j.g. Rriarr; the Vulcan lieutenant j.g. T'Lirin; the Martian human lieutenant Gian Sortollo; and the Matalinian lieutenant Feren Denken. With the exception of their shuttle pilot, Ensign Olivia Bolaji, everyone aboard was outfitted in stealth suits and helmets. These garments, based on the isolation suits worn by Federation social scientists while covertly observing prewarp species, were utterly black on the surface. But when their internal systems were activated, they holographically duplicated the background behind the wearer, thus providing highly effective personal camouflage.

Even with their stealth systems turned off, the suits' helmets not only helped disguise the identities of the away team members, but were also equipped with electronic auditory enhancers and heads-up in-helmet displays whose optical sensors provided what amounted to 360-degree vision. The suits also afforded their wearers a degree of resistance to directed-energy weapons, though field tests suggested that it wasn't wise to allow oneself to take more than a single direct hit.

Vale listened as Keru went over the team's mission profile and contingency plans yet again. He seemed extremely concerned about leaving any member of the team behind, no matter the reason, and assigned them to work in pairs. Keru was to go with Rriarr, T'Lirin and

Sortollo were a pair, and Denken and Vale were to be the third duo.

Looking out the *Handy*'s forward viewport, Vale saw that columns of black smoke were wafting into the sky. As the cloaked craft drew nearer to the prison's squat, gray structures, she caught sight of dozens of figures moving with frantic speed. Armed Romulan security personnel were scrambling throughout the outer levels of the structure, whose walls were arranged in three concentric circles. At the center of it all lay a massive complex that the shuttle's scans—hampered as they were by seemingly random subterranean veins of refractory metals—revealed extended six or more stories underground; Tuvok's biosignature was emanating from deep within that central structure. Vale looked toward the sprawling surface prison yard near the innermost circle; here a swarm of armed Remans was massed, firing at the walls of the surrounding structures—and at the guards who dared to peer over those walls or shoot back.

"I can get us over the prison," Bolaji said. "But there's no clear place to land that probably won't be swarming with Romulan skimmers any minute. Jaza tells me seventeen of them are already en route."

"And with the transporter scramblers operating, we still can't beam Tuvok out, or beam ourselves in," Keru said, looking at the forward window. "We're going to have to get in there the hard way." He turned back toward the others on his team. "Remember those swift descent air assault exercises we've been doing, folks?"

"How could we forget, O Fearless Leader?" Denken said with a lilt in his voice that didn't quite conceal his nervousness. Vale nodded as the rest of the strike team made positive noises and double-checked their equipment.

Keru grinned through his helmet's open faceplate.

"Then it looks like it's about time to put theory into practice."

Vale couldn't fault Keru's plan. Though it was old-fashioned, she didn't doubt it was the best way to enter the prison undetected—or at least as stealthily as possible under the circumstances. She pointed toward the top of one of the low buildings, where a handful of Remans had overpowered the guards near what appeared to be a landing bay for hover vehicles.

"Get us as close as you can to that rooftop down there, without crossing into the prison's antitransporter fields," Vale said. "We'll beam directly to the dorsal hull, come down firing. Once we reach the roof we'll have a high, defensible position. With a little luck, the Romulans on the outer perimeter will never even know we were here." She turned back toward the others. "Phasers on heavy stun. Keep your beams narrow, and keep an eye on the proximity sensors in your helmets so we don't hit each other. Watch your backs—it's pandemonium down there."

She pointed to one of the side viewscreens, then raised her wrist-mounted tricorder. "Tuvok's biosignature is still coming in strongly, and I read two clear paths to reach him." She was grateful that the fistrium and kelbonite *Titan*'s sensors had detected from orbit didn't seem to be interfering significantly with the *Handy*'s sensors, or the away team's tricorders, at close range. "Whoever reaches Tuvok first will signal the rest of the team. Then we'll all get the hell out of there."

Vale turned back toward Bolaji and caught her wincing and rubbing her protruding stomach. "Are you all right?"

"I'm fine," Bolaji shot back tersely. "Just a kick."

Let's hope that's all it is, Vale thought, then turned back to face the others. "Let's move, people."

As Bolaji held the cloaked shuttle in position hovering over the rooftop, Keru began keying commands into the transporter console. T'Lirin and Sortollo activated their stealth systems and silenced gravity boots, turned invisible, then vanished in the shimmer of a transporter beam. Vale looked through the front window, though she could see no sign of either of them as they glided invisibly downward toward the rooftop.

As Keru and Rriarr repeated this maneuver and began their gentle descent, Vale saw two of the escaped Reman prisoners cast squinting glances toward the essentially invisible shuttlecraft. *Damn,* she thought, *they must have heard the transporter or the gravity boots. Their ears are a lot more sensitive than we thought.* Their weapons at the ready, Vale and Denken were next to materialize on top of the shuttlecraft *Handy,* toward which the Remans had already raised their rifles. Luckily, Vale and Denken managed to squeeze off the first shots.

Even as the stunned Remans toppled, the phaser blasts caught the attention of a dozen or so other prisoners who were already beginning to swarm onto the roof. But moments later, Vale's proximity sensors revealed that Keru and Rriarr were down on the rooftop, crouching behind what appeared to be a large air-conditioning unit as they began spraying the angry Remans with phaser fire. Sortollo and T'Lirin had taken cover nearby, firing into the melee as well.

Moments later, Vale's and Denken's gravity boots touched the roof's hard surface, where the rooftop rioters were all sprawled unconscious.

"Thanks for leaving some for us," Vale said, grinning behind her face shield. The acrid smell of ozone hung in the air.

"You'll get your chance to shoot at something soon enough," Commander Keru responded, his deep voice sounding slightly tinny in her helmet.

As the team members forced open a door and cautiously lowered themselves into the prison facility, Vale had little doubt that *Titan*'s security chief was right.

"So much for stealth," Keru muttered. He realized belatedly that he had badly underestimated the efficacy of the Remans' nonvisual senses.

Four angry Remans were running toward them now. Though the away team had extinguished all the lights—and though the team's stealth suits seemed to be functioning perfectly—the Remans were apparently able to locate them as though they were caught in a searchlight's glare.

Rriarr leapt into the air, hissing as the large Reman approaching him swung a metal bar, narrowly missing his helmeted head. Grasping a pipe hanging from the ceiling, the Caitian flipped himself over and past his attacker and landed in a crouch behind him. A two-handed jackhammer blow to the base of the Reman's skull drove the man down, making him lay still.

But Keru didn't have time to watch Rriarr's back at that moment; he was involved in a close-quarter combat situation of his own. They had entered a room that had scanned as empty, only to face an explosion from beyond the doors on the darkened chamber's far side. The blast had knocked them both off their feet, tossing their weapons out of reach. A swarm of angry Remans immediately piled inside, and Keru's night-vision visor revealed opponents who were armed, enraged, and numerous. Though the room was as dark as the night that was enfolding the prison yard, the Remans zeroed right in on Keru and Rriarr. Keru had never expected the darkness to slow down the Remans, who were born and bred to it; he merely hoped that it would conceal the away team's presence from any Romulans they might encounter.

Already having downed three of the Remans with his hands, Keru was grabbed from behind by another of them. Unable to break the Reman's grip, Keru pushed backward with his feet, slamming his attacker into a wall. As the blow loosened the bear hug, Keru stamped down hard on the upper arch of the Reman's foot, causing the bone within to crack loudly.

The Reman released him momentarily, but Keru had to duck to avoid the swinging roundhouse blow of another club-wielding thug. He heard the club connect with flesh above him, then a bellow of rage as he sprinted to one side. He turned to see the larger of his attackers now pummeling the other Reman who had just accidentally struck him.

Keru looked around for the phasers they had dropped, and wasn't surprised when he failed to find them. Then he noticed that a smallish Reman prisoner had scooped them up, and was, at that moment, attempting to fire at him. He moved quickly toward the Reman—who couldn't have been more than a preteen—unconcerned. The phasers were specially tuned to the circuitry in the gloves of the stealth suits they were wearing. No one who wasn't wearing the gloves could fire them.

Another Reman charged him. He crouched, using a martial arts technique that he had learned from one of the older Guardians in the caves of Mak'ala back on Trill. Keru struck two fingers up toward the Reman's throat, sweeping one leg out at the same time. The Reman tumbled over his shoulder, carried by the kick and his own momentum, a strangled gurgle of pain replacing his guttural attack cry.

Keru stood and walked toward the Reman youth, who was now quaking with fright. "Boo!" he said, putting his gloved hands up. Panicked, the youth dropped the weapons and ran for the outer corridor from which the Remans had entered the room.

Quickly retrieving the phasers, Keru palmed one and whirled to face their remaining Reman attackers. Double-checking his helmet's panoramic sensor display, he confirmed that none were left standing. Rriarr was crouched on all fours, breathing heavily, but in far better shape than any of the escaped prisoners who lay sprawled about the floor.

"Are you all right?" Keru asked.

"Just winded," Rriarr said, his esses rendered slightly sibilant by his prominent canines. The Caitian's helmet visor was raised, revealing golden, vertical-pupiled eyes that probably rivaled the night-vision system built into the stealth suits. "But if my tail weren't tucked into this damned suit, I suspect there'd be another big chunk missing from it after that little dustup. Give me a second to catch my breath."

Keru spoke into the mouthpiece in his helmet. "Commander Vale, how goes it?"

"Not good," came the exec's response. "We got ambushed in one of the corridors. They sliced Denken up pretty badly. I'm putting a field dressing on him now, but if we don't get him back to Titan soon, I'm afraid he's going to lose the arm."

Stifling a curse, Keru let out his breath in a whoosh. "Sortollo, report."

"We're holding steady up here, but the Romulan skim-mers have definitely arrived. Right now, they're under heavy fire from escapees in the prison's outer perimeter. But it's only a matter of time before one or more of the skimmers makes for the roof you used to get inside."

"I'm getting intel from Titan *that confirms this,"* Bolaji said, breaking in. *"I'd say we've got five minutes, maybe less."* She paused for a moment, then came back on, her voice sounding strained. *"Commander Keru, you're posi-tioned closest to Tuvok. My scans show he's located two chambers past you, but something strange is going on there. We've got a group of life signs approaching him, heavily armed."* She paused again, and Keru thought he heard a moan. *"They're coming up from underground. I'm feeding you the data now."*

Keru saw a rough electronic map flashing on one sec-tion of his helmet's faceplate, and he turned to Rriarr. "Let's go get him. Double time." Into his mouthpiece, he said, "Commander, get Denken back to the *Handy*. Rriarr and I are going in after Tuvok now."

In the corridors leading away from the first chamber, Keru and Rriarr found only unconscious or dead Reman prisoners and Romulan guards. As they neared the en-trance to the second chamber, Keru felt his already-elevated adrenaline levels beginning to peak. *I'm probably going to need anesthezine to get to sleep tonight,* he thought. *Assuming I manage to make it back to* Titan.

Weapons at the ready, the pair burst into the final dark-ened room, firing at the first Reman prisoners that ap-peared on their night-vision displays. As the rioters began to fall under their phaser barrage, Keru saw a huge, battle-scarred Reman standing beside a shabbily dressed, dark-skinned Romulan on the far side of the ragtag cluster of escapees. Keru also quickly gathered from the Romulan's actions and appearance that he was working with the Remans, a fellow prisoner rather than a captured prison guard.

"Hold fire!" Keru said to Rriarr as they both sought cover behind a stone pillar.

He shouted over the return fire, and the aggressive shouts of the Remans. "Commander Tuvok?"

A moment later, the Remans quit firing. "Who are you?" The voice that filled the sudden silence was shaky and hoarse, but clearly had not come from a gravel-throated Reman.

Still hunkering behind the pillar beside Rriarr, Keru quickly considered his options. No one at the prison knew that they were Starfleet officers, but to gain Tuvok's cooperation, he knew he was going to have to reveal that fact. He hoped that decision wouldn't come back to haunt him.

"I'm Lieutenant Commander Ranul Keru, *U.S.S. Titan*," he said. "I'm here to extract you, and I'm running out of time."

"How do we know you aren't Romulans?"

Keru realized that even if he and Rriarr had been seen at all, they wouldn't have looked like Starfleet officers, thanks to their stealth suits. He could think of but one way to prove his identity. He reached into a flap on his stealth suit's equipment belt and plucked out a small backup transceiver unit. The rectangular, silver-colored device was about the size of his thumb, and for discretion's sake lacked the distinctive chevron-shape of standard Starfleet combadges; but a Starfleet intelligence operative like Tuvok would surely recognize it for what it was.

"I'm tossing you my communicator," Keru said. He threw it in the direction of the group of escapees, and was gratified that he hadn't heard the small device clatter to the hard floor. *Someone caught it.* "You can use it to contact our personnel in orbit, or on the surface."

"Yhaim hraen teidr!" This voice clearly belonged to a Reman. Peeking from behind the pillar, Keru saw that the speaker was the large Reman who stood beside Tuvok. The quintet of remaining Remans lowered their weapons as one, apparently in response to their leader's order. Some of them looked less than happy about it, though Reman facial expressions were hard to fathom, with or without night-vision gear.

Keru heard the man whom he assumed to be Tuvok speaking to the large Reman at his side, but couldn't clearly parse what was being said, even with his helmet's auditory enhancers. Finally, the Vulcan approached. He was holding the combadge.

"I am Commander Tuvok," he said. "I will go with you, Commander Keru. But I must insist that those who assisted me in my escape accompany—"

Tuvok was interrupted as the wall exploded inward behind him, showering the room with stone, metal, and dirt. The force of the explosion blew even the sturdiest of the Remans off their feet, and cracked the column that Keru and Rriarr had been using as cover. Keru felt something heavy fall on him, and a bright nimbus of pain flared in his left hip and leg.

Fighting to keep himself from blacking out, Keru sat up and pushed at the heavy chunk of masonry that was pinning him down. A disruptor blast skipped off his helmet; he saw a brilliant flash just before his internal faceplate displays went abruptly dark.

Dropping his head back down to make himself less of a target, Keru groped in the darkness for his again-missing phaser. Effectively blinded and pinned, he could hear a ca-cophony of shouts and cries in Romulan, all of them com-ing from the direction of the blast.

Then he felt a gloved hand pressing down against his. "Stay still, Commander," Rriarr said. "They've got us pinned down good." With his other hand, Keru lifted his helmet's faceplate. Despite the darkness, he saw the gleaming golden eyes of his subordinate officer, who was on his belly to stay out of the line of fire. A flash of disrup-tor fire revealed the dirt and dust that clouded the air and dusted Rriarr's deactivated stealth suit.

As the seconds ticked slowly by, the gabble of Romu-lan voices seemed to be growing steadily fainter. Rriarr cautiously poked his head up, then turned to Keru.

"Whoever they were, they're gone now."

"Good. Now get this stuff off me," Keru said, pushing at the heavy chunks of shattered stone and duraplast. Rriarr strained with him in vain, then cast his bright eyes past the debris. Though Keru couldn't see it, he could hear someone moving on the other side of the pile of debris that still pinned him down.

Keru groaned in pain as the rubble shifted and fell away from his body. Though he could see only the silhouette of his rescuer, Keru realized who it was: the hulking, battle-scarred Reman who had stood at Tuvok's side. Limned in the blaze of a searchlight whose beam leaked in through a shattered exterior wall, the Reman was covered in dirt, sweat, and green blood, some of which had to be his own.

The Reman reached for Keru's hand, helping him up. "They took Tuvok," he said.

"Who?" Keru winced as another jagged lightning bolt of pain shot down his left leg. He saw Rriarr checking the room carefully, his weapon in his gloved hand.

"Other Remans. Ten of them, maybe more. They weren't prisoners."

Rriarr was now nearing the portion of the wall that had exploded inward. "There's a tunnel here, Commander. Looks old. I think they—" He stopped and listened, then looked back at Keru. "Commander, is your comm working?"

Keru shook his head. "Dead. My helmet got hit." *And I gave away my backup transceiver,* he thought ruefully. *Wonderful.*

"Bolaji says that the Romulan police skimmers are on their way in now," Rriarr said. "If we don't get back to the *Handy* in the next two minutes, then we aren't going to get home."

"You have a way out?" the Reman asked.

"We have a cloaked shuttle," Keru said. He pondered the situation for a moment. They could conceivably go after Tuvok and his Reman abductors, but there was no guarantee of success. And besides, not only was he injured, but so was Denken. He didn't like the prospect of leaving Tuvok in the hands of people who were most likely hostiles. But he had to consider the safety of his teammates, each one of whom he considered every bit as important as the man they had been ordered to rescue.

"From the last thing he was saying, it seems that Tuvok wanted us to take you and your . . . associates with us." Keru looked at the large Reman, appraising him in the intermittent glow of the searchlights that came through the shattered walls.

"We helped each other to escape," the Reman said. He gestured toward another pile of debris, which covered several Reman bodies. "The others must have been too close to the explosion. Kachrek is missing. Perhaps he is pursuing those who took Tuvok. I must follow as well."

The Reman turned as if to leave. Then his legs buckled beneath his considerable weight and he sank to his knees.

"You won't make it ten meters in the shape you're in," Keru said to the Reman before turning to face Rriarr. "Tell Christine and Olivia that we're on our way. We'll have to come back later for Tuvok." Ignoring his own pain, he threw an arm around the injured Reman and helped him get to his feet.

"Commander Vale isn't gonna like this," said the Caitian. "And neither will the captain."

Keru shrugged. "Yeah. And Admiral Akaar won't be pinning any medals on my chest either. But as security chief, it's my call to make." *You think I like having to leave anybody behind?* he wanted to shout as a particularly clear image of his beloved Sean appeared in his mind's eye.

As the motley trio retraced their steps swiftly through the chambers that led back toward the roof, they encountered no further resistance. The injured Reman actually seemed to help support Keru's weight, despite his own bleeding multiple wounds.

Focusing past his own steadily escalating pain, Keru wondered about the group of Remans that had just come and gone, apparently with the express purpose of taking Commander Tuvok. *If they aren't prisoners, then who are they? Did they know Tuvok's identity? And if they knew about a tunnel running underneath the prison, then why didn't they help the other Remans use it to escape?*

They reached the rooftop, where they found Vale waiting for them. Her damaged suit's stealth system was deactivated. "Everybody else is already aboard the *Handy,*" she said, pointing toward a conspicuously empty space on the landing bay, where Bolaji had apparently taken the risk of setting down the cloaked shuttlecraft. "Where's

Tuvok? And who's our guest?" Keru noticed that Vale's hand hovered near her phaser as she eyed the fierce-looking, though clearly injured, Reman.

"Tuvok's been taken," Keru said. "This Reman's a friendly, and in need of medical attention. I'll explain later."

As Vale led everyone at a run across the rooftop, the group heard the whine of a skimmer engine, and moments later disruptor blasts ripped into the stone roofing tiles all around them.

"Open the hatch!" Vale called out, and Keru saw T'Lirin inside the aperture that suddenly appeared out of thin air, a floating window that displayed a narrow slice of the shuttle's otherwise invisible interior.

Rriarr and Vale reached the doorway first, but as the Reman pushed Keru across the threshold, a blast from the approaching skimmer punched through the prisoner's shoulder, splattering green ichor on everyone.

The Reman began to slump to the rooftop. "Help me get him aboard!" Keru shouted, and T'Lirin, Sortollo, and Rriarr all grabbed hold of the downed prisoner. They managed to drag him aboard and shut the hatch just as the skimmer came about for another pass.

"Get us out of here, Olivia!" Vale shouted.

"Yes, sir," Bolaji called back, her voice sounding intensely strained.

Vale helped Keru into a seat behind Bolaji, while Sortollo opened a fresh medikit. "Help the Reman," Keru said, wincing. "Just give me a little triptacederin. That ought to hold me until we get back to *Titan*."

As Sortollo and Rriarr began to work on the Reman, Keru looked at Vale. "There was another group down there looking for Tuvok. A Reman group. It looks like they escaped into a tunnel that runs under the prison."

Vale nodded, scowling. "This planet seems to have way too damned many tunnels."

The ship lurched to the side, and Vale and Keru turned toward Bolaji.

"Enemy fire? Is our cloak not working?" Vale asked as she seated herself in the copilot's chair.

"No," Bolaji said weakly. "Something's wrong. The baby is . . ." She trailed off, her skin suddenly ashen, her hand trembling as she pointed downward.

Keru looked down and saw a puddle of clearish liquid pooling beneath Bolaji's chair. It was stained with streamers of crimson.

"Oh, shit!" Vale exclaimed, her fingers tapping at the control panels in front of her. "I'm taking over."

Still waiting for the painkiller he knew wasn't going to come unless he got the hypo himself, Keru hoped that this wasn't a portent of away missions to come. He and Denken were both seriously injured, as was the Reman escapee, whose wounds might very well prove mortal. On top of that, Bolaji was going into premature labor.

And they had failed to bring back the man they had come to rescue. The mission was a failure.

An urgent beeping from a nearby sensor console caught Keru's attention, and elicited a triumphant smile. He read the data he saw there a second time, just to be certain.

"Christine, I may have some good news."

Her concentration intent on the forward window and her instruments, Vale replied without turning around. "It had *better* be good news."

"I've got a fix on Tuvok's location," Keru said as still more data appeared on the console. "And I've just picked up a *second* Vulcan biosignature."

He also noted that both life signs now seemed to have

moved beyond the reach of both Vikr'l Prison's transporter scramblers and the troublesome underground deposits of refractory metals that had intermittently thwarted their sensors up until now. Forgetting his own injuries, Keru allowed himself a broad grin as he began entering commands into the panel before him as swiftly as he could.

Chapter Eighteen

ROMULUS

The Remans moved swiftly through the darkened tunnels, relying mostly, no doubt, on their finely honed nocturnal senses. Tuvok was glad that two of them were carrying him between them. Had they forced him to run alongside them, he no doubt would have tripped repeatedly, smashing into the rocky ground and likely breaking his malnourished and probably brittle bones.

Because the passageways were nearly pitch black, Tuvok found the sense of rapid forward movement disconcerting. The loud, rhythmic susurration the Remans made as they breathed and ran in the darkness might have frightened most sentient beings, but Tuvok had conquered his fear of the dark when he was a mere child of nine. He had run away from his home after the death of his pet *sehlat,* which had precipitated a disagreement with his parents over whether or not pets possessed a *katra.* Embarking on the *tal'oth* survival ritual—the four-month version of the more modest, seven-day rite of passage called the *kahs-wan*—he had faced many of his childhood fears while crossing the searing desert known as Vulcan's Forge before returning home.

Now, he didn't know where the Remans were taking him, and his body was still jangled from the explosion at the prison. Logically, his abductors seemed to mean him no harm. He didn't know if he was the only one they had extracted from Vikr'l, but the Remans seemed to have come specifically for him. Even now, they were fleeing farther and farther away from the Romulan guards who had by now probably begun taking Vikr'l back from its rioting inmates.

Time seemed to pass with immeasurable sluggishness, although Tuvok knew that only minutes had elapsed since his capture. He wondered what had become of the Starfleet officers who had come to rescue him. He still clutched the communicator badge that one of them had thrown to him. He couldn't risk using it now—there was no guarantee that he would reach anyone capable of beaming him out of the tunnels he knew often contained sensor-obscuring ores—but he found its presence comforting nonetheless. Other than his memories and dreams, the transceiver was the only reminder of who he had been prior to his seemingly interminable incarceration in the hellish Vikr'l Prison.

Suddenly, Tuvok noticed light emanating from the rough-hewn tunnel walls, and he heard a Reman voice shouting from somewhere farther ahead. Another Reman voice, even farther away, echoed toward them. Unlike the deep, gravel-filled voices the Remans used in ordinary conversation, these vocalizations were piercing, echoing shrieks that reminded Tuvok of the mating calls of Tiberian bats.

Soon, Tuvok found himself inside a wide, high-ceilinged stone chamber that appeared to have been scooped out of the surrounding rock by one of the angry deities of ancient Vulcan mythology. The rocky cavity was dimly illuminated by glowsticks mounted in the rugged walls. Perhaps a dozen Remans were there awaiting their arrival, and Tuvok realized that the cave was some kind of assembly room.

"You are the one called Rukath?" The voice was harsh and low, clearly Reman.

Tuvok turned, trying to figure out which of the shadowy figures had spoken. "Yes," he said simply.

"And yet you are not Romulan," a large, dusky-hued Reman said, stepping forward. Tuvok saw that his clothing was not that of an escaped prisoner. Like several of the others who stood nearby, he wore a gray-armored military uniform. Though battered, the uniform suited his ramrod-straight bearing. "You are Vulcan."

Tuvok wondered how the man knew this, but remained silent.

The Reman approached him closely enough for Tuvok to feel the steam of his exhalations into the cavern's chill air. "You need not confirm this fact," he said, then gestured as another Reman stepped forward. "My brother, Duwrikek, sensed this about you while you were imprisoned together."

Tuvok recognized the raggedly dressed Reman male, Duwrikek, as one of those whom Mekrikuk had allowed to accompany them in their bid to escape. Apparently, Tuvok wasn't the only prisoner these people had extricated from Vikr'l after the explosion.

"Did you rescue anyone else from the room where you found me?" he asked.

"No," Duwrikek said. "Many were injured or killed.

Trying to move them would have slowed us down too much."

Shuddering inwardly at the Reman's pragmatic coldness, Tuvok tried to reconstruct exactly how his current circumstances must have come about. Somehow, Duwrikek and his brother had communicated while one of them was incarcerated. The pair probably shared a stronger mental link than did most Remans, and thus had been able to connect even though they were separated by a considerable distance. But how had the Reman leader known where and when to send his troops? The logic eluded him. No matter how tough and determined the Remans might be, it was difficult to believe that they could have penetrated a maximum security prison near the Romulan capital without help from someone on the ground.

"Who are you?" Tuvok asked the Reman. "And how did you know to find me?"

Squaring his shoulders, the Reman seemed to grow even taller. "I am Colonel Xiomek, commander of the Reman Kepeszuk Battalion. And you, Vulcan-turned-Romulan, are of little importance to me. However, your presence seems to matter a great deal to the one who now offers hope to my people."

Hearing a shuffling sound coming from the other side of the cavern, Tuvok turned his attention away from Xiomek. Given what the Reman had just said, he wasn't overly surprised to see the white-robed, craggy-faced older Vulcan entering, surrounded by his small coterie of armed Romulan confederates and bodyguards.

"Ambassador Spock," Tuvok said with a respectful nod. "It would appear that I owe you a debt of thanks."

Spock took several steps closer. He stopped, then raised his right eyebrow as he cast an appraising eye on

Tuvok. Seeming more interested in Tuvok's condition than in receiving his gratitude, he said, "The time you spent in Vikr'l has done you ill, Rukath. Or should I say, Commander Tuvok?"

Tuvok nodded. He could see no point in trying to maintain a Romulan cover identity that had obviously failed to stand up to telepathic scrutiny. "It has been a most trying time for me." He still wasn't certain precisely how long he had been detained, but information gleaned from the prison computers just prior to opening the gates had led him to believe that his confinement had lasted more than sixty standard days.

"No doubt you are wondering about the purpose of this meeting," Spock said. He gestured to his Romulan followers, then to Xiomek. "After all, the goal of my mission of Unification is to bring the Romulan and Vulcan peoples together."

"I assume that you see the chaos that would surely result from a Romulan-Reman civil war as antithetical to Unification," Tuvok said.

"Indeed. It would be greatly distracting, to say the least."

Tuvok almost winced at the seeming impertinence of the ambassador's remark. Then he heard Xiomek and the other Remans chuckling in apparent approval of what they evidently considered Spock's droll humor.

Tuvok immediately revised his opinion of Spock's manner. *He knows how to speak to these people in a way they understand,* he thought. *Diplomacy is clearly best left to those with the skill and temperament to carry it out.*

"I must further assume that you have found some common ground among all three races," Tuvok said aloud. He wasn't certain what that commonality was, but if anyone could negotiate peace between the Romulans and the Re-

mans, on his way to unifying Romulus and Vulcan, it was
Spock.

"Two standard months ago, I told you that the tensions
between the Romulan Senate and the military factions
were swiftly headed toward a breaking point," Spock said.
"None of us could have guessed how swiftly the crisis
would come to a head, nor what the ramifications of Shinzon's actions would be.

"While you were incarcerated, the Romulan Star Empire was brought to the very brink of ruin. Although logic
dictated that the Unification movement would stand little
chance of success in the current climate of political up-
heaval, I have attracted more followers to my cause than
ever before. And not solely from the obvious sources."

He paused for a moment, steepling his fingers before
him. "I have come to realize the value of brokering rap-
prochement and peace with the Remans. The Federation
seeks peace only with whoever controls the Romulan Star
Empire's levers of power; but it has underestimated the
will of those within the Empire who believe that the established power structure on Romulus has reached the end of
its useful life."

"Surely you realize that whoever currently controls Ki
Baratan's political and military hierarchies will never step
aside voluntarily," Tuvok said.

A look akin to sadness played across Spock's eyes.
"Yes."

Tuvok felt a deathly chill slowly ascend the length of
his spine. "It sounds as though you are working with the
Remans to engineer an outright armed rebellion. Have you
been away from Vulcan so long that you have forgotten the
teachings of Surak?"

Spock gestured toward Colonel Xiomek. "The Remans
have not moved against the Empire, although I can assure

you they have the capability of doing so. Were that to occur, the fires of violence that still burn within the Romulan heart might be stoked beyond anyone's ability to bank them again."

And what would become of your life's work then? Tuvok thought, nodding. "I see," he said aloud.

"I am attempting to show the Reman leadership the need to curb their people's desire for revenge, and to seek other methods of redress and social change," Spock continued. "They may even have a better affinity for pure logic than that of our Romulan cousins—at least, those who reject out of hand the path of Unification."

Though his respect for Spock's accomplishments and expertise remained vast, Tuvok could not deny his growing sensation of foreboding. "You cannot be unaware of the dangers inherent in trying to engineer even a nonviolent revolution," Tuvok said, turning the cool communicator over and over in his left hand. "If you were to cause a civil war here, however inadvertently, your name would be—"

"Reviled forever," Spock said brusquely, interrupting. "My reputation matters little when placed in the balance against the cause of Vulcan-Romulan Unification."

The needs of the many outweigh the needs of the few, Tuvok thought, recalling an aphorism from Surak's *Analects.* "But are you really willing to risk engendering further violence—merely to advance the uncertain end of Unification?"

Spock paused, staring pensively off into the darkness. He seemed about to answer when Tuvok noticed a rippling shimmer begin to gather in the air around the aging diplomat. A millisecond later, he saw it appear around himself as well, and felt the familiar, momentarily vertiginous tug of a transporter beam.

The rocky cavern walls and shocked faces of the Remans and Unificationist Romulans were replaced by the smooth and comparatively sterile interior of a Starfleet shuttlecraft. Tuvok found himself standing on a narrow transporter pad, alongside Spock, whose surprise was being expressed entirely through his right eyebrow. Turning, Tuvok then saw a bearded Trill who was clad in a battered black utilitarian suit, no doubt designed for stealth operations. He wasn't sure whether or not he had seen the man before. *Commander Keru?*

The Trill favored Tuvok with a grim smile as he swiped his hand downward over the transporter controls on the console beside him.

As he dematerialized yet again, Tuvok couldn't help but wonder what effect Spock's unplanned departure from the caverns beneath Romulus would have on his supporters.

Chapter Nineteen

The shimmering curtain of light released him, and Tuvok found himself standing beside a moderately surprised-looking Spock on a much wider Federation transporter stage than the one the shuttlecraft had carried. He presumed that they were now aboard the very starship from which the shuttlecraft had originated.

"Lieutenant Radowski to bridge," said the young male human Starfleet officer who stood behind the transporter room's sleek control console.

"Go ahead, Lieutenant," replied the resonant, businesslike voice that issued from the junior officer's combadge.

"They're both on board, Captain."

"Good work. I'm on my way."

The next moment, the doors whisked open to admit a pair of armed personnel who were obviously security guards. Seeing their hard stares, Tuvok remained where he was on the transporter stage. He was mildly surprised to see Spock step off the stage and onto the deck.

"Please remain where you are, sir," one of the guards said.

Spock obediently stopped, though his craggy features betrayed determination rather than fear.

Less than a minute later, a tall, bearded Starfleet officer followed the armed personnel into the chamber, accompanied by a petite, dark-haired humanoid woman. Tuvok recognized them both immediately. So, too, apparently, did Spock.

"Captain Riker," Spock said. "Commander Troi."

"Ambassador Spock," Riker replied, nodding to the security guards. They both remained attentive, though their demeanor relaxed from vigilant suspicion to an obvious dawning awareness of the ambassador's identity.

Riker and Troi turned toward Tuvok, who decided that the ideal moment to introduce himself had arrived. "Commander Tuvok, currently on detached duty with Starfleet Intelligence. Permission to come aboard, Captain?" Tuvok allowed himself to be pleased by his discovery that he had not been so weakened by his prison ordeal as to have entirely forgotten Starfleet protocols.

"Granted," Riker said. "Welcome aboard *Titan*."

Tuvok replied by moving down from the stage to stand beside Spock. Tuvok realized only then that the ambassador had pointedly *not* asked anyone's permission before he had stepped down onto the deck.

"I must confess to some surprise at your presence here, Captain," Spock said, fixing his gaze squarely upon Riker. "Your arrival has greatly complicated my work on Romulus. I must return to the Remans quickly if I am to finish dissuading them from their war plans."

"You're welcome," Riker said with an ironic shake of his head. "Excuse me, Mr. Ambassador, but I was under the impression that we just *rescued* you."

" 'Rescue' from the company of an ally and negotiating partner is hardly necessary, Captain," Spock said dryly.

Mention of the word "rescue" had a bracing effect on Tuvok's fatigued mind. "Captain, regarding Mekrikuk—the Reman who was helping me escape when your rescue team reached me—do you know if he managed to escape as well?"

Riker nodded. "He's suffered some pretty serious injuries. My chief of security has already beamed him directly to our sickbay, along with our shuttle pilot and one of our security officers. But my chief medical officer is confident that they'll both pull through."

"I am gratified to hear that, Captain. I would almost certainly have died in that prison if not for Mekrikuk."

"I see. Dr. Ree will do everything he can." The captain looked Tuvok up and down, obviously taking in his distressed, bloodied clothing. Tuvok supposed that Riker was also inventorying his many visible scrapes, cuts, and bruises—to say nothing of the forehead surgery he had obviously undergone in order to pass unnoticed among the Romulans. "I want you to report to sickbay, too, Commander Tuvok."

Though he was inclined to argue that his injuries weren't that severe, Tuvok merely nodded silently.

The transporter room door slid open once again. Yet another Starfleet officer entered the room, ducking because the doorway had not been designed to accommodate his atypical height. Although Tuvok had not seen the silver-haired Capellan in decades, he recognized him immediately—and felt a surprising rush of pleasure at his presence, in spite of what had passed between them some thirty years ago. Silently cursing the extent to which his lengthy prison ordeal had obviously compromised his emotional control, Tuvok carefully schooled his features into an unreadable mask.

"Admiral," Tuvok said after glancing at the pips on the other man's collar. When had Akaar been promoted to *fleet* admiral? "You are looking well."

A grin slowly spread across Akaar's lined face. "But you have certainly looked better, my old friend. I am pleased to see you, Tuvok. I had begun to fear that the Empire's current upheavals had proved to be your undoing."

"As had I, Admiral," Tuvok said, his voice hoarse, his throat suddenly feeling as dry as Vulcan's Forge. He was grateful that the admiral had the sensitivity not to try to touch him.

"We both should have known better," Akaar said, no doubt remembering more carefree times, when they had first served together aboard the *Excelsior.*

But the moment quickly passed, and Akaar turned his attention elsewhere. "Ambassador Spock."

Something perilously close to a human smile touched the ambassador's lips. " 'Spock' will be sufficient, Admiral."

"Spock," the admiral repeated, the single syllable sounding almost awkward. "I am pleased, also, that you are unharmed."

"While I, too, am gratified to see you again, Admiral, now is not the best time for reunions. I must return to the Remans immediately, so that I may prevent a likely war and return to the task of reuniting the Vulcan and Romulan peoples."

Tuvok thought that Spock had made a good point. Perhaps now was not the best time to have summarily yanked the ambassador away from his emotionally volatile Reman allies. Would his sudden disappearance cause them to panic and take some precipitous action? Knowing what he did about the ships and weaponry the Remans had quietly accumulated during the Dominion War, he believed that they could cause a good deal of damage if given sufficient reason.

Tuvok noticed that Akaar's already solemn expression had subtly shifted toward outright grimness as he responded to the ambassador's request. "I regret that I cannot do that, Ambassador. At least not yet. We have pressing matters to discuss first." Akaar then turned to address Captain Riker. "And the transporter room is a less-than-ideal place to do that, Captain."

"Of course," Riker said. Turning his gaze toward Spock, he added, "Ambassador, Admiral, please accompany me and Commander Troi to my ready room." To Tuvok, he said, "Commander Tuvok, I'll have one of my people escort you to sickbay."

Tuvok quietly shook his head, displaying what he hoped Riker would take as persuasive determination. "I believe that can wait, Captain. As Admiral Akaar has said, we have pressing matters to discuss first."

Striding forward in silence, Riker led Deanna, Admiral Akaar, Ambassador Spock, and Commander Tuvok— whom he had included in the meeting at the insistence of both Vulcans—across the bridge and into his ready room.

Akaar was the first to take a seat, settling on a tall chair that was situated directly in front of the captain's desk. His eyes firmly fixed on Spock, the admiral made a simple, blunt declaration. "Ambassador Spock, the Federation Council has decided to formally withdraw all of its covert support for your Unification movement, effective stardate 57088.8. I am sorry."

That's only about a month from now, Riker thought.

But Akaar wasn't finished. "The council also requests, and requires, that you cease your activities here and return to the Federation for debriefing."

Trying to conceal his surprise at these revelations, Riker took a seat behind his desk as Deanna sat on a couch beside Tuvok, who was still clad in the distressed Romulan civilian clothing he'd been wearing at the time of his rescue. Though the bruised and battered Tuvok was clearly in need of medical attention, he was just as obviously determined to take in this meeting first.

Ignoring the seat he'd been offered, Spock remained standing, his expression impassive and all but imperturbable. He turned away from Riker's desk to face Akaar.

"I already know," Spock said, betraying no trace of emotion.

For the first time that Riker could recall, Akaar looked genuinely surprised. "You *know?*"

Spock seemed almost to enjoy the admiral's momentary discomfiture. "I have my resources. The council, it would seem, perceives my work here to be a potential impediment to its own peace efforts. And perhaps even a danger."

Akaar merely stared silently at Spock without denying his assertion.

Riker glanced at Deanna, who was shifting uncomfortably next to Tuvok; he'd known her long enough to see that she was reacting to someone's particularly strong emotional spike.

"Admiral, I came to Romulus to *request* Ambassador Spock's *temporary* return to Earth," Tuvok said. Though he spoke quietly, Riker could see from the set of Tuvok's jaw that he was the source of Deanna's distress. "However, I was told beforehand that Unification had the council's full support. When did the council reverse itself?"

"The initiative began the day the council learned of the assassination of the Romulan Senate," Akaar explained.

"The day the Romulans took me prisoner," Tuvok said, apparently staring off into some horrible memory hole. Recalling his own recent maltreatment as a prisoner of war on Tezwa, Riker shuddered involuntarily.

Grave-faced, Akaar nodded to Tuvok. "Much changed that day. The formal decision to order Spock's return came later, after several weeks of . . . spirited closed-door debate. I am sure I need not remind anyone here how profoundly and quickly the fall of the Senate changed the Federation's relationship with the Romulan Star Empire."

"Indeed," said Spock. "But I trust that the council's decision does not comport with the wishes of President Bacco."

"It does not. But the Federation president is not an autocrat. She can be overruled by the council. Perhaps if you had been present on Earth weeks ago for the meetings you had scheduled with the president and the security council, the outcome of the council's deliberations might have been different."

"I might have come to Earth per those plans, had I believed the council to be persuadable. And had the post-Shinzon Romulan-Reman political landscape left the Unification movement in less desperate need of my direct guidance."

Riker wondered briefly why the ambassador hadn't had any official communication with anyone in the Federation for more than seven weeks, his disagreements with the council notwithstanding. Then he decided that Spock, who had somehow maintained a subterranean existence on Romulus through four praetorships and the assassination of an emperor, knew better than anyone when it wasn't safe to put one's head up.

"We're here to help calm down the political landscape, Mr. Ambassador," Riker said. "By doing everything we can to build an understanding between all the competing Romulan and Reman factions."

His right eyebrow rising, Spock looked toward Riker. "Curious, Captain. The Federation Council decides to cease supporting Unification, the one political movement on Romulus that holds the greatest hope of achieving lasting peace. Then, in place of that support, it sends a flotilla of armed ships."

Riker shook his head. "Ambassador, this is a relief convoy. Not an attack wing."

"And we are operating our 'flotilla' out in the open," Akaar pointed out, "rather than continuing a program to covertly run supplies to what can only be described as an illegal dissident group."

"Indeed," Spock said, nodding and steepling his fingers before him. "However, the distinction you have drawn might be too subtle for either the Romulan or Reman eye."

"I think you may be selling these people short, Mr. Ambassador," Deanna said. "Particularly the Romulans."

"Not at all, Commander Troi. In fact, I believe I understand Romulan psychology far better than anyone else here. Paranoia is etched deeply into their culture and character. Why else would the large star map that adorns the floor of the Romulan Senate make such a prominent display of the Neutral Zone, the symbol of everything that either inhibits or threatens the Romulan Empire?"

Riker watched Deanna silently concede the point, and had to admit himself that Spock's observation made sense.

He couldn't help but wonder if the Federation Council, for all its good intentions, might not have taken this component of Romulan psychology sufficiently into account.

Spock turned to address Riker. "Colonel Xiomek tells me that your convoy appears to consist of four Starfleet vessels, accompanied by three heavily armed Klingon warships."

"That's correct," Riker said.

"And *Titan* is one of Starfleet's twelve new *Luna*-class vessels, is she not?"

"Right again, Mr. Ambassador." Riker wondered how the ambassador was able to stay so up to date on such relatively recent developments within Starfleet. Of course, he could have learned a great deal about the *Luna*-class starships being developed at Utopia Planitia during his most recent visit to Earth two years earlier.

"Which means," Spock continued, "that *Titan* is hardly unarmed herself."

Riker's brow crumpled involuntarily into a frown. "If you're aware of the *Luna* program, then you know that its purpose isn't to wage war."

"I understand, Captain. Just as I understand that good intentions are necessary but insufficient requirements for success here."

"The Federation cannot simply stand by and do *nothing,* Mr. Ambassador," Akaar said. "Nor can the Klingon Empire, for that matter. You know as well as I do that billions of deaths could result from the sudden collapse of the Romulan Empire, and the accompanying unconstrained spread of its weapons technologies across two quadrants."

Spock's eyes narrowed. "I have never been more keenly aware of anything in my life, Admiral. This is a proud but gravely wounded empire. One that is arguably more susceptible to provocation now than at any other time since the Vulcan and Romulan peoples became sundered from one other. And both Romulus and Remus are all but certain to experience a mutual bloodbath unless they fundamentally reorient their social priorities."

"And you offer a cultural reunification with Vulcan as the solution to the Empire's woes," Akaar said.

"Given the Empire's current vulnerabilities, Unification—tempering the Empire's ingrained violence with the discipline of Vulcan logic—could well be the last viable chance for peace. It may be the only way to guarantee a secure future for both the Romulan and Reman peoples." He paused before adding, "And it may bring Vulcan a step closer to becoming truly whole."

Riker couldn't help but admire Spock's idealism. But he also had the real world to consider, as well as the immediate future. "You could be right, Mr. Ambassador. History might even prove that someday. But we don't have the luxury of hindsight right now. We have to worry first about the short-term survival of billions of people. Unification is just too long-term a goal and too lengthy a process to provide the kind of immediate stability the Romulan Empire needs in the here and now."

Spock nodded somberly. "Your analysis may indeed prove to be the correct one, Captain. Nevertheless, I must caution you: Romulus and Remus are both caught in the grip of fear, one of the more incendiary of the emotions. The presence of a heavily armed outworld contingent such as this convoy could well ignite that fear—thereby bringing about the very societal collapse we all seek to prevent. Imagine for a moment how the Klingons would have reacted to such an intrusion after the Praxis explosion nearly laid waste to Qo'noS."

"But we're not 'intruding,' Mr. Ambassador," Deanna

pointed out. "The Romulan praetor has *requested* our presence here."

"Tal'Aura," Spock said, "is a praetor whose authority is opposed by a strong plurality, if not a clear majority, of the Empire's citizenry. Supporting her is a dangerous gamble."

"We're not supporting *any* particular faction here," Riker said, feeling a surge of pique rising and doing his best to squash it back down. "Our goal is to help them all hammer out a mutually acceptable power-sharing arrangement."

"The Remans have yet to be included in any such discussions," Spock pointed out. "Therefore they might be forgiven for doubting your goodwill. And perhaps that of the Federation Council itself."

Riker felt his own frustration continuing to rise. "We're trying to include *everyone* in the power-sharing talks, Mr. Ambassador."

"That is wise, Captain," Spock said. "Please allow me to assist you by returning to the Remans. Unless, of course, your intention is to arrest me for having failed to respond more promptly to the council's diplomatic recall order."

Riker leaned forward, meeting Spock's gaze squarely. "Mr. Ambassador, my intention has always been to *rescue* you. And then to ask you to return the favor by helping me accomplish a damned difficult peace mission. However, your fate isn't entirely up to me." His questioning gaze lit upon Akaar.

"Conducting unauthorized interstellar policy on behalf of either the Federation or a Federation member world is a serious offense," Akaar said. "Especially after the council has issued a formal order of diplomatic recall."

"Indeed," Spock said. "However, I have . . . resisted

such orders before without suffering any serious consequences."

"That was before Shinzon changed everything," Akaar said. "Certain members of the council are nervous enough to wish to see you in irons, Mr. Ambassador. However loudly Councillor Enaren may sing your praises, both Gleer and zh'Faila continue to characterize your activities as unacceptably dangerous under the current circumstances. Even T'Latrek of Vulcan voted in favor of the recall order."

"I am not surprised," Spock said. "Fear exists in abundance on *both* sides of the Neutral Zone. And fear trumps logic all too often."

"It's too bad the council has no way of knowing for certain whether or not you ever actually *received* the recall order, Mr. Ambassador," Riker said, allowing a slight smile to tug at his lips.

"A logical assessment, Captain," Spock said, then turned to face Akaar. "Am I under arrest, Admiral?"

Akaar mirrored Riker's smile. "I doubt I could trust myself to carry out such an order, Starfleet discipline notwithstanding. I have not forgotten that you and my namesakes saved my life, and that of Eleen who bore me, more than a century ago."

"Then allow me to return to my Reman negotiating partners now," Spock said. "Before they overreact to my sudden departure by—"

An almost shrill voice from Riker's combadge interrupted the ambassador. *"Ensign Lavena to Captain Riker."*

Riker tapped the device on his chest. "Go ahead, Ensign."

"The new sensor nets have just picked up a whole fleet of incoming warships, Captain. Several dozen strong.

They're entering orbit around Romulus. And they're loaded for bear."

"More Romulan military vessels?" Riker asked, rising from his chair.

"Yes, sir. But Jaza's scans say they're crewed by Remans."

Chapter Twenty

Maybe Spock was right after all, Riker thought as he left his ready room just ahead of Deanna, Akaar, Spock, and Tuvok; he bounded through the doors and toward the center of *Titan*'s bridge as the others hastened to follow.

Christine Vale—her short hair still somewhat disheveled after the raid on Vikr'l Prison—was already relinquishing the central command chair, moving toward the seat located on its immediate right. But she remained standing, her small frame fairly vibrating with tension.

"Red alert! Shields up!" Riker shouted as he seated himself in the command chair while Deanna took the seat at his immediate left. "Hail the lead ship, Mr. Keru."

"Shields up. Hailing again, Captain," said the tactical officer. Unlike Vale, he still wore one of the black stealth suits the away team had been issued for the prison rescue operation. His suit was torn, bloodied, and caked with dust: he had obviously spent as little time as was permissible getting patched up in sickbay following the rescue raid.

"We started hailing them right after the sensor web detected their launch from Remus," Vale reported. "Their only response has been to drop their cloaks."

Which means either that they know there's no longer any point to maintaining their cloaks, Riker thought. *Or that they're about to attack Romulus.*

Or both.

Riker leaned forward as he studied the image on the bridge's panoramic central viewscreen. The cloud-streaked blue-brown orb of Romulus stood out in sharp detail, the curving shadow of its terminator temporarily consigning half of the planet—including Ki Baratan—to darkness. Two of the planet's four airless, rocky moons were visible as well, each of them in half phase, poised on the twilight boundary between day and night.

Beyond lay the pockmarked orange hellworld of Remus, which appeared to be only a quarter the size of Romulus because of its relative distance from *Titan.* Though it was co-orbital with Romulus, Remus had an eternally broiling day side as well as a perpetually frozen night side. Less than half the planet's bright side was visible, dominated presently by its ever dark and frozen hemisphere.

Harsh white sunlight glinted off the gray-green hulls of what appeared to be dozens of vessels, which were flying in formation and dropping in a long graceful arc from uninviting Remus toward the cool blue world that *Titan* orbited. The incoming fleet's trajectory confirmed that it had just crossed the shallow gulf of cisplanetary space—a span scarcely larger than the distance between Earth and Luna—that separated Remus and the fleet's obvious target, the surface of Romulus itself.

Vale quickly consulted one of the consoles built into the arm of her chair. "None of these ships are on the cutting edge of Romulan design, Captain. Most of them are *Amarcan*-class warbirds. Some appear to be Klingon cast-offs that might be *K't'inga*-class or even old D-7s. There are even a few horseshoe-crab–shaped birds-of-prey that have to be at least a hundred years old."

"They must be decommissioned ships, then," Riker said, nodding his understanding. "Mothballed long enough ago that the Romulan military wasn't keeping a close enough eye on them during the last few sudden management changes in Ki Baratan."

Vale shrugged. "Maybe so, Captain. But wherever the Reman crews got these ships, they're relatively well armed—and they outnumber us nearly six to one. They're more than a match for us, maybe even with our Klingon escorts."

"They're charging their weapons systems, sir," Keru said, his voice steady, though pitched a bit higher than his customary baritone. "And their shields are going up."

"Alert the rest of the convoy," Vale said to Keru.

"And tell the commanders of the *Phoebus, T'rin'saz,* and the *Der Sonnenaufgang* to get their ships into a higher orbit," Riker added. "They're not equipped for combat, and I want them out of the line of fire."

"Aye, sir," Keru said, already working the companel.

Riker turned toward Vale and noticed then that her gaze had drifted, just for a second, toward a conspicuously blank space on the bulkhead beside the main turbolift. It was the spot they had reserved for *Titan*'s dedication plaque, once the captain and first officer finally agreed on exactly what they wanted to have engraved on it.

"How could the Romulan military lose track of so many warships?" Deanna asked, shaking her head incredulously.

"This kind of thing has happened before," Riker said. "After the Cold War of Earth's twentieth century, a lot of questions were asked about the whereabouts of Russia's Black Sea Fleet, as well as its stockpiles of weapons-grade nuclear material."

"Mr. Keru, any sign of Romulan planetary defenses?" Vale asked, turning toward the aft tactical console.

The large Trill shook his head. "I'm picking up a gabble of planetside communications, Commander. The local defenses are trying to respond, but they seem to be in disarray."

"Just as they probably have been ever since Shinzon's attack on the Senate," Riker said.

Glancing aftward, the captain saw that Akaar was standing silently beside the turbolift, making his stolid presence as unobtrusive as a man his size possibly could. Ambassador Spock and Commander Tuvok, still clad in the Romulan civilian garb they had been wearing at the time of their rescue, stood flanking him. All three men seemed to be taking conspicuous care not to get in anyone's way. Riker momentarily considered ordering the malnourished-looking Tuvok to report to sickbay, but decided to leave that for later; like Akaar, Spock, and everyone else on the bridge, Tuvok's attention was riveted to the drama that was unfolding on the bridge's central viewscreen.

"The sensor nets are picking up intermittent tachyon emissions," said Jaza, turning from the science console. "They may indicate the presence of other nearby cloaked vessels. And they don't match the tachyon profile of General Khegh's warships."

"So whose ships are they?" asked Vale, who was still standing before her chair as she studied the main viewscreen.

"They're apparently Romulan," Keru said.

"More Remans?" Deanna said.

Riker shook his head. "I'd bet real money that they have Romulan crews." He felt certain that Commanders Donatra and Suran wouldn't have left the Romulan capital so utterly open to a Reman sneak attack, which they surely must have suspected was coming. *But they might not have been able to post a large force—either because of dissension within their own military hierarchy, or out of fear of provoking Tal'Aura, Durjik's hard-liners, or even the Tal Shiar.*

Ambassador Spock stepped down into the center of the bridge, simultaneously facing Riker, Vale, and Deanna. "Captain, you see before you an eloquent argument in favor of returning me to the Reman leadership. Immediately."

Riker sighed. "You may be right, Mr. Ambassador. Unfortunately, I'm afraid the opportunity to do that may already have passed." Spock treated him to a withering glare as the captain moved up to the upper portion of the bridge, passing Akaar and Tuvok as he crossed to the tactical station.

"Any response yet from the Remans?" Riker asked Keru.

"No, sir. I'm continuing to hail."

"And there's still no definitive evidence that the Romulan military is intact enough to mount an effective defense," Vale pointed out. "The Remans have a lot of ships, and there are a hell of a lot of soft targets down there." She was still standing, bouncing slightly on the balls of her feet. Once again, Riker noticed that her gaze lit fleetingly on the missing dedication plaque.

Looking toward the screen that displayed the approaching Reman fleet, Riker said, "Mr. Keru, get me General Khegh."

A moment later, the image of Romulus and the Remanoperated flotilla that threatened it shrank and withdrew to the upper left quadrant of the screen. The rest of the image area was now dominated by the ruddy illumination of the *Vaj*'s crowded bridge; in the foreground was the grinning, jagged-toothed face of the commander of the local Klingon forces.

"This is an exhilarating spectacle, Captain Riker, is it not?" Khegh said, punctuating his observation with a coarse guffaw.

"That wouldn't quite be how I'd describe it, General," Riker said, standing before his command chair. "You've received my tactical officer's alert. You know that the Remans are in control of those incoming vessels, and that the Romulans might not be able to defend themselves from them. We can't just sit by while Romulus is decimated."

"Captain, my government didn't send me here to fight on behalf of honorless Romulan petaQ," Khegh growled. *"We are here, in large part, at the request of our Reman allies—not their former slavemasters."*

"Damn it, General, the Klingon Empire hasn't abandoned its Dominion War alliance with the Romulans, and you know it."

Khegh pursed his lips as his rheumy eyes narrowed in anger. *"True, Captain. But I will shed no Reman blood this day."*

Riker tried to reign in his own escalating irritation with the Klingon, without complete success. "Then I'd appreciate it if you'd give the Romulans the same consideration. Please don't do anything to help the Remans attack Romulus, General."

Khegh bared two rows of discolored, highly asymmetrical teeth. But he was not smiling. *"I will take your request under advisement, Captain,"* he said before abruptly vanishing. On the screen, nearly forty Reman-crewed vessels entered the troposphere of Romulus. Rarefied gases began to ionize against their hulls, each ship creating a spectacular orange streak over the planet's night side that resembled a meteor burning up during its terminal descent.

Riker had a sickening feeling that Romulus and Remus both were about to witness a great deal more fire and burning. *"Ghuy'cha',"* he whispered, repeating one of the first of the many colorful Klingon curses he had learned over the years.

He knew that brute force wasn't going to work here. What he needed instead was a diplomatic solution. He had one of the Federation's most celebrated diplomats at his disposal. But there seemed to be no safe way to deliver him to where he was needed most: the immediate presence of the Reman leadership.

"What are you planning to do, Captain?" Akaar rumbled.

Riker exchanged a significant glance with Vale, then turned to look into Deanna's eyes. He knew that they both supported his unspoken decision, and understood that he couldn't stand by idly while Reman slaughtered Romulan wholesale. He might be forced to fire *Titan*'s weapons, even though this was ostensibly a mission of peace. *Hell, I have to do something to stop this,* because *this is a mission of peace.*

He turned to face the admiral's cool stare, though his words were for his conn officer. "Ensign Lavena, prepare to change our heading. Intercept the lead Reman vessel."

"Aye, Captain," the Pacifican said, her nervousness plain even through the slight muffling caused by her hydration suit's rebreather unit.

"I'm finally getting a response from the Remans, Captain," Keru said, sounding both excited and apprehensive. "The transmission appears to be coming from the lead vessel."

"On screen, please," Riker said, putting on his best poker face.

The hard visage of a Reman warrior appeared on the screen. Though the illumination in the Reman-occupied warship was dim, Riker could see that the other man's skin was as pale as the snows of Mount Denali.

The Reman's voice sounded like a slow rockslide, and was as deep and cold as an Alaskan glacier. *"Federation vessel. Do not attempt to interfere with us. You will not be warned again."*

"This is Captain William Riker of the Federation starship *Titan*. Please identify yourself."

When he spoke, the Reman's lips parted, displaying a proliferation of sharp, serrated teeth. *"I am Xiomek, colonel of the Kepeszuk Battalion and commander of all the Reman Irregulars. I speak now as the voice of the Reman people."*

That's pretty convenient for me, if it's true, Riker thought, recalling Spock and Tuvok having mentioned Colonel Xiomek during their brief walk from the transporter room to the ready room. Spock had explained that Reman military and civilian leaders were really one and the same, and that they had a fairly quick turnover because of their refusal to conduct warfare from the rear. Spock had explained his belief that Xiomek wielded serious influence over his people, and Riker was therefore inclined to believe it—especially now that Xiomek had shown himself to be in charge of what was probably every piece of ordnance the Remans had at their disposal.

"And I speak on behalf of the United Federation of

Planets," Riker said. "I am here on an errand of peace. Please break off your attack."

Xiomek tipped his head in apparent confusion. *"We have made no attack as yet, Riker. And whether or not such an attack occurs is entirely up to the Romulan praetor, to whom we have just issued our demand."*

Riker pondered the fact that Xiomek had not, in fact, begun firing on any targets on the ground, at least not yet. *It must mean he hasn't gotten wind of that first diplomatic meeting that Tal'Aura kept him out of,* he thought. *At least, not yet.*

Aloud, he said, "And what is it you've demanded, Colonel?"

"We want Ehrie'fvil."

"Come again?" Riker glanced quickly at Deanna and Christine, both of whom shrugged.

Then Riker saw Xiomek and Spock nod silently to one another by way of greeting. Deanna glanced significantly at Riker, as if to confirm the two men's already apparent mutual respect.

Spock turned to face Riker. "Ehrie'fvil is the name of a small, all but uninhabited continent located in Romulus's southern hemisphere," he said with the quiet confidence of an academic authority. "It is roughly the same size as Earth's Greenland, and possesses similar climatological characteristics."

Facing the Vulcan ambassador, Riker said, "He's asking for a whole continent?"

"This isn't the first time the matter has come up. Neither crops nor animals can flourish in the harsh, dry, tide-locked climate of Remus. This has made the Remans dependent upon those who have enslaved them for centuries. It is no surprise that such an unbalanced relationship would give the people of Remus cause to covet the abundance of their planet's companion world. However, the Remans have never before attempted to seize Romulan lands using the direct threat of military force."

"We have been confined to Remus, and to the darkness of the dilithium mines, for as far back as our history records," Xiomek said. *"There we have provided all the toil necessary to power the fleets of the Empire. No more. No more will we be forced to dwell in lands blighted by the Empire's insatiable greed."*

Facing Xiomek again, Riker said, "You are in a position to do a great deal more than seize land, Colonel. How do we know your people won't also exact revenge against the Romulan people you've been laboring for all these centuries?"

Xiomek bared his fangs again in what might or might not have been a smile. *"You do not know that, for I can make no such guarantee. But you have no choice other than to accept my words at face value. As well as my assurance that this man"*—the Reman colonel pointed a long-nailed, gnarled finger directly at Ambassador Spock—*"has already made every effort to dissuade us from engaging in unnecessary bloodshed.*

"I, however, will decide how much bloodshed is necessary, Captain—based upon whether or not you or anyone else attempts to stop us from claiming the land and water and air that should have been ours long ago."

In response to a glance from Deanna, Riker gestured to Keru, who momentarily interrupted the audio portion of his exchange with Xiomek. The Reman colonel continued to glower silently at the bridge crew from the main viewscreen.

"I sense that Xiomek is being sincere, Captain," Deanna said.

"And I can confirm that about half the Reman ships are headed directly for Ehrie'fvil," said Keru. "The rest of them are leveling out their descent."

"Heading?" asked Vale.

"They're remaining in the upper atmosphere, and appear to be heading for positions over major cities all around the planet."

"So they're daring us to follow them down there for close-quarters combat," Riker said.

"Or warning us not to," Deanna said.

"We're not built for that, Captain," said Vale, looking slightly worried.

Riker nodded. Like most starships, *Titan* had not been designed for flight within a planetary atmosphere, let alone for atmospheric combat.

"And there's no way we can engage the Remans without inflicting a lot of harm on the innocent civilians down below," Deanna added.

Vale sighed. "We just have to hope that there are enough cloaked Romulan ships nearby to encourage Xiomek's fleet to back off quickly."

Riker looked toward Jaza, who was shaking his head. "I'm afraid there's no way to know for sure, Captain. Our enhanced sensor nets notwithstanding."

Riker gave another hand signal to Keru, who reactivated the viewer's audio pickup. "What are your terms?" he asked the Reman. He hated feeling so helpless, but he knew he had little choice.

"*If we encounter resistance, we shall bombard the cities of Romulus. And I promise that Ki Baratan, the praetor's pride, will be one of our prime targets in that event.*"

Spock stepped forward. "But you *will* encounter resistance, Xiomek. Surely you must realize that. This is

Romulus. And the people you seek to intimidate are *Romulans.*"

As if cued by the ambassador, Jaza spoke up, an edge of real fear audible in his usually serene voice. "Captain, four *D'deridex*-class warbirds and three more *Mogai*-class vessels are decloaking over the northern continent. They're charging weapons and closing with the Reman-crewed vessels located nearest to Ki Baratan."

Lovely, Riker thought, struggling to keep his shoulders from sagging under the oppressive weight of near-despair. *We haven't even had our first full peace conference yet, and we're already spiraling down into all-out war.*

But he saw that Xiomek had lapsed into what Riker thought—or at least fervently hoped—was a thoughtful silence. The colonel had obviously heard Jaza's report, and the Reman's own bridge crew had no doubt informed him, perhaps telepathically, of the new tactical situation.

"*We* will *engage the Romulans, Ambassador, if our former masters force our hand,*" Xiomek said, his dark, hooded eyes now fixed squarely upon Spock. "*But we will agree to delay our bombardment of their cities for four* veraku—*provided no one attacks us. The praetor and the Romulan military have that long to cede Ehrie'fvil to us completely, or else Romulan blood will flow like the waters of the Apnex Sea.*"

Along with how much of your own people's blood, Xiomek? Riker thought ruefully before fixing Spock with a questioning glance.

"Four *veraku* is approximately four point one eight of your hours, Captain," Spock said in response to Riker's unspoken question.

"*You must excuse me, Captain,*" Xiomek said, his fangs actually seeming to lengthen as he spoke. "*It appears that I am about to become rather busy.*" And with that, his chalk-white image disappeared from the central portion of the screen, which switched to a broad view of the graceful curve of Romulus's night side, whose surface was illuminated by the lights of scores of cities and towns. Riker had no doubt that lightninglike traceries of disruptor beams and torpedo detonations would soon overwhelm those distant hearth fires, abruptly turning much of the planet's night side into day.

"A single *Mogai*-class warbird has just moved to intercept Xiomek's attack wing in the upper atmosphere," Keru reported, studying his tactical console. He looked up at Riker. "It's the *Valdore,* Captain."

"Donatra's ship," Riker said, noting on the tactical display that this particular impending battle was the one that lay closest to *Titan*'s current flight path. *Why haven't the Romulans scrambled more defenses?* he wondered, noting that the planet's orbiting defense platforms remained oddly silent. Had the Remans somehow sabotaged them, or had the rapid descent of their warships into the upper atmosphere rendered them useless?

"The *Valdore* is already effectively surrounded by six *Amarcan*-class warships," Keru said, nodding. "They're smaller and not as well armed as the *Valdore,* but . . ." He trailed off.

But they outnumber her, Riker thought, completing Keru's analysis.

"At least the Klingons are behaving themselves," Ensign Lavena said as she fed some minor course adjustments into the conn station.

For the time being, Riker thought, hoping Khegh would be content to enjoy the shedding of Romulan blood vicariously. *But if things begin to go seriously against the Reman attack force, can we count on the Klingons to stay on the sidelines?*

"True enough, Ensign," Deanna said. "And we can also be thankful that Xiomek hasn't obliterated any Romulan cities yet."

Standing anxiously near her seat, Vale raised both hands, displaying crossed fingers. "Let's hope whatever defenses the Romulans can scramble keep his fleet too busy to try. In the meantime, we have to make a decision: Do we help the Romulans?"

Seated beside Riker, Deanna was silently asking him the very same question. Riker could feel Akaar's gaze boring into his back. He studiously ignored it.

"No," he said, squaring his shoulders and addressing everyone on the bridge. "We came here to broker a peace arrangement. Not to take sides in a civil war." No one argued with him. Turning his head, Riker saw that Akaar and Tuvok were standing by quietly, evidently no better able to see a way out of this developing catastrophe than he was. Spock, however, was quietly scowling at him, as though convinced he could have averted this confrontation if not for *Titan*'s interference.

If not for my *interference,* Riker thought, beginning to wonder if the ambassador might not be right. But he took heart from the fact that Spock was no longer insisting that he be sent back to Xiomek now that the battle had been joined. Even the ambassador seemed to acknowledge that the solution to the current mess now had to come from one man: Captain William T. Riker.

Riker saw then that Vale was once again staring at the blank spot on the aft bulkhead. This time she was pointing toward it as well.

"I told you it was bad luck to leave Utopia Planitia without a dedication plaque," she said, speaking quietly enough so that he doubted anyone else had heard her.

His brow furrowed involuntarily. "No, you didn't."

"Okay," she whispered after a beat. "Then I should have."

Except for the red-alert klaxons, silence reigned on the bridge. Every eye was on the viewscreen, where hell had begun to erupt in the skies over Ki Baratan. Riker was thankful, at least, that the convoy's three aid ships had managed to get themselves out of harm's way, at least for the moment.

"Incoming!" shouted Keru.

The bridge lights flickered as *Titan* shuddered from a sharp, forceful impact.

Commander Donatra's bridge shook violently. Sparks and flame flashed across the oval-shaped chamber as yet another salvo of disruptor fire pummeled the *Valdore*. Ozone and smoke stung her nostrils as electrical fires tested the battered warbird's fire-suppression system to its limits. Her right side ached as old wounds flared back to livid, angry life.

"Forward shields are failing, Commander," cried Centurion T'Relek from the primary tactical station. Two decurions and an antecenturion were sprawled nearby on the deck, dead or dying.

Despite that, Donatra remained encouraged. *They're still merely trying to coerce us into backing off,* she thought. *They haven't strafed the cities yet.*

"Return fire, all tubes!" The bridge rumbled again from yet another direct hit. With shaking hands, the centurion launched another fusillade.

Donatra spun her chair toward the stoic young female decurion who was operating the communications console. "Have our reinforcements responded yet?"

The decurion shook her head gravely. "The Remans

must be jamming us locally, Commander. I can't even tell if our initial message got through to offworld elements of the fleet. Local units seem to be rallying, however."

Donatra silently prayed that this would suffice to drive the Remans off, or at least dissuade them from trying to transform Ki Baratan into a charred crater.

Just before the *Valdore*'s recent communications difficulties began, Donatra had managed to intercept a fascinating subspace exchange between Xiomek and Captain Riker. She knew of the outrageous demand Xiomek had just made, as well as his threat to immolate the Romulan capital, as well as other cities, within four *veraku* should the Empire fail to accede. She had heard his threat to attack immediately should his own forces be assailed. She wondered if she could afford to take the colonel at his word.

It shouldn't have made any difference either way. She was a Romulan military officer, and her world was in peril. Though she was badly outnumbered, she knew she should engage the enemy now. She wanted nothing more than to put a decisive end to the Reman threat, even if that meant risking everyone under her command, and courting the abrupt destruction of most of Ki Baratan.

But if there is to be any chance of our reinforcements arriving in time to overwhelm these wortu, Donatra thought, *then I may have no choice but to find another way.*

"Withdraw!" she shouted, despising herself. "Get our attack wing clear of jamming range as quickly as possible. We have to raise the reinforcement fleet immediately."

The *Valdore* shuddered in protest for several moments after the flight controller executed her commands. Donatra breathed a silent prayer of thanks to the Gatekeeper of Erebus when the singularity drive finally engaged. The ozone-tainted air gradually cleared, though the atmospheric recirculators whined in protest.

"Damage procedures, all decks!" she shouted into the ship-wide comm channel, then settled heavily back into her scorched command chair. There had been neither the time nor the opportunity to repair the *Valdore* properly after the severe punishment the warbird had received from the *Scimitar,* Shinzon's flagship. Though Colonel Xiomek's weapons were far less potent than Shinzon's, they might very well have reopened some of *Valdore*'s recent war wounds.

Donatra watched the gently curved main viewer, which showed a crescent-shaped Romulus falling rapidly away into the infinite night. No pursuit was in evidence.

Donatra was both relieved and heartsick. *Does this mean that Xiomek is too preoccupied with carrying out his threat to destroy Romulus to go after me?*

She forced such thoughts from her mind. There was very important work to be done, and she needed to focus all her attention on it.

"Resume trying to raise our reinforcements," Donatra ordered, after dispatching the remaining three ships of her attack wing to a high polar orbit over Romulus. The *Valdore* was now on a different course, heading unescorted back toward the Great Bloom, the last known position of the reinforcement fleet that Donatra had left in Suran's care.

"Immediately, Commander," said the decurion at the communications post.

Once again, the *Valdore* received no response. Everyone on the bridge listened intently to the static-laced silence, which seemed to last for at least half a *verak*.

Then, abruptly: "Commander!" The tactical officer

began pointing animatedly at the central viewer, where another vessel was decloaking.

"Alert status!" Donatra said, rising. The old burns on her leg and torso rudely reminded her of their presence yet again.

A split second later, she recognized Suran's flagship as it became visible in the empty space before the *Valdore*.

"Helm, match our velocities. Hail them."

Relief warred with apprehension within Donatra's breast. Her old wounds were now itching so fiercely they almost seemed to burn. *Where is the rest of the fleet?*

Suran's face appeared on the main viewer. He looked haunted, his sunken eyes resembling frightened animals engaged in a desperate search for some means of escape.

"Suran. What is the status of our reinforcements?"

He stared at her in silence, his face contorting into an angry, accusatory expression. *"You should have listened to me, Donatra, when I warned you not to entrust our fleet to the Great Bloom."*

Donatra felt her patience with her emotionally volatile colleague beginning to wane. When she spoke, her voice sounded brittle in her own ears. "Suran. Where. Are. Our. Ships?"

"They're gone, *Donatra. As though they had never been."*

She sank backward into her chair as though she had just been slapped. Her heart turned to ice.

Akhh! I have signed my people's death warrant!

Chapter Twenty-one

Riker was both grateful and annoyed that the new command seats came equipped with automatic safety harnesses. Triggered into operation by *Titan*'s momentarily overloaded inertial damping system, the automatic restraints had deployed quickly enough to prevent the violent impact of the first attacker's barrage from throwing him to the deck. But he was not in the habit of allowing himself to be pinned down, especially in the middle of a combat situation.

"Report!" he shouted as he reached for the manual release control, located on the left arm of his chair.

"Shields holding at seventy percent," Keru said from his post at the aft end of the bridge. "Phasers are armed and ready."

Riker knew that under normal circumstances, returning fire would be one of his prime options. But this situation was anything but normal. Old and new Romulan ships— vessels crewed by opposing Remans and Romulans—

were moving quickly to engage one another in the night skies over Romulus. It was difficult to tell the two sides apart, let alone determine with certainty which side had attacked *Titan*.

"Any idea who hit us?" he asked.

"It's not immediately clear," Jaza said, his hands playing over his console. "Both the Romulan and Reman ships are firing at each other. I'm not certain that salvo was even meant for us."

Riker looked to the forward viewscreen, where he saw what must have been several dozen ships engaged in aggression. Angry red disruptor beams ionized the night sky, briefly seeming to entangle one vessel with another in a lethal cat's cradle. "Give us some distance," he said. "Maybe we took fire because we're too close."

As Lieutenant Rager and Ensign Lavena entered course corrections into their respective conn and ops consoles, Riker turned to Vale, who was seated at his right. "Tell the *Phoebus, T'rin'saz,* and the *Der Sonnenaufgang* to withdraw from disruptor range."

"Yes, sir," Vale said, tapping commands into her armrest console. The Starfleet aid ships had already moved to a one-thousand-kilometer orbit over Romulus, but that still wouldn't necessarily keep them entirely out of harm's way if the gunners on either side of the Romulan-Reman conflict decided to target the convoy deliberately.

Riker started to turn toward Tuvok, Spock, and Akaar, intending to ask the admiral to escort both Vulcans down to sickbay, when another blast rocked the ship. A spray of sparks arced out of a conduit above the upper corner of the main viewscreen, which blacked out a moment later. Riker stumbled to one side, thrown against a railing as *Titan*'s inertial dampers kicked in, righting the deck.

"Get that screen back on line," Riker ordered, swallowing a curse. "In the meantime, activate every other available monitor so we can see what's happening out there."

As he moved to the aft end of the bridge, several monitors had already taken up the forward viewscreen's slack.

"Shields down to forty-eight percent, Captain," Keru said. Riker could hear the timbre of concern in his voice.

"The Klingons are moving in toward us, but they're not firing at the Romulans," Jaza said. "They appear to be taking up defensive positions between *Titan* and the skirmish line."

"Circling the wagons," Riker heard Deanna say while he studied one of the tactical displays and considered his options.

He spared a quick glance toward Akaar, Tuvok, and Spock. The expressions on all three faces were inscrutable, but Riker knew they were probably contemplating the same question he was; how to defend the ship without actually engaging in—or escalating—the developing battle. *If the Klingons are holding back,* Riker thought, *then Khegh must have decided that the Romulans have him overmatched, and that today isn't such a good day to die.*

The turbolift doors opened, and a pair of engineers stepped onto the bridge, carrying their tools on a small hovering platform. Riker barely spared them a glance.

"Mr. Keru, can you target just the weapons on those ships?" Riker asked. If *Titan* could force both sides to stop firing at each other for at least a while, then some other more permanent solution might present itself.

"Hard to say, Captain," Keru said, frowning at his monitors. "We've taken some damage. But I think I can get a lock on the weapons of some of those older ships the Remans are using."

"Lieutenant Rager, get me Khegh," Riker said. A moment later, the scowling visage of the burly Klingon general appeared on one of the monitors.

"A touchy situation, is it not, Captain Riker?" Khegh said, baring his yellow teeth in a fierce smile.

"General, we need to stop the hostilities," Riker said. "Do you have any influence over the Remans?"

Khegh's smile disappeared. *"They seem to have chosen their course, Captain. I doubt we could dissuade them."* He assayed a guileless expression, but failed miserably. *"And truthfully, why should we want to?"*

"We are prepared to target only the weapons systems of the Reman ships," Riker said, feeling a trickle of cold sweat begin to run down the back of his neck. "Can you engage the Romulans, *without* destroying their ships?"

"Where is the fun in that?" Khegh asked, grinning again. He turned and barked an order in Klingon, addressing his crew. *"Besides, I thought you wanted to keep us from fighting these treacherous Romulan* petaQ."

"Believe me, asking you to fire on Romulan ships isn't my first choice," Riker said. "But we need to stop this war before it gets completely out of hand."

He wasn't surprised when Khegh signed off without acknowledging him.

"The Klingons are breaking away from us," Vale said, looking up from her console. "Our shields are still at less than half-strength, Captain. Staying out of harm's way would be as good an idea for us as for our convoy ships."

Riker slapped the combadge on his chest. "Riker to engineering. We need to get our shields back to full power, Ledrah. Now."

"We're already working on it, sir," the chief engineer's calm voice replied.

Riker strode back down toward his chair, aware that the

eyes of his wife had been on him for the last several minutes. He could feel her calming influence, even though she wasn't speaking aloud.

He turned toward Keru. "Mr. Keru, you may fire when ready, but I do *not* want any of those ships destroyed. Just make sure they can't take any more potshots at anyone else."

"Yes, sir," Keru said.

Tuvok stepped toward the captain's chair. "Captain Riker, if you require additional help, I was the tactical officer aboard *Voyager* for seven years. I can assist Mr. Keru if you have a targeting console to spare."

Riker nodded curtly. "Glad to have your help, Commander. Two good marksmen are better than one." He turned to see the forward viewscreen flicker to life for a moment, then wink out again. In that instant, Riker caught a glimpse of one of Khegh's Klingon battle cruisers swooping in toward one of the newer Romulan warbirds, while a phaser burst from *Titan* lanced out toward an older, Reman-crewed ship.

"Sorry, sir," the engineer said, holding up a pointed spanner. "We'll have it back up in just a moment."

Riker noted that the pair working on the viewscreen were the Polynesian twin ensigns. He could never tell them apart, so he was glad in this instance that he could just use their mutual surname. "As quickly as you can, Ensign Rossini."

"I've tried hailing Praetor Tal'Aura, but our signal apparently isn't getting through," Deanna said, looking up from the console she had snapped down from the side of her chair. Her dark eyes grew wider, and he felt her speaking directly into his mind.

This is not your fault, Will. I'm not even sure that Ambassador Spock could have prevented this, regardless of what he believes. He might only have delayed the Reman attack.

Small comfort, Imzadi, he thought in response. *It feels as if we're trying to keep a boat from sinking with a bucket brigade.*

She frowned slightly at his boat reference, and he was certain she was remembering their honeymoon. Suddenly, an urgent voice pulled his full attention back to the crisis at hand.

"Captain, one of the Remans is closing on our port bow! Collision course!" Rager's voice was high-pitched, though not panicked.

"Evasive maneuvers!" Riker roared.

The viewscreen flickered back on just in time to display an obsolete D-7 cruiser barreling toward *Titan,* filling almost the entire image area.

Then the incoming vessel appeared to pull away. Riker felt intense relief.

Until the other ship was hit by some other vessel's disruptor fusillade, breaking her hull into burning, atmosphere-venting fragments that careened in every direction.

One rather large, jagged piece was headed straight for *Titan*'s new evasive heading.

"All decks, brace for impact!" he shouted into his combadge. He saw Lavena and Rager frantically entering commands, but he knew that even their considerable skills wouldn't be enough.

A cacophonous sound rent the air, and Riker felt himself thrown violently backward. The lighting dimmed to near-darkness, lit only by a shower of sparks. Amid the blare of klaxons and the tortured moans of strained structural integrity fields, Riker heard a scream, and a wet sound. Then he crashed against something hard, a flare of pain igniting within his left shoulder.

A few seconds ticked past before the bridge's emergency lights kicked on, bathing the scene in an eerie orange glow. Will struggled to sit, aware that he had landed near his command chair, his back up against the upper-level support frame for the bridge's raised aft work stations. He heard Deanna moan, and saw her sit up from where she was slumped over her chair's armrest, held in place by the autorestraints.

Riker placed his hand against the deck, feeling something wet and warm there as he turned toward Vale's chair. He saw that she was sitting in it, held in place by her harness; she looked dazed, though not obviously harmed. An errant thought flickered through his mind: *Clearly the lesson here is to stay in my chair.*

As Riker struggled to his feet, he heard the other members of the bridge crew moaning and moving around him. He stooped near the conn, where Ensign Lavena lay after evidently having opened her restraints; her suit had sprung a leak, and its fluids were rapidly spilling onto the deck. Riker realized that this was the source of the moisture he had felt on the deck, and was thankful that it wasn't anyone's blood.

"Everybody, sound off," he said, turning. In quick succession—though accompanied by many moans and groans—Lavena, Rager, Jaza, Deanna, Vale, Akaar, Tuvok, the Rossini twins, and three other members of the bridge crew called out their names.

Which left only Keru.

Riker turned to see Tuvok kneeling beside one of the aft consoles. "Captain, your tactical officer is badly injured."

Riker tapped his badge, as Deanna and Christine rushed to the upper level. "Riker to sickbay. Prepare for incoming wounded." He sighed, and turned to Jaza as the science officer moved back toward his station. "Status report."

The Bajoran ran a shaky finger across his console's monitor, following as he read. *"Titan* was turning when she was struck. We were lucky. We appear to have sustained only minor hull damage. There's a small breach on deck five, and emergency forcefields are already in place. But our shields were overloaded by the impact."

"How badly?"

"They're down to thirty percent, Captain. Sir, we *can't* take another hit like that."

"Will." Deanna was calling him from the upper part of the bridge, aloud this time.

"Contact Khegh, Rager. We're going to need the Klingons protecting our flanks."

"Will!" Deanna's voice had become more insistent. He moved in behind her, steadying himself against a console as he looked down.

Ranul Keru lay in a crumpled heap, contusions about his face from the console circuitry into which he had crashed. But of far, far more serious concern was the spanner that protruded from his chest. Deep red blood oozed out around what he recognized as one of Ensign Rossini's tools.

Then he noticed that the large Trill was not breathing, either.

Simultaneous to this observation, Vale tapped her combadge. "Vale to transporter room four! Beam Commander Keru directly to sickbay. Sickbay, prepare a trauma team. We're beaming Mr. Keru directly to you. He's critically injured."

As the shimmering curtain of energy surrounded and dissolved Keru, Deanna stood. Riker saw that her eyes were wet. "I could barely feel him, Will. I don't know if he's going to make it."

Not caring how the gesture would look to Akaar or anyone else, Riker gathered Deanna into his embrace. He looked over her head at Vale.

"Let's get this ship running again," he said grimly.

SEVERAL MINUTES EARLIER

Olivia Bolaji had screamed so much that her voice was hoarse, and not even all the asinolyathin in sickbay seemed to be of any help.

Ogawa checked the biobed display again, then kept her voice as low and calming as possible as she addressed her infuriated patient. "I'm sorry, Olivia. I don't see any change. If we don't get your baby out now, we'd be risking both of your lives."

Axel Bolaji stood near the biobed, his dark-hued hand now purplish from the hard squeezing Olivia had been giving it. "He's four months early. Will he survive?"

"There are always risks, but we'll make certain they both do fine, Axel," Ogawa said. Though it was rare in modern Federation medical experience, human babies still occasionally arrived prematurely.

"Noah wasn't premature, but he had a difficult birth," Ogawa said, giving Olivia a small smile. *Calling thirty-two hours of labor "difficult" is a bit of an understatement,* she thought. *I was ready to yank him out with a tractor beam if he'd taken a minute longer.*

"You're sure the transporter won't hurt him?" Olivia asked, wincing.

Ogawa shook her head side to side. "We'll be using a

small, confined transporter beam. It's the least invasive procedure we can do." She gestured out toward the rest of sickbay. "I'm going to need Dr. Onnta's help though, since he has the most experience in this arena. I'm going to go get him now. The sooner we get this done, the better it'll be for the three of you."

The Bolajis nodded, and Ogawa turned and exited the OB/GYN room, deactivating then reactivating the bio-isolation field as she left. She made her way to Surgical Three, where Dr. Onnta and Dr. Ree were working on Lieutenant Denken. The young Matalinian had been grievously injured during the raid on Vikr'l Prison, and lay unmoving in the surgical bay.

Ogawa was about to ask how the surgery had gone when she noticed that Nurse Kershul was wrapping Denken's severed right arm up in cloth.

"You weren't able to save his arm?" she asked.

Ree shook his head, the sensor cluster's bright surgical lights making his scales look almost iridescent. "Whatever they cut him with in the prison was poisoned. We were barely able to stop it from spreading throughout his nervous system. Another five minutes and he would have lost seventy-five percent of his mobility, another ten and he would have died."

"He has that to be thankful for then," Ogawa said. She was always careful to be positive around trauma patients, even those who were sedated or even apparently unconscious; she knew that their subconscious minds often heard everything being said in the room, and that their waking minds might later access those memories.

The red-alert klaxons suddenly came on, startling everyone in the room. Although the klaxons were quieter here in sickbay than up on the bridge, they were no less effective.

"Bridge, what is the nature of the emergency?" Ree asked, speaking into a wall-mounted companel.

"*Just being careful, Doctor,*" answered Lieutenant Commander Jaza. "*We're pretty close to some ship-to-ship combat between the Romulans and the Remans, and we don't want to be drawn into it.*"

Ree's double eyelids blinked several times in rapid succession. "Is *Titan* in danger, Commander?"

"*I really can't talk now, Doctor. I'll try to get back to you. Bridge out.*"

Onnta sighed heavily. "Let's hope we *won't* be engaging in any battle either. Whatever beef the Remans have with the Romulans, it isn't our fight."

Ogawa nodded. Ever since Andrew had died fighting the Dominion War, she'd had little stomach for armed conflict, and an increasing contempt for those who were too quick to resort to it. She excused herself for a moment to call Noah, to make certain he stayed put in their quarters.

Back to the matter at hand, Alyssa, she silently chided herself. *There's a new life about to be born. Try to focus on that.*

"If you're available, Dr. Onnta, it's critical that we deliver Olivia Bolaji's child as soon as possible," Ogawa said, gesturing toward the OB/GYN room.

"Yes, of course," Onnta said, doffing his bloody surgical gown. "Mr. Denken is sleeping soundly. Have you prepped the equipment?"

"Of course, sir," Ogawa said, nodding. She liked the gold-skinned Balosneean doctor well enough, despite his often absentminded air—and the fact that he often spoke to her as if she were a second-year med student. It only bothered her slightly now, but if his attitude didn't improve soon, she'd find the time to share with him exactly how much field experience she'd had after nearly a decade of service aboard two starships named *Enterprise*.

"I'd like to come along to observe," Dr. Ree said, his tail switching to one side behind him. He scratched at his chin absently with one of his long, multijointed fingers. "I have been treating Mrs. Bolaji regularly, but found no warning signs of this premature labor."

As the trio strode toward the OB/GYN room, Onnta let out a sigh which Ogawa took to be one of relief, though it could as easily have been born of frustration. "Busy day. I'm glad every shift isn't like this," he said.

Both Ogawa and Ree nodded. In less than an hour, they'd treated not only Bolaji and Denken, but also the various nicks and scrapes that other members of the away team had suffered. And then there was the large, unconscious Reman, whose injuries had apparently been less severe than Ogawa had originally feared. Remans, it seemed, were made out of pretty stern stuff.

"How is our Reman guest?" Ogawa asked.

"Resting comfortably," Ree said. "He's a tough one, if a bit of a bleeder. Given the number of scars on his body, it seems he's endured several lifetimes worth of battles and close calls. At the rate he's healing, I expect he'll be mobile again within days."

The three of them re-gowned themselves, then Onnta switched off the OB/GYN room's bio-isolation field. They entered the room, and Ogawa was pleased to see that nothing had gotten worse, though Olivia was still clearly in both distress and discomfort. However, it seemed that the combination of morphenolog and asinolyathin was finally easing Olivia Bolaji's pain.

Onnta set about his job efficiently, and Ogawa took mental notes as they worked together. She suspected that Ree was doing so as well; after all, transporter surgery was one of Onnta's specialties, and they both could learn a great deal from him. Ogawa rolled the incubator bay closer to the bed as Onnta discussed the procedure with the Bolajis. Here, with a conscious, lucid patient and her husband, Onnta's bedside manner was impeccable, if ever-so-slightly condescending.

"Do you have any further ques—" Onnta said just before being thrown to one side, along with anything that wasn't bolted to the deck.

"Something just hit the ship," Axel said, righting himself even as the deck leveled out.

"Sickbay to bridge," Ree said into the nearest companel. Of the three medical personnel in the room, he had remained the most stable when the deck had shifted. Ogawa noticed that he was using his tail almost as a tertiary leg, and that Ree's dewclaws had dug deeply into the carpet.

"Now's not a good time, Doctor," Jaza said. *"We're taking fire. Try to lash down the breakables. Bridge out."*

Ogawa prayed that Noah would be safe enough in their quarters.

"You need to get to the bridge," Olivia said, grimacing from the pain.

Axel clasped his left hand over the top of the one she held his right in. "Aili's going to do fine up there. If they need me, they'll call me. But right now, it's more important for me to be here with you."

Onnta set about resetting the delicate transporter device. It hung from a radial arm on a wheel-mounted floor stanchion.

Ogawa felt a surge of sickening fear in the pit of her stomach a nanosecond before the room rocked once again, more violently this time. *Noah!*

After they had all righted themselves the second time,

Onnta looked toward Ogawa and Ree. "I can't work under these conditions. If the ship gets hit again while I'm operating, the transporter might glitch."

Ree looked up at the display monitor positioned above the biobed, his double eyelids nictitating. "We may not have a choice, Doctor. We don't know how long the ship will be in combat, and Olivia's biosigns are already stressed as it is. We may just have to hope that we don't experience another jolt like that."

Ogawa watched as Onnta considered Ree's words, then looked back at the biobed display, which showed dangerously high blood pressure, as well as signs of incipient edema and preeclampsia.

"Okay, we go for it," he said finally, moving the radial arm back into position, recalibrating it for a second attempt.

Four tense minutes later, a tiny, twenty-five-week male preemie materialized within the incubator bay, and immediately began crying lustily. As Ogawa clamped the newborn's umbilical cord—which had materialized severed and cauterized as part of the transport process— Onnta concentrated on beaming out the remainder of the cord, along with the placental tissue that had nurtured the child during its gestation.

"Is he all right? Can I hold him?" Olivia asked. She had stayed awake through the whole procedure, fighting off the effects of the anesthetics.

A chime sounded from the wall-mounted comm unit's speaker. *"All decks, brace for impact!"* The voice belonged to Captain Riker.

Ogawa barely had time to secure the incubator before the entire room rocked again. She felt herself crash into the biobed as the lights dimmed, and heard Olivia, Onnta, and Axel scream.

• • •

His chest was so full of pride that he thought he would burst. None of the work he had done on either the Defiant- *or* Intrepid-*class starship design teams during his years at the Utopia Planitia Fleet Yards could even come close to the triumph of experiencing the maiden voyage of the first ship he had designed in toto.*

The field tests for the prototype U.S.S. Luna, *the first of its class, had been completed the previous week, and now the newly minted vessel and the eager young personnel who flew her were on their first "real" voyage out of the Sol system. The permanent crew had become a cohesive, well-oiled unit over the last few months of "fit-and-finish" testing, and he couldn't be happier. He had even begun to date the ship's hydroponics chief, a winsome—and single—Efrosian woman named Dree, whose long white hair almost reached the floor behind her. She was better for him than the last woman he had been romantically involved with, whose husband had been less than understanding after he had discovered the real nature of their "working relationship." Unlike Efrosians, humans had rather quaint and curious notions about marital fidelity and sexual propriety.*

So now, as he stood on the bridge at Captain Fujikawa's request, he felt better than perhaps at any other time in his life. He watched the stars rush toward them on the forward viewscreen. Though he had seen this sight hundreds of times before, it all seemed new because of the current circumstances. He could scarcely wait to make love to Dree while viewing those stars from his luxurious guest quarters.

Then, the ship had shuddered, interrupting his self-satisfied reverie. In the instant before the computer systems triggered an alarm, he felt it, a sensation almost imperceptible to anyone not intimately familiar with the vessel's innermost workings. He knew what had happened even before the computer announced it. An explosion in the engine room. But he didn't know why it had happened. And he could never have predicted what was about to happen next—

"Dr. Ra-Havreii? Are you all right?"

The voice was insistent, calling to him from another time, another place, another disaster. Dr. Xin Ra-Havreii forced himself to open his eyes, feeling pain flaring through his shoulder. The acrid air assaulted his delicate sense of smell, carrying with it a perspiration born of fear. He also inhaled the metallic aroma of ozone, and a bouquet of scents that reminded him uncomfortably of barbecued sweetbreads.

The voice that had awakened him belonged to Ensign Crandall, an eager-to-please young human engineer who talked far too much. But Lieutenant Commander Ledrah liked him, and since it was her engineering team, Ra-Havreii never said anything untoward to the youthful babbler.

Ra-Havreii had quickly collected his thoughts, taking stock of his physical being as short-term memories flooded back into the forefront of his mind. "Yes, I'm all right," he said. He had come down to engineering at the first sign of trouble with the Remans, having viewed the approaching conflict from the VIP quarters Commander Troi had provided for him. As always, the gracious—and quite fetching—Ledrah welcomed his aid and advice, especially once *Titan* had sustained a direct attack that threatened to compromise not only her shields, but also her structural integrity fields.

A second attack had prompted Ledrah to dispatch the none-too-bright Rossini twins to the bridge to fix the main viewscreen there. Ra-Havreii suspected that the pair had barely passed their engineering classes at the Academy, and would have thrown them off the crew, along with Crandall, at the first available opportunity, had this been his crew. But, as he kept reminding himself, this was *not* his team. He felt fortunate that he got any play at all in Starfleet these days, given that the bastards at the Starfleet Skunkworks were less forgiving than a menopausal Betazoid. And he assumed that if he wanted to maintain his welcome aboard *Titan* for any appreciable length of time, then he'd best keep his intimate past relationship with one particular menopausal Betazoid discreetly concealed from Captain Riker's wife.

While Ledrah had worked feverishly at one engineering station, trying to bring the shields and structural integrity fields back up to full power, Ra-Havreii had worked at another console, located near the warp core. Then, the comm units had chimed.

"All decks, brace for impact!" Captain Riker had shouted.

Ra-Havreii couldn't remember what had happened next, until the moment when Crandall had shaken him awake.

"What happened? How long have I been out?"

"Something crashed into the ship," Crandall said. "Most of our systems are down."

An atonal voice called from the other side of the room, past the warp core. Ra-Havreii recognized it immediately as that of the partially cybernetic Choblik trainee, Torvig Bu-Kar-Nguv. "We need help over here. Commander Ledrah is hurt!"

Crandall helped Ra-Havreii to his feet, and the pair of them limped around the room. The other dozen or so engineers converged on the spot as well. By the time Ra-

Havreii approached, one of them was already by Ledrah's side, scanning her with a tricorder.

The Efrosian shipbuilder didn't need scans to tell him what his keen olfactory senses already had. Ledrah had been cooked by the explosion of one of the plasma relays. The relay's suddenly unchecked energies had ripped through her console and literally roasted her where she stood.

Two Luna-*class ships. Two engineering disasters.*

He was suddenly back aboard *Luna,* where it sometimes seemed his career had both begun and ended.

"Sir?" Crandall was saying, probably not for the first time. "We really could use your help."

This child seems to be in even worse shape than I am, Ra-Havreii thought, suddenly ashamed of his despair and emotional paralysis.

Then he decided that there was only one thing he could do to keep himself from taking a dive straight into the warp core.

He stepped to the bulkhead and tapped a console there. "Captain, this is Dr. Ra-Havreii. Lieutenant Commander Ledrah is dead. Unless you have any objections, *I* will take over the engineering section for the duration." *Or until I blow it up, just like the* Luna.

Long ago, Ra-Havreii had heard an Earth phrase: "That which doesn't kill us makes us stronger."

Right now he wanted to kill whoever had said that.

"You ought to have stayed clear of the combat zone, Captain. You have my word, Captain, that your ship will not be deliberately attacked. At least not so long as you continue to refrain from firing on our *vessels,"* Colonel Xiomek said from the main bridge viewscreen, his long fangs bared.

"I've already instructed my officers to cease fire," Riker said, sparing a glance at Tuvok, who had agreed to take over Keru's tactical station for the time being. "But you realize that we were only targeting your weapons, not actively seeking to destroy your ships."

"Truly, it matters not," Xiomek said in supercilious tones. *"Were you not allied with the Klingons, and were you not holding Ambassador Spock hostage, your ship would have been destroyed for attacking us after you allowed your ship to wander too close to our battle against the Romulan oppressors. You should consider yourself fortunate."*

Riker didn't rise to the bait. He could feel Deanna, Vale, Akaar, and Spock all watching him to see what he was going to do next. The situation was precarious, and no scenario he could think of, either from his Academy training or from his two decades serving aboard Starfleet vessels, showed him an easy way out. There didn't seem to be any practical way to separate the Romulans and the Remans before a lot more blood was spilled, and the promise of peace was lost, perhaps forever.

Come on, Will, he thought. *Outside the box.* He was uncomfortably aware that Xiomek was still waiting for a response, though he had probably been silent only for a second or two. Finally, he reconsidered a far-fetched idea he had briefly considered earlier, only to allow his own reticence to quash it.

"Colonel Xiomek, I have a proposal to make to you and the Reman people. What if the Federation were to offer you official protectorate status until such time as full-scale power-sharing talks with Romulus can begin? That way, you could—"

Xiomek snorted, interrupting him. *"You can barely protect your own crew. How do you propose to protect us?*

Humans, it would seem, are too soft and weak to properly protect anything. And need I enumerate to you how many of my people's current woes were caused by a human? Shinzon had many grand plans, but the benefits they brought to the Reman people were fleeting at best."

Riker was about to respond, but Xiomek held up his hand. *"Captain, I have more important matters to deal with right now than you and your offers that give us nothing. You have the safety of your ship. Be grateful, stay back, and let us forge our destiny without your interference."* Then the screen went blank.

Riker let out his breath, his shoulders sagging as though deflating. He wanted to let out a string of Klingon curses fit to melt the deckplates, but he somehow held his tongue. Facing Akaar and his own bridge crew right now was bad enough without displaying any further weakness. The last thing he wanted to do now was look as ridiculous as Khegh.

And then it hit him. *Khegh.*

He whirled around, doing his best to suppress a sly smile. "Christine, you have the bridge. Ambassador Spock, would you please accompany me to my ready room? I believe I'm going to need some expert diplomatic assistance."

He moved toward the door to his ready room, catching Deanna's eyes for only an instant.

Don't worry, Imzadi, he thought. *I think I've finally got this thing figured out.*

Chapter Twenty-two

U.S.S. TITAN

The fighting had stopped, at least for the moment.

Troi sensed both incredulity and admiration radiating from the otherwise inscrutable Tuvok. *If he doesn't report to sickbay soon, he's liable to fall down.* But the skies over Romulus still teemed with hostile, Reman-crewed warships, and Tuvok's assistance during their attack had proved indispensable. The outbreak of hostilities had kept the intelligence operative too busy to submit to a thorough examination in sickbay, though he had found the time to exchange his torn and bloodied Romulan traveling cassock for a standard-issue Starfleet duty uniform.

Tuvok, who was working at Lieutenant Commander Keru's tactical station, looked toward the center of the bridge, where Troi and Vale sat. "Whatever Captain Riker did, it appears to be working," Tuvok said. "Although more than half of their vessels remain fully operational—and able to continue fighting—the Remans are withdrawing."

"Confirmed," Jaza said, his eyes trained on the science station's scanners. "The Reman attack fleet has begun falling back toward Remus."

The ready-room door swished open. Troi turned and watched as Will strode briskly back onto the bridge, followed a moment later by Ambassador Spock, who moved across the bridge with supple grace.

The turbolift doors slid open, and Troi saw Akaar step onto the bridge after a brief absence that the admiral hadn't seen fit to explain to anyone. Perhaps he had needed some privacy in order to consult his local covert intelligence resources; she assumed he was looking in on the twilight power struggle that doubtless continued on the ground, even as the battle in the skies over Romulus reached a tentative conclusion, or at least a stalemate.

The tension that suffused the admiral's body reminded her of her own current uncharacteristic emotional state. She had been angry and frustrated—and frankly still was—at having been excluded from whatever ad hoc plan Will had apparently just hatched to convince the Remans to break off their aerial assault on Romulus.

Troi looked back at Vale, who was already rising from the command chair Will had left in her care less than half an hour earlier. *I can understand Will ordering Christine to stay out here on the bridge while he and Spock did gods-only-know-what in the ready room. Somebody has to tend the rudder. But I'm the diplomatic officer. I should have been in on whatever plan they've come up with.*

She tried to set aside her own wounded pride, though without complete success. Whatever deal Will and the ambassador had just negotiated behind closed doors, it was clear to Troi that neither of them wanted anyone else to share responsibility in the event their improvised plan were to result in catastrophe.

Troi recalled something Data had observed about her husband many years earlier: During battle, William Riker tended to rely on conventional strategies and tactics less than a quarter of the time. *Perhaps this is just another one of those inspired occasions,* she thought.

"Well?" Akaar said as Will and Spock came to a stop before him.

"I believe we were successful, Admiral," Spock said. "At least so far."

"The Remans are no longer shooting at us," Akaar allowed. "Or overtly menacing Romulus. Those are satisfactory results, I should think."

Will spread his hands. "But only temporary ones, unless we take the next step, and quickly. Now the Romulans have to stand down as well, or else there really *will* be hell to pay. And if that happens, we won't have a prayer of stopping it again."

"The Remans have moved against Romulus, using the Empire's own ships," Akaar said. "The Romulans will expect to strike back decisively. And immediately."

"Indeed," Spock said, his jaw set in a grim line. "Though the Remans did very little real damage to Romulus, this incursion has no doubt dealt a serious blow to Romulan pride."

Troi knew that the Remans could have laid waste to much of Ki Baratan before the planet's disorganized defenses finally mobilized themselves. She also knew that it was foolish to expect the Remans' restraint to inspire any gratitude from the Romulans.

But that restraint did give her reason to hope that Colonel Xiomek might be amenable to making an honorable peace with his Romulan neighbors.

Will offered Akaar an ironic half-smile. "And we thought it was going to be hard to persuade the Romulan factions to work together again."

"Few things are quite so persuasive as a phaser pointed at one's head, Captain," Akaar observed dryly.

"Sensors are picking up another pair of warbirds approaching Romulus, Captain," Tuvok reported. "They're dropping out of warp now, on an intercept heading toward the retreating Reman fleet. I have identified one of the warbirds as Commander Donatra's vessel, the *Valdore*."

Will took several steps toward Tuvok's station. "Hail her, Mr. Tuvok. She and Suran weren't privy to the, ah, *deal* that Ambassador Spock and I just struck with our Reman friends. We can't afford to let her undo it."

A few moments later, Donatra's face appeared in the wide viewscreen's center. Troi hadn't seen her look so careworn since immediately after the battle against Shinzon. Troi sensed a profound feeling of loss. Had someone close to Donatra died during the Reman attack?

"Captain Riker. I'm glad to see your vessel hasn't been too badly damaged during this . . . unpleasantness."

Troi quietly shook her head at Donatra's gift for understatement. "Unpleasantness" hardly did justice to an armed battle involving dozens of starships. *And maybe at least that many casualties,* she thought.

"We're fine, thank you," Will said to Donatra. "But that's not my main concern at the moment. I need you to break off your pursuit of the Reman fleet."

Donatra regarded him as though he had just grown a second head. *"Excuse me?"*

"Please listen to me, Commander. Captain Picard and I trusted you during the Shinzon affair. Now I'm asking you to return the favor."

"We're being hailed," Tuvok reported.

"By whom?" asked Vale.

Tuvok turned toward Vale, and both of his eyebrows went aloft simultaneously. "Praetor Tal'Aura."

Troi could sense Will's self-confidence rising, outpacing the background of apprehension he was still emanating. She couldn't help but be reminded of the many poker games during which he'd tried, without complete success, to conceal the fact that he was holding a very, very good hand.

"Put her on the screen, please, Mr. Tuvok. Let's have a three-way conversation."

Tuvok entered a command into his console, and Donatra's face moved into the lower right-hand corner of the viewscreen, displaced by a similarly sized square at the top right that contained the images of both Praetor Tal'Aura and Proconsul Tomalak.

"Captain Riker, how dare you intervene on behalf of the Remans?" Tal'Aura snapped angrily. *"You have overstepped your authority."*

"It wouldn't be the first time, Praetor."

Once again, Troi felt a surge of confidence waxing within her husband and captain, as though he'd just been dealt a hand containing four aces. *I hope you know what you're doing, Will.*

Troi hardly needed her empathy to see that Tomalak was nearly beside himself with fury, and that Will seemed to relish his old adversary's discomfiture. *"This is outrageous!"* Tomalak roared. *"The Remans have just launched a sneak attack against us—and now you attempt to prevent us from punishing them for their treachery! Why have you taken their side?"*

"The only side I'm on, Proconsul, is that of peace,"

Will said, then nodded to Tuvok. "Hail the lead Reman ship, Mr. Tuvok, and patch the colonel into this conversation."

Tuvok entered several commands into his console. The cutout images on the viewscreen moved again to accommodate the appearance of yet another face.

A fierce, glowering Reman face: Colonel Xiomek.

On the remainder of the viewscreen's image area, Donatra's warbird—and a second warbird that Troi presumed to be the flagship of Commander Suran—continued closing on the eighteen or so battered Reman-controlled vessels that had survived the fighting in the skies over Romulus.

The outcome of the *next* impending battle—if it proved unavoidable—seemed by no means certain, though it promised brutal deaths for many. And the very real likelihood of the start of general Romulan-Reman warfare that could spread like a brushfire across the entire Romulan Star Empire as other breakaway vassal worlds, such as Miridian or Kevatras, joined in on the Remans' side.

"The Klingon vessels escorting us have just veered off from our convoy, Captain," Tuvok said, a look of concern etching his dour, bruised features. "They appear to have begun chasing Commander Donatra's ships."

Troi's heart sank. "So much for hoping that Khegh will stay out of the fight," she said quietly.

Everything seemed to be spiraling very rapidly out of control. She looked at Will. Almost instinctively, her empathy reached out toward him, drawing strength from his unflappable aura of resolve and confidence.

And she silently prayed that he had a solid reason to feel that way.

"*Commander Donatra,*" Tal'Aura said in a tone of icy command. "*Under the authority of the praetorship of the*

Romulan Star Empire, I order you to take down the Reman flagship. Do not allow the Klingon dogs who are pursuing you to interfere with what you must do."

On the screen, Donatra was speaking inaudibly with someone outside the view of her visual pickup. *Battle preparations,* Troi thought.

Troi struggled to keep herself calm. Seated beside Will, she placed her hand on his, and he responded by grasping it gently. She noticed only then that he, too, was experiencing some nervousness, though he still seemed far less apprehensive than everyone else present, except perhaps for Ambassador Spock.

"The Klingons are still closing on the Romulan vessels, Captain," Tuvok said. "Their weapons are charging."

"Let's hope that's just Klingons being Klingons," Vale said in a near-whisper. "And not the start of a very long and nasty war."

Donatra suddenly resumed looking straight ahead into her visual pickup. *"Excuse me, Praetor, but I do not recall the Romulan military announcing its formal support of your praetorship as yet."*

"Commander Donatra, I could order you executed," Tal'Aura said, almost growling. *"This is insubordination."*

Donatra smiled. *"It would be. If I were your subordinate."*

Will released Troi's hand and stood before his command chair. His face was almost as emotionless as a Vulcan's as he addressed the Reman whose visage still scowled down from the upper left corner of the main viewer.

"Colonel Xiomek, I would be honored if you would inform the praetor and the proconsul of the bargain you have just made."

Xiomek nodded, then replied in low, sepulchral tones. *"I, Colonel Xiomek, commander of the Reman Irregulars' Kepeszuk Battalion, speak on behalf of the entire Reman people. The planet Remus has just accepted temporary protectorate status."*

The notion of a Federation protectorate inside Romulan space stunned Troi momentarily. But she did her best not to show her intense surprise, taking a cue from an admirably poker-faced Vale.

Tal'Aura jabbed a finger toward whatever apparatus was sending her image to *Titan. "You have gone entirely too far, Riker! The Federation Council could not have authorized you to establish a protectorate within Romulan territory—even a temporary one."*

"Besides, Captain," said Tomalak, *"we overheard your initial offer of protectorate status. Xiomek rejected it out of hand."*

Will held up a hand in a placating gesture, his expression mild and reasonable. "You're absolutely right about that, Praetor, Proconsul. I assure you both, the Federation has no intention of establishing a protectorate here."

"And even if we wanted to do that," Troi said, "we couldn't—not without violating both the Armistice of 2160 and the Treaty of Algeron."

"You are contradicting yourselves," said Tomalak, continuing to fulminate. And Troi clearly sensed that Will was greatly enjoying the proconsul's discomfiture. *"Is it too much to ask that you start making sense?"*

"Fair enough, Proconsul." Will turned momentarily toward Tuvok. "Patch in General Khegh, please."

A moment later, Khegh's grinning, snaggletoothed visage appeared on the lower left quadrant of the viewscreen. *"Perhaps Captain Riker was not making himself plain, Praetor Tal'Aura, Proconsul Tomalak, Commander Do-*

natra. Humans use many words when few would serve far better. It seems to be an all-too-common flaw among Federation nationals."

Tal'Aura sniffed. *"You seem rather discursive yourself, for a Klingon,"* voicing the very observation that had just occurred to Troi.

"A fault no doubt acquired during many years spent away from Qo'noS, serving in the Klingon Diplomatic Corps."

"A Klingon diplomat," Tomalak said. *"Now there's an oxymoron if I ever heard one,"* Troi realized only now that the proconsul and the Klingon officer had encountered one another before; from the mutual antipathy she sensed, they had almost certainly faced off in battle, either literally or across a negotiating table.

"No more so than 'Romulan nobility,' " Khegh replied, with a smoothness that might have impressed a Vorta.

Troi understood only then that she had badly underestimated Khegh. As, no doubt, had everyone else present. *Except maybe for Will.* Clearly, he wasn't the only player here who liked to keep his cards very close to his vest—until the time to show his hand inevitably arrived.

"Enough," Tal'Aura said. *"Come to the point, Khegh, if you please."* It was clear that Tal'Aura also already knew Khegh, and that she bore no more love for him than did Tomalak.

"Very well," said Khegh. *"Remus is now a protectorate of the Klingon Empire, at the request of Xiomek, the lawful representative of the Reman people. On a purely temporary basis, of course, and with only a nominal presence of Klingon Defense Force personnel and matériel. For now."*

Troi's surprise intensified, her growing admiration for Will's diplomatic talents displacing her earlier pique at having been kept out of the loop. There was a truly elegant logic behind this idea. *The Federation gets to avoid offending the Romulans, while furnishing the Remans with protectors who share a similar warrior ethic—and at the same time giving the Romulans a new neighbor they won't be eager to cross while their homeworld defenses are as badly diminished as they are right now.*

"*You cannot be serious, Klingon!*" Tal'Aura said, wide-eyed and aghast. Troi noticed then that only two people on the bridge did not seem to share the praetor's intense surprise. Ambassador Spock was one of them.

Will, an almost infinitesimally small smile tugging at his lips, was the other.

"*Oh, I am* deadly *serious, Praetor,*" Khegh said. "*We have much to discuss. The precise timetable of our withdrawal, for one. Which, of course, will depend upon how quickly the Reman people are given access to the land, water, and other resources so abundant in Ehrie' fvil.*"

"*This is an even worse idea than allowing a Federation presence here!*" Tal'Aura declared.

Troi had to concede that the praetor had a point, at least from a security standpoint. With a beachhead located so close to Romulus, the Klingon Empire would have an enormously favorable vantage point from which to observe their old enemies. And perhaps to do more than observe.

"*It sounds like a viable plan to me, Praetor,*" Donatra said with a sly smile, surprising Troi yet again. "*Commander Suran concurs with me—and with my appraisal that your objections will amount to nothing without the support of the Romulan military.*"

"*Commander Donatra, you are a traitor to the Empire!*" Tomalak growled. "*When, exactly, did the Klingons buy you?*"

"That is an ironic charge indeed, coming from the paid lapdog of a self-styled, self-appointed praetor," Donatra said, the outward calm of her voice doing little to conceal a roiling, volcanic undercurrent of anger. *"Suran and I may have just saved the Empire from itself."*

"That is patently absurd," Tal'Aura said.

"Is it really, Praetor?" said Will. "It seems to me the sudden appearance of a Klingon stronghold right on your back porch ought to provide encouragement to you and the other Romulan factions."

"Encouragement?" Tal'Aura's expression was a study in puzzlement.

Will nodded. "To work together. To set aside your differences. To prevent your Empire from becoming utterly fragmented, perhaps beyond repair. I predict that Senator Durjik's hard-line faction, for one, will be much friendlier to you now, at least for the foreseeable future."

Troi could certainly see the logic behind that. Politicians of Durjik's stripe tended to thrive on fear. It was their stock in trade.

But a possible showdown with Durjik's hard-liners wasn't the first difficulty that lay ahead. Will still had to deal with the immediate problem of calming Praetor Tal'Aura before she decided to do anything rash. And Troi didn't doubt she could still do so, even without the support of Donatra and Suran.

Troi recalled having read about a standoff between the leaders of two great rival nations on her father's homeworld, an event that had occurred more than four centuries ago. These two powerful men had brought their respective countries to the very brink of nuclear annihilation before achieving a fragile compromise, that others later built into a durable, if imperfect, peace. Troi now sensed a similar tension growing between her husband and Praetor Tal'Aura; she could only hope that they would resolve it as successfully as had Earth's ancient cold warriors.

Then, abruptly, Troi sensed the cloud of hostility and tension beginning to lift.

"This is only a temporary arrangement, you say?" Tal'Aura said, squaring her shoulders.

"Completely," Will said, nodding. "We can negotiate a 'date certain' for a complete Klingon withdrawal. And, as General Khegh and Chancellor Martok himself have both pledged, the Reman-Klingon protectorate arrangement requires only a minimal Klingon military presence on Remus. The whole thing would only last until the Remans become self-sufficient, resource-wise. And their successful development of Ehrie'fvil would certainly bring that about, quickly."

The Klingon protectorate would definitely have to end, Troi thought, *once the Romulan military recovers enough strength to force the issue. And we can probably add to that a little friendly Starfleet persuasion—if the Klingons decide to overstay their welcome. Very neat.*

"Praetor!" Tomalak said, protesting. *"I cannot believe you would actually consid—"*

"Kroiha!" she shouted, cutting him off. *"You may approach Romulus, Captain Riker. You and I clearly need to have another face-to-face meeting."*

Will bowed his head respectfully, no longer displaying any of the puckish acerbity that he had used to get the praetor's attention. "Whenever you wish, Praetor. My crew and I are at your disposal."

"Just make sure that Khegh and Xiomek are prepared to discuss the details of this . . . arrangement."

"And Durjik?"

"As you say, Captain, he should fall neatly into line

now. Let me *worry about him. I will contact you when we are ready to assemble."*

And with that, the images of Tal'Aura and Tomalak abruptly vanished from the screen. After brief farewells, Donatra and Xiomek did likewise.

Akaar and Spock stepped down into the command well, both regarding Will with obvious respect.

"Well played, Captain," Akaar said.

"Indeed," Spock said.

Will looked upward, studying the tall Capellan's deeply lined face, which showed just the slightest hint of a smile.

"If you don't mind my saying so, Admiral, you've been pretty silent through this whole business."

Akaar raised an eyebrow in a curiously Vulcan manner. "Did you expect me to interfere, Captain? This is your mission, after all. I had faith that you would improvise a suitable solution. Had it been otherwise, Admiral Ross and I would have selected another captain and another crew."

"Thank you, sir," Will said. Troi was surprised to see him actually smile back at Akaar.

Will gets it now, she thought. *He's finally accepted that the admiral isn't out to wreck his first command.*

And that he's not Kyle Riker.

"I think you may have overlooked something, Captain," Vale said with a wry smile.

"And what's that?" Will said.

"You didn't invite the Tal Shiar to our little teleconference."

"Somehow I think they'll get the message," Troi said. "It's what they do, after all."

"And why didn't we hear directly from Suran?" Vale wanted to know.

Troi thought that was a good question. And possibly also an unanswerable one. Were Donatra and Suran really in complete agreement about how best to handle Praetor Tal'Aura and the Remans? She recalled having sensed some discord between them during that first meeting in Ki Baratan.

"Maybe the new Klingon-Reman arrangement will keep the peace between Donatra and Suran the same way Tal'Aura expects it to keep Durjik in line," Troi said. "But I think we can let Donatra worry about that for the moment."

"Exactly," Will said, clearly not in the mood right now to find dark clouds inside his silver linings. There would be plenty of time later for that. For now, there was a real prospect for peace. Tenuous and balanced on a knife's edge, to be sure, but also substantial enough to offer a genuine cause for hope.

Chapter Twenty-three

In spite of himself, Riker felt he was the least of the three people present in his ready room, now that the crisis had been averted. Akaar and Spock sat on the other side of the desk from him, discussing the resolution of the immediate Romulan-Reman conflict, and what was to come next. They all knew that what they had done today was merely a stopgap measure. But now the way was clear for the Federation to send in specialists from the Diplomatic Corps to help work out the fine details of the Klingon administration of a Reman protectorate. Riker was well aware that the deal he and Spock had brokered between the Klingons and the Remans might have unpredictable consequences down the road.

For the moment, the result was peace, however fragile it might be. And that was infinitely preferable to the alternative.

"Admiral, do you think you could see your way clear to allow Ambassador Spock to return to his work with the

Unification movement and the Remans?" Riker asked, posing the question that he felt was the elephant in the room that Akaar had so far ignored.

Seated in the tall chair before Riker's desk, Akaar regarded him with a testy expression. "You are fully aware of the Federation Council's wishes, Captain."

"As am I, Admiral," Spock said calmly, looking Akaar in the eye. The ambassador was sitting, hands folded in his lap, in one of the ready room's other "visitor" chairs.

Riker knew well that Spock was fully capable of defying authority if the stakes were high enough. Spock's hijacking of one of the earliest starships named *Enterprise* to the forbidden world of Talos IV, and his subsequent acquittal by a Starfleet court martial, were common knowledge. Therefore Riker could empathize with the respectful yet wary expression he saw on Akaar's lined face.

"I believe that I *shall* return to Earth to meet with President Bacco and the Federation Council," Spock continued. "Such was my plan prior to the upheavals caused by Shinzon, after all."

"But what about your ongoing Unification work on Romulus?" Riker asked. "Commander Tuvok tells me that when he first tracked you down, you weren't willing to leave Romulus, even for a short time."

"Given the presently changing fortunes of the Romulan Star Empire, logic dictates that workable solutions will require expansive minds. Perhaps my views will be seen as expansive."

"But what if the president or the council tries to keep you from going back to Romulus?" Akaar asked.

"I have returned to Earth on more than one occasion since I began my association with the Romulan dissident movement. Federation authorities have never attempted to interdict me."

"But suppose they decide to do it *this* time?" Akaar asked. "Do you plan to return to Romulus afterward, regardless of whatever the council or President Bacco decides?"

Spock put his hands in front of his face and steepled his fingers against his lips. "My mission is infinitely more complex and dangerous than it ever was before, Leonard. Where once my task was to reunite the Romulan and Vulcan cultures via the logical teachings of Surak, I must now do so while helping the Romulans and Remans overcome their long-standing mutual hatreds. To adopt the ways of Surak, the removal of hatred is a necessary first step."

"I will take that as a 'yes,' " Akaar said, smiling grimly.

"If you must," Spock said, sounding like a patient teacher working with a willfully obtuse child. "However, I have faith in my ability to persuade both the president and a council majority to resume the Federation's support of the Unification movement."

"Faith, Mr. Ambassador?" Riker said. "Are you sure that's entirely logical?"

Spock nodded, as though acknowledging at least the appearance of a paradox. "There were times, Captain, when faith in the power of logic was all that sustained Surak himself. It will suffice, I should think."

"I hope you are right," said Akaar. "You may find Councillor T'Latrek of Vulcan difficult to persuade. Not to mention Councillor Gleer of Tellar. That one would surely tax the patience of even Surak himself."

"Indeed," Spock said, his craggy face taking on a determined cast. "But if logic was an easily attainable goal, there would be little need for diplomats."

Akaar inclined his head. "Or for Starfleet."

"Admiral, will you be joining your advisers and Ambassador Spock on *Der Sonnenaufgang?*" Riker asked, unable to suppress a smile himself. All three of the convoy's Starfleet cargo vessels were due to depart for re-supply in Federation space within the hour. Very soon, Starfleet vessels would be making regular freight and personnel runs to assist Romulan and Reman alike in rebuilding the infrastructure of their respective worlds—under the watchful eyes of both Starfleet Command and Klingon Governor Khegh of the newly instituted Reman Protectorate.

Akaar's small smile widened. "You will not get rid of me quite that easily, Captain. I intend to stay aboard *Titan* until her stopover at Starbase 185."

"If you must," Riker said dryly.

Akaar let out a hearty laugh, while Spock turned to regard Riker with a raised eyebrow.

Deanna Troi walked toward sickbay slowly, unable to suppress a slight feeling of trepidation. It was one thing to see a Reman from the safe remove of the bridge viewscreen. But it was quite another thing to know that a Reman was aboard *Titan,* waiting for *her.* He had specifically requested to speak with the ship's diplomatic officer.

Entering sickbay, Troi gently rapped her knuckles against the plasteel wall beside the biobed where the creature lay. "Commander Deanna Troi. You asked to see me?" she said, willing a professional calm into her voice despite the restless churning of her belly.

The large Reman opened his eyes and turned his head to look at her. He was draped with a powder blue blanket, but she could see deep scars crisscrossing his torso, giving his fish-white flesh a texture reminiscent of broken concrete.

"Thank you for coming, Commander," he said, his voice low and deep as a gravel pit. "Pardon me for not getting up to greet you, but your captain has had me restrained as a security measure. Over the objections of your healers. And your Commander Tuvok, I might add."

Troi noted that the Reman was, indeed, restrained by a forcefield. She knew that Will was taking a reasonable precaution in keeping a former Vikr'l Prison inmate confined in this fashion. But she also wondered whether she would have felt shock rather than relief at the sight of his treatment had he been a member of some other species.

"I hope you can understand our caution, given the circumstances, Mister . . ." She trailed off, eyeing him inquisitively. She'd heard his name spoken only once.

"Mekrikuk," he said. "My name is Mekrikuk. Like the mountain range on my homeworld. And I certainly do understand why Starfleet personnel might distrust me, given the actions of Shinzon and his Reman followers. Although I have become somewhat used to confinement, I must say you are more civilized in your treatment of prisoners than were the Romulans."

"You are not technically our prisoner," Troi said, moving to stand near a side wall. "You will be released to the Remans as soon as you're judged well enough to travel."

Mekrikuk bared his fangs in what she thought might be an approximation of a smile. "And what if I do not wish to rejoin my people?"

"I'm sorry," Troi said. "I just assumed. We can return you to the Romulans if you would like. Though why you would wish to return to a people who imprisoned you—"

"I don't wish to be returned to *either*," Mekrikuk said, interrupting her. "Did Tuvok not tell you?"

"Tuvok is in surgery right now, having his . . . facial alterations removed," Troi said. She was intrigued now. "What was he supposed to have told me?"

Mekrikuk looked back toward the ceiling, but he was

clearly focusing on something much farther away. "I hope to see Tuvok when he has recovered. When we were imprisoned together, we talked of many things. He told me much about the space beyond what I have known. Though I have been to other worlds, to fight in the war against the Dominion, I have known no life other than my existence serving the Romulan Star Empire. Tuvok gave me hope that I might seek a new life were we to escape from Vikr'l.

"Hope that I might find refuge within the Federation." He turned to look at her again. "I hereby renounce all ties to my life as a Reman and to the Empire. I ask you for political asylum, Commander Troi."

Troi struggled to keep the look of surprise off of her face. "Well, we can certainly take that under consideration. I will discuss the matter with the captain. I think I can at least guarantee you a fair hearing." She knew from previous experience that once any sentient being made a formal asylum request, Federation law required a starship captain to grant a formal asylum hearing unless another government could demonstrate a lawful claim of custody. She had to wonder, though, how Mekrikuk's former status as a prisoner of the Romulan justice system would factor into the proceedings.

"That calms my spirit," Mekrikuk said, smiling again, his sharpened teeth bared.

Troi flinched involuntarily, then did her best to return his smile.

"May I ask you something else, Commander?" Mekrikuk said.

"Certainly."

He looked back toward the ceiling. "I sense that you are uncomfortable around me. Have I done something to offend you? Or is it because I am Reman?"

Troi felt twin fires of anger and embarrassment flare within her. "I understand that some Remans have telepathic abilities, Mekrikuk. Most cultures consider it a violation of privacy to use them on others without permission." The irony of her own words hit her a moment later. *I read people's emotional states all the time without their permission.*

"You misunderstand me, Commander," Mekrikuk said, frowning. "I did *not* use the mind-touch to perceive your distress. The mind-touch requires much effort. But noticing your behavior in my presence does not. You seem to shrink away from me, as though repelled. I apologize if my question was intrusive."

Troi blinked slowly, realization dawning on her. Throughout this entire mission, the horrific memories of the telepathic assault she had suffered at the hands of Shinzon—an act made possible by the psionic abilities of his Reman viceroy—had never been very far from the surface. Ever since it had happened, she'd managed to hide her feelings from everyone except Will. But this Reman had seen right through her pretenses, and her empathic talents told her that his denial of having used telepathy on her was sincere.

So much for my sanctimonious lectures on diversity, she thought. *That'll teach me to tease Will about being afraid of Dr. Ree.* She had never felt so deeply ashamed of herself before.

"No, Mekrikuk, I should apologize to *you*," she said. "I have allowed a past ordeal to color my view of all Remans, yourself included."

Mekrikuk shrugged. "I suspect that Remans are no more like one another than are the members of other species. I have seen members of my people who were beauty personified. I have seen those who were pure, distilled hatred. And I have seen those who cross from one side to the other, and every shade in between."

He looked back at her, and she saw an apparently bottomless well of pain in his hard, dark eyes. "But I believe myself to be unique. Not because I am a Reman who chooses to leave his people. Nor because of the experiences that have shaped who I am today. I am unique because I am Mekrikuk. Just as you are unique because you are Deanna Troi. Neither of us could be anyone else."

Haltingly, trusting her empathic sense of his lack of ill intent, Troi approached the biobed more closely and deactivated the restraining field. She reached toward him and grasped his hand in hers. It felt cool and rough, like unpolished marble. Its nails were long and sharp, reminding her of the delicately tapered claws of Dr. Ree, whom she knew was one of the gentlest souls she had ever encountered.

"We're *all* unique, Mekrikuk," Troi said quietly. "And I will try to do my best to remember that in the future."

"Will Uncle Ranul ever wake up?" Noah Powell asked, his eyes as big as saucers.

Alyssa Ogawa stood behind her son in the isolation room, stroking his sleek black hair. "We don't know yet, sweetie," she said. "Sometimes people in comas wake up, and other times they just sleep forever."

"Rule of Acquisition Number One Hundred and Three: Sleep can interfere with . . . well, a whole lot of things." The voice behind them was grating and female. Ogawa knew that it belonged to Dr. Bralik before she even turned around.

"Hello, Bralik," she said agreeably.

"Hi, Alyssa," Bralik said, pulling something from her tunic. She held it out toward Noah. "And how are you, little grub? I brought you some candy!"

Noah scowled. "I didn't like that last stuff you gave me. It tasted yucky."

Bralik's eyes popped wide. "The honey beetle clusters? Oh, I'm hurt."

Ogawa tapped her son on the shoulder. "Noah, I thought I taught you to be more polite than that."

Noah sighed dramatically and held out his hand. "Thank you for the candy, Aunt Bralik." She deposited a hard bar of a translucent, greenish substance in his hand. He sniffed at it tentatively. "What is it?"

"Slug Slime," Bralik said, smiling. "Now why don't you go get Auntie Bralik some water, and she'll forget your lapse in manners."

As soon as Noah had scampered out of the room, Ogawa asked, "What *was* that?"

Bralik shrugged. "Slug Slime? I don't have any idea what's in it. But grubs of all species seem to like it."

Ogawa snorted as Bralik sat on the chair that Noah had vacated, bringing herself level with the biobed where Ranul Keru lay.

"How is the furball, really?" Bralik asked, putting her hand on Ranul's, atop his chest.

"We were able to get the tool out of his chest without causing much additional damage," Ogawa said. "But he also sustained a significant head injury during the collision. There's a good deal of brain swelling. We don't know when he'll wake up."

Bralik squinted back at her. "There's not a question of *if* he'll wake up, is there?"

Ogawa sighed, but didn't say anything. She didn't want to admit, either aloud or even in her own mind, the possibility that Keru might die. He'd become a great friend to her aboard the *Enterprise,* and a wonderful "uncle" for Noah, and their relationship had grown even stronger since they had come aboard *Titan.*

"That's the spirit," Bralik said, winking broadly and aiming her words in Keru's direction. "He'll *definitely* wake up then. It's just a question of when." She turned back to face Ogawa and said, "Rule Number Two-hundred and sixty-seven: If *you* believe it, *they* believe it."

Noah returned with the glass of water he'd been sent to fetch. "Here, Aunt Bralik."

"Thanks, grub," Bralik said, taking it. "I'm gonna need it, since I'm going to read your Uncle Ranul a story." With her free hand, she extracted a book from her tunic.

Noah grinned. "A pirate story?"

Bralik smiled. "Of a sort. Not for little boys, though."

Ogawa looked at the spine of the book. She was only able to make out a few words of the title, but they were enough to tell her that it was *definitely* too steamy for young ears.

"Come on, Noah, we need to check in with Dr. Ree before we leave. Mommy's had a long shift today."

"Okay. 'Bye, Aunt Bralik. 'Bye, Uncle Ranul." Noah left the room ahead of Ogawa.

" 'Bye, grub," Bralik said.

"Good night," Ogawa said with a smile. As she exited, she heard Bralik behind her, talking to Keru.

"Now before I start this story, I've got to warn you that Kent will be by later, but I'll make sure he doesn't try to hold your hand or anything. Once you wake up, I'll help you find a way to let him down gently. You know me. The soul of tact."

As she walked away, Ogawa heard the sound of

Bralik's book falling to the floor, followed by the Ferengi's soft, ragged, uncontrolled sobs.

"Are you sure you're up to this?" Christine Vale asked.

Dr. Xin Ra-Havreii rubbed his temple. "Becoming your chief engineer? Well, some of my colleagues would undoubtedly think it beneath them. But they haven't had quite the thrill-ride of a career that I've had."

Vale sat on the edge of Ledrah's desk. She still expected to see the Tiburon woman sitting there, her bluish hair spiked upward. In her place sat the middle-aged Efrosian male who had designed *Titan* and had overseen her construction.

"I heard about what happened aboard *Luna*," she said quietly. "But I also know you were cleared of any culpability."

Ra-Havreii offered her a wan smile. "Cleared of all culpability is very different from being found innocent, Commander. You may not blame me, and Starfleet may not blame me, but the men and women of Utopia Planitia don't share that magnanimity. Nor do the families of *Luna*'s crew."

Or yourself, Vale thought, as Ra-Havreii lapsed once again into woolgathering.

"I'm not sure this is a good idea at all," Vale said. "Being a starship's chief engineer isn't quite the same as working at Utopia Planitia. Thanks for offering to take over in engineering, but—"

Ra-Havreii suddenly came out of his funk. "I think I *need* to do this job, Commander. At least until you find a permanent replacement."

"But why?"

"Perhaps to maintain what I have helped to create," he said. "And perhaps . . . to atone," he said. Once again, he lapsed into pensive silence—though he was staring straight at her chest. *Deanna, you just may have your work cut out for you,* Vale thought. *I hope I don't regret this, but I need a good chief engineer.*

She knocked on the desktop, then pointed to her eyes with forked fingers. "Hey, eyes *here.*" Once she had the engineer's attention again, she continued. "Okay, so the first rule, now that I outrank you, is this: no pity parties on my watch. I've never worked in engineering, though I've helped the SCE on a few missions. But I come from a long line of peace officers, and let me tell you, they were none too happy when I left the family business to enroll in the Academy.

"It didn't seem to matter to them that I went into security while in Starfleet. Or that I've gotten a whole pile of commendations over the years. Hell, I haven't even told them that I'm the first officer of *Titan* yet. I may not be exactly living up to their expectations, but I'm damn well doing a good job at something I think is important."

Ra-Havreii stared her straight in the eyes, almost defiantly. "Having your peers think you're a dangerous failure is a bit different from disappointing your family."

"Yes, it is," Vale said. "But the biggest difference is how you react to it. So you've had two tragedies on your watch? This ship, *your* ship, held together today, and you're a big part of the reason for that. And there's no reasonable way you can blame yourself for Nidani's death. You didn't dump that hull debris on top of *Titan,* and it's awfully hard creating a contingency plan that'll be of any use when something like that happens. An earlier class of ship might not even have *survived* today's battle."

She stood up and extended her hand. "I'm ecstatic that

Titan's designer will now be our chief engineer, for however long we are privileged to have you, Doctor Ra-Havreii. And I hope you'll join me in tossing all the old ghosts right out the nearest airlock. I'm sure the journey ahead of us will be interesting enough without hauntings."

Ra-Havreii stood and shook her hand, but Vale could see in his eyes that he still wasn't quite ready to exorcise his demons.

Captain William Riker was glad that the most egregious of his chores was finally behind him. After consulting with Admiral Akaar and Ambassador Spock—the latter of whom had just departed for Earth aboard the *Der Sonnenaufgang*—Riker had made a complete report to Starfleet Command, informing them in detail about his delicate, improvisational Romulan-Reman peace plan. Admiral Ross hadn't seemed displeased with the outcome of the mission, despite the unorthodox methodology, though Riker knew that all that really mattered in the long run was the Federation Council's opinion, and that of President Bacco. Akaar assured him that when he returned to Earth after this mission, he would champion Riker's peace plan with all the influence at his disposal.

But now, Riker had more pleasant matters to attend to before retiring for the evening with his lovely wife. He saw Nurse Ogawa exiting sickbay with her son, but they had moved down a branching corridor before he'd had a chance to speak with them. He entered the medical facilities, glad to see that things had calmed down considerably there. He'd been down here earlier, to speak to Tuvok.

Until Ranul Keru recovered, if ever, Riker knew he was badly in need of at least a temporary tactical officer and security chief. He had offered the combined job to Tuvok, citing both his assignment aboard *Voyager* and the advanced tactical training classes the Vulcan had taught for many years at Starfleet Academy. Thankfully, Tuvok had been easier to persuade to take a posting on *Titan* than had Vale. Tuvok had agreed to take over the position, at least until Keru recovered.

Riker had just heard from Christine Vale that Dr. Ra-Havreii would also be staying aboard for the foreseeable future, taking over the duties of the late chief engineer Ledrah. Riker intended to contact Ledrah's family tomorrow, to break the bad news to them himself; later that day, he would conduct a shipboard memorial service.

In the meantime, he sorely needed to hear whatever good news there was aboard this ship.

Riker saw Dr. Ree, and pointed toward the OB/GYN chamber. "Is Olivia awake yet?" he asked.

"Yes, Captain," Ree said. "She is with the baby now. They're both doing well." He retracted his arms for a moment, bringing them in closer to his chest. "Well, small mammals make me hungry. Care to join me in the mess?"

Riker smiled at the doctor's attempt at humor, remembering the bloody abattoir of a meal he'd recently seen Ree consume in the mess hall. After politely declining the invitation, he said, "Thank you for your excellent work today, Doctor." He extended his hand.

Ree shook his hand and smiled a predatory smile. "Why, thank you, Captain. And allow me to thank *you* for keeping the ship in one piece."

Disengaging with a nod, Riker turned and proceeded toward the birthing room. Stepping just inside the door, he saw Olivia Bolaji lying in the bed beside the incubator that housed her premature infant. The impossibly tiny-looking child was wrapped in a royal blue blanket, asleep. Axel

Bolaji was sitting in the chair nearby, also sleeping, one arm up on the bed next to his wife.

"Hi," Riker said quietly. "I just wanted to say hello to our newest crewman."

"Come in, Captain," Olivia said, smiling the radiant smile that Riker had seen nowhere else except on the faces of new mothers. "He's beautiful. I can hardly wait to hold him."

Riker looked down at the sleeping infant, its skin almost purplish brown, and as wrinkled as a raisin. The child wriggled a bit in its sleep, and Riker wondered how much the tiny creature weighed.

"Have you named him yet?"

"Yes," the now-awake Axel Bolaji said, stretching and yawning. "His name is Totyarguil. In the Aranda language of the Australian Aborigines, it means 'the eagle star.' "

" 'Totyarguil,' " Riker repeated. "May you bring us all luck, little eagle star."

The child's deep blue eyes opened briefly, momentarily reflecting the dim illumination of the room. But Riker saw that the darkness and light at play there in those eyes looked as deep, as infinite, and as mysterious as the universe itself.

Chapter Twenty-four

The meeting with Tal'Aura, Tomalak, Durjik, Donatra, and Xiomek had gone far more smoothly than Riker had expected. But it was the end of yet another extraordinarily long day, and the weary captain could tell that Deanna was as exhausted as he was even before they had finished materializing in transporter room four.

But Deanna also evidently shared his upbeat mood. "I think we're really beginning to get through to them," she said, walking arm-in-arm with him along the corridor that led to their quarters. "Tomalak is going to be a tough sell, and Donatra seems to hate him almost as much as she despises Tal'Aura. On the other hand, I'm sensing that Tal'Aura is beginning to trust us. As is Xiomek."

"Meaning that they trust us more than they trust each other," Riker said as they reached the door to their quarters. "Which isn't all that much."

"True enough. But it's as good a place to start as any

other," Deanna said, placing her palm on the control pad mounted on the wall. The door obediently opened in response, and they entered.

Deanna dropped wearily onto the couch. "Once the permanent diplomatic team reaches Romulus, I think we'll start seeing some real progress toward a permanent power-sharing agreement."

"No doubt," he said, settling down beside her. "Especially if Akaar turns out to be right about Spock being with the team when it arrives. Tal'Aura might not be thrilled about having a social dissident like Spock involved in the process, but it ought to make the Remans happy."

"I sense that Tal'Aura is well aware that the last thing she needs right now are unhappy Remans," she said.

He nodded. It was clear to him that the Remans still had plenty of reason to be unhappy. They needed strong leadership, and Xiomek seemed to excel at supplying just that, at least so far. Riker could only hope that whatever knack had enabled Xiomek to survive the Dominion War—and to survive his own penchant for commanding from the front lines—would keep the Reman colonel, as well as the current improvised peace arrangements, alive. At least long enough for Ambassador Spock and the Federation Diplomatic Corps to help craft a more permanent peace.

"So, when do we get under way?" Deanna asked. He knew that she was as eager as he was to bring *Titan*'s current diplomatic detour to a conclusion.

"Sometime tomorrow, after the first Reman homesteader ships touch down on Ehrie'fvil. I want to give Christine and Tuvok a chance to evaluate Commander Suran's plan to provide security at the settlement sites. *And* make sure that Khegh doesn't get too assertive in enforcing Ehrie'fvil's status as part of the Reman Protectorate." He paused, then added, "I'm looking forward to putting all this behind us."

She leaned backward into him, and fairly purred with contentment when he began rubbing her back. "Me, too. Happy New Year, by the way."

He paused in his ministrations to her back. With all the frantic activity of the past couple of weeks, he had somehow completely lost track not only of Christmas, but had also failed to note the arrival of a new year and a new decade. The year 2380 had sneaked up on him like a shrouded Jem'Hadar.

"My God. It's already Elvis Presley's birthday," he said. "I must be getting old and distracted."

She turned toward him. "Not old, Will. Seasoned."

"Ugh. You know I hate that word."

"I just mean that the gray in your beard suits you. You've earned it. As for 'distracted,' let *me* handle that." She looked up at him expectantly.

He bent down to kiss her.

Then his combadge abruptly shattered the moment. *"Vale to Captain Riker."*

Though two decades of Starfleet service had conditioned him to the inevitability of such interruptions, he was never happy about it. He sighed, then tapped the badge a little harder than was strictly necessary.

"Go ahead, Christine."

"It's Commander Donatra. Her ship has decloaked just astern of us, and she wants to talk to you right away."

He stood and straightened his uniform jacket. "Pipe her down here, Christine."

"Aye, sir."

Riker took a seat behind the desk in the small office nook located just outside the bedroom. He touched a control on the interface console located there, and its small viewscreen lit up, displaying the white-on-blue emblem of the United Federation of Planets.

A moment later, this was replaced by the image of Commander Donatra, who looked even more distressed than she had during the battle in the skies over Ki Baratan. The background behind her was a neutral green; she seemed to be transmitting either from her ready room, or perhaps from her personal quarters.

"Commander Donatra," he said. "What can I do for you?"

"Is this channel secure on your end?"

Deanna approached, making herself visible to Donatra while he entered a few quick manual commands into the desktop terminal.

"It is now, Commander," Riker said.

"I'm afraid I need your assistance, Captain," Donatra began without further preamble. *"There's no one else I can turn to."*

He glanced quickly at Deanna, whose dark eyes were wide with alarm. She was confirming what he had already concluded: Something had gone very, very wrong. Perhaps catastrophically wrong.

"I sense your reticence, Commander," Deanna said. "I am the only one here besides Captain Riker. If my presence makes you uncomfortable, Commander, I would be hap—"

Donatra interrupted her. *"No, Commander Troi. There's no reason for you to leave. My folly will no doubt soon be common knowledge anyway."* She seemed almost on the verge of tears.

"But you obviously have enough confidence in us to come to us first," Riker said, once again more than a little grateful for the bond that Captain Picard had created with Donatra during the battle against Shinzon.

She paused, looking away toward something that might have been parsecs distant. She seemed to be gathering her thoughts and emotions around her like tattered garments.

"During the confusion that followed the elimination of Praetor Hiren and the Senate," she began at length, *"Suran and I gained access to a large complement of warbirds. These vessels and their armaments were, shall we say, subsequently unaccounted for.*

"Obviously, we needed to keep the existence of these vessels a secret, and their location concealed. I convinced Suran that the best place to hide the fleet was within the gravimetric and subspace flux zone surrounding the Great Bloom."

"Great Bloom?" Riker asked.

"Forgive me. The Great Bloom is our designation for the spatial anomaly located only a handful of veraku *away from Romulus at high warp. You have no doubt observed the phenomenon yourselves, and have given it another name. It's centered in the very spot where Shinzon's vessel exploded after our engagement with him."*

"The spatial rift," Deanna said quietly.

"Why are you sharing this with us, Commander?" he said aloud.

"Because . . ." Donatra began, her voice faltering momentarily before she found the strength to continue. *"Because the entire fleet has vanished. Every ship. Every officer. Every enlisted crew member. All gone, without leaving so much as a body or any identifiable debris. Suran and I have been searching the region for two full* eisae, *but to no avail."*

"You think your ships have fallen into the event horizon of the spatial rift," said Deanna.

"The Great Bloom's center is the only place we've yet

to search directly, because our sensors cannot penetrate it. But it is the likeliest place."

"And you want us to help you find them," Riker added.

"Yes."

Riker understood that yet another fairly monumental decision was now expected of him. He was more than passing familiar with the Romulan aphorism "He who rules the military rules the Empire." And it seemed fairly obvious that helping the Romulan military faction acquire—or reacquire—large quantities of ships and arms could jeopardize the already delicate balance of power that now existed between the mutually opposed Romulan factions and the Klingon-protected Remans.

But leaving those ships lost, he thought, *where they might fall into the hands of gods-only-know-who might be an even worse idea.*

"I am taking the Valdore *into the center of the Great Bloom, Captain. With or without your help. I intend to give my crew the order in a moment."*

Riker had seen enough spatial rifts over the course of his career to understand the extreme danger inherent in flying into one. But ever since Commander Donatra had joined forces with the *Enterprise* crew against Shinzon, Riker had regarded her almost as a comrade-in-arms. Her cooperation during the recent Reman attack and the subsequent power-sharing summit had only solidified that working relationship. How could he let her face such a terrible risk alone?

He came to a decision. *"Titan* will accompany you to the edge of the rift, Commander."

"But not over its edge. You disappoint me, Captain. I thought you had more courage."

Riker answered with an involuntary chuckle. *Does she really expect to manipulate me by calling me "chicken"?*

"There's courage and then there's suicide," he said. "I'll do my best to help you recover your ships and crews. But I'm not interested in helping you atone for losing them by throwing yourself off a cliff."

Her eyes narrowed, but it was obvious she had no desire to alienate him by venting her anger on him. *"And what will merely standing on the cliff's edge accomplish?"*

"Titan has sensors that I'll wager are a good deal more sensitive than anything aboard the *Valdore.* Perhaps they can tell us just how dangerous that cliff really is."

She took this in with a curt nod. *"Very well, Captain. The* Valdore *will depart for the Great Bloom in five of your minutes."* And with that her image vanished, to be replaced by the white-on-blue UFP symbol.

"You're welcome," Riker said to the screen before tapping his combadge. "Riker to bridge."

"Vale here, Captain."

"Change of plans, Commander. We have to make best speed for the spatial anomaly we observed on our way here. I want us under way in five minutes. Please coordinate our departure with Commander Donatra's staff aboard the *Valdore.* They'll be leading the way."

"May I ask what this is all about?"

He tapped a string of commands into his console. "I'm sending the recording of my conversation with Donatra up to my ready room. Once you review it, you'll know as much as Commander Troi and I do."

"I'm all over it, sir. Vale out."

He turned to face Deanna. Taking her hands, he said, "Seems to me we won't be needed on the bridge until *Titan* reaches the rift."

"And how long will that take?" she asked.

He performed a rough calculation in his head. "At least a couple of hours."

With a sultry smile, she pulled him directly toward the bedroom.

The rift's most striking feature, Riker thought, was its color. Or rather, its *colors*. Great loops of energetic orange and iridescent green stretched for hundreds of kilometers from the rift's invisible core, twisting and entwining themselves about the phenomenon that Donatra had called the Great Bloom. On the bridge's wide central viewer, Riker could see the sea-green hull of Donatra's warbird limned in the glow.

"Keep us at station, Mr. Bolaji," Riker said. "Five hundred klicks from the event horizon."

"Aye, sir," replied Chief Axel Bolaji, as he entered a string of commands into the conn station. He was helping fill in for Ensign Lavena while she recuperated in the aquatic environment of her quarters; Lavena had become dangerously dehydrated when her suit had ruptured during the battle over Romulus. "Keeping station."

"I am still detecting tachyon emissions indicative of a nearby cloaked ship," said Tuvok, who already looked a good deal healthier than he had during the recent Romulan-Reman skirmish.

"It must be one of Khegh's ships," Deanna said.

Riker nodded. "The Klingons certainly would have noticed the *Valdore* approaching us, even if they couldn't eavesdrop on our conversation with Donatra. And our early departure from Romulus must have made them even more curious."

"The Klingons must be counting on the rift's energy discharges to help hide their presence from us," Vale said. "Lucky for us they underestimated our new sensor nets."

"There's a terrific quantity of energy here, Captain,"

said Jaza. When he had heard that *Titan* was going to get right up close to the rift he had until now been forced to admire from afar, he had come straight to the bridge, insistent upon relieving his gamma-shift counterpart at the science console. "And the intense background radiation signature I'm reading confirms the phenomenon's probable origin: the detonation of the *Scimitar*'s thalaron device."

"Can the sensors image anything at the rift's center?" Vale asked, seated in the chair at Riker's immediate right. She seemed as eager as Riker was to avoid dwelling on the thalaron weapon that had killed Data.

"Not yet, Commander," said Cadet Dakal. "I'm going to increase the gain." Dakal touched his console, entering a command.

Hell unleashed itself at that precise moment. The placid, glowing tendrils of energy that surrounded the rift's event horizon suddenly crackled with agitation, like the tentacles of some legendary kraken preparing to strike at its prey. Then the viewscreen was awash in blinding light for an instant, just before the bridge was plunged into absolute stygian darkness.

For a timeless interval, Riker thought he had ceased to exist. The ship's gravity seemed to have failed along with the lights, and he felt as though he were plunging in freefall through an infinite void.

His command chair grew comfortably solid beneath him, and the sensation of weightless disorientation gradually passed as the dim red emergency lighting kicked in. Alarm klaxons blared. Mercifully, Vale ordered them silenced.

"Ship's status?" he shouted, then turned to see that everyone was still at their stations, though all present were wide-eyed with surprise. Once again the automatic restraints had activated, and everyone was struggling out of them, Riker himself included. The main viewscreen was working, but displayed only a hash of random static.

After a beat, everyone working on the bridge sounded off. Then, over the intercom, each department head reported in.

"We'll have power restored in a few minutes, Captain," Dr. Ra-Havreii reported from the engine room. *"I only wish I knew what just happened to us."*

"That makes all of us, Commander," Riker told *Titan's* new, if provisional, chief engineer. "We'll let you know once we figure it out ourselves." He turned toward the science console, beside which stood both Jaza and Dakal, the latter of whom appeared to be utterly guilt-stricken. "Any ideas about that, Mr. Jaza?"

The bridge doors slid open before Jaza could answer. Riker turned in time to see Admiral Akaar step out onto the upper level.

Intent on his scanners and monitors, Jaza said, "My best guess is that the rift's energies somehow interacted with our scanning beams."

The static that dominated the main viewscreen settled down to the prosaic image of black space, punctuated by countless stars. Riker didn't recognize any of the constellations. But then, he didn't expect to, so deep inside Romulan space.

"Meaning what?" Riker asked.

Jaza looked up, his expression mild. "We've been drawn over the edge of the rift's event horizon, Captain."

"Then—where *is* the rift?" Riker asked, gesturing toward the main screen, which stubbornly continued to display nothing but stars and trackless empty space.

Tuvok rose from his tactical station, an almost haunted look on his face. "It appears that the question isn't where the *rift* has gone, Captain. It is where *we* have gone."

Riker was liking this situation less and less. "Meaning?"

"Meaning I have begun running comparisons of the stars in this volume of space with our stellar cartography database. *Titan* seems to have abruptly shifted position."

"Shifted," Riker said, cold fingers of dread clutching at his guts. "Shifted how far?"

"My preliminary estimate is a distance of about two hundred and ten thousand light-years."

Riker tried to get his mind around that. "That would take us well outside the Milky Way galaxy." Pointing toward the star-dappled viewscreen, he added, "That hardly looks like intergalactic space."

Jaza, who had apparently been attempting to check out Tuvok's findings, straightened up from the console he had been hunched over. "That's because we seem to be inside one of the Milky Way's small, irregular satellite galaxies. I'll want to consult with Lieutenant Pazlar to make sure, but I think we've landed smack inside the Small Magellanic Cloud."

Riker noticed then that Tuvok and Akaar had both turned visibly pale.

"Neyel territory," Akaar said quietly.

Tuvok nodded. "So it would seem."

"You two have been here before," Riker said. He wasn't asking a question.

"Yes," Akaar said. "On *Excelsior.* Over eighty years ago. The Neyel made this place their home centuries ago, long before the Federation came to be."

"These . . . Neyel," said Vale. "Is that what the locals call themselves?"

"Yes," Tuvok said, impassive but still pale with obvious surprise.

"Humanoid?" Deanna wanted to know.

"More than that, Commander," Akaar said. "The Neyel are *human*."

Riker felt his jaw drop involuntarily, his gaze turning back to the viewscreen. *Humans? Out here?*

And as *Titan* sailed on through the alien galaxy, her captain wondered what else awaited them among those unfamiliar stars.

THE VOYAGES OF THE
STARSHIP TITAN

CONTINUE IN

THE RED KING

ABOUT THE AUTHORS

MICHAEL A. MARTIN's solo short fiction has appeared in *The Magazine of Fantasy & Science Fiction*. He has also coauthored (with Andy Mangels) several *Star Trek* comics for Marvel and Wildstorm and numerous *Star Trek* novels and e-books, including this volume and *Titan: Book Two—The Red King* (forthcoming); *Star Trek: Worlds of Deep Space 9 Book Two: Trill—Unjoined; Star Trek: The Lost Era 2298—The Sundered; Star Trek: Deep Space 9 Mission: Gamma Book Three—Cathedral; Star Trek: The Next Generation: Section 31—Rogue; Star Trek: Starfleet Corps of Engineers* #30 and #31 ("Ishtar Rising" Books 1 and 2); stories in the *Prophecy and Change* and *Tales of the Dominion War* anthologies, as well as in the soon-to-be-released *Tales from the Captain's Table* anthology; and three novels based on the *Roswell* television series. His work has also been published by Atlas Editions (in their *Star Trek Universe* subscription card series), *Star Trek Monthly, Dreamwatch,* Grolier Books, Visible Ink Press, and Gareth Stevens, Inc., for whom he has penned several *World Almanac Library of the States* nonfiction books for young readers. He lives with his wife, Jenny, and their two sons in Portland, Oregon.

ANDY MANGELS is the coauthor of several *Star Trek* novels, e-books, short stories, and comic books, as well as a trio of *Roswell* novels, all cowritten with Michael A. Martin. Flying solo, he is the best-selling author of many entertainment books including *Animation on DVD: The Ultimate Guide* and *Star Wars: The Essential Guide to Characters,* as well as a significant number of entries in *The Superhero Book* from Visible Ink Press.

He has written hundreds of articles for entertainment and lifestyle magazines and newspapers in the United States, England, and Italy. He has also written licensed material based on properties from many film studios and Microsoft, and his comic-book work has been published by DC Comics, Marvel Comics, and many others. He was the editor of the award-winning *Gay Comics* anthology for eight years. Andy is a national award-winning activist in the gay community, and has raised thousands of dollars for charities over the years. He lives in Portland, Oregon, with his long-term partner, Don Hood, their dog Bela, and their chosen son, Paul Smalley. Visit his website at www.andymangels.com.

STARSHIP TITAN DESIGN CONTEST
ENTRY DEADLINE: AUGUST 15, 2005

OFFICIAL RULES
NO PURCHASE NECESSARY.

The following Contest is intended for viewing and participation in the United States and Canada only (excluding Quebec). Do not enter this Contest if you are not located within the U.S. or Canada.

Contest begins at 12:00 a.m., Eastern Standard Time on March 29, 2005, and ends at 11:59 p.m., Eastern Standard Time on August 15, 2005.

PURPOSE
Pocket Books is offering *Star Trek* fans with an aptitude for ship design the opportunity to design the *U.S.S. Titan*, the starship of Captain William Riker, which was established but not seen in the feature film *Star Trek Nemesis*.

ELIGIBILITY
This contest is open to *Star Trek* fans age 18 or older as of March 29, 2005. Open to legal residents of the United States and Canada (excluding Quebec). Void in Quebec, Puerto Rico, and wherever prohibited or restricted by law. Employees and their immediate family members (or those with whom they are domiciled) of the Sponsors, their par-

ent companies, subsidiaries, divisions, related companies and their respective agencies and agents are ineligible.

JUDGING AND NOTIFICATION

All designs will be judged by the *Star Trek* editorial staff at Pocket Books, together with *Star Trek* designers Doug Drexler, Michael Okuda, and Rick Sternbach; Associate Producer, *Star Trek: Enterprise* David Rossi; Senior Director of Licensed Publishing for Viacom Consumer Products Paula M. Block; and Manager of Licensed Publishing for Viacom Consumer Products John Van Citters, all of whom are fully qualified to apply the stated judging criteria. Entries will be judged on the basis of originality (25%), execution (25%), consistency with the *U.S.S. Titan* Concept Notes (25%), consistency with *Star Trek* Starfleet style (25%). The winning design will be published in an upcoming *Star Trek: Titan* novel, and will be used as the basis for cover art on the same book. The winning designer will be credited on the novel's copyright page. In the event that there is an insufficient number of submissions received that meet the minimum standards determined by the judges, the prize will not be awarded.

Contest results will be announced on or about October 2, 2005. Winner will be notified by telephone and/or by email on or about September 29, 2005. The decisions of the judges with respect to the selection of the winners, and in regard to all matters relating to this Contest, shall be final and binding in all respects.

The winner's name and winning entry will be posted online at

www.startrekbooks.com/titancontest

PUBLICITY

Winner grants to Pocket Books the right to use his or her name, likeness, and entry for any advertising, promotion, and publicity purposes without further compensation to or permission from such winner, except where prohibited by law.

FORMAT FOR SUBMISSION

Designs must be based on the *U.S.S. Titan* Concept Notes created for the novels, which appear at the end of this document. Submissions must be in the form of general plans (i.e., technical illustrations), and must include the following five external views:

- side
- front
- back
- top
- bottom

All files submitted must include the designer's name, address, telephone number, and email address.

Designs must be submitted via email to
titancontest@simonand schuster.com
in the following electronic format:

- jpeg
- CMYK color
- 14" x 9" at 300dpi

All submissions must be received by 11:59 p.m., Eastern Standard Time, August 15, 2005.

The decision of the judges with respect to the selection of the winner and in regard to all matters relating to this contest shall be final.

No responsibility is assumed for late, lost, damaged, incomplete, technically corrupted, illegible, or misdirected entries, or for typographical errors in the official rules or Contest materials. All entrants must have a valid email address. In case of dispute as to identity of entrant, entry will be declared made by the authorized account holder of the email address submitted at time of entry. "Authorized Account Holder" is defined as the natural person who is assigned an email address by an Internet access provider, online service provider, or other organization (e.g., business, educational, institution, etc.) responsible for assigning email addresses or the domain associated with the submitted email address. A potential winner may be requested to provide Sponsor (defined below) with proof that such winner is the authorized account holder of the email address associated with the winning entry. Any other attempted form of entry is prohibited; no automatic, programmed, robotic or similar means of entry are permitted. Sponsor, its affiliates, partners and promotion and advertising agencies are not responsible for technical, hardware, software, telephone or other communications malfunctions, errors or failures of any kind, lost or unavailable network connections, Web site, Internet, or ISP availability, unauthorized human intervention, traffic congestion, incomplete or inaccurate capture of entry information (regardless of cause) or failed, incomplete, garbled, jumbled or delayed computer transmissions which may limit one's ability to enter the Contest, including any injury or damage to participant's or any other person's computer relating to or resulting from participating in the Contest or downloading any materials in the Contest.

All entries must be original and the sole property of the entrant. Please retain a copy of your submission. All entries and any copyrights therein become the property of Pocket Books and Paramount Pictures and will not be returned. By entering, entrants hereby transfer and assign all intellectual property rights (including, but not limited to, copyright and trademark) in and to the drawing and description, to Sponsors. By entering, entrants agree to abide by these rules and grant to Sponsors the right to edit, publish, display, promote, broadcast and otherwise use their entries without further permission, notice, or compensation, in any media now known, or hereafter developed.

By entering, entrants release Pocket Books, Paramount Pictures and their respective project partners and their respective parent companies, subsidiaries, affiliates, divisions, advertising, production, and promotion agencies from any and all liability for any loss, harm, damages, costs or expenses, including without limitation property damages, personal injury and/or death arising out of participation in this contest, the acceptance, possession, use or misuse of the prize, claims based on publicity rights, defamation, copyright infringement, trademark infringement, invasion of privacy or the violation of any other intellectual property rights.

No cash substitution, transfers or assignments of prize allowed. In event of unavailability, Sponsor may substitute a prize of equal or greater value.

Sponsors reserve the right, in their sole discretion, to cancel, terminate, modify, or suspend the Contest should (in their sole discretion) virus, bugs, non-authorized human intervention, fraud or other causes beyond their control corrupt or affect the administration, security, fairness or proper conduct of the Contest. In such case, judges will select the winners from all eligible entries received prior to and/or after (if appropriate) the action taken by Sponsors. Sponsors reserve the right, at their sole discretion, to disqualify any individual they find, in their sole discretion, to be tampering with the entry process or the operation of the Contest or the Contest Web site.

CAUTION: ANY ATTEMPT BY AN ENTRANT TO DELIBERATELY DAMAGE ANY WEB SITE OR UNDERMINE THE LEGITIMATE OPERATION OF THE CONTEST MAY BE A VIOLATION OF CRIMINAL AND CIVIL LAWS AND SHOULD SUCH AN ATTEMPT BE MADE, THE SPONSORS RESERVE THE RIGHT TO SEEK DAMAGES FROM ANY SUCH PERSON TO THE FULLEST EXTENT PERMITTED BY LAW.

Sponsors will be collecting personal data about participants online, in accordance with their respective privacy policies. Please review each Sponsor's privacy policy at

**http://www.simonsays.com/content/feature.cfm?sid=33&
feature_id=1610**

and

http://www.startrek.com/startrek/view/privacy.html

By participating in the Contest, entrants hereby agree to each Sponsor's collection and usage of their personal information and acknowledge that they have read and accepted each Sponsor's privacy policy.

All taxes, if any, are the sole responsibility of the winner. Winner may be required to execute and return an Affidavit of Eligibility and a Liability/Publicity/Rights Transfer Release and all other legal documents that the Sponsors may require within 15 days of attempted notification or an alternate winner may be selected. In the event the winner is considered a minor in his/her jurisdiction of residence, the winner's parent/legal guardian will be required to sign and return all required documentation within the prescribed time period.

Sponsors: Pocket Books, 1230 Avenue of the Americas, New York, NY 10020 and Paramount Pictures, 5555 Melrose Avenue, Los Angeles, CA 90038

U.S.S. TITAN CONCEPT NOTES

The Ship:
U.S.S. Titan, NCC-80102, *Luna*-class. The *Titan* is a mid-size Starfleet vessel, approximately 450 meters in length (larger than the *U.S.S. Voyager,* smaller than the *Enterprise*-D; go to **www.startrekbooks.com/titancontest** to see size comparison), with a crew complement of 350. *Titan's* hull configuration is comparable to other established Starfleet vessels.

The *Luna*-class is Starfleet's newest-generation long-range explorer, a starship *not* built specifically for combat, but like the *Constitution*-class of the previous century, a vessel designed for a long-term multipurpose mission into uncharted space. Equipped with conventional tactical systems (deflector shields; phasers; quantum torpedoes), *Titan* also boasts state-of-the-art propulsion and cutting-edge scientific equipment, as well as being a testbed for experimental science tech not yet available on other classes.

The *Titan* is manned by the most varied multispecies crew in Starfleet history, with humans taking up less than 15% of the 350-member crew. The diversity of the crew is intended to facilitate stories that will explore the ways that beings of different cultures, biologies, psychologies, and physical appearances learn how to work together, or fail to, depending on the circumstances they encounter.

Titan has eight shuttlecraft of various sizes.

The story behind the *Luna*-class:
The *Luna*-Class Development Project was initiated in 2369 in response to the discovery of the Bajoran wormhole, and originally conceived as leading a planned Starfleet wave of deep-space exploration in the Gamma Quadrant. The project was spearheaded by Dr. (Commander) Xin Ra-Havreii, a Starfleet theoretical engineer at Utopia Planitia. Field testing on the prototype *U.S.S. Luna* was under way by 2372 in the Alpha Quadrant, and construction of the fleet was scheduled to begin the following year. Unfortunately, contact with the Dominion and the subsequent outbreak of hostilities mothballed the project indefinitely, as Starfleet redirected its shipbuilding resources to the production of vessels better suited to combat.

Upon the war's end in late 2375, Dr. Ra-Havreii correctly judged that the Federation's cultural psychology would eventually shift back toward its pre-war ideals, and pushed to have the *Luna*-class revisited as a major step toward resuming Starfleet's mission of peaceful exploration (even though the class would no longer be assigned exclusively to the exploration of the Gamma Quadrant). Construction of an initial fleet of twelve *Luna*-class vessels was completed by 2379, and the *Titan* was offered to William T. Riker, one of many command officers eager to put the strife of the last decade behind them.

The *Luna*-class fleet:

The ships of the *Luna*-class are all named for moons in Earth's solar system:

Amalthea	*Callisto*	*Charon*	*Europa*	*Galatea*	*Ganymede*
Io	*Luna*	*Oberon*	*Rhea*	*Titan*	*Triton*